LONG DANCE HOME

SECOND VOLUME IN THE GOOD NEIGHBORS SERIES

WRITTEN BY JOHN R. & JANET M. DANN
ILLUSTRATED BY JANET M. DANN

DANNWORKS

Friday Harbor, WA

BOOKS BY JOHN R. DANN

Song of the Axe

Song of the Earth

Song of the Gods

The Good Neighbors

S.C.R.A.M. - The Chernobyl Connection

Storm in August

* * *

Reviews of books by John R. Dann

Song of the Axe by John R. Dann
Forge Books, a subsidiary of St.Martin's Press

"Impressive research lends flintiness to a work that holds up
well indeed to Jean Auel's *Earth Children* trilogy ."
—Kirkus Reviews

"In his sweeping cast of thousands tale, Dann tackles the
culture of the Ice Age in sparse, biblically tinged prose. Potent,
this prehistoric epic is a dizzying amalgam of legend, myth,
archaeology, warfare and romance."
—Publishers' Weekly

"Five Stars. A winner. For those who relish prehistorically set
tales, John R. Dann's novel is the right stuff."
–Harriet Klausner,
Amazon.com Customer Reviews.

"Suffused in the mythology and mysticism of an ancient era, and in the tradition of *Clan of the Cave Bear*, this mesmerizing saga will enthrall a broad spectrum of readers."
—Margaret Flanagan, *Booklist*

"The amazing story of Eena and Agon and their progeny will thrill anyone who delights in prehistoric reads and will entice the reader who looks for supporting archaeological finds along with an author's fantasy."
—Ruth B. Hill, author of *Hanta Yo*

"I am particularly impressed by the strength of the writing which is clear, forceful, and very much to the point. An amazing recreation of an utterly bygone era. There is barely a wasted word in the whole novel. Dann knows how to draw strong characters and to create and maintain tension."
—R. Garcia y Robertson, Author

"Drawing upon solid research from many disciplines, Dann presents a well rounded and believable portrait of life 30,000 years ago. Against this background his characters spring to vivid life. He accomplishes this with a style many more experienced novelists will envy."
—Morgan Llywelyn, Author

"Dann's world of cave men and women trying to survive the physical challenges of a prehistoric landscape is so authentic it allows the reader to transcend the enormous liability of time before time."
—Robin Hamilton, Editor, *The Islands' Sounder*

"A prehistoric epic in the vein of *The Clan of the Cave Bear* series." —*The Times/Post Intelligencer* (Seattle)

"We have seven copies of *Song of the Axe*, and they are always out."
—Librarian, Seattle Public Library

Long Dance Home

Second Edition (as Irina)
Fully revised and reprinted in 2017 by Janet M. Dann

This is a work of fiction. All characters portrayed in this
book are fictional, and any resemblance to real people or
incidents is purely coincidental.

Illustrations by Janet. M. Dann
Cover design & interior layout by W. Bruce Conway
Printed in the U.S.A. on recycled paper

Published by DannWorks
Friday Harbor, WA

ISBN: 978-1-7334951-1-0

Library of Congress information will be provided by
publisher upon request

Dedication

This book is dedicated to my father, John R. Dann who instilled in me a love of adventure, other cultures, and a great appreciation for the land and people of South Dakota. It is also dedicated to my South Dakota relatives.

—Janet M. Dann

* * *

Acknowledgements

I wish to first acknowledge and thank my husband, Tso-lo, who has provided support, encouragement, and suggestions which have contributed to *Long Dance Home* and enabled the book-writing process.

Of course without my father's strong start of this story, it never would have happened. I thank him for that and for asking me to finish his book. It has been an honor and pleasure to do so. Thank you, Daddy!

My mother, Barbara Dann, was also of tremendous help and support, as usual. She was an ever-willing proofreader, resource for the time period, financier, and cheerleader. Thank you, Mother!

I also wish to thank my cousin Gary Dann for his expertise in farming and remembering stories of how folks managed in the '30s.

My nephew Hanan Dann provided guidance re: Jewish names and food, and strongly discouraged me from making Mrs. Epstein's son a doctor or lawyer, for which I thank him.

Cam and Jeanette Ainsworth are contemporaries of my father who contributed greatly to understanding the roads, cars, and finances of the time, and who also provided support and encouragement. I am ever grateful to them.

Veronika Doherty, a friend from New York City, went out of her way to remind me of the ins and outs of *the city*, and took me on a refresher tour. I thank her for her invaluable help.

W. Bruce Conway - Publishing Services in Friday Harbor, Washington, has also been of invaluable assistance in publishing this project. I thank him for his support, knowledge, and encouragement.

I also want to thank Andrew Seltser for his assistance in proofreading and editing the manuscript, and his guidance in punctuation.

Finally I want to acknowledge my brother John, and sister Cathy, for their support and encouragement.

Characters

JOSIF and IZABELLA DACIA – A Romanian couple who emigrated from Romania to Oklahoma via Ellis Island in 1920. At the time they had children: ALEXANDER, two and a half, and MARIE, an infant. ALEXANDER died in 1929, and Marie is now thirteen. The other children, ROSE, ten, CAROLINE, eight, and MICHAEL-JOSEPH, seven, were all born in Oklahoma.

UNCLE JON and AUNT MAGDA – Emigrated from Romania with JOSIF and IZABELLA, JON is JOSIF'S uncle on his father's side. All the DACIA adults were involved in opposing the resurgence of the Iron Guard in Romania and left that country looking for a better place to live.

IRINA TATARANU – The last of the DACIAS in Romania. JOSIF'S sister, Sophia's daughter. Lead dancer in the Romanian State Dance Ensemble and marked for death by the Iron Guard.

FRITZ and AUGUST WAGNER – Ages twenty-three and nineteen, are neighbors of the DACIAS.

GEARHARD and GERTRUDE WAGNER – aka GRANDPA and GRANDMA, raised FRITZ and AUGUST after their parents died during the Spanish Influenza Epidemic of 1918.

DEBEN CEASCU – Lead male dancer of the Romanian State Dance Ensemble, and member of the Iron Guard.

PETRU BUSCAN and DRAGOS AMANAR – DEBEN'S henchmen in the Iron Guard and also dancers in the ensemble.

CORNELIU CODREANU – Head of the Iron Guard who has meetings in the castle of VLAD TEPES, aka VLAD the IMPALER, aka DRACULA.

PRIMO *the BULL* MORETTI – Chicago mob boss who has set up a cover identity as MR. JOHNSON in Sioux Falls, South Dakota while he looks for the body of his brother ANGELO, and cash and jewels which were stolen from him while he was in prison.

GINA CAMPANELLA – Posing with PRIMO as MRS. JOHNSON, PRIMO's current woman.

FRANKIE MALDONADO – PRIMO's cousin and a button man.

RED MC GUIRE – Farmer turned gangster who works for PRIMO.

ARNOLD ARIOSTO – Neighbor of the DACIAS. Also brother of BELLE LAMB and nephew of FRANK ARIOSTO, an honest and strong sheriff who was killed by C.D. LAMB. ARNOLD inherited the Lamb farm from BELLE after her death.

THE LAMBS – C.D., aka Clarence, and VINCE LAMB came from Chicago. VERNE LAMB was married to BELLE ARIOSTO who died of cancer. JULIUS LAMB, their son, was responsible for ALEXANDER DACIA'S death. All the LAMBS are now dead.

ZEKE VOLAKIS – Greek mob boss in Sioux City, Iowa.

KOSTAS and ACHILLES PAPADOPOULOS – Nephews of ZEKE VOLAKIS on his sister's side.

HELEN STEPHANOS – Involved with ACHILLES PAPADOPOULOS and the Greek mob, but fell in love with TONY TURELLO, ANGELO'S wife's brother's son who was working for the Italian mob.

SHERIFF BUTCH BENNARD – Sheriff of the county, and his deputy, HAROLD TORKLESSON.

MRS. EPSTEIN – A Jewish woman of compassion, wisdom, courage, and wealth who befriends IRINA on board *The Atlantia*.

MIHAI CELAC – Coordinator of the Romanian State Dance Ensemble's tour of Europe and the U.S.

EAMON JONES – Activity director on *The Atlantia*.

ONE DOLLAR in 1932 was the equivalent of eighteen dollars and seventy-two cents in 2019.

Table of Contents

Synopsis of Fate Be Damned

Fate be damned was the attitude Romanian immigrant, JOSIF DACIA, took when he left Romania with his wife, IZABELLA, two children, ALEXANDER and MARIE, and his AUNT MAGDA and UNCLE JON for a life of hope and opportunity in America. In Romania, many believe that one's fate is determined, and cannot be changed. Then there are the others who take the future in their own hands, who will fight to determine their own fate, strong and fixed on the American dream, who will let nothing stop them. JOSIF DACIA is one of those.

From Ellis Island, the DACIA family migrated west until becoming sharecroppers in Oklahoma. When their farm blew away in the *Dust Bowl*, the DACIAS drove their team of beloved plow horses, PETER and PAUL, north looking for a farm to rent, or even buy, in South Dakota. Along the way, JOSIF resists all offers of help which he deems charity, and angrily pushes north.

In the town of Centerford, in southeastern South Dakota, the DACIAs find a farm, and because of their driving passion to own land, sign a mortgage for a one hundred and sixty acre farm with a total price of $3,200, and monthly payments of one hundred and twenty-eight dollars, plus any principle they could afford. Josif sets a personal goal of two hundred dollars per month, hoping to pay for the land in his lifetime to hand down to his eldest son, twelve-year-old ALEXANDER.

In farm country, your neighbors are part of your life; you can try to ignore them, but they share boundaries with you, as well as the weather. Like a spider's web, one strand cannot be disturbed without impacting all the others. Most of the DACIA'S neighbors were hard working farmers, trying to make a living against the increasing odds of drought and a struggling economy. Then there was the neighbor who was looking for big easy money through bootlegging disguised as farming.

The WAGNERS were the honest farmers. GRANDPA and GRANDMA WAGNER were raising their grandsons, sixteen-year-old AUGUST, and twenty-year-old FRITZ, solid, raucous boys who loved to fight anyone, and play pitch with the neighbors.

The LAMBS were the family with an uncle and brother from Chicago who were associated with the mob, CLARENCE, aka C.D., and VINCE. The Centerford farm was owned by VERNE LAMB, and his wife, BELLE. VERNE'S son, JULIUS, and VERNE are bigoted, and furious that the DACIAS are renting neighboring land that once belonged to BELLE's family but had to be sold for back taxes.

C.D. has arranged for a huge still to be brought to VERNE'S farm. He destroys VERNE'S current small still, and takes over the farm. VERNE and VINCE are brothers, but there is no love lost between them. VERNE is furious with VINCE and C.D., but has no choice except to go along. BELLE is dying of cancer, JULIUS is still in school, and VERNE needs a supplemental income besides farming.

ALEXANDER and JULIUS attend the local one room school house together. There, JULIUS torments ALEXANDER, and ends up knocking him down and kicking him in the ribs until he becomes unconscious. ALEXANDER has broken ribs and is taken to the hospital in Sioux Falls when he develops pneumonia.

C.D. appears to be a fumbling, mild-mannered old man, but he is a conniving and evil person who soon becomes known to the DACIAS as a *strigoi*, a vampire-like creature in intent. A *strigoi* sucks the life and vitality from living things. not by sucking blood, but by evil acts and lies. After death, they can become literal bloodsuckers. Garlic and crucifixes are the trusted *strigoi* deterrents.

C.D. kills two gangsters who accompanied the still to the LAMB farm, and has VINCE and VERNE bury them in the silage pit behind the barn. Unseen by the others, C.D. hides a lock-box of money and jewels in the pit. This is loot which he stole from incarcerated Chicago mob boss, PRIMO MORETTI, before leaving Chicago.

C.D. also kills the local sheriff, framing the DACIAS, and plots to have the DACIAS burned out. The DACIA men are arrested, ALEXANDER dies in the hospital, and VERNE and C.D. kill each other back on the LAMB farm. VINCE and JU-

LIUS who are drunk and have been sent out to do more violence, set up their own death when a can of gasoline in the back seat tips over, and they cause an explosion when they light their cigarettes.

When the truth is discovered about who killed the sheriff, the DACIAS are released. The WAGNERS and other neighbors who have come to the aid of the DACIAS participate in ALEXANDER'S funeral. After the forty day mourning period, a feast is held by the DACIAS for the neighbors, and people of many ethnicities attend. It is during this time of community support and comfort that the DACIAS realize, they belong, and indeed have become Americans.

Prologue
February 1932

The drought which began in the late 1920s in parts of middle America gradually expanded in the 1930s to cover the center of the continent. Farmers and small towns- people of the Great Plains suffered greatly from the drought because the marginal rainfall that allowed them to exist in *good* years now became almost nonexistent. The land became parched, and each year the crops withered and died under the blazing prairie sun.

Already caught up in the disaster of the *Great Depression* which had begun with the market crash of *Black Thursday* on October 24, 1929, the farmers found themselves in the company of the laid-off industrial workers of the cities.While the men and women of the cities sold apples on street corners and stood in bread lines, the farm people mortgaged their land in order to borrow money from the banks to buy seed and plant their crops each spring.

Although the farmers prayed for rain, each summer saw their corn plants turn brown and brittle, their oats, rye, and barley shrivel and die. Great clouds arose and swept over the land, blotting out the light. Tumbleweeds, rolled and bounced by the wind, collected in huge piles in fence corners. Cattle became gaunt and chewed at ancient straw stacks. The people too became gaunt. Their faces were lined and careworn from the heat and dust, and from watching the sky.

* * *

In Europe another cloud began to sweep over the land: not a dust cloud, but the black cloud of Fascism and racial hatred.

* * *

In a poor section of Bucharest, Romania, three men in dark clothing and carrying iron bars approached a small bakery which stood between a shoe repair shop and a dance studio. The shoe store and dance studio were unlit, but a dim light showed through the plate glass front window of the bakery.

In the interior of the bakery, the men saw a young man and woman standing at a wooden table, mixing dough for the morning loaves of bread. The young couple had dark curly hair, and they smiled and spoke with each other happily as they worked.

One of the men spoke. "Dragos, Petru, break down the door." Iron bars smashed the window and heavy boots kicked in the door, and the men rushed into the little shop. Iron bars slammed into the man's skull, and as he fell dying to the floor, the young woman screamed and tried to go to him.

Strong arms seized her and threw her on the table between the piles of dough. The men rammed huge lumps of dough into her mouth and raped her, while she struggled helplessly to breathe and finally shuddered and lay still.

One of the men dipped his fingers in a pool of the man's blood, and with a triumphant look on his face, wrote on the bakery wall.

* * *

That same night, a blizzard swept in from Canada and roared across Montana and Wyoming into the Dakotas, bringing below-zero temperatures and driving icy snow across the fields and huddled farm buildings in the dark night.

A grove of cottonwood, soft maple, and box elder trees sheltered a strange little house and the weathered barn and sheds of a farm in southeastern South Dakota. Wood smoke whirled into the storm from the old brick chimney of the house, and the light of a kerosene lamp glowed cheerfully from a window.

From inside the little house came the sound of singing accompanied by a violin, *tambal* and pan pipe. Women's voices blended in a wild and primitive harmony, sad at times, then wildly exuberant and joyful.

If an observer could have peered in through the window, he would have seen, playing their instruments, two dark, mustachioed, wiry men; two women, one young and exotically beautiful, and the other, older, sturdy, and still beautiful; three girls, and a very young boy. This was the Dacia family, Romanian immigrants who had come to America to find freedom and land of their own.

Chapter One
Irina Tataranu

Across the Atlantic Ocean, in Bucharest's Civic Opera House, the Romanian State Dance Ensemble performed to a packed house of dignitaries, government officials, and wealthy citizens.

The lead dancers, Deben Ceascu and Irina Tataranu, performed brilliantly, dancing with such vigor and grace that the audience applauded before and after each of their solo appearances. During the ensemble dancing, the eyes of the audience followed Deben and Irina, enchanted by the attractive couple and the artistry of their dancing.

As well as Romanian folk dances, the ensemble also performed some classical ballet. One of the dances was a wedding dance, performed by the whole company, but featuring Deben as the bridegroom and Irina as the bride.

When Deben lifted Irina in the air and then lowered her at the end of the dance, his hands found her breasts as her feet touched the floor, and he smiled possessively at her as they turned to bow to the audience.

Deben, handsome and athletic, and Irina, lovely and equally athletic, were showered with bouquets of flowers at the end of the performance, and in the gala reception that followed, the two dancers were surrounded by admiring men and women who toasted them with champagne.

The women basked in Deben's virile manliness, and each man looked at Irina with lustful eyes, and a desire to possess her.

* * *

The next morning when Irina came to open her dance studio, she walked past her building to the bakery next door to say good morning to her dear friends, the young couple Aaron and Esther Horowitz, who would be placing their loaves of newly-baked bread on the shelves.

Irina gazed in shocked surprise at the smashed window of the bakery and then, upon entering the room, looked with horror at the bodies of her friends and the bloody words on the wall: *Death to the Jews.*

Chapter Two
April, 1932 - The Letter

Josif and Uncle Jon came in from the fields at 4:00, shortly after the children had returned from school, and were watering the horses at the stock tank when a 1929 Chevy chugged into the long driveway. Josif recognized the car; it belonged to the mailman who drove by on the county road every weekday. But the mailman had never before stopped at the Dacia's farm.

The mailman halted the car in front of the house and impatiently tooted the horn. As Josif left Uncle Jon with the horses and walked toward the car, the mailman stuck his head out the window. "You Josif Dacia?"

"Yes," Josif replied. "I am Josif Dacia."

"You oughta have a mailbox. I can't come runnin' in here every time you get mail."

"I sorry. We never need mailbox before," Josif said apologetically.

"Well you do now. You got a letter."

Josif pushed back his cap and stared at the man. "For me?"

The mailman held up a battered envelope. "It's got your name on it. The address is all mixed up, like whoever wrote it never learned how to write an address. I showed it to Horace Bowman and he said it was for you, alright. He wanted to bring it out to you, but I told him, I said,

'Horace, the mail has to be delivered by the official United States mailman.' That's me."

He handed the envelope to Josif. "Here it is. Now I gotta get back to my route. You folks see to it that there's a mailbox out by your driveway. I can't come drivin' in here every time you get some mail." The mailman turned the Chevy in a big circle through the barnyard and out into the road, then headed north toward the Wagner farm.

Josif stared in disbelief at the envelope, then hurried to the house and entered the rickety porch. The children, who had been playing outside, followed closely behind.

Josif held the envelope out toward Izabella and Aunt Magda who were watching from the kitchen doorway. He spoke in Romanian as the adults often did when excited or in a hurry. "Look! From home! A letter!"

The women froze in place and stared at the envelope in Josif's hand. "A letter!" Aunt Magda touched the cross at her neck. "God's will it is not bad news!"

Izabella's eyes were wide. "Who sent it, Josif?"

Josif placed the envelope in the center of the kitchen table. "It is from Ploesti."

The children gathered around the table, but sensing the seriousness of the letter did not pester the adults with questions, watching and listening with somber, curious faces.

Uncle Jon stamped dirt from his shoes, then removed them, and left them on the porch, entering the kitchen and hanging up his cap on the hook by the door. He eyed the envelope and touched it gingerly with a calloused finger, studying the stamp and writing. "A letter from Ploesti, from the old country!"

"I do not trust it." Josif scowled at the envelope. "The Iron Guard may have sent it. We know no one in Ploesti."

"The Iron Guard...." Aunt Magda crossed herself.

Uncle Jon shook his head. "It would have all sorts of official seals... not the Iron Guard." He pulled at his mustache. "Unless they were trying to trick us."

Aunt Magda brought the kitchen knife to Josif. "Even though Satan himself may have sent it, you will have us all dying of curiosity if you don't open it, Josif. Simply reading it cannot harm us."

Josif looked at his name and address on the envelope. It was printed with scrawling letters, as though the writer had been working hurriedly, or didn't know English:

JOSIF DACIA
CENTERFORD FARM
STATE SOUTH DAKOTA. AMERICA

"No one we know writes like that." Josif touched the letter with the point of the knife. "How could they have known where we live?"

"Sofia," Izabella said softly. "It is from your sister. Remember, you sent a letter last winter, hoping she was still alive. Only she could know our address here."

Aunt Magda held the letter out eagerly to Josif. "By all the saints, open the letter. You are driving us mad!"

Josif held the letter in one hand, the knife in the other. "Sofia is dead. She fought with the partisans."

Izabella touched Josif's arm. "She could have escaped."

"Antone was killed. I saw him die. How could she have lived?"

"Open the letter, please, Josif."

Josif inserted the blade of the knife beneath the flap of the envelope and sliced it open. He withdrew a folded white paper. He unfolded it and silently read the letter, while the family watched him, scarcely breathing. When he had finished, he looked up at them. "It is probably a trick by the Iron Guard. They say Sofia's daughter is alive."

Izabella's eyes shone with excitement. "Irina! She was only nine years old when we left Romania. Thank

God she is still alive! Read it to us, Josif!"

Uncle Jon spoke. "The Iron Guard no longer rules our land. Maybe it is not a trick."

"The letter would have us go to New York City to rescue Irina," Josif said disbelievingly.

"Please, Josif. Let me read it," Izabella implored.

Josif handed her the letter. "Read it then."

Izabella read the letter through. When she had finished her eyes were moist with tears. "Sofia is dead. But Irina is alive. Listen. I will read it to all of you." She read the letter aloud in her clear, soft voice:

10 March, 1932. Bucharest
My Dear Uncle Josif,

God has brought your letter to me. Passed from friend to friend, it finally came to my hands. I cannot tell you what joy I felt in reading it, except to learn of Alexander's death. I am so sad about that.

Yes, I am still alive, even though I am the last of your family still in Romania. My mother died a year ago, peacefully, in the arms of friends. However those friends have been killed and I suspect I am also marked for death.

I dare not mail this letter to you, but will give it to a friend who will try to mail it from another city.

I am going to try to escape to America. My mother changed our name so those who killed my father could not find us. I am now Irina Tataranu, lead female dancer of the Romanian State Dance Ensemble. We are coming to America on 20, August this year to perform in New York City. While there, I am going to escape. And I will become an American, just as you are. I can hardly wait. Do not try to write to me. If you can come for me, good. If not, I will find a way to come to you.

Your loving niece,
Irina.

Izabella held the letter to her heart. "Sofia is dead, but Irina is still alive! And she is coming to America!"

Josif shook his head. "I still believe it's a trick. How could she have survived the war, the Iron Guard?"

"Strange things happen in war time," Uncle Jon said with authority. "Men have crawled alive off battlefields where every square foot of earth has been torn by shells."

"The war maybe. But Sofia fought with the partisans. I trust no one in Romania now. All our family, all our friends, are dead." Josif pointed to the letter. "Even if Irina is alive, the letter could have been intercepted and read, then mailed on to us to deceive us."

"She asks you not to write again," Aunt Magda said. "If the Iron Guard wanted to have her betray herself or us they would not ask that."

Izabella nodded. "I feel that Irina wrote the letter. She is in danger; we must help her escape when she comes to America."

Josif stared at her. "How could we help her? Would you have me drive Peter and Paul to New York City? We have been there. That is where we arrived in America. It is a big, busy city."

"We will get an automobile."

"An automobile! When oats are thirty cents a bushel and the corn withers in the heat and drought?"

"Aunt Magda, the girls, and I will embroider table-cloths. People in America pay well for embroidery."

Aunt Magda nodded. "Remember that big farm woman in Nebraska?"

"I remember her. Trying to have the Lady's Aid Society give us shoes." Josif scowled. "You cannot earn enough money embroidering tablecloths to buy a car. Of course, I want to help my sister's daughter, but we must use what money we have to pay off the mortgage. I will not be in debt, there is no question about that!"

Chapter Three
Primo *the Bull* Moretti

On the same day that the Dacias received the letter from Irina, Primo *the Bull* Moretti was discharged from federal prison at Leavenworth, Kansas.

Primo was only five foot seven inches tall, but he was called *the Bull* because he was as wide as a door, weighed over two hundred pounds, and had once charged a rival – striking him in the chest with his head, breaking the man's ribs, and causing them to puncture the man's heart and lungs, killing him. He had a thick neck, coarse features, and emotionless eyes like a reptile.

The warden had a final conversation with Primo. The warden stood

Jail Cell

six foot four and was not a slender man, nor was he gentle or soft-spoken, but he spoke politely to Primo.

"We hope things are gonna work out okay for you, Mr. Moretti."

Primo stared coldly at the warden.

The warden forced a smile, showing big yellow horse teeth. "Your friends have come. I let them bring their car right up to the gate."

"What? You yellow-toothed jackass! You think I owe you something for that?" Moretti yelled at him.

"N-no, of course not, I just hope you're not gonna hold your stay here against us. I tried to do the best I could for you."

"Sure you did," Primo said with his eyes fixed on the warden's. "I got one piece of advice for you, you son-of-a-bitch: don't come to Chicago."

The warden shifted his feet uneasily. "Don't worry. I'm not comin' to Chicago. No Sir. Chicago's one place I don't intend to visit."

Primo continued staring at the warden. "You fucking piece of shit."

The warden's eyes moved nervously to the big clock on the wall. "Well, Mr. Moretti, it's time." He took a step backward and gestured at the door. "Good bye Mr. Moretti. Like I said, I hope you're not gonna hold your stay here against us. We were just doing our jobs."

Primo ignored the warden and pushed past him. "Go fuck yourself."

A black Cadillac waited for Primo outside the prison gate, and two men in dark suits greeted him; one held the rear door open for him. Primo did not look back at the prison as he entered the Cadillac.

One of the men climbed in beside the driver. Frankie Maldonado was in his early forties. He had a neatly trimmed black mustache, greying temples, and wore a

navy blue pinstriped suit. His nails were manicured, he wore a diamond pinky ring, and he had applied his sweet smelling hair treatment liberally. He was a *button* or *hit* man. Frankie Maldonado was a cousin who had grown up with Primo. He was happy taking orders and he was trusted.

The other man went around the car and joined Primo in the back seat. Although this man wore the mandatory dark suit, he looked more like a misplaced farmer than a gangster. The red skin of his lower face and neck suggested years in the fields, and his eyes held the squinty and challenging look of one who has battled the weather. "You say the word, Bull, and we can go take care of anybody that bothered you," he said matter-of-factly.

Primo shook his head. "Forget it, Red. Those cocksuckers aren't worth our time. There's something else I want you and Frankie to take care of."

"Name it, Bull."

"We're gonna take a trip. As soon I get back to the city and straighten a few things out, I, you, Frankie, and Gina are going for a trip to the countryside."

"Oh yeah? Maybe do a little *pheasant hunting* or somethin'?" Red smiled knowingly.

"Yeah, while I've been in the can, some of my assets went missing. Seems they went missing about the same time Clarence Lamb moved that big still to South Dakota and Angelo and Lou also went missing. I don't care about Lou, but Angelo was my brother. The Lambs are all dead, so I figure they're somewhere on that Lamb farm. Or those fuckin' Greeks in Sioux City may have had a connection to that rat C.D. Lamb. He was always ready to betray someone if it was to his advantage. They haven't violated my territory yet, but they're too close and I'd love an excuse to wipe 'em out."

"That would give us a lot more territory too," Red commented, smiling.

"While I was in the joint I made arrangements for Angelo's wife's brother's son, Tony Turello, to move down to Sioux City to check out some of the hang-outs in the Greek section. We'll see what he finds out, then take *appropriate* action."

Red leaned back in his seat and smiled. "It's good to have you back, boss, it was getting real dull."

Chapter Four
The Guitar

A week later, shortly after dinner, the Wagner brothers came into the Dacia barnyard in their 1930 Pontiac. Wearing large sweat-stained fedoras, permanently grease-stained overalls, and rangy and strong as plow horses, they were arguing as usual as they came up the walk to the porch.

Fritz, the elder and larger, spoke in a voice loud enough to make the rusty screens shake as he glared at his brother. "No you ain't, August, goddamnit. We got too much work to do for you to go runnin' off down there!"

"Well, hell, it ain't gonna take no time for me to go down there and show 'em what I can do!"

August gestured toward Josif, Uncle Jon, and seven-year-old Michael-Joseph, who had come out onto the porch. "Wait'll Joe and his Uncle Jon hear about my big offer. They'll tell you the same thing I did. This is too big a deal to pass up!"

The brothers were at the porch steps by then, and they held out shovel-sized hands to the Dacias. Fritz spoke first. "I come down here to get you folks to help me talk some sense into this idiot. He wants to go runnin' off to Yankton!"

August glared at Fritz. "He's just jealous 'cause I got an offer from Herman B. Henty to sing on his radio show."

"Sing!" Fritz glared at August. "He sounds like a coyote with turpentine on his ass!"

August looked at Uncle Jon for understanding. "He don't know nothin' about music."

"I know when I hear a pig caught under a fence!" Fritz hauled out the makings for a cigarette.

"It's yodelin'." August said proudly. "I learned how to do it from Herman B. Henty." He spoke to Josif. "Wanna hear me do it? I got my guitar out in the car."

"Joe and his uncle don't wanna hear you howlin' away." Fritz rolled his cigarette, then lit it with a big kitchen match which he snapped alight with his thumbnail. He looked at Josif with concern. "He'll scare all the stock outta the barnyard."

"Hell I will!" August turned and strutted back to the Pontiac. He reached in the back seat, lifted out a big Spanish guitar, and came back to the porch, proudly holding out the guitar for the Dacias to admire. "This is Monkey Ward's special model." The guitar gleamed with fancy nickel-plated ornamentation and had a gaudy leather strap fastened to each end to form a loop.

Uncle Jon whistled. "That is something! I would like to hear that!"

August looked triumphantly at Fritz. "Hear that? They wanna hear me play and yodel!"

"They said they wanted to hear the blankety blank guitar! Not you. Let Joe here play it."

Josif shook his head. "I never play one of these."

"Well, it don't matter," Fritz said, "August ain't gonna play it neither."

"The hell I ain't!" August placed the guitar strap around his neck and ran his sausage-sized fingers across the strings. "I'll just tune it up a little first."

"It don't matter whether he tunes it or not," Fritz said. "August's been tryin' to play that thing for two weeks now and me and Grandpa know enough to get outta the house.

"Grandma must need to get her ears cleaned out again 'cause she thinks he's making music."

August finished adjusting the strings. "I learned four chords already. Now I'm gonna sing and yodel *In the Jail-house Now* by Jimmie Rodgers and Elsie McWilliams."

The Dacias stared at August in amazement as he sang. Unlike his speaking voice, which was like the roaring of a bull calf, his singing voice was clear, melodious, and in perfect pitch, although somewhat loud. Then August broke into a yodel.

Yode a lay dee, yode a lay dee, yode a lay dee hoooooo, yode a lay dee, yode a lay dee, yode a lay deeeeee. This was delivered in a high semi-falsetto. While Fritz's comparison to the howl of a turpentined coyote was possibly justified, the yodeling compared quite well to that of the yodelers of Germany and Austria with whom the Dacias were familiar.

As August finished, Fritz looked at the Dacias for confirmation of his judgement. "Now you heard him; ain't that about the worst noise you ever heard?"

"He don't know good singin' when he hears it." August struck a chord on the guitar. "Ain't many people can yodel."

Michael-Joseph had watched open-mouthed as August performed. Now he spoke. "Holy shit!"

Josif cuffed his son. "Michael-Joseph" he said sternly, "talk like that and you will be kneeling on corn for a week."

"Yes Papa. But I wanna learn to sing like August."

August looked triumphantly at Fritz. "See there? I knew they were gonna like it!"

"Joe and his Uncle Jon ain't said nothing yet. They're prob'ly 'bout ready to puke."

The Wagner brothers glared at one another, their big fists clenched.

Josif asked, "Is to yodel an American way of singing?

We only hear in mountains in Europe."

"Darn tootin' it's American! You don't have a radio, so you may not have heard him, but Jimmie Rodgers is the most famous yodeler ever!" August stroked the guitar again. "Us cowboys do it all the time."

"Cowboy, is it?" Fritz blew smoke out of his nose. "He's been readin' that *Wild West Weekly* so much his brains is all scrambled. Now he thinks he's a singin' cowboy!"

August ignored this. "I'm goin' down to Yankton next Saturday night. Station WNAX. Herman B. Henty himself is gonna listen to me."

Fritz stamped out his cigarette on the porch. "Herman B. Henty is prob'ly gonna shoot himself." He took a deck of cards from his overall's pocket. "Put that stupid guitar back in the car an' we'll have a game a pitch."

Chapter Five
Chivaree

It was hard for the Dacias to believe that the rains were not coming as usual. Huge storm clouds arose in the west and swept over the plains with flashing lightning and booming thunder, yet not a drop of rain fell on the ground.

But the Dacias' fields still looked as though they might produce good crops because of the peculiar lay of their land. The creek which flowed along the south border of their farm had overflowed out into the fields during the flooding caused by the March thaw of the winter snow, and the low, southeast corner of the farm had been covered with a large shallow pond until early April.

While this prevented the Dacias from planting as most of the other farmers had, the residual moisture in the soil had kept their crops and hopes alive.

The family spent long evenings discussing how they might find enough money to buy a used car and get to New York City to help Irina escape from the dance troupe. Izabella, Aunt Magda, and the three girls worked at their embroidery as the family talked, making tablecloths which they hoped to sell in Centerford. But the family realized that at five dollars each, they needed much more money than could be supplied by the tablecloths.

They owed the bank one hundred and twenty eight

dollars a year in interest alone, plus any extra money they could put down on the principle. Josif dreamed of paying two hundred dollars a year and of paying off the loan in less than twenty-five years, but feared that would not be possible.

In previous summers Aunt Magda had made large batches of *tuica* and sour cherry brandy from the orchard fruit that Uncle Jon harvested, and these were bottled and stored in the root cellar under the kitchen floor. One evening Uncle Jon showed a dollar-fifty to the family.

"Mr. Bowman bought three bottles. He said I could sell all I had in Sioux Falls or Sioux City."

Aunt Magda's eyes flashed. "You know it is against the law to do this. You will become as bad as the terrible Lambs who made alcohol to sell in their barn."

Uncle Jon protested. "This is only fruit juice which has aged. It is like selling oats or corn that have grown on our land. Besides, you have made more than we can drink in a year. Why shouldn't we make some profit from our labors?"

Aunt Magda stood up taller and looked sternly at Uncle Jon. "The *tuica* is only for our use. It is part of our daily lives and we don't sell it. When you are in jail for selling this alcohol you will think differently."

Josif interceded for Uncle Jon. "When I hauled barley to Centerford a week ago, the man in the elevator said that soon it will be legal to sell alcohol in this country. It is being talked about in the United States Congress."

Marie, who was thirteen, added, "Mrs. Horsefall told us about it in civics class. There will be an amendment to the United States Constitution. It will be called *Repeal.*"

Rose and Caroline, ten and eight, agreed, nodding their heads. Michael-Joseph spoke up eagerly. "August said Mrs. Bowman is gonna have a damn fit."

Izabella placed her hand over her little boy's mouth.

"Michael-Joseph," she said sternly, "you promised not to talk like that any more."

"I forgot, Mama."

Josif scowled at Michael-Joseph. "You forget one more time and you will go to your room and kneel on corn for an hour!"

"I won't forget, Papa, not in the house."

"Not anywhere, Michael-Joseph! You understand?"

"Yes, Papa." Michael-Joseph looked at the floor and said nothing. Suddenly he brightened. "I'm gonna get a guitar when I get big." His eyes were wide with excitement. "I'm gonna yodel like August does."

Before either parent could respond, there was the sound of a car leaving the main road and turning in the driveway.

Aunt Magda peered out the window. "A car is coming! And at this time of the night!"

They all rushed to the windows of the living room and watched as the headlights of a car shone in the driveway and moved toward the house. Josif and Michael-Joseph ran into the kitchen and with Uncle Jon stepped out into the porch as the car stopped in front of the house.

The Wagner brothers climbed from the car and came up to the porch. "I hope you folks ain't gone to bed yet," Fritz said conspiratorially. "We got some news."

"Yeah," August added. "There's gonna be a *chivaree*."

"Shut up, August," Fritz said. "I was gonna tell Joe and his uncle that if you hadn't come buttin' in."

"What is *chivaree*?" Josif asked.

"Why hell, everybody knows that," Fritz said. "Ol' Ansel Peterson and that old lady who was keepin' house for him went and got hitched."

"We just found out about it." August said. "We got to go *chivaree* 'em tonight before they get away."

Fritz scowled at August. "Will you let me tell this for

Christ's sake?" He looked past the Dacias into the kitchen. "We ain't got time to come in. Get your guns and anything else you can make noise with: old plow shares, discs, iron bars, hammers, buckets ...."

August grinned. "We're gonna scare hell outta 'em."

"What have these people done wrong?" Josif asked.

"They ain't done nothin' wrong." Fritz jerked his thumb to the southeast. "They just got married. We gotta *chivaree* 'em."

"So we can have a dance." August grinned again. "We're gonna haul 'em outta bed and make 'em promise to put on a dance for everybody."

"But why do you need guns?"

"To scare 'em. Ain't you never been to a *chivaree?*"

Fritz scowled at August. "They don't have to have you explain that. They musta had *chivarees* where they come from, back in the old country. Everybody has *chivarees.*"

Josif looked thoughtful. "Maybe we had different name. When we have wedding in our country we have dance. Everybody dance. Sing and eat and drink *tuica* and dance."

"That's it, Joe! That's just what we do here." Fritz waved toward the car. "Get your noise-makin' stuff and climb in. We gotta get there quick and surround the place."

"Women come? They have to get dressed up for dance."

"We ain't gonna dance yet. Not for about a week. And I sure wouldn't bring your women along now unless they like to go runnin' through the fields in the dark and shootin' off guns." Fritz looked down at Michael-Joseph. "Mike here can come. Just keep outta the way so you don't get tramped on if things get rough."

"What you mean, *rough?*" Josif asked.

"If they get ornery and try to get away." Fritz replied.

"Then we gotta run 'em down."

"Bring your lanterns and some torches," August said. "There ain't no moon out tonight. Ol' Ansel can run like a jack rabbit, and that old lady is mean and tough as a mink. If they get a head start we're gonna have one hell of a time catchin' 'em."

Josif looked at Uncle Jon, then at Michael-Joseph. "We like to come to dance, but we better stay home to-night."

"Well, suit yourselves," Fritz said with some disap-pointment, "but you're sure gonna miss all the fun. Every-body from ten miles around is gonna be there."

"We thank you," Josif said. "You tell people who marry that if they like, we make wedding music for their dance."

"Say, that ain't too bad an idea." Fritz stuck out his big hand and shook hands with Josif and Uncle Jon. "Lou-ie Broozey ain't gonna play for weddings no more since he got put away up in the pen at Sioux Falls. After we nail ol' Ansel for a dance, I'll tell him you folks might like to make some music at it."

August added, "I'll be goin' down to Yankton Satur-day night to take that job playin' on the radio, but maybe if I ain't too busy I could show you guys how to play at ol' Ansel's dance."

Fritz snorted. "You ain't gonna get any job playin' on the radio. Once Herman B. Henry hears you soundin' like a coyote, you'll be right back at the farm sloppin' hogs."

"Hell I will," August said. "You wait and see."

The Wagner brothers glared at each other and then lurched toward their car, still arguing.

When the car had gone out into the road, Josif, Uncle Jon and Michael-Joseph went back into the house where the women and girls watched from the living room. Aunt Magda spoke severely to Uncle Jon in Romanian.

"They are going to kill that poor old man and his wife. You should have stopped them!"

Uncle Jon winked at Michael-Joseph. "They are not going to kill them. Mr. Bowman told me about this thing they call a *chivaree*. They just have a little fun. They make a lot of noise around the house, and when the married couple comes out, they just make them promise to have a dance for everybody."

Aunt Magda frowned. "And chase them through the fields with guns and torches! What a terrible thing to do!"

Michael-Joseph looked up at Izabella. "Next time I wanna go with Fritz and August. I wanna have fun too!"

The next evening after chores were done, Mr. Bowman came to the Dacia farm in his Overland. Mr. Bowman reminded the Dacia children of the picture of Abraham Lincoln that hung on the front wall of their schoolroom, but Mr. Bowman differed from Abraham Lincoln in several ways. Mr. Bowman's nose was a deep red color, which when he became excited glowed like a tail light on an automobile, and he had a fondness for anything alcoholic, which he called cough syrup. He had come to see Uncle Jon.

Mrs. Bowman was opposed to Mr. Bowman's liking of cough syrup. She belonged to an organization called the WCTU, which fascinated the Dacias with its hint of mystery. In addition, Mrs. Bowman was the social leader of the neighborhood, being the perennial president of the Ladies Aid Society of St. Olav.

After Mr. Bowman and Uncle Jon had gone into the granary together, and after Mr. Bowman had placed something wrapped in a gunny sack in the Overland, the two men joined Josif in the barn, where he was currying the horses. Mr. Bowman related the events of the night before to Josif and Uncle Jon.

"Ansel and Maud Peterson gave that *chivaree* crowd

a real surprise. They left a short candle burning in their bedroom upstairs, then they must've gone out and hid somewhere around their farm. Well, after the crowd surrounded the house, they saw that upstairs light go out, and they figured it was time to act. But with all their shooting and banging and hollering, nobody came out of the house, so the Wagner boys and some of that rough crowd from Kronberg went in to drag Ansel and Maud out of bed. And there wasn't anybody there!"

Uncle Jon slapped his thigh. "We should have gone, Josif!"

Mr. Bowman chuckled. "Then Ansel's oldest boy, Ture, says, 'Well, Pa sure fooled you. Look at that!' And he pointed off across the fields, and there were the lights of a car on the road to Centerford, going fast, about two miles away. Of course everybody ran off and got in their cars and tried to catch them."

Mr. Bowman removed a flask from his coat pocket and offered it to Uncle Jon. "Try this, Jon, and you too, Josif. It's from a supply I had put away in the hay mow some years ago. Tell me what you think of it."

Uncle Jon thanked Mr. Bowman and took a polite sip. He passed the flask to Josif. "That is good stuff," he said. Josif took a mouthful, nodded in agreement and gave the flask back to Mr. Bowman. Mr. Bowman took a good pull and licked his lips. He gave the flask to Uncle Jon again.

"This was made by a man named Louis Broozey, a musician. I had stored it in the hay mow after I had finished its brother and only discovered it this morning when I was pitching some old hay down to the cows. I had forgotten it was there. It must be ten years old."

Uncle Jon took another drink. "It has aged well. It should be given a medal."

"Fritz Wagner said last night that man named Broozey

was now in prison," Josif said to Mr. Bowman.

"He is. Louis Broozey used to have a dance band and a still. He farmed up north of here. Unfortunately, he was not in our county. The sheriff there was not as lenient as Frank Ariosto, and Louis was sent to jail for bootlegging and other things around four years ago, just before you folks arrived here."

"Frank Ariosto was good man."

"He was. When Clarence Lamb killed him, the county lost the best sheriff it ever had."

Josif recalled with anger and sadness the four Lambs: Clarence, Verne, Vince and Julius.

Clarence, aka C.D., a little white-haired man who looked as innocent as a kindly grandfather, and who had killed Sheriff Frank Ariosto, and tried to have the Dacias take the blame for it.

Verne, dark-faced with hatred, who had cursed at Josif and his family.

Vince, Chicago hoodlum who had searched the Dacia women, placing his hands on them, and who had smashed Josif's violin as they stood with guns pointed at them.

And Julius, Verne's son, who had kicked Alexander again and again as he lay helpless in the schoolyard, so that Alexander had died.

But now the Lambs were all dead: Clarence with Verne's axe in his skull, Verne who lay dying from Clarence's bullet as Josif held his grandfather's knife to Verne's throat, Vince and Julius who had ignited the gasoline they were bringing in their car to burn Josif's house and barn and murder his family and horses.

Uncle Jon put his hand on Josif's shoulder. "Drink, Josif. The Lambs are all dead now."

"Yes." Josif took the flask. The whiskey burned his throat, burned the memories. He gave the flask back to Mr. Bowman. "We thank you. Is good whiskey."

Uncle Jon eyed the flask. "Did *chivaree* people ever find married people?"

Mr. Bowman drank again and gave the flask to Uncle Jon. "That was the best part. As the mob jumped into their cars, the lights on the Centerford road disappeared. Just disappeared. Like the car had never been there. Well, the whole bunch raced their cars over that way, but they never did find anything. They finally came back to Ansel's farm to pick up their plowshares, buckets, and old discs and things, and there were Ansel and Maud sitting at the kitchen table playing cards with three lamps lit. Ansel came to the door, and said, 'Why, if we'd known you folks were comin' we would've had some coffee ready, wouldn't we Maud?' And Maud came to the door and she said, 'My, my, what're all of you folks doin' out this time a night?'"

Uncle Jon returned the flask to Mr. Bowman who took another pull. "You should've seen the faces of all those people. But I give Fritz Wagner credit. He and August were up front, and Fritz never even dropped his cigarette; he said, 'Well we just come over for a little pitch and a cup a coffee. Usually when we do that we get invited in.'

"And Ansel said real polite, 'Well you boys sure are welcome, but it's kinda late now. I'll tell you what we'll do. If we can find a band we'll put on a dance for all of you and your womenfolk at the Pavilion a week from this Saturday night. Me and Maud are gonna take a honeymoon for a week, but we'll sure be back for that dance!'

"And Fritz said, 'Well, I think I got a band for that dance'; and he mentioned you folks."

Josif looked pleased. "We talk with Fritz and August that night. I tell them we be happy to play for wedding dance."

"That's what Fritz said. But August didn't quite see it that way." Mr. Bowman smiled and took another drink from the flask. "I'm cleanin' this up a little. As you know the Wagners use some real choice words. Anyway, August said, 'Blankety blank it, Fritz, I was with you, blank it, when Joe Dacia said he would play for the blankety blank dance. You ain't the one that got the band all by your blankety blank self!'"

"Then what Fritz say?"Uncle Jon asked.

"He said, 'Blank it, August, shut up. Me and Ansel here are tryin' to get this blankety blank dance organized.'"

Chapter Six
The Dance

The Wagners and Bowmans drove the Dacias with their instruments to the Pavilion Dance Hall, which was located a few miles south of Centerford. The dance was to start at 8PM, and the two cars pulled into the grounds of the Pavilion at 7:30 to allow the musicians time to tune their instruments to the piano.

The dance hall was a large, once-white, one-story, decaying wooden building which sprawled in a five-acre patch of cottonwoods and box elders. It belonged to a big Norwegian farmer named Knut Knutson, who greeted the Dacias and the Wagners at the dance hall entrance.

Knut stared at the Dacias' instruments. "Ain't you got any saxophones or trumpets or drums?"

Josif shook his head. "My uncle play Romanian instrument called *tambal* and I play violin. Aunt play pan flute, daughter play piano. The others sing and clap to music."

August hoisted his big guitar case. "I got my guitar. An' Ture Peterson is comin' with his saxophone."

As the Dacias and Bowmans walked into the dance hall and towards the raised platform of the bandstand, Knut eyed August suspiciously. "You ain't plannin' to cause any trouble here tonight, are ya, August?"

Fritz snorted. "The only trouble he's gonna cause is

he's gonna make everybody wanna puke. He thinks he's a cowboy singer."

August ignored Fritz's comments. "I been down at Yankton playin' for Herman B. Henty on WNAX. He thinks I'm pretty damn good."

Knut looked in disbelief at August. "You been playin' on WNAX?"

"Well, I guess so. Herman B. Henty said if I got any better he might hafta look for a new job."

"That's a buncha B.S.," Fritz said. "From what I heard, Herman B. Henty had to head for the hospital after listenin' to August."

"He was headin' for the hospital anyway, damn you, Fritz," August countered. "Besides, I came in second. Now you can't say that ain't good."

"Oh sure," Fritz said, "There was prob'ly only two of you there. How in hell could you keep from comin' in second?"

"There was six of us, damnit! I would've come in first, but Herman said he felt sorry for Myrna. He told me that private-like afterwards."

"Who the hell is Myrna?" Fritz asked. "And how come Herman B. Henty felt sorry for her?"

"Somebody grabbed her family's farm when they were out in California lookin' for work. Now they're stayin' with relatives." August looked at his fingernails. "I'm gonna get her to come up this way sometime. She kinda likes me."

Fritz rolled his eyes. "She must be feeble-minded if she goes for you."

"She ain't neither, Fritz. Wait'll you see her."

"Yeah, I can hardly wait. You ain't answered my question yet. Who the hell is she? Some old lady that's gone queer?"

"Goddamnit Fritz, I'm gonna show you. On top a that, I'm gonna pound the shit outta you if you make fun of her!"

"You're gonna pound the shit outta me? Why you stupid jerk, I can whip you with one hand tied behind me!"

Knut stepped between the two brothers. "You two cut out your damned arguing and fighting. I ain't gonna have it here in my dance hall. The only reason I let you in tonight is because of the Bowmans and that bohunk family." He held up a big fist. "Now cut it out or I'm gonna knock hell outta both a ya!"

"Jesus Christ, Knut, what're you gettin' so damned upset about? Me and August was just havin' a little discussion."

"Well, have your discussion outside, not in here." Knut scowled at the two brothers. "Now August, you get your ass up on that bandstand and help them people get set up. Fritz, I'm gonna make you my official bouncer for the night. Anybody tries to start any trouble, you give 'em the bum's rush."

August climbed up the wooden steps onto the rickety bandstand where the Dacias were gathered as Josif tuned his violin to a leprous-looking upright piano at which Marie sat striking a single note. The piano had been painted white at some earlier age, but now the paint was yellowed and peeling with dark patches of the original cracked varnish revealed like sores. Brown-burned cigarette trails lay like rusty bolts over the upper surfaces of the piano, and sticky rings left by wet glasses of pop decorated the music shelf.

But the piano fit well with the decor of the dance hall. Streamers hung in limp loops around the bandstand railing, and similar streamers hung from an ancient light fixture in the dance hall ceiling, sagging out to the walls like the strands of a giant spider web. The interior walls and ceiling of the building were bare wood, and the crude wooden booths and benches which lined the walls were beaten and battered. Near the entrance was the *bar*, a room filled with crates of pop, which was separated from the main room by a long counter of planks.

August brought his Montgomery Ward guitar from its case and looped the strap around his neck. "Let 'er rip, Joe. I'm ready." He struck a chord, so dissonant with the piano and the violins that the Dacias shuddered.

Josif placed his violin carefully on top of the piano. "Piano is bad. Is what you say? Not tune? I had to change tune of violin. Maybe guitar need that too."

August grinned. "That piano ain't never been tuned. Knut's too blankety blank tight." He adjusted the tension of the guitar strings, plucking them as he did so. "The stupid book that came with this didn't say nothin' 'bout tryin' to play with a beat-up old piano like this, but Herman showed me how to do it. I'll have this here guitar tuned in about five seconds." Then as Josif and Uncle Jon and the rest of the Dacias watched and listened in disbelief, August brought the guitar in tune with the wretched piano.

He played a few chords. "Here comes Ture. Now we can get goin'."

A lanky, red-headed, pimply-faced, blue-eyed young man climbed up the steps to the bandstand carrying a big beaten-up instrument case. He knelt and opened the case and took out a large golden saxophone. "Hey, August, that sure is one heck of a guitar." He pronounced it *gi-tar*.

"Monkey Ward's best." August introduced the Dacia family: "These are the folks we told you about at the *chivaree*. They're gonna play with us."

"Nice ta meet ya," Ture said. He took a mouthpiece from the case, attached it to the saxophone, and licked the reed. He looked at Marie, "Play a B flat, will ya?"

Marie, who had taken piano lessons from Mrs Horsefall, the schoolteacher, played the note with the pedal down while Ture sounded the saxophone and adjusted it. The tone Ture produced was big and smooth. He said to

38

the Dacias, "You folks know *Where the Blue of the Night Meets the Gold of the Day?*"

Josif shook his head. "We don't know."

"Ain't you never heard it on the radio?"

"We don't have radio."

Ture stared at the Dacias. "What was you gonna play tonight?"

"Wedding songs."

"What kinda wedding songs?"

"From our country. From Romania. *Hora* for decoration of fir tree first. People dance while bride get nice clothes on. But you play American song first."

Ture looked hard at August and drew him aside. "Holy Christ! You told me they could play for this dance. I ain't standin' up here making a horse's ass outta myself trying to play some kinda Gypsy music about whores!"

"You already made a horse's ass outta yourself," August replied. "And who said anything about whores!"

"He did. He said they were gonna play a whore!"

"A 'Hora,' you dumb shit! It's a kinda dance in their country. Just shut up and play that blue night stuff and they'll learn it."

"Learn it!" Ture said, his voice rising in exasperation, "We don't have time for them to learn it!"

"Just stop complainin' and play the damn music like I told ya. They didn't take no five years to learn to write their names like the way you did."

Ture took a step closer to August. "Maybe you wanna step outside. We'll see how long it takes you to learn how to keep your goddamn mouth shut!"

Uncle Jon spoke quietly to Josif in Romanian. "They are going to fight. We had better get the women and children off this bandstand."

Josif handed his violin to Uncle Jon. "I'll try to stop them."

He stepped between August and Ture and said politely, "You play music on saxophone and guitar. We play it with you when we hear it once."

Ture stared at Josif again. "You hear it once and can play it?"

"We learn music in our country that way."

Ture licked his reed. "I don't believe it, but I'm gonna give it a try." He scowled at August. "If this don't work, I'm just purely gonna beat the crap outta you." Ture brought the mouthpiece of the saxophone up, licked the reed again, and began to play *Where the blue of the night....* The Dacias listened to the melody one time through. Then Josif joined in with his violin, playing the melody with Ture. Uncle Jon accompanied him on the *tambal*, Aunt Magda played a haunting version of the melody on her pan flute, Marie at the piano played chords, while Izabella and the children clapped their hands in time to the music.

August now played chords on his guitar, first the same as Marie on the piano, then striking off into uncharted territory of his own.

Ture widened his eyes in surprise and brought sounds from his saxophone that equalled the improvisation of a New Orleans jazzman. The combined sound of the instruments became rich and full, and the music held a haunting mixed beauty of Romanian music and the powerful wail of the saxophone. Finally Ture raised his saxophone and blew a set of ending notes.

"By golly, that sure was good! You let me start off and we ain't gonna have any problem!" He shook hands with Josif. "Lemme hear some of your music now. That fir tree dance."

Josif nodded. "Is *Hora*. Has eight beats instead of three." He played the melody on his violin.

Ture said, "That sure don't sound like any American dance, but I kinda like it. You and your family get goin' with it and I'll just kinda play soft and join in." He glanced at August. "I didn't think you'd be able to play worth beans. Where'd you learn them chords?"

"I just made 'em up," August said modestly.

"Well, they ain't too bad." Ture licked his reed again and nodded at Josif. "Let 'er rip!"

As the Dacias played the *Hora*, people began to enter the dance hall, farmers in their Sunday suits with tight-necked white shirts and gaudy neckties, and farmers' wives with marcelled hair, flouncy dresses, silk stockings, and sturdy high-heeled shoes.

They stared at the strange dance orchestra with puzzled faces, but as Ture joined in with the familiar sound of his big saxophone, husbands and wives formed couples and gingerly two-stepped around the dance floor, the men shuffling determinedly forward with their hapless wives forever dancing backward.

Ture Peterson watched the entrance door as he played, and suddenly he raised his saxophone and brought the number to an end. "Pa and Maud just came in. I'm gonna play, *Ain't She Sweet*, then, *Yes Sir, That's My Baby*. You folks join in when you think you know 'em!"

At 10:00 Mr. Bowman came up on the bandstand, bringing along Ansel and Maud, who beamed with happiness and excitement. Ansel, sixty years in age, had outlived two wives, and now had married his spinster housekeeper, fifty year old Maud.

Mr. Bowman and Ansel had slipped outside periodically for sips of Mr. Bowman's *cough syrup* which he carried in a flat bottle, but other than the fact that Mr. Bowman's large nose was glowing more warmly than usual, and that Ansel Peterson was slightly unsteady on his feet, they gave little indication of having almost emptied the bottle.

Mr. Bowman carried a hat, and he bowed graciously to the bride before he spoke. "By golly, Ansel and Maud,

I've taken a count, and eighty-six of your friends are here tonight!" Loud clapping erupted from the crowd. Mr. Bowman continued. "You all have been having a good time dancing, and Knut has plenty of pop left, so we're all gonna keep on havin' a good time." He bowed to the band. "I want to thank Ture Peterson and the Dacia family and August Wagner for the music. How about it folks? How about a big hand for the band!"

The crowd clapped again, but someone shouted, "August Wagner can't play worth beans!" August put his guitar down.

"Who said that?"

A big, yellow-haired Scandinavian pushed forward from a group of young men, staggering drunkenly. "I did. Art Swenson. What you gonna do about it?"

"I'll show you what I'm gonna do about it, you goat-faced north end of a horse goin' south!" August leapt down the rickety steps from the bandstand and pushed his way through the crowd toward the Scandinavian. Knut stepped in front of August.

"August, I told you I didn't want no trouble here to-night. Now you and Art cut it out or I'm gonna have my bouncer throw you both out!"

"Oh yeah? Well, your bouncer's my brother."

"It don't matter. You cause any trouble and he's gonna throw you out!"

Art Swenson brayed contemptuously. "Haw haw haw! One Wagner tryin' to throw the other one out! I gotta see this! It'll be like two jack-asses kickin' an' pawin' at each other!"

Fritz came through the entry door. "What the hell is goin' on here? I just get through givin' the bum's rush to a buncha town idiots and I hear somebody callin' me a jackass! Who said that?"

"I did," Art said. "And I got some Kronberg guys here with me who ain't afraid of you Wagners!" Five big yellow-haired toughs slouched forward to stand belligerently behind Art.

Knut directed a fierce scowl at them. "You guys cut it out! I ain't having any trouble in my dance hall! If you wanna fight, go out behind the building like everybody else does!"

"There's only six of these Kronberg deadbeats," August said. "I can handle 'em right here by myself."

"Damn it, August," Fritz said. "Quit buttin' in when me and Knut here are tryin' to talk. I'm the bouncer here tonight. Now get back up on that bandstand or I'll throw you out along with these Kronberg jokers."

"You ain't throwin' me out. I'm part of the band."

"It don't make no difference. I'm the bouncer. I get to throw anybody out that starts causin' trouble."

"The hell you do! You ain't havin' all the fun. This jackass insulted me. I get to throw 'im out!"

"Listen, you stupid jerk. Get this through your thick head. I'm the bouncer!"

Art turned to his band of toughs. "This sure is funny. These Wagner boys ain't got brains enough to figure out who's supposed to be the bouncer."

Fritz turned slowly to face Art. "What'd you say?"

"I said you ain't got brains enough to figure out who's the bouncer."

Fritz hit Art Swenson in the stomach so hard that Art flew backward in a V shape with his yellow hair and big feet trailing behind him as he slammed into his cronies and brought three of them to the floor with him. Fritz scowled at them. "I'm the bouncer. Don't go buttin' in when me an' August here are tryin' to talk. I'll take care of you and your chicken-shit buddies in a minute."

"Damn it, Fritz," August complained. "Now you took all the fun outta it. Those Kronberg sissies was mine. I oughta knock hell outta you!"

Fritz turned to face August again just as Mr. Bowman stepped beside Knut Knutson. "By gracious," he said. "You boys are the limit. Now both of you stop this arguing and help pass the hat around for Ansel and Maud."

"Hell, Horace," Fritz said. "You don't hafta get so damned upset about it. Me and August was just havin' a little discussion. We'll be glad to help pass the hat; lemme just heave these Kronberg guys out first."

"Holy Christ Fritz, use your head," August said. "Pass the hat around first, then throw 'em out. Otherwise you ain't gonna get any money out of 'em."

"Listen August, whaddaya think I am, stupid?" Fritz took a wad of bills and a large handful of change from his pocket and dropped it in Mr. Bowman's hat. "I got this much already from those town guys I had to throw out."

He turned and hauled Art Swenson up off the floor with one hand and held a big fist in front of his face. "I'm collectin' at least fifty cents a piece. You and your jackass buddies cough it up now and I'll just throw you out. Try to get smart and I'll beat the crap outta you, one at a time or all together. How do you want it?"

Art was still gasping for breath. He fumbled with his wallet and dropped a dollar bill into Mr. Bowman's hat.

Fritz glared at the rest of the Kronberg gang. Five one dollar bills appeared and went into the hat.

"By gracious," Mr. Bowman said. "I think we should let these boys stay and enjoy the party. They're just farm folks like the rest of us. You boys get your hats and pass them around through the crowd. Ansel and Maud promised to pay for the dance hall and the band, but we're gonna see to it that they don't come out short."

"Hell, Horace," August said, "I thought we was supposed to have fun at this dance. This is gonna be like a ladies' aid meeting. When me and Myrna get hitched, we're gonna have a real party."

Fritz scowled at August. "What the hell are you talkin' about?"

One of the Kronberg boys snickered. "If she likes August she must be some blind, homely old maid."

August charged past Fritz and leapt onto the six Kronbergers, his big fists hammering, and a tumbling mass of fighting bodies rolled like a huge Russian thistle blowing across the dance floor.

Fritz turned to Horace Bowman. "Go ahead with your passin' the hat, Horace. I'll just throw August out with them Kronberg jerks."

The band received eight dollars from Ansel Peterson for playing at the wedding dance. August and Ture would only take two dollars a piece, leaving four dollars for the Dacias. In addition, Ture gave Michael-Joseph an old Albert-keyed B flat clarinet and showed him how to finger it and make a decent tone.

Michael-Joseph learned quickly how to play the clarinet, and he easily developed the loud harsh tone so loved by Balkan musicians for that instrument.

The band received requests to furnish music at other dances in that area, and Josif's wallet began to swell with two dollar bills and singles. The band had developed a unique style, a combination of American popular music, Balkan dances, and cowboy yodeling which fascinated the people of the mixed racial communities of South Dakota.

The dances were not without incident. Men were fascinated by Izabella's, Aunt Magda's, and Marie's exotic beauty, and at the second dance the Dacias played for, two drunken men accosted the Dacias after the dance as they walked toward the Bowman and Wagner cars.

"How about a dance?" one of the men, a big Dane

from the town of Swanborg asked Izabella. "I'll bet them red boots of yours would really stir up the dust out here if you had a man dancing with you."

Josif stepped in front of Izabella. "She is my wife. Our women dance only with their men."

The man stood half-a-foot taller than Josif. He guffawed. "Prob'ly 'cause they ain't never danced with a real man. Why don't you just go take a piss while I do a little waltz with your wife?"

Josif took his knife from his belt. "First we fight."

The man stared at the knife. "I ain't got no knife. You wanna fight, we'll use our fists." He made a fist. "Come on, you danged Gypsy!"

Josif spoke to Uncle Jon. "Lend me your knife. I will give this man mine."

Uncle Jon handed his knife to Josif. "Give it back when you have cut him enough, Josif. I want to slice this other man up a little. He has been looking at my bride like a sick calf."

Josif held out his knife to the man. "Now you have a knife. Hold it in your knife hand while my uncle ties our other hands together."

The man's face became pale in the sickly glow from the dance hall lights. "I ain't fighting that way."

"You want to dance with my wife, you fight that way."

"Hell, I just wanted to have a friendly little dance." The man backed away. "I didn't mean nothin' by it, mister."

The Wagner brothers and Horace Bowman came from their cars. "If you want me to, Joe," Fritz said, "I'll knock the shit outta these guys."

"I thank you. But I think man not understand how we fight." Josif smiled at the men. "We not be enemies. I want to be good neighbor. You shake hands, tell me your name, we be friends. My name Josif Dacia."

The man held out his hand. "You're damn right. Put 'er there! My name is Jens Jensen. I ain't stupid enough to knife fight with nobody that fights with his hand tied to mine!"

Mr. Bowman removed his flask from his coat pocket. "By golly, I believe this calls for a libation." He handed the flask to Josif. "Jen's folks have always been good friends to me and Beatrice. You two share a little drink now and you'll be good friends from now on."

Josif drank from the flask and handed it to Jens Jensen. "You want to, I show you how to fight with knife. Is good to know when you get wife."

Jens took a long guzzle and handed the flask back to Josif. "Damn right. But I think maybe fists is good enough for any of these guys that live around here."

* * *

August took offense easily if local toughs made remarks about his playing and singing, and almost every dance ended in a free-for-all fight with men being sent crashing through windows, rolling down stairs in tangled masses, or engaged in fist fights on the urine-soaked ground behind the dance halls. Ture loved to fight almost as much as did August, but to save his knuckles and fingers for the saxophone, he requested that Fritz accompany the group as bouncer at two dollars a night.

By this time the band was so popular that it brought in large crowds, and it received eight to ten dollars for each dance. The Dacia earnings slowly built up, but remained inadequate to make the mortgage payment, feed and clothe a family of eight, prepare for a long cold winter, buy a car and finance the long trip to New York City.

Chapter Seven
Explosion

On a clear Thursday evening in June, the Dacias were standing in their yard looking at sheet lightning to the west; wondering if it would develop into rain when something suddenly flashed in the northern sky, a white burst of light shooting up from the dark horizon. As the family gazed in amazement, a tremendous explosion boomed far to the north. The earth seemed to shake with the blast, and the horses whinnied fearfully from their pasture behind the barn.

Aunt Magda crossed herself. "That was not thunder!"

"Holy Mother of God!" Uncle Jon stared to the north. "It sounded like the big cannons the Germans used! Has this country gone to war?"

Josif felt a strange sense of foreboding, as when three years before he had heard the huge trucks from Chicago come to Verne Lamb's farm in the night. That night there had been omens of death as his eldest son, twelve year old Alexander, lay wounded in his bed from a beating from his neighbor's son, Julius Lamb. He saw that the three girls pressed close to Izabella. Michael-Joseph had taken his hand. "If it was war, we would hear more guns. I think something big has exploded up near Sioux Falls."

Yard lights came on in the farmyards to the west, tiny points of light on the dark sweep of land that stretched away toward the Missouri River. Then the lights of a car showed through the cottonwoods; it approached from the north, coming fast. It roared into the Dacia driveway, and they recognized the Pontiac and its occupants, Fritz and August Wagner.

Fritz leaned his head out of the driver's side window. "Climb in! We're headin' up north!"

August pushed his head in front of Fritz. "We're gonna see what the hell happened."

"Shut up, August," Fritz said. "Don't come buttin' in when me an' Joe an' Jon are tryin' to talk."

"Well, I don't hear nobody talkin' but you. I was just tellin' 'em why we're headin' up north."

"Damnit, August, I'm gonna whomp you good if you don't stop interruptin' me. Joe and his uncle here don't need you tellin' 'em why we're headin' up north. They can figure that out for themselves."

"We wonder what can make such big explosion," Josif said. "Took sound so long to get here, must be very far away."

"Yeah, I figured that," August replied. "It was twenty-five miles away."

"You figured that?" Fritz snorted. "I'm the one that explained that to you. And you got it all wrong as usual. The damned explosion was thirty-five miles away."

"It wasn't neither! It was only twenty-five miles away! You gotta say, 'One mile away gonna thunder and rain like hell,' for every mile. I got up to twenty-five. you left out the 'and rain'."

"Jesus H. Christ!" Fritz exclaimed. "It wasn't no twenty-five miles! I bin countin' miles for lightnin' a hell of a lot longer than you have, and I always get it right. You gotta say, 'One mile away, gonna thunder like hell.' There ain't no guarantee it's gonna rain!"

"Sayin' it's gonna rain don't have nothin' to do with

whether its gonna rain or not," August said. "You put in the rain part so you get the right number of miles away the blankety blank storm is!"

"Listen August," Fritz roared. "I'm gonna explain it to you one more time. Countin' miles don't have nothin' to do with rain. It's the goddamned thunder you're listening for! Not the stupid rain! You ain't got sense enough to come in outta it if you did hear it. I'm right and you know it."

August snorted in exasperation. "Oh sure, you're always right! You've missed so many times it ain't even funny! How about that time lightnin' struck that bohunk's barn over in Iowa? You said it was thirty-five miles away. The next day we found out it was only thirty!"

"Well, you dummy, you said it was twenty-seven! You wasn't any more right than I was!" The brothers glared at each other.

Josif spoke to Uncle Jon in Romanian. "If they keep on arguing like this, they are going to start fighting right in their car." He said to Fritz, "If you go to explosion, I like to go with you, but rest of family better stay home. I think something bad happen."

Fritz turned his attention from August. "Well, we sure ain't gonna miss it. You hop in the back seat and we'll get the hell up there before everything cools down."

"Can I go too, Papa?" Michael-Joseph asked.

Michael-Joseph was seven years old. Josif studied the little boy's face. He saw that Izabella had taken Michael-Joseph's hand. Michael-Joseph was her only son after Alexander had died, and she had become overly protective.

"Someday Michael-Joseph will be the man in this family" he said sternly. "He will go with us."

They drove north on Highway 77, which led to Sioux Falls. Car lights stretched ahead and behind them, all going north.

"All these dumb farmers are gonna be up there gawkin' at everything and blockin' the roads," Fritz complained. "I don't know how they all got ahead of us."

"They wouldn't have," August said, "if you hadn't set there braggin' about how you could figure how many miles away lightning was."

"Damnit, August, you was the one that kept interruptin' me all the time. Now we gotta creep along behind all these old ladies! Whatever the hell happened is all gonna be cooled off by the time we get up there."

A siren wailed behind them and then quickly upon them as a car with bright red lights roared past on the wrong side of the road. "Holy Christ!" August said. "That was Butch Bennard goin' eighty miles an hour in his new V-8!"

Fritz swung the Pontiac out from behind the car ahead of them into the left lane and followed the V-8. "If the sheriff can pass all these dummies, so can we. I'm gonna follow right behind him. Anybody headin' south is gonna head for the ditch when they see Butch comin' at 'em!"

"Yeah," August shouted, "and we'll follow him right to where the explosion was! He must'a picked it up on his radio!"

"Listen, August, why the hell do you think I'm followin' Butch? I had that figured out the minute I heard his siren."

Fritz drove with one hand while he fished for tobacco and papers in the bib of his overalls. "Now that we're out from behind all them slowpokes we got clear sailin' all the way." He held the bag of tobacco in his teeth while he peeled a paper out, then with one hand and his teeth, he pulled the bag open, filled the paper, and rolled a cigarette. He licked the edge of the paper and rolled the cigarette shut. Then he closed the bag with the assist of his teeth and tucked it back in his pocket. Next he hauled out a big kitchen match, which he snapped alight with his thumbnail, and lit the cigarette. He shook out the match flame and dropped the match-stick remnant into his pant cuff.

"This is the best damn way to get up to Sioux Falls there is. We got this side of the road all to ourselves." The speedometer needle pressed up against the sixty mile an hour mark.

August peered at the speedometer. "Hell, Fritz, give it some gas. Butch is gettin' way ahead of us."

Fritz glared at August. "Shut up, August. You know damn well Butch's got a special transmission in that V-8, and we ain't never gonna be able to keep up with him."

"Well, if I was drivin' I'd sure as hell keep up with him."

"The hell you would. I already got this thing floorboarded. Now shut up and let me do the drivin'."

Michael-Joseph had watched from the backseat with round eyes as Fritz built his cigarette. "Damnit, Fritz," he said, "Hand me the makin's. I wanna roll a cigarette."

Josif gave him a hard look. "You are not rolling a cigarette and watch your language."

"I wanna make one with one hand the way Fritz did!"

"You start making cigarettes, next thing you want to start smoking them. You do that and I take my belt to your behind."

August looked back from the front passenger's seat. "Hell, Joe, it'll make a man outta him. I been smokin' 'em since I was ten years old."

Fritz snorted. "Yeah, and look at you. I think they stunted your brain, if you ever had one." He looked back at Josif. "The dummy started smokin' just because I did. Hell, I was fourteen."

"Yeah, and I s'pose that made you so smart!" August said. "And watch where the hell you're goin'!"

Still looking backward, Fritz glanced to the side and pulled the car back from the edge of the ditch. He scowled at August. "I don't need your help in handlin' a car. I can drive just as good looking backwards an' having a smoke as anybody else can looking out the damned windshield all nervous-like, like some old lady just learnin' to drive."

"Oh sure! And how many times have you put a car in the ditch? Five times! That's how many!"

"It ain't five times! It don't count when you're practicin' somethin.' I ain't never put this car in the ditch since I learned how to do it."

"The hell it don't! If you put it in now, you'd say you was still practicin'! It don't matter when you do it. Even if you put the car in the ditch the first time you try it, it counts."

Fritz shook his head in disgust and spoke to Josif, "He's so bull-headed there ain't nothin' will change his mind unless I give him a good whompin'. I ain't got time to do that now, so you're just gonna hafta ignore him." He turned to face forward. "That damn Butch is gettin' ahead of us. I'm gonna see if I can get a little more speed outta this car."

As they sped north, the number of cars on the right side of the pavement began to decrease, and ahead of them they saw the bright lights of the sheriffs V-8 move back to the other side of the road. "By God," Fritz said. "We're finally gonna get ahead of all these nervous Nellies!" He passed the last car and swung in front of it. "Now we'll just follow Butch to wherever the hell that explosion was!"

After about five more miles, the brake lights of the V-8 flared far ahead of them, and the sheriff's car made a right turn. Fritz yelled, "He's headin' off toward the Minnesota border!" He continued at full speed until they came almost to the intersection, then braked the Pontiac and skidded around the corner. Ahead of them the lights of the sheriff's car shone dimly and faded away in a choking cloud of dust.

"Jesus Christ, Fritz," August yelled. "Keep up with him! If you lose him now we'll never find the damned explosion!"

"How in hell do you expect me to keep up with him when we gotta plow through this goddamned dust?"

Michael-Joseph leaned forward in his seat and said excitedly, "I can hear Butch's siren, Fritz! He just turned off to the north." Then they saw the bright red lights of the sheriff's car to their left, no longer hidden by the dust, moving fast, then slowing as the brake lights flared up.

"He's stopping!" Fritz swung the Pontiac in a sharp turn onto a high, newly graded road bed. "It's by this goddamned new road they're makin'!"

Police cars and an ambulance lined the road ahead, their red roof lights glowing eerily. Fritz braked to a stop just behind Butch's V-8. "Every damn cop in Sioux Falls must be out here!" he said excitedly.

They climbed from the car and hurried along the row of police cars toward a dark group of men who stood about twenty yards off the road, waving flashlights. All the men wore police uniforms except for a big man in a cowboy hat and two men in white clothing.

A powerful smell of explosives caught at their throats, and an aroma of hot earth filled the air, as when a huge bonfire has overheated the soil beneath it. The men seemed strangely silhouetted against the night sky, as though they stood on the edge of a cliff.

Then, as the Wagners and Dacias came closer, they saw a great crater in the earth, just beyond the group of policemen. In the glare of the flashlights smoke slithered up from the pit, and heat radiated from the crater as if from a furnace.

Fritz spoke to a burly man in uniform. "Holy shit, Butch! What blew up?"

The man turned to look at Fritz. "The goddamned powder house." He stared at the Wagner brothers. "I might of known it was you two guys. I oughta lock you both up. What the hell made you think you could follow me down the wrong side of the road when you didn't have no red lights or siren?"

"Well shoot, Butch, all them farmers was pokin' along, cloggin' up the road like they was goin' to a Sunday school picnic. With you clearin' the way for us, we got up here in time to help out."

"Yeah," August added. "We'll help you figure out what happened."

"Shut up, August," Fritz said. "Me and Butch here don't need you buttin' in when we're trying to talk and get this thing straightened out."

Butch scowled at the Wagners. He tapped his sheriff's badge. "You see this? I'm the sheriff. This dad-blasted explosion happened in my county. I'm the one that's gotta figure this thing out. If I want help I'll let you know. You understand?"

"Hell, Butch," Fritz said. "You don't need to get all excited. Just tell us what happened and we'll help you figure it out."

"The goddamned powder house blew up! The road construction crew stored their dynamite in it, and it blew up. That's what happened! Any idiot can figure that out!"

Butch glared at Josif. "Who told you to bring that kid up here? We got enough problems without having him fall in this crater or somethin'. You get him back in whatever car he came in and keep him there!"

Josif looked at Michael-Joseph and put his hand on his shoulder. "You go back to car like sheriff said. We be there soon."

Michael-Joseph gazed off to the west where about twenty feet away a low mound of earth rose above the field. "Papa, I hear something. A lady is calling."

The men stared at Michael-Joseph. The big man wearing the cowboy hat turned from the line of officers who stood on the edge of the crater. "What'd you say, boy?"

"A lady is calling." Michael-Joseph pointed. "Over by that little hill."

The men listened silently, holding their breaths. "I hear lady too," Josif said, and several other men nodded in agreement.

Butch stared at the hill. "I don't hear a damned thing." He pulled his revolver from his holster and aimed his flashlight at the small ridge of earth. "I'm goin' over there."

The group of men and Michael-Joseph walked cautiously toward the mound of earth, the officers playing the beams from their flashlights back and forth over the ground and at the ridge. Butch climbed up on the ridge and shone his flashlight down on the other side. "Holy Christ!" He said in awe.

They all climbed up the slope of dirt to look. A woman lay face-down in a shallow ditch just beyond the base of the incline. She wore a blue and red dress, and she called weakly over and over, "Help me."

TOMMY GUN

Then they saw that the red parts of her dress were blood.

Butch turned toward the men next to him, "Get that goddamned ambulance over here fast!"

One of the men in white ran back toward the line of vehicles while his companion scrambled down the ridge and into the ditch to examine the woman. "Holy shit! These are bullet wounds." He held up his hand. "Bring me one of those flashlights."

He moved the disc of light over the woman's body. "She's been shot about five times!" He lifted her wrist and held it, looking at his wrist watch. "She must be made outta iron! Can you hear me, lady?"

"Help me. Don't let him kill me."

Butch leaned over the woman. "What the hell are you doin' out here?"

"Help me."

"Where's your car? You live around here?"

"Help me, please!"

"How'd you get here? You walk from some farm?"

"Please."

The ambulance headlights swept around, aimed at the group of men and approached, levering up and down over the rough ground. The ambulance stopped and the driver left the motor running and the headlights on as he leapt out and pulled a stretcher from the rear doors. He ran with it to the woman. "Get the hell outta the way, Butch. Everybody shine your flashlights down here so we can see!"

The man kneeling by the woman spoke quietly to her. "We're gonna get you in the ambulance now." Together the two men gently turned the woman over onto her back and lifted her onto the stretcher. "You'll be in the hospital in fifteen minutes."

"Wait one goddamned minute." Butch glared at the men. "I'm the county sheriff, and you're not hauling her off 'til I question her. We gotta find out what happened here before she dies!"

"Jesus H. Christ, Butch, she's still alive! We gotta get her to the hospital!"

"With five bullets in her? She ain't got more than about thirty seconds left. Now you two sons-a-bitches get back while I question her or I'll slap the cuffs on botha you!"

Butch elbowed the men away and bent over the woman. "Who shot you? Who was it?"

"Where's Tony?"

"Tony? There ain't no Tony around here."

One of the policemen picked something up from the ground. "Shit!"

Butch looked up at him. "What?"

"Look at this!"

"What the hell are you talkin' about, Merle?"

"Come up here and look at this."

"Holy Christ, I'm trying to get some facts before she kicks the bucket. What the hell are you talkin' about?"

"I think maybe I found part of Tony. I found his finger."

"No!", the woman cried out.

Butch looked at Merle. "How in hell is she still in one piece?"

"I crawled away... he was shooting at Tony... then the blast came...."

"Who shot you? Tell me now!"

"I'll never tell... don't shoot me again...."

"I'm the sheriff. I ain't gonna shoot you. Now you gotta tell me who shot you and why."

"I'll never tell...."

"Look, lady. You been shot five times. You're gonna die. Nobody can hurt you more than that. Now tell me who shot you and why so I can get the bastards!"

The woman stared up at the sheriff. In the glare of the flashlights the men saw that her face was beautiful. She spoke weakly. "He thought I had betrayed him to the Chicago mob and knew where the money was. But all I did was fall in love. Where's Tony?" Her head slumped to the side.

The ambulance driver felt the woman's wrist, then the side of her throat. "She's told you all you're going to hear from her now, Butch. She'll be lucky to survive the ride to the hospital."

* * *

The Wagner brother's Pontiac roared into the Dacia driveway after midnight. The whole family rushed to the kitchen porch as the car circled the barnyard, stopped in front of the house to let Josif and Michael-Joseph out, and then roared out the driveway.

Izabella knelt and hugged Michael-Joseph as he came into the porch, then looked up at Josif. "We were so worried about you.° We thought you had been in an accident," Izabella said speaking Romanian.

Michael-Joseph shook his head and spoke in English, as was becoming a family pattern: the adults speaking in Romanian when at home or speaking amongst themselves, and the children speaking in the same conversation in English. This was easiest for all and kept adults and children familiar with both languages. "Fritz can drive facing backwards."

Izabella hugged him more tightly. "Thank God you are still alive."

Aunt Magda raised her hands. "They are crazy boys, they will kill themselves if they're not careful!"

"Did you find out what the explosion was?" Uncle Jon asked.

"Somebody blew up a storehouse full of dynamite. The sheriff was there and many men."

"Why would anyone blow up the dynamite?"

"To get rid of someone maybe. Michael-Joseph heard a woman calling for help. She had been shot."

Izabella and Aunt Magda touched the crosses at their necks. "Shot?" Izabella asked.

"Five times!" Michael-Joseph held up his right hand with fingers spread.

"And she could call for help?"

"She was dying," Josif said. "They didn't think she'd make it to the hospital."

Izabella's eyes filled with tears. "How awful. The poor woman."

Michael-Joseph spoke up brightly. "They found a man's finger."

The women and girls stared at him.

Josif explained. "Someone set off dynamite maybe to get rid of the woman and a man. The man must have been blown to pieces."

"They found only his finger?"

"Yes."

Aunt Magda crossed herself. *Strigoi!* she said looking around warily.

Izabella drew the girls close. "Come inside! Evil spirits roam in the darkness!"

"It was way up east of Sioux Falls," Josif said. "We are safe here."

Michael-Joseph shot an imaginary pistol. "Gangsters did it."

"Gangsters!" Aunt Magda crossed herself again. "Like the ones who killed the sheriff?"

"That was three years ago. And those men are all dead." Josif closed the kitchen door, shutting out the night and things hidden in the darkness.

The three girls had been listening silently, their eyes wide. Marie, the eldest, asked, "How could only the man's finger be left?"

Michael-Joseph happily explained. "Butch said the man must have spattered like ketchup all over the goddamned fields." He threw his arms open. "Ka-blooey!"

Aunt Magda shuddered. "Don't talk about such things."

Josif cuffed Michael-Joseph. "What did I tell you about swearing?"

"I'm sorry, Papa."

Uncle Jon pulled at his mustache. "How could the woman not be blown up?"

"She was in a ditch about twenty feet from the powder house. She must have crawled there before the explosion."

"After she was shot five times?" Uncle Jon whistled. "That was one tough woman."

"She was." Josif spoke sternly to his children. "Everybody get to bed now; it's very late."

After the children were in bed, Josif closed the kitchen door and spoke quietly to the adults as they sat around the kitchen table in the lamplight. "Before the woman passed out, she said the man who shot her thought she had betrayed him to the Chicago mob and knew where some money was. When I think of the Chicago mob, I think of those murdering Lambs. I hope there is no more trouble at that farm. Arnold Ariosto is a nice man. He doesn't need trouble from any Chicago mob."

Aunt Magda stared through the window into the darkness and crossed herself, "God's will that no more evil men come this way."

Chapter Eight
A Game of Pitch

That Friday evening the Wagner brothers appeared as usual, carrying a greasy deck of cards and arguing loudly as they came up to the porch.

"Dammit, August," Fritz bellowed. "You got that all wrong just like you always do."

"I ain't neither," August replied. "Butch told me just exactly what I said."

"Butch didn't tell you nothin'! Me and Butch was talkin', and you stuck your nose in."

"Butch was talkin' to me just as much as he was to you."

"No he wasn't. I'm the one that asked Butch. I said, 'How's things?'"

"Well I was there too, for crying out loud. I could've said, 'How's things?' just as well as you did!"

By this time the Wagners were at the porch steps where Josif, Uncle Jon, and Michael-Joseph waited to greet them. "August is dumber than usual tonight," Fritz said as he shook hands with the Dacia men and joined them on the porch. "I'm prob'ly gonna hafta explain how to play pitch to him all over again."

"How to cheat, you mean," August protested. "He's the world champion expert on that. Besides, I know the rules better than he does."

Fritz waved a big fist under August's nose. "See this? You try harpin' on any of your stupid rules tonight and I'm gonna jam it right down your throat."

Josif held the kitchen door open. "Come in. We have coffee getting ready."

The Wagners clumped into the kitchen and seated themselves in their usual chairs at the table. They tipped back their hats, and built cigarettes with papers and tobacco hauled from the pockets of their blue-striped overalls.

Fritz lit his cigarette and blew smoke toward the ceiling, then glanced at the kitchen stove. "I s'pose that coffee must be about ready now, ain't it?"

Josif nodded. "Michael-Joseph will bring it."

As Michael-Joseph proudly poured four cups of coffee and brought sugar and cream, Fritz shuffled the cards and dealt them. August objected, "Jesus H. Christ, Fritz, you're supposed to let somebody cut them cards first!"

"Not the first hand. It ain't necessary. You only hafta cut 'em after we played awhile and all the suits get kinda gathered together." Fritz picked up his cards and studied them. "Two spades."

August threw his cards face-up on the table. "I ain't playin' with no cards that ain't been cut! Look at that hand! There ain't a face card in it."

"Well it ain't my fault that you can't get good cards. Now you spoiled this whole hand." Fritz threw his cards down in disgust. He turned to Josif. "You prob'ly didn't hear what I was trying to tell August when we drove in. He's so blankety blank stupid he's got what Butch Bennard told me all mixed up, just like how he plays pitch."

"I ain't got nothin' mixed up, and Butch told it to me just as much as he did to you." August looked at Josif for support. "Butch said that woman we found all shot up in that ditch was still alive when they got her to the hospital."

"I told you he had it all mixed up," Fritz said. "The way he tells it, you would think she got to the hospital and died. She ain't dead yet. She's still alive."

"She is still alive?" Josif shook his head. "How could she live with five bullet wounds?"

"She must be tough as hell." Fritz took a long drink of coffee.

"Butch said she had done some talkin'," August added.

"See, that's where you got it all wrong, August." Fritz grinned in triumph. "Butch said she was doin' some talkin'. That means she's still alive. If you say it like you did, that she had done some talkin', then it sounds like she's dead now."

"It doesn't either sound like she was dead now. If she had done some talkin', that doesn't mean she couldn't still be doin' some talkin'."

Fritz looked to the ceiling in disgust. "He can't get nothin' through his head. I try, but it just ain't no use."

"Did sheriff say what woman said?" Josif asked.

"Gangsters did it," Fritz replied. "Seems like one Chicago gangster crossed another and stole millions in cash and jewels and then hid all that loot. He also may have killed the first gangster's brother and another guy in the process. That woman, Helen, and *Tony the finger* were supposed to be spyin' on each other but fell in love and betrayed their own families. They were tryin' to steal dynamite so that they could defend themselves from the mob and get the money all for themselves."

"That plan didn't work out," August added knowingly.

Fritz snorted. "Of course it didn't, you idiot. Any time you get shot five times, or blowed up so you only got a finger left, your plan didn't work out! You sure got a pathetic way of statin' the obvious."

August ignored Fritz and spoke to Josif and Uncle Jon. "The sheriff said her name is Helen Stephanos, which sounds Greek they say. She was all delirious and kept begging him not to tell Zeke. The only gangster he knew of named Zeke is some Zeke Volakis in Sioux City, who also happens to be Greek."

"Well, it don't matter anyway," Fritz scoffed. "The only gangsters we had around here were those goddamned Lambs, and they're all dead. Explosions and murders in Sioux Falls, Greek gangsters in Sioux City, don't none of those things have nothin' to do with us here."

Not unless those evil Lambs hid some 'things' and some 'ones' on the Ariosto farm, Josif thought. *Then it could have a lot to do with us here.*

Chapter Nine
Arnold Ariosto

Saturday morning Josif walked to Arnold Ariosto's farm, going south across the stone bridge that arched over the creek, then west for a mile along the road that separated the Ariosto farm from the farms to the north, then south to the driveway that led to the white house and the big red barn where the huge still had been hidden.

Three years ago Josif had crossed the fields in the night toward those buildings, carrying his grandfather's knife with the intent of killing Clarence, Verne, Vince, and Julius Lamb in revenge for the death of his son, Alexander. There Josif found Verne Lamb dying from a gunshot wound, and had spared his life.

That same night Josif learned that Verne had killed Clarence Lamb with an axe, and that Vince and Julius Lamb had died in a gasoline explosion. Died as they came to burn Josif's house and barn and to kidnap Ellen Olson, who had brought Izabella home from the hospital in Sioux Falls where Alexander had died. Shortly afterwards, Verne's wife Belle had died of cancer.

Arnold Ariosto was Belle Lamb's younger brother, her only living relative since Clarence had killed their uncle, Sheriff Frank Ariosto. He had inherited the farm after Verne's and Belle's deaths, and was working hard to make a go of it by himself.

Now Josif walked in the daylight to help a neighbor, rather than in the night to kill his enemies. Meadowlarks sang from the fence posts, the rising sun illuminated the broad fields with their green rows of sprouting corn, and the fresh morn-

ing air filled him with energy. Yet now a sense of impending danger prevented him from glorying in the beauty of the world.

Arnold Ariosto was in the barnyard working at a two-row corn cultivator, bolting on grease-covered shovels. He stood up and wiped his hand on a piece of burlap before he shook hands with Josif. He was a powerfully built young man, on the tall side, with dark wavy hair, and the same strong and capable look as Sheriff Ariosto. He smiled at Josif. "What brings you over here so early in the morning, Mr. Dacia?"

Josif looked serious. "I come to tell you about something. You hear that big explosion couple nights ago?"

"I was over in Yankton, but we heard it there. Sounded like it was up by Sioux Falls."

"Fritz and August Wagner take Michael-Joseph and me up there. Somebody blow up powder house full of dynamite."

"On that new road they're building?"

"Yes."

"Do they know who did it?"

"Woman shot, but she said gangsters from Chicago or maybe Sioux City. She almost die."

Arnold's eyes became steely hard. "They shot a *woman?*"

"Yes. And blew up man."

"Did they identify the woman and man?"

"Identify?"

"Know their names? Who they were?"

"Woman was almost dead. Sheriff said she had Greek name; she ask for man name Tony. They were in love. Only one finger was left of him."

Arnold tipped back his fedora, and stared at Josif. "The man was blown to pieces, but the woman lived?"

"Before explosion she crawl away from little house where dynamite was. Was very strong woman. Was shot five times. Some bad people wanted her to tell something. She said more things in hospital."

"What?"

"Man who shot her want to find out about much money stolen by gangster. He said Greek woman betrayed him. Was very angry."

"I guess so to do that to a woman."

"The man, Tony, was from different mob. He was looking for money and for brother of Chicago gangster, and another man. This brother never return to Chicago. I hope all this have nothing to do with this farm, but I have wondered, how did Clarence and Vince Lamb drive two trucks and one car out here? I am afraid this farm may not have finish with trouble. You our neighbor. I want you to know what is going on. I not want you be killed."

Arnold's face hardened, and his eyes held a cold look

of determination. "Don't worry, if any damn gangsters come nosing around here, I can deal with 'em." Then he smiled at Josif. "I thank you for coming to warn me. You're a good neighbor." He held out his hand to Josif. "If I can help you and your family in any way, please let me know."

Chapter Ten
Sofia's Daughter

After the death of her partisan husband, Sofia Radulescu, née Dacia, took the last name *Tataranu* in order to escape from the enemies of her family. When the *Great War* ended in 1918, Sofia brought her eight-year-old daughter, Irina, to Bucharest where Sofia supported them by teaching ballet and ethnic dancing in a small studio in a poor section of town.

Irina had spent her childhood in the forests and mountains of Romania with the partisans who fought for the freedom of their country. She had learned to run silently, to hide in caves and under fallen trees, to make forced marches through snow and storm, to sense danger, and to shoot accurately with a light carbine and pistol. She was schooled by Sofia in reading and writing and the history of her country.

Attending the public schools in Bucharest, Irina did so well that upon finishing high school, she was recommended for the university under a government scholarship. At the university she studied history and philosophy, and joined a group of students who spent their evenings in cheap cafés discussing poetry, politics, and the future of their country.

Two of Irina's best friends were Aaron and Esther Horowitz, a young couple who operated a small bakery next to Sofia's dance studio. Aaron and Esther had spoken passionately against the evils of dictators and tyrants, and revealed to Sofia and Irina that they had fled from Russia after the Bolshevik revolution. When Sofia became ill, Aaron and Esther were like family to the sick woman and the young Irina, bringing food to them, and helping to care for Sofia in her last days.

After Sofia's death, Irina lived alone in the tiny flat and earned her living by continuing to teach in the dancing school as well as completing her studies a year early. An accomplished dancer and teacher at nineteen, she auditioned for the Romanian State Dance Ensemble, and was accepted. A beautiful girl, she danced with such artistry and passion that she advanced through the ranks until in 1932, at age twenty-two, she became the lead female dancer.

For the first time in her life, she had enough money to move to a small apartment which had running water and a bathtub. She even bought a few pieces of attractive clothing for herself: a simple black dress, a flowered summer dress, satin underclothing, silk stockings, a small fashionable hat, and a pair of small black leather dress shoes with slender heels. These things she cherished and treated as works of art, wearing them only after bathing in the luxurious bathtub, and then only to church and important receptions.

As a dancer in the ensemble, she had acquired beautiful folk costumes of the various regions of Romania, making most of the costumes herself, embroidering them with the intricate peasant patterns of her country. But for everyday wear and for rehearsals, she wore secondhand clothing, clean but often patched.

She had never forgotten the rough times of the partisan life, or the almost penniless days after the war when her mother struggled to establish her dance school. Irina spent her salary carefully, saving most of it in a small box under the floorboards of her flat.

Then in the summer of 1932, Irina found Aaron and Esther murdered in their wrecked and desecrated bakery.

Irina had seen death in her years with the partisans, but the cruelty and hatred she saw evidenced in the bakery, the method of death, and the bloody words on the wall, sickened and horrified her.

Shortly after the murders, Irina discovered that she was under almost constant surveillance: shadowy figures in the dark streets below her flat, men watching her from alleys, hooded figures following her. When she found that someone had entered her apartment and searched through everything in it, she was angered and alarmed.

Her university friends spoke behind their hands of similar experiences, and warned her that her friendship with Aaron and Esther had endangered her life. It was then that Irina decided to defect when the Dance Ensemble went to America. And when Uncle Josif's letter to her mother had reached her, she sent the letter Josif had received, having it secretly mailed from Ploesti by a friend. Now she counted the days until August 14th, when the Dance Ensemble would sail for America.

Chapter Eleven
All for the Fatherland

At midnight in a forest glade ten miles from Bucharest, dark figures assembled, members of the Legion of the Archangel Michael, known as the Iron Guard. Deben Ceascu trembled with excitement as their leader, Corneliu Codreanu, strode into the center of the circle of waiting men. Codreanu saluted, a powerful sweeping motion with his right arm. "All for the Fatherland!"

The men returned the salute. "All for the Fatherland!"

"Blood and soil!" Codreanu held high a small cloth bag.

"Blood and soil!" Each man held aloft a similar bag.

"Death to the Jews!"

"Death to the Jews!"

"One national community of the quick and the dead!"

"One national community of the quick and the dead!"

"Roll call of our fallen comrades!"

A man stepped forward with a black book. Another man held a torch over it. The first man read from the book:

"Antonescu, Mihai."

The men shouted, "Present!"

"Balcic, Ghiorghiu."

"Present!"

"Costinescu, Anton."

"Present!"

"Dragomir, Nicolae."

"Present!"

The list of names continued through the alphabet. All the dead men were present.

Codreanu and the men saluted.

"Bring our comrade, the martyr Iuliu Puscariu," Codreanu ordered. "Seven years he has lain in the soil of our beloved country."

Four men carried a long wooden box to the center of the circle and placed it in front of Codreanu. Four other men brought in an ornate casket with silver and gold decorations, and placed it beside the wooden box. The man with the torch held it above the box while the four men opened the lid. Tenderly, lovingly, they lifted a skeleton from the casket and placed it on a white sheet which lay on the ground near the ornate casket.

The men cleaned the bones of the skeleton, carefully removing every vestige of decomposed skin and flesh with scrapers, knives, brushes, and wet cloths, and finally polishing the bones with dry cloths. Then the skeleton was placed in the ornate coffin.

Codreanu and all the men saluted.

Codreanu intoned, "Now let the soul of our comrade depart from his body. Vengeance will be ours. Ten men will die for every one of our martyrs." He held up slips of paper, "I have here the names of ten men who must die. Form yourselves into nine groups. Each group will take one slip of paper. Make your plans carefully. Work in secret. Kill anyone who could or would betray you. Even your friends, wives, or lovers if necessary."

Codreanu held up one of the slips of paper. "This man is mine. I will need only one of you to work with me. He knows already that I have chosen him. Now, the rest of you form into groups and take a paper with a name on it. Then we will transport our comrade's bones to the cemetery his family has chosen."

* * *

After the burial, Corneliu Codreanu met secretly with the man he had chosen to help him. The meeting was in a windowless basement room in Codreanu's home. The chosen man was Deben Ceascu.

Codreanu showed Deben the slip of paper.

Deben swallowed. "The Premier? Ion Duca?"

"He must die. The king's mind is poisoned against us by Duca."

"But the king would send troops against us if we kill Duca."

"He must not know. The Iron Guard must appear innocent."

"How can we not be blamed for it?"

Codreanu smiled. "Because we will not do it."

"I don't understand...."

"A woman will kill him."

Deben stared at Codreanu. "A woman?"

"Duca is always surrounded by his bodyguards. It is not likely that a man can get past them. A woman will not attract the guards' attention."

"But where can we find a woman who is willing to do this?"

"You are still a member of the National Dance Ensemble?"

"I am lead dancer."

"Yes. And your partner is Irina Tataranu. A beautiful dancer?"

"Yes."

"You will make her want to kill Duca."

"Irina kill Duca? Impossible. She knows nothing

about guns, about killing. And why would she want to kill Duca?"

"She knows more about killing than you think. And we will make her want to kill Duca."

"What do you mean? How can we do that?"

Codreanu smiled. "Listen and I will tell you.

* * *

The next day Deben Ceascu spoke to Irina after rehearsal. "Come to the Ileana Café at 8:00 tonight."

"Why?"

"Because I tell you to."

"That is not a good enough reason."

Deben scowled at her. "Becoming lead female dancer has made you insolent. If I say the word, you will be removed from the Ensemble."

"You are not the director."

"No, but the director will do as I say. If you are not careful, you will be back in your pitiful studio teaching unwashed peasant girls."

Irina looked down at the floor, not letting Deben see her eyes.

"Think twice about your insolence." Deben's voice was domineering. "You have given me fine thanks for getting you the lead dancer position."

"*Getting* me the lead dancer position?!' Irina said scornfully. "I earned that position myself." Then looking hard at Deben she said, "and do not touch my breasts while we are dancing! You have no right."

"Try to stop me," Deben said smugly. *You* have no rights."

"Why do you want me to come to the café?" Irina spat at him with disgust.

"There's something I want to tell you. It's for your own good."

78

"Is it about dancing?"

"It is more important than that."

"Tell me now."

Deben lowered his voice. "We cannot talk here. Be at the café tonight."

"You will tell me then?"

"Yes."

Irina felt angry and wary, but wanted to hear what Deben had to say. "Then I will come."

"Good. I can do many things for you. Do not forget that."

"I won't," Irina said quietly, feeling her sense of rage and unease grow.

Deben smiled at her. "Now you are acting as you should."

That evening Irina walked the dozen blocks to the Ileana Café and found Deben waiting for her at an isolated table in the back of the room. He motioned her to the chair opposite him. "You're late."

"I walked."

"You should've taken a streetcar."

"I have no money for streetcars."

"You are always so frugal. You should have more money than you claim you do. You must hide your money under the floor in your apartment."

Irina said nothing to this, but felt vulnerable. Deben pushed a glass and a half-empty bottle of red wine toward her. "You don't have to worry; I paid for this."

She poured a little of the red wine into her glass. "Why did you have me come here?"

"To help you. To keep you out of prison."

She looked steadily at him. "Why should I be put in prison?"

"The government suspects certain people."

"Suspects me?"

"Yes."

"Of what?"

Deben lowered his voice. "You are suspected of being Jewish."

"I am not Jewish."

"You associate with Jews."

"I associate with my friends."

"You have associated with Jews."

"What if I have?"

"Ion Duca plans to kill all the Jews in Romania."

"I don't believe it. He could not be that cruel."

"You saw what happened to your Jewish friends in their bakery."

Tears came to Irina's eyes. "They were good people. It was horrible."

"Ion Duca had them murdered."

"Why? Why were they killed in such a terrible way?"

"He hates the Jews. He will arrest and interrogate anyone who has associated with them."

"How do you know what the Premier will do?"

"I am associated with a group of patriots. We know everything that the government plans to do. We can help you."

"I have done nothing wrong. And Ion Duca was a friend of my father and mother. I don't need your help."

"Your parents thought that too."

"What do you know about my parents?"

"That they were killed by Ion Duca."

Irina stared at Deben in disbelief.

"We have proof. Your father was betrayed by Ion Duca. Your mother was secretly poisoned by him. His men have been spying on you. They intend to arrest you, inter- rogate you." Deben leaned forward and spoke in a harsh whisper with an almost gleeful look on his face. "Do you know what the state does to those they interrogate? Have you heard of the guards in the prisons? Women are raped and tortured without mercy, again and again."

"The king would not let such things happen," Irina said sitting back in her chair and looking at Deben with distaste.

"The king knows nothing. The premier, Ion Duca, rules. His men will make you confess."

"I have nothing to confess."

"That doesn't matter. They will torture you until you do confess. You will confess to anything to stop the pain."

Irina shuddered. "No one could stand that."

"That is why you need friends."

"I have friends. Dancers, fellow students, teachers..."

"They can do nothing. You need powerful friends."

"Like you?" Irina said with sarcasm.

"Like me. Our group fights for freedom. We can help you."

"We leave on tour in two weeks. Surely I will be safe then."

"You will not go on the tour. You will be in prison. No one can help you then, except me. You are nothing without me."

Irina threw her wine in Deben's face. She said coldly, "You are the one who searched my flat! You lie to me about my parents, about Ion Duca. He was a friend of my father and mother. You are my enemy, not Ion Duca." She marched from the café, her back straight, her chin up.

* * *

The next night, Deben Ceascu came to Corneliu Codreanu's house. In the secret room he told Codreanu of Irina Tataranu's reaction. Codreanu listened intently.

"You did not mention the name of our organization."

"No."

"The girl is courageous and intelligent. She will have to be convinced of Ion Duca's guilt in some other way."

"Our people could arrest and interrogate her, making her believe she has been taken by Duca's men."

Codreanu frowned. "I knew her father and mother. I would rather not have her raped and tortured."

"She will be raped and tortured if she kills Duca."

"No. She will die quickly. She must not live to incriminate us. One of our men will shoot her in righteous anger the moment she kills Duca."

Now Deben understood the genius of Corneliu Codreanu.

Codreanu placed his hand on Deben's shoulder. "One of the attributes of our organization is patience. We have waited as long as ten years to avenge the death of one of our patriots. Use psychology on the girl. Slowly, slowly, bring her to the point where she will, before all things, desire to kill Ion Duca."

"There is one problem."

"What?"

"Our Dance Ensemble leaves on tour in two weeks."

Codreanu was silent, thinking. "You must have other dancers who can take her place."

"We have, but none as good as Irina."

"No matter. Non-Romanians will not know the difference. You must forget my words about patience. Sometimes we must act with the speed of a striking serpent. Have her arrested and interrogated."

"Interrogated in the usual way?"

"Yes. But not so she dies. Your men must make her believe that Duca ordered her arrest and torture. Once she believes in Duca's complicity in her parents' deaths, in her Jewish friends' deaths, in her torture, she will have only one wish – to kill Duca. When the time is right you will *rescue* her; tell her how she can kill Duca; that you will help her. Codreanu raised his arm in salute. "All for the Fatherland!"

"All for the Fatherland!" Deben repeated with conviction.

Chapter Twelve
Flight

After Deben told her of the horrors of the prisons, Irina had prepared for flight. She brought her mother's pistol from its hiding place under the floorboard and kept it by her bed. She obtained boy's clothing that fit her slender body, and in her bag she placed her money, a compass, flashlight, matches, knife, bottle of water, light blanket, a cross, garlic, cheese, and hard bread. She would be ready when the time came.

The time came that night when Irina awakened, sensing the approach of something evil. Quietly, quickly, every sense alert, she grasped the pistol that lay on her bedside stand, slipped out of bed, and tiptoed to the window overlooking the street three floors below. She opened the curtains slightly and peered down. In the dim light of a distant street lamp, two black automobiles pulled up to the curb in front of the apartment house and squatted there, ominous as two huge black spiders.

Irina drew back from the window. Hurriedly in the near darkness of the bedroom, she pulled on wool socks, threw off her nightgown, and dressed in a boy's dark trousers, shirt, jacket, and cap. Then she tied on rough leather shepherd's sandals. She grasped the pistol and the bag that stood by her bed, then crept silently to the door of her apartment and cautiously opened the door a crack.

On the stairway below, heavy feet made the steps creak. She silently opened the door and stepped into the corridor, locking the door behind her. She ran down the corridor without sound, her feet light as falling leaves. The fire escape lay at the far end of the corridor, and as heavy footsteps sounded at the top of the stairs, she pushed open the double windows only enough to allow her to step through and onto the fire-escape. She ran down the iron steps as nimbly as a cat, dropped lightly the last six feet onto the ground, and ran into the darkness.

A forest lay some miles to the north of the city, and Irina fled toward it through dark alleys, side streets, and country roads. Once a speeding car roared toward her and she hid in a weedy ditch, invisible in her dark clothing. When she came to the forest, she melted into it as easily as an animal of the night.

Her childhood with the partisans had toughened Irina and taught her to survive under conditions that could not have been endured by the untrained. Now she headed north toward the Transylvanian Alps. Wild as any mountains in Europe, the lofty crags and ghostly forests of the Transylvanian Alps had been Irina's home and held no fears for her.

She planned to cross the mountains and go to Cluj where she would take a train to the Adriatic Sea, and then a ship to America.

She crossed a shallow tributary of the Danube in the first light of morning and slept in a wooded ravine until nightfall, then skirted the city of Ploesti in the darkness and entered the foothills of the Transylvanian Alps shortly after midnight. She slept in a thicket and was awakened at dawn by the sound of sheep and a flute.

She peered from the thicket and saw a flock of about one hundred sheep being herded up the hillside toward her by two brown and white dogs. Behind the sheep came

ROMANIA

a peasant boy in a belted smock, cloth leggings, huge paw-like leather boots, and a round topped hat. He carried a bag from one shoulder, a staff under one arm, and held a wooden pan flute to his lips, playing a hauntingly beautiful tune as he walked.

The dogs scented Irina and crouched to the ground, gazing intently at the thicket. The boy lowered his flute and drew a knife from his belt.

Still hidden, Irina sang:

In fields of sweet-smelling grass, tell them to bury me...

The boy stared in wonder at the thicket. Irina called, "Don't stop." She rose to her feet and smiled at the boy.

He lowered his knife. "You know *Miorita!*"

"*The Lamb.* The song is so sad, so beautiful.

They will gather and will cry blood tears.

85

The shepherd knows that he will be killed by his friends, but accepts his fate and his death, and his sheep mourn with him as he prepares to die." Irina sang another line from the song.

"Tell them that at my wedding a star fell…"

The boy slipped the knife back under his belt. "How do you know *Miorita*?"

"I learned it long ago from my mother." Irina came out of the thicket, moving slowly so as not to antagonize the dogs or frighten the sheep.

The dogs looked back at the boy, then came to Irina and licked her hands. The boy slipped his flute into his pack. "You are not dressed like a shepherd. How can you know a song of the shepherds?"

"My people lived in the mountains."

"Are they shepherds?"

"They are dead. They fought for our country."

The boy considered this. "Is that why they died?"

"My father, yes. My mother fought beside my father. She lived then, but now she is dead."

The boy nodded. "My father is dead."

"Your mother lives?"

"She is sick. After the avalanche killed my father last winter, she became sick. She wants to die."

Irina saw the sadness in the boy's eyes. She came closer to him. "Now you are the man."

"Yes."

"How many winters have you lived?"

"Twelve. How many winters have you lived?"

Irina crossed herself mentally. "Fourteen."

The boy studied her. "You have small hands and feet, and you have no beard. I think I can put you on your back in a fight."

Irina deepened her voice and scowled at him. "I am very strong." She pointed to a fallen tree. "Could you jump over the trunk of that tree?"

The boy looked at the tree. "No one could jump that."

"Move the sheep ahead where they will not be frightened. Then watch."

The boy whistled to the dogs, and they moved the sheep forward past the thicket and held them there. Irina put her bag on the ground, ran lightly toward the fallen tree, and leaped easily over the trunk. She circled back to the boy. "Do you still want to fight me?"

"You must be a Gypsy. They came to our village once and did magic things. They stood on each other's shoulders with a girl on top. They threw the girl up in the air and caught her. They walked on a rope tied between two trees."

"I can do those things, but I am not a Gypsy."

"How can that be?"

"My people lived with the Gypsies during the war," Irina said, again lying to the boy.

"Why are you here in the mountains?"

"I want to go to Cluj Napoca."

"Why?"

"My aunt lives there." She smiled at the boy. "I could help you take the sheep up into the mountains."

"Wolves live in the mountains."

"I am not afraid of them."

"Spirits of the undead fly among the peaks after the sun sets. They take the life from the living. They prey on the young and the weak," the boy said quietly, noting Irina's reaction.

"I do not fear the *strigoi*." Irina said as matter-of-factly as she could. "There are things you can do to keep them away, like a cross and garlic. I have a cross and some garlic;

do you have either?"

"Of course," the boy replied, feeling more confident of Irina's possible helpfulness in the mountains. "I always carry garlic when I go to the mountains and I always wear a cross around my neck."

"We could take turns sleeping," Irina said smiling. "You can have half my bread."

"You have bread?"

"Yes. And cheese."

"Let me see."

Irina opened her bag and took out the bread and cheese, and her knife.

The boy stared at the bread hungrily. "Let me taste the bread."

Irina sliced off a piece of the bread and gave it to the boy. He sniffed it, then broke off half and chewed it slowly, wonderingly, his face showing his delight. He put the other half in his bag. "I have never had such bread. It is like cake. What is your name?"

"Alexander."

"Let me taste the cheese," he demanded.

Irina gave him a piece, and he sniffed it as he had the bread, then ate half of it. "Your cheese has little taste." He reached into his bag and pulled out a chunk of white cheese from which he cut a thin slice with his knife. He handed the piece to Irina. "Taste this."

Irina sniffed the cheese, then tasted it. The powerful aroma and taste of fermented sheep milk brought tears to her eyes. "I remember this. It is cheese of much character."

The boy smiled. "Our people say it smells like the feet of angels..."

" ... and tastes like heaven," Irina finished.

They laughed together. The boy held out his hand. "You can help me and the dogs take the sheep into the mountains."

She gripped his hand. "Thank you. What is your name?"

"Carol."

"Your name is that of our king."

"Our king who has gone." The boy spat. "Michael made a better king."

Irina nodded in agreement. "His turn will come again. He is still young. His grandmother, the Dowager Queen Marie, is a good and strong woman."

"My father saw her once. She wore white furs and was beautiful."

"She still is beautiful."

"You have seen her?"

"Once when I was in Bucharest."

"And did she wear white furs?"

"From her head to the floor. And her white fur hat had a jewel and a pure white feather on its front. She is the most beautiful queen in the world."

"I wish I could have seen her. But I wasn't even born yet when my father saw her."

Irina nodded sympathetically. "Sometime maybe you will see her. Maybe you will see the king too. He wears a white robe over his uniform, and a great red cross is on the robe. I think he is trying to be a good king now."

"How can he be a good king when he leaves our country and lives with Magda Lupescu?"

"Kings do strange things. He was forced to abdicate."

"What does that mean, *abdicate?*"

"To leave his throne."

Carol studied her face. "Where did you learn that word?"

"In school."

"We never learned that word in school."

"But you know about King Carol and Magda Lupescu."

"Everybody in our village knows about them." The boy hoisted the bag's strap over his shoulder. "We have to get to the hut before dark. Cut a staff from a tree in case wolves come. Stay beside me until you know the dogs and the sheep. Listen to my whistles."

"I will. What are the dogs' names?"

"The one with the white eye is Star. The one with the mane and the torn ear is Lion."

"They are good names." Irina went to a tree and cut off and trimmed a branch to make a shepherd's staff. She smiled at Carol. "I am ready for wolves."

He lifted her bag from the ground. "Don't forget this. I would not have you leave that bread behind." His hand supported the bottom of the bag as he passed it to her, and he looked up at her in surprise. "You have a gun!"

"Yes."

"Why?"

"Bandits."

He scowled at her. "My people are not bandits."

"Not your people."

"Who, then?"

"Bad men from the city."

"What would they do here in the mountains?"

"Steal your sheep."

"What would men from the city do with sheep?"

"Put them in trucks and haul them off to be slaughtered."

Carol looked at her suspiciously. "How do I know you are not working with them? You might have come to kill me!"

Irina shook her head. "That is not true." She pointed to her bag that Carol still held. "You take the gun. Carry it in your bag."

"You would give me the gun?"

"While we are together. When I leave you I must have the gun again."

"Why? I thought you were going to visit your aunt. Are you going to kill somebody?"

"I may have to."

He looked knowingly at her. "Someone is after you."

"Yes."

"Why?"

"They killed friends of mine. They want to put me in prison."

Carol thrust his hand into the bag and pulled out Irina's pistol. He studied it, sniffed it, and pulled back the hammer. He aimed the gun at the fallen tree.

Irina stopped him. "Don't shoot."

"Why not?"

"Because the men who search for me may not be far away."

Carol turned and studied the forested foothills below them, then ahead at the wild crags and massive peaks of the Transylvanian Alps thrusting into the cobalt blue Romanian sky. "I see no men."

"No."

"I could shoot you."

"You wouldn't."

"Always I have wanted my own gun. Now I can shoot anybody I want to. I can be a chieftain."

"A good chieftain does not waste ammunition. The bullet you waste might be the one that could have saved your life. The pistol only has eight cartridges."

"You have more."

"No. Look in the bag."

He rummaged in the bag. "What is this thing?"

"My compass."

"I have heard of them. How does it work?"

"It tells directions." She showed him how the compass worked, and he became so fascinated by it that he gave her the gun in order to have his hands free. When she explained magnetism to him he grasped the concept immediately and tested the compass again and again, his face alight with the joy of acquisition of knowledge and understanding. He insisted on carrying the compass as he signaled the dogs and began to move the sheep up the mountainside. Irina quietly placed the pistol back in her bag and followed the dogs, Carol, and the sheep.

Chapter Thirteen
Camp at the Mountain Hut

All day they climbed north, and the flat lands behind them fell away while the great loop of the Danube appeared to the east, and before them the mountains thrust higher into the sky. But as the sun swung down into the valleys to the west, the craggy peaks darkened and a feeling of ancient spirits crept over the mountains. Ragged grey clouds dragged like torn capes over the sheep and shepherds, and a low moaning caused the dogs to show the whites of their eyes and to raise the hair on their necks.

They came to a pine forest, and Carol and Irina collected fallen branches and each carried a large bundle of them as they continued up the mountain. Then Carol pointed in the gathering darkness to a low structure ahead of them in a grassy hollow, a crude hut made of rough stones, roofed with heavy branches and flat slabs of rock. "We stay there tonight."

A narrow stream ran through the hollow, and the sheep and dogs drank thirstily while Carol and Irina dropped their loads of branches by the hut and then drank upstream from the animals. When the sheep began to graze, the dogs disappeared into a rocky glen and Irina asked Carol with some concern, "Why have they gone?"

"They go to bring our supper." Carol dropped his bag near a charred spot in front of the hut. "Bring grass for the bed while I build a fire."

Irina gathered armfuls of dry grass and spread them to form a narrow bed against an inner wall of the hut, then brought more which she spread against the opposite wall. She noted a crude door of woven branches against the inner front wall and saw that it could be slid along the wall to seal the doorway. Carol watched from where he tended a tiny fire, then peered into the hut. "Why have you made two beds?"

"I have always slept alone."

"We will be warmer in one."

"I can't sleep with another person."

He shrugged. "Sleep where you want, but if you find a *strigoi* hovering over you in the night, don't blame me."

"You believe in *strigoi?*"

"Of course."

"Have you ever seen one?"

Carol made the sign of the cross. "I hope I never do."

"Have your people seen them?"

"There are many stories of them."

Irina shuddered.

Carol lowered his voice. "Our people make a cross of tar over their doors." He pointed to the stone lintel of the hut. "My grandfather made that cross many years ago."

"Then we should be safe."

"We need more." Carol took a dried garlic plant from his bag and hung it from the end of one of the roof branches above the doorway. "This will keep most *strigoi* away."

"Most?"

"If a *strigoi* is very determined or hungry for someone else's life force, he will need more than one garlic plant to keep him away."

Irina pulled her jacket closer around her, and looked into the thickening shadows. "I have some garlic too. I will rub it around the door and put some in each of our beds."

At this moment two dark figures leaped toward them

from the shadows. Irina felt an instant of terror, then she recognized Lion and Star, each with a large hare hanging from its mouth. Carol patted the dogs and praised them as they dropped the hares in front of him. "Good Lion. Good Star. You have brought us our supper."

Irina patted the dogs and rubbed their ears. "Good dogs. You will protect us tonight, too."

Carol shook his head. "Dogs and horses fear *strigoi*. If the dogs run from us in the night, hold your cross before you and pray, for the *strigoi* will be near." He slipped his knife from his belt and started to skin one of the hares. "Skin the other one. Do as I do."

Irina took her knife from her bag and grasped the other hare. She expertly skinned and gutted the hare, working so easily and fast that she finished before Carol. She wiped her knife on the grass and smiled at him.

He stared at her. "You must be a Gypsy. Only Gypsies can skin a hare that fast."

"Didn't you believe me? I told you I am not a Gypsy."

"I don't know what to believe about you."

They selected three branches from their wood pile and made a spit on which they hung the carcasses of the hares above the fire. As the meat sizzled and browned the aroma made their mouths water, and the dogs joined them, eyeing the meat and drooling. "How did you train them to bring the hares to you?" Irina asked.

Carol smiled. "They like cooked meat better than raw." He ruffled Lion's coat. "But they have already eaten one hare apiece before they came to us. They cannot wait."

Irina patted Star's head. "They are good dogs."

They were ravenous with hunger, and when the meat was only half-cooked they began cutting brown dripping slices off the outside, ecstatically tasting the hot juices, sinking their teeth into the hot flesh, eating as their primitive ancestors must have eaten after a kill.

They were sharing the meat with the grateful dogs when the dogs suddenly raised their heads and stared into the darkness, their noses sampling the air. Then they whined softly and crouched down on their stomachs. Irina felt a coldness on her back. "Something watches us."

Carol nodded. "It is the old one. He smelled our meat."

"The old one?"

"He has lived here forever."

Irina's fingers found the cross at her throat "He will not hurt us?" Carol called into the darkness, "Come, we have meat for you."

Something shuffled into the dim light of the fire – a bent creature covered with ragged furs. Owl eyes gleamed from beneath forked horns, and it seemed that a long thick tail dragged behind the apparition. The dogs crawled toward it on their stomachs, still whining softly.

Irina felt a powerful and ancient force, primal as the mountains, emanating from the strange being. The smell of bear, wolf, horse, and deer came to her nostrils, and she sensed a mystery as old as the earth. The beast stared at her, then approached, sniffing the air; its eyes widening. It began to make eager noises and saliva dripped from its mouth. A strong musk scent filled the air. The creature reached out toward Irina and began to make motions of mating with its hips.

Irina tensed and leaned away. She pulled out her knife and held it so that it pointed at the creature. "Leave me alone and be gone!" she said harshly.

The being howled in frustration and anger, and reluctantly backed away into the woods, whining and growling as it went.

Carol gazed into the darkness, then at Irina. "The old one has never acted like that or gone away before without eating." Carol looked at her suspiciously. "Why?"

"I don't know."

Carol got up and placed his foot in his baggy boot next to her slender foot. "My foot is twice as big as yours!" He pointed accusingly at her. "You're a girl!"

"No."

"Yes. The old one knew." He backed away from her. "You have lied to me."

Irina lowered her head. "I am a woman. I lied to you because evil men seek me." She gathered up her possessions and placed them in her bag, then she patted each one of the dogs. "I'm sorry. I will leave now."

Carol watched her silently for awhile, then spoke,

"Why do the men seek you?"

"They think I'm Jewish."

"Did you steal something?"

"I stole nothing."

"You took milk from their cow. Jews do that."

"I took nothing."

"Then why do they seek you?"

"They want to do bad things to me."

"What bad things? Whip you?"

"Worse than that."

"What?"

"I don't want to tell you."

"Tell me."

"They said they will torture and rape me, again and again."

Carol stared at her. "Because you are Jewish?"

"I am not Jewish."

"Why do they think you are?"

"Because I had some Jewish friends. The men killed them."

Carol sat silently, thinking. "We hate the Jews in our village," he said.

"Do you have Jewish neighbors?"

"No."

"Do you know any Jews?"

"No. But I saw one once. He would have stolen our cow."

"Did he?"

"My grandfather chased him away. Jews are worse than Gypsies."

"The Jews I knew were a man and his wife. They were young and had fled from Russia. When my mother became ill they helped care for her. They were good people. They had a small bakery near my mother's dance studio. They gave us bread and soup when my mother was sick and dying."

Carol shook his head. "They cannot have been Jews."

"They were. Men came in the night and killed the man. They raped the woman and suffocated her until she died. The men wrote, *Death to Jews* on the wall with their blood. I saw their dead bodies and the writing in blood."

Carol squirmed uneasily, not looking at Irina.

"If the men track me, they will kill you and your dogs. I will go now."

"No."

"I must."

"In our village, the men protect the women."

"I am not of your village."

"You are a woman."

She lifted her chin. "I can protect myself."

"If you go, you will shame me."

"You would rather die?"

"Yes."

Irina studied Carol's face in the firelight. "I have lied to you in another way. I told you I was fourteen years old. I am really twenty-two. You are only twelve."

"It doesn't matter. I am the man." Carol pointed to the hut. "You will sleep inside. The dogs and I will sleep outside the door. You will be safe. Don't shame me by running away in the night."

Irina touched his shoulder. "I will not shame you."

* * *

Corneliu Codreanu, founder of the Iron Guard, summoned the leaders of each *cuib* or *nest* of thirteen men to meet with him in the Bucharest forest at midnight. The men came secretly and heavily armed.

Codreanu, dressed in white, riding a white horse, appeared from the shadows. He addressed the men without leaving the saddle. "The legion of the Archangel Michael must strengthen itself. We have failed to complete the mission which would have resulted in the death of Ion Duca. We will regain our strength by meeting our dead comrades in a glorious celebration of blood and earth at our castle in the mountains. A castle that was home to one of the greatest patriots of our homeland. A patriot who killed the Turkish invaders by the thousands. I need not tell you his name.

"We will meet at the castle at midnight, three nights from now. Inform your men to come by train and motor coach to the nearest villages, then on foot to the castle, keeping hidden in the forests and mountains. Anyone who betrays us by his actions will be killed."

"Will we have the cleaning of the bones?" a man asked.

"Bring no bones. Our meeting is for a different reason." Codreanu stared at the man. "Ask no more questions." He turned the white horse and rode into the forest, disappearing like a white ghost in the darkness.

Irina dreamed in the darkness of the hut. The men of the black cars were crouching. Crouching like ravenous, crazed beasts, ready to strike at the first sign of movement from their prey.

She awakened. She lay unmoving, all her senses alert. Slowly the sense of horror lessened and disappeared. It had been a dream. Silently, she crept from her bed of grass and tip-toed to the entrance of the hut.

The sleeping forms of Carol and the two dogs lay between the hut and the dim redness of the dying coals of the fire. One of the dogs raised its head and stared at her, then the other dog did the same. She backed quietly toward her bed and the dogs lowered their heads. *I am safe here now*, she thought. *The men are still far away, and they could not know where I am, but I know the dream was to warn me. I will not let these good dogs and that boy be killed if the men come.*

Chapter Fourteen
The Castle of Vlad Tepes

For three days Irina, Carol, and the dogs moved the sheep higher into the Transylvanian Alps. In late afternoon of the third day, black clouds boiled up in the west and the ominous rumble of distant thunder told of an approaching storm. By some strange structure of the mountains, the thunder echoed back and forth between the peaks in a continuous growling as though a great beast hovered above them and threatened the shepherds and their flock. The sheep responded by crowding together and crying piteously, while Lion and Star gazed with white eyes at the darkening sky, flattening their ears uneasily as the thunder increased in volume.

Carol pointed with his shepherd's crook. "An old castle stands just beyond those peaks. If we can get there before the storm hits, we can drive the sheep into the ruins of the stables."

With the help of the dogs, they forced the flock up a narrow trail that led over the bony spine of the mountain and down into a wild landscape where amid contorted peaks and twisting valleys, an ancient castle stood – a fortress of towering vertical walls topped by round spires and sharply-peaked roofs. On the top of the highest roof a tower rose like a spearhead into the lightning-lit, black rushing clouds. The structure contained only a few small,

deep windows, giving an impression of gloomy corridors, dark rooms, and dank dungeons. The place had such an air of evil that Irina drew back and touched the cross at her neck. "Does anyone live there?" she asked.

Carol crossed himself. "A man from our village went through the doors and part-way up the turret. He had taken a dare to prove to his sweetheart how brave he was, and it happened to be on St. Andrew's night, when the *strigoi* are most active."

Carol looked intently at Irina. "You know that *strigoi* can take the form of an animal?" Irina nodded uneasily. "Well, he was met by a huge wolf with red eyes. It growled and snapped at him, and chased him from the turret into the black night and down the mountain. If he had not been wearing a cross that hung on his chest and another that hung down his back, and had garlic in all his pockets and around his neck, it would have killed him. He said he could feel its icy breath on his neck and sense the evil coming from it. When he got back to the village, his hair had turned completely white and he had aged twenty years; he could barely speak. He was never the same after that."

Irina shuddered. "I would rather stay outside in the storm than go near it. See how the dogs cringe."

"We have to save the sheep. In a bad storm they will run and fall over the cliffs. The old stables will give us shelter." He pointed. "They are away from the castle. My father and my grandfather brought sheep to them before."

"I would not stay here. Take the sheep to the stables if you must, but let me go on. There will be no shame to you."

"You could die in the storm."

"I would rather risk that. Evil surrounds us, comes closer."

"You know this?"

"Yes."

The dogs crouched, growling deep in their throats. They stared in one direction, then another, now showing their teeth. Carol stared at the dogs, then at Irina. "Men are coming... from all directions...the dogs know...."

"I must go, now!"

"No. Shepherds and their sheep have the right to be in the mountains in the summer to find food when the snow has gone. Even if the men find us, they will not hurt us or take the sheep. It is *transhumanta*, an ancient law."

"I am not a shepherd."

"You look like one. Don't speak if they find us." Carol looked up at the approaching storm. "Quick! Help me get the sheep into the stables!"

They herded the sheep down toward the stables, the dogs working hard and fast, racing to move the stragglers, keeping the terrified sheep together as lightning crackled and thunder exploded, while the roaring sound of a great wind came from the wall of churning clouds which was now less than a mile away.

As Carol, Irina, the sheep, and dogs ran through the crumbling stone walls of the stable entrance and under the shelter of a roofed section, a man on a galloping white horse came from the valley floor upward toward the castle and into the stables.

The horseman was clad in a white uniform, and as he looked down at them from the wild-eyed steed, Irina realized that he was the most handsome man she had ever seen. His dark eyes burned with passion and intelligence, his body was that of an athlete and his voice of a man of culture, of learning.

"You have done well to bring your sheep to shelter." He smiled at them. "I came to help, but you and your dogs have already accomplished that." He leapt out of his saddle as easily as a circus performer and handed the reins to Carol along with a silver coin. "Please put Vlad in a stall. Friends of mine are coming for the night, and I must welcome them before the storm is upon us."

Carol gazed at the coin, then at the man. "They are coming here, to the stable?"

"No. To the castle."

"You will go into the castle?"

"Certainly. It was the home of a great patriot."

"People in our village say it is the home of evil spirits."

"It is the home of brave spirits. Spirits of men who fought for the Fatherland. Men who gave their blood for the earth of Romania." The man's eyes shone as though a fire burned in them. "I must go now. Do not leave the stable until sunrise. Do not tell anyone of what you may hear or see, or you will die."

He turned away from them and ran toward the castle, moving so fast that he seemed to float above the ground. Then as they watched, it seemed in the lightning's glare that the dark figures of many men swept like ghosts toward the castle and disappeared into the dark entrance just as the storm struck.

In an instant all was driving wind and rain, blinding lightning, and deafening blasts of thunder. The castle glowed like a great electric bulb for a moment and then disappeared in the raging storm.

Carol and Irina led the white horse into a stall and then crouched with the dogs, trying to hold the terrified sheep in the farthest corner of the stable as the wind tore at the building and rain hammered on the roof. Voiceless in the roaring of the gale, they could only pray and wait, grateful that they had found shelter from the storm, fearful that the spirits of the castle might be swirling about them.

Finally the fury of the storm abated as it moved on to the east. Carol and Irina crept into the roofless entrance to the stables and above them saw the gibbous moon sailing through torn black fragments of clouds. Carol pointed to the castle. "Look!"

The castle stood tall and menacing in the intermittent moonlight, and every window from the lowest to the top tower held a fiery red light. Then from it came the sound of men chanting, deep voices in an ancient solemn litany.

Irina shuddered. "They sing of blood and death. So the Spartans must have chanted as they prepared for battle."

"Who were the Spartans?" Carol asked.

"Ancient Greek warriors. They fought with great bravery, expecting to die."

"Are the man and his friends expecting to die? Like the shepherd in *Miorita* do they accept their fate and prepare for it? Is that why they chant?"

"They chant to kill."

"Are these men of our country?"

"Yes."

"Who do they want to kill?"

"Jews, Turks, Russians, Hungarians, strangers."

"Why?"

"They believe that all the troubles of our people are caused by those who are not true Romanians."

"How do you know this?"

"I believe they are the ones who killed my friends. I think they are the ones who pursue me."

"How can you know?"

"They are chanting, 'Everything for the Fatherland!'" It is the war cry of the legionnaires of the Iron Guard, The Legion of the Archangel Michael." Irina spoke to Carol with urgency in her voice. "We must sleep now. We must leave here early in the morning before the men come. I do not believe that it is our fate to die here, and I want to make sure."

They awoke in the first dim light of morning. As they prepared to bring the sheep from the stable, Carol spoke quietly to Irina, "The man with the white horse came to help us drive in the sheep. He gave me this coin. I think he is a good man."

Irina said nothing. Carol stared at her accusingly. "You said the men were coming to torture and rape you. The man saw you and left you here. He could have taken you into the castle to do those things."

"He did not recognize me."

"He has never seen you. I think you are lying to me."

"No. His name is Corneliu Codreanu, leader of the Iron Guard. He sends out death squads to kill those he hates."

"Codreanu? He is the man on the white horse?"

"Yes."

"We know of him in our village. He wants to make things better for us. He is a good man. When he comes for his horse, I will thank him. He loves the peasants. He loves our country."

"We must leave now. If he sees me again he may recognize me."

"How will he recognize you? Does he know you?"

"He may. Until I fled to the mountains, I was a dancer in the State Dance Ensemble. My picture has been in the newspapers; he may even have seen me dance."

A man spoke behind them. "He has seen you dance."

Irina spun around to face the speaker. "Deben!"she said with a look of shocked dismay.

"Yes, Deben. The one who warned you of Ion Duca."

"How did you...?"

"Find you? Our leader recognized you." Deben said smugly. "You have come a long way," he added with irritation.

"I never should have stopped here," Irina replied, unable to keep the frustration from her voice.

"You will be glad you did. Ion Duca's men are in the mountains searching for you. They would have taken you in a few more days. You know what would happen then." Deben turned away from Irina and smiled at Carol. "You have done well to have helped my friend. What is your name?"

"Carol."

"A good name." Deben held up a silver coin. "Go saddle and bridle the white horse. Bring him to me and you will have this coin."

Carol looked at Deben. "You will not hurt her or take her. Try and I will set the dogs on you."

"You are a fierce boy."

"She is my friend."

"And mine. I care for her as you do. Now bring the horse."

"I go, but I will be watching you."

When Carol had gone, Irina said, "It was your men who came to my apartment!"

"No. Ion Duca's men came."

"How can I believe you?"

"Come with us back to Bucharest. We will protect you. You have my word and the word of our leader. You saw him before the storm. You must have seen that he is a good man."

"You lie. You will put me in one of your jails."

"We will keep you from Ion Duca's jails."

"While I am tortured in one of yours."

"The Dance Ensemble leaves on tour in a week. We can smuggle you onto the trains and ships, keep Duca from finding you. Once in America I will see that you are lead dancer again. The American newspapers and radio will make so much of you that Ion Duca would not dare abduct you when we return. He wants America to loan money to him."

"I don't trust you."

"Would you rather have Duca's men take you? There will be no trip to America, no dancing, no photographs. There will be only pain, degradation, and death. I can save you from that."

"Why do you claim you want to help me?"

"You don't know?"

"No."

"I want you to be my wife."

"Your wife?!"

"I have thought about it for a long time."

Irina stared silently at Deben.

"You will have fine clothes, a fine house, servants."

Deben placed his hand on her arm. "Come back with me to Bucharest. I have an automobile in the village."

Irina said nothing. Deben's fingers closed possessively around her arm. "I must go back to the castle now. At sunrise I will come to get you." He pointed at the surrounding mountains. "There is no use in trying to escape. We have men guarding every pass, every trail."

"I will never go with you," Irina said defiantly.

"You will." He pressed against her and whispered harshly, "If you try to escape or kill yourself, the boy and his dogs will be killed."

"No! You could not be that cruel!" Irina said, twisting her arm out of Deben's grasp.

"Come with me or they die. It is for you to decide." Deben called to Carol. "How is Vlad, Carol?"

Carol came toward them with the horse. "He is ready."

Deben gave him the coin. "Irina decided to go with us. She will be safe with us, and you can leave with your dogs and sheep. Because you have helped her, our leader will see that your village is helped."

Carol looked into Irina's eyes. "Do you want to go with him?"

"Yes. It is best that I go."

Deben stepped between them. He spoke to Carol. "I will take the horse to our leader now. Stay with Irina until I come for her." He turned toward the castle, and leading the white horse disappeared into the gray mist of the morning.

Carol drew Irina back into the deep shadows of the stable. He whispered to her, "Don't be afraid. Let me have your pistol. I'll kill him when he comes back to get you."

"No. You must not try to kill him."

"I'm the man. The man protects his women. Give me the gun."

"No."

"Are you going to kill him?"

"No."

He touched her arm, gently. "You are going to kill yourself. Our women would do that."

"I am going with him."

He stared at her in disbelief. "You told me what they would do to you."

"I was wrong. I will have fine clothes, a fine house with servants. I will dance again and go to America. When we come back, you can visit me in my fine house in Bucharest."

"He was lying to you, I could tell."

"No, You must not think that. You must think of me in my fine clothes and my fine house. I will dance for you, and we will talk about the time that we brought your sheep up through the mountains."

"Why are you crying?"

"Because I'm so happy." She wiped her eyes. "They are coming now. Take the sheep and go." She hugged him. "I will never forget you."

She knelt, and hugged and petted the dogs. As they licked her hands, she said, "Goodbye Lion. Goodbye Star. You are good dogs. I will remember you always."

Chapter Fifteen
Cat and Mouse

Primo *the Bull* Moretti and Gina Campanella, registered as *Mr. and Mrs. Albert Johnson*, occupied one of the best suites in the Palace Hotel in Sioux Falls. Liberal with their tips, they were popular with the staff and management. Primo's fifty dollar suits, Gina's beauty and stylish dresses, and the new black Cadillac which was polished daily in the hotel garage did nothing to lessen their reputation. All in all, they brought to the hotel an aura of big money and power, and rumor of gangland connections only added to the respect and awe with which they were regarded.

Because of the gangland rumor, Primo's appearance of great physical strength, and his emotionless face and flat, black eyes, men were very careful in their relationship with Mr. Johnson. They never asked questions of him, were always civil, never attempted to be familiar, never looked into his eyes unless he spoke to them, and never, ever seemed to be looking at Gina.

When it was learned that the Johnsons had donated large sums of money to the Sioux Falls Chamber of Commerce and two hospitals, the civic fathers and leaders in the community were impressed, and any talk of gangsters was quickly quashed. The people of Sioux Falls and the surrounding small towns accepted Mr. and Mrs. Johnson as beneficent additions to the community.

One exception to that line of thought was Sheriff Butch Bennard of Lincoln County. Butch Bennard who, with his new Ford V-8 with the special transmission, passed the Wagner brothers in their speeding Pontiac heading north the night the dynamite in the powder house blew up east of Sioux Falls.

"Goddamned gangsters did it," Butch told Harold Torklesson, his lanky and newly- hired deputy that Sunday while they opened the office. "They're back again. Just like that damn bunch of Lambs that had that big still back in '29."

"Hell," Harold replied. "Them Lambs are all pushin' up daisies."

"I know that, Harold. I didn't say them Lambs blew up the powder house. I said some new bunch of gangsters has showed up."

"I ain't heard of no stills lately."

"Nobody said there was any stills, Harold. Whoever blew up that powder house was after a lot of money. We gotta find out who."

"How're we gonna do that?"

"I'm making you a special investigator, Harold. You're gonna work undercover."

"Whaddaya mean, undercover?"

"I mean you're gonna keep your badge in your pocket, and your gun in the car. You're gonna go up to Sioux Falls and look around. You ain't been deputy long enough for anybody to recognize you."

"I ain't no G man, Butch."

"I know that. I'm gonna help you get started." Butch spread the Sioux Falls Sunday paper out on his desk. "See this? Some guy named *Johnson* has been spreading money around."

"So?"

"So I seen him coming out of the Palace Hotel with a good-looking broad and climbing into a big new Caddy. If his name is Johnson, I'll eat my hat. The guy looked like Al Capone."

"Al Capone is in the Atlanta Federal Penitentiary. He ain't in Sioux Falls."

"I know that, Harold. What I'm tryin' to tell you is that this Johnson guy prob'ly has a name like 'Caparetto' or something. What I wanna know is, what's he doin' in Sioux Falls?"

"You want me to go up and ask him?"

"No, Harold. I don't want you to go up and ask him. That would be about the stupidest thing you could do. I want you to go up there and keep your ears open." Butch smacked his hand down on the newspaper. "Now go put on your Sunday suit and get up to Sioux Falls. I want you to find out what the hell is goin' on."

* * *

At 10:00 that morning Harold Torklesson, in his blue Sunday suit, ambled into the lobby of the Palace Hotel, trying to look inconspicuous. He purchased a newspaper at the stand and settled uneasily into a big leather chair behind a potted palm. He pretended to be reading the paper as he sat with one leg crossed nonchalantly over the other.

After an hour, Harold's stomach told him it was time to eat. In addition, the man behind the reception desk kept glancing at him, making Harold uneasy. He rose from the chair and walked casually to the counter. He leaned one elbow on the counter. "Anywhere a fella could get a cuppa coffee around here?"

"The coffee shop's down those stairs." The man studied Harold's hand-painted necktie. "Could I help you with anything? A room maybe?"

"Naw. I was just waitin' for somebody. I guess he ain't comin'."

"It doesn't look that way."

"You don't mind me settin' in that chair?"

"Not as long as you're a customer here. You live here in Sioux Falls? I don't believe I've seen you before."

"Well usually I'm goin' over to the stockyards or somewhere."

"Oh, you're a farmer?"

"Well, more of a cattle feeder. I ain't in love with sittin' on a cultivator all day."

"I can understand that."

"Ya. I like to move around, see the big cities."

"Is that right?"

"Oh, ya. Omaha, Sioux City, Minneapolis...."

"That so?"

"Yup. Minneapolis. Now there's a town for you." Harold looked knowingly at the man.

"I never been there."

"Is that right? Well, I suppose not many people from Minneapolis get out this way either. Course you'd know more about that than me, what with you workin' in the hotel here."

The man nodded. "We get 'em from all over. Lot of 'em come here pheasant season."

"Sure. So some of them stay in the hotel here? Bring their guns in and everything?"

"We're filled right up in hunting season. Some of 'em make reservations a year in advance!"

"Well, I'll be! That long ahead! How about here in June? You get anybody as far away as Minneapolis then?"

"Sometimes."

"Is that so?"

"That's right."

"I thought I saw in the paper that that Carlson or

Hanson guy who gave so much money to the hospitals came from Minneapolis. The name sure fits Minneapolis with all them Swedes up there."

"You mean Mr. Johnson?"

"That's the name. I always get them names mixed up."

"He's not from Minneapolis."

"He isn't?"

"No. He comes from Chicago."

"Is that so?" Harold took his elbow off the counter. "Well, I guess I'll just mosey on down to that coffee shop and get a cuppa coffee and a sweet roll or somethin'. It's been nice talkin' to ya."

"Same here. If that friend of yours shows up, I'll send him down."

Harold waved a hand. "If he ain't here by now he ain't comin'." He turned and walked casually to the stairs that led down to the coffee shop, his new Montgomery Ward yellow oxfords squeaking on the marble floor of the hotel. But instead of stopping for coffee and a sweet roll, he hurried past the counter and out the coffee shop's street entrance. He had some undercover information for Butch and he could hardly wait to tell him.

* * *

Harold returned from Sioux Falls and reported to Sheriff Butch Bennard in the County Courthouse in Centerford. The room was the same one where Clarence Lamb had shot and killed Sheriff Frank Ariosto three years before.

"He's from Chicago!" Harold said excitedly.

"Son-of-a-bitch! I thought so!" Butch brought his feet down off his desk. "You sure of that?"

"Got it right from the horse's mouth."

"Who?"

115

"The guy behind the desk in the hotel."

"You didn't let him know you was a deputy?"

"Heck no. I just sat there awhile readin' the paper and then went and had a talk with him."

"You had a talk with him? What about?"

"Oh, farmin', feedin' cattle, pheasant huntin'...."

"Pheasant hunting?"

"Sure thing."

"And he told you this Mr. Johnson came from Chicago?"

"Yup." Harold studied his fingernails.

"Did anybody see you talkin' to this guy?"

"Nope."

"You sure?"

"Sure I'm sure."

Butch studied Harold upward from his Montgomery Ward shoes to his painted necktie. "Harold, get into your uniform, and grab your gun; we're goin' out to that Lamb/Ariosto farm and nose around a little. That's where the gangsters were before and as sure as Bob's your uncle, if they're back, that's where they'll be headin'. This is gonna involve some real good police work, so keep your eyes open for clues."

* * *

On the day before Harold's undercover job, Red McGuire drove his Model-T truck in through the driveway of the old Toovey farm and up to a sagged-roof shed that served as a garage. Primo's gleaming Cadillac was already in the shed beside Frankie Maldonado's Packard.

The dry grass stubble crunched under his heavy work shoes, and small grasshoppers jumped and flew out of his way, making sharp clicking noises with their wings, as Red hurried into the dilapidated farm house he and Frankie had rented.

Primo, Gina, and Frankie sat at the kitchen table

with a bottle of Canadian whiskey between them. All day Friday and that Saturday morning, Primo and Gina had been involved in dedication ceremonies at two projects his donations had helped sponsor. Primo hated every moment of the speeches and festivities, but knew he had to maintain his carefully established cover and reputation, so he had grinned and painfully borne it. Now he was not in a good mood and was anxious for news regarding his real business dealings.

Primo motioned for Red to sit down, and pushed a glass toward him. "You find out anything?" he asked harshly.

Red quickly poured himself half a glass of the whiskey and took a large swallow. "I sure did, Boss," he said wiping his mouth with the back of his hand. "I found Tony and followed him. He went to Sioux City and met a girl at a café near the Athens Supper Club. They obviously knew each other and had a real intense conversation.

Then they suddenly got up and left. I followed, real casual-like, and was headin' for my truck to follow 'em when I saw Achilles Papadopoulos come out from behind a building across the street. He was acting real casual-like too, so of course I was suspicious. He got into a little roadster and waited a minute, then started to follow Tony and the girl. It was gettin' dark, so I was able to follow them without bein' seen."

Moretti's eyes narrowed as he focused on Red's story. "Where'd they go?" he demanded.

"They went up towards Sioux Falls and turned off at that road construction job just easta town. Achilles cut his lights and so did I. I followed from a ways back and with the dust and the darkness I wasn't seen. When they stopped at the powder house, I parked outa sight behind some shrubs, and snuck up behind some boulders where I could watch and listen."

Primo's fists clenched. "What happened?"

"Seems the girl was Helen Stephanos, Achilles's girl friend, and an agent for Volakis. She and Tony met and fell in love while spyin' on each other's gangs. They wanted dynamite to fake their deaths so that they could run off together. Achilles was real pissed. He had a lot of questions, and he sent her a bullet with each one. First though he kneecapped Tony so that he couldn't interfere."

Primo bolted upright. "That son-of-a-bitch! I'll kill him!" He stared intently at Red. "What happened next?"

"Well the *questioning* revealed that Tony and Helen didn't know anything about the money C.D. stole from you except the same rumor that we heard. That he hid a lock-box full of money and jewels."

Primo glared at Red and growled, "Then what?"

"Then Achilles started to question Tony, and the girl crawled off into a ditch. Tony managed to throw himself in front of the powder house as Achilles was letting loose with his Tommy gun, and the whole shebang blew up. Achilles figured out what Tony was up to just before the explosion and dove behind a boulder. After the explosion he ran to his roadster and lit out. I stayed hidden until the sheriff arrived, then mingled with the crowd."

"So, the Greeks caused that explosion! I'm not surprised; those rotten sons-a-bitches!" Primo struggled to keep himself under control. "You found out nothing about Angelo?"

"Nothing about Angelo, Bull. All that was left of Tony was a finger."

"Goddamnit! Those fucking Greeks are getting too sure of themselves. Those *strunzi* need to be dealt with."

"You just give the word."

"First we must find the money and Angelo." Primo clenched his fists again. "That rat C.D. should be glad he's dead. I'd love to have questioned him. It just proves that except for you, Red, you can only trust family. Tony betrayed me for love, but he was Angelo's wife's brother's son. His blood was too thin to put respect first in his life."

"You know that on my honor I would never cross you, Bull. You gave me justice when there was none. I am forever indebted to you."

"I know that, Red, you're a stand-up guy. You would make a good Italian."

Before his association with Bull, Red had worked the family farm in central Illinois, until the bank foreclosed on it. In Red's mind, this had resulted in his wife miscarrying and dying. Then his son ran away to California and hadn't been heard from since, and his teenage daughter had married the widowed neighbor and died with her baby in childbirth.

Red had appealed to his senators and to President Hoover who had their staff write back saying that the whole country was suffering, that better times were around the corner, and to hang on.

Then Red drove to Chicago and found Primo Moretti and appealed to him. Within a week, the banker and his family were dead, and Red had found a new livelihood.

To Red, the elimination of the banker and his family was right and just, but it did not stop the anguish in his heart, the feelings of failure, nor the rage. Working with Primo provided an outlet, but his *jobs* never fully satisfied him, and Red found himself looking for harsher and coarser ways to vent his fury.

* * *

Primo studied his whiskey glass, then looked up with the cold stare of a reptile. "So we know Achilles and thus Volakis are responsible for Tony's death. We know C.D. was worse than a low-life snake in the grass, and that he is the one who stole from me while I was in the joint. He was probably also responsible for Angelo's death. All his operations were at that Lamb farm. Now it's owned by Arnold Ariosto, Verne Lamb's brother-in-law. That's where we'll find Angelo, and that's where we'll find my money." He leaned forward in his chair and looked at Red, Gina, and Frankie.

"Now listen to me. I have jobs for all of you. Red, I and you will pay a visit to this Arnold Ariosto. We'll see if he seems reluctant to help us search or like he might go blabbing to the sheriff. We'll explain that there are other ways to search a farm, and that sometimes it's easier to look around if all the buildings are gone... and the people."

Red smiled. "I get the picture, Bull."

"We'll go in your truck so that we don't attract attention.

"Then I want you to visit those bohunks at the farm next to Ariosto. They must hate the Lambs as much as I do since they were responsible for their son's death. See what they know about Angelo, the money, or any Greeks nosing around."

"You bet, Bull."

Next Primo turned to face Gina and Frankie. "Gina, I want you to visit Zeke, soon-to-be-dead, Volakis. Tell him nothing. Don't let him know that we know who killed Tony. Find out what he knows. Be nice to him. Lead him on. But give him a message. The money and Angelo are my business, in my territory. Any interference or sudden windfall of money and jewels to anyone other than myself will be seen as a personal insult to me. A very serious lack of respect. I would not be happy or merciful. Tell him that.

"Frankie, you drive Gina down to Sioux City. Rent two rooms in a hotel near the Athens Supper Club. That's Volakis' place.

"Gina, you get cleaned up real pretty when you go

to see Volakis. He'll try to tempt you to betray me and to come over to him. Let him think you might. Get his guard down with you. We can use that later. But do not disappoint me with bad behavior."

Gina shifted uncomfortably in her seat. "You know I'm your woman, Bull."

"Frankie, stay out of sight, but if she isn't back to her room at the agreed time, you go make *inquiries*."

Frankie's eyes lit up. "It would be my pleasure, Boss."

Primo *the Bull* Moretti stood and pushed back his chair. He regarded his three gang members with narrowed and menacing eyes as he began the litany of wrongs performed against him by Volakis. The litany of wrongs that justified vengeance, no holds barred vengeance.

"His nephew has killed one of my family. He has invaded my territory and caused an explosion and disruption in my city. He thinks he has a right to look for my money."

Primo's fist crashed down on the table, causing the whiskey glasses to jump. His face became red and his eyes bulged. Gina cringed as he hurled his whiskey glass past her, smashing into the wall, and bellowed, "He thinks he has a right to look for my money and my brother's grave! He shows me no respect! He has no honor! He and all his men will be rubbed out! *Morto!* Gone from the face of the earth! On my mother's grave, I swear it!"

* * *

Within an hour, Red and Primo were pulling into Arnold Ariosto's driveway. Red loved this kind of a job. He didn't have to be subtle or deceptive; he could just deal out fear. He loved to watch defiance turn to begging. Loved it. This sort of thing was the real payoff from working for Primo Moretti.

He stopped the truck near the barn and got out leaving Moretti in the vehicle with a .45 pointed at Ariosto through the door.

Arnold came out of the barn to greet him.

"You one of the Lambs?" Red inquired, without any of the usual pleasantries.

Arnold stiffened at Red's brusqueness, but answered anyway. "My sister was married to Verne Lamb; they used to own this place. Why?"

"My boss wants to know. He thinks his brother and some of his property are hidden here. Whaddaya know about that?"

"No more than what was in the papers. That business was three years ago. I've been working this farm since then and I haven't found anything. Tell your boss he's barkin' up the wrong tree."

"My boss don't take kindly to being called a dog." Red smiled, but his eyes were cold. He reached into his overalls' pocket and pulled out a pistol. "Why don't you show me around? I'm real interested in where the still was located and what's out back." He gestured to Primo, who joined them, now with his gun in the open.

Arnold saw there was nothing to gain by going against armed men, and led Red and Primo into the barn where the still room was concealed in the wall. He opened the small entry door and flipped the light switch revealing sacks of grain and oats stored inside. "This room is usually free of vermin," he said.

"This room could contain a corpse if you don't watch your fucking mouth!" Red said while shoving his pistol into Arnold's back. "Show us around back."

Arnold led Red and Primo out of the barn and along a path, to the back of the barn. Red stopped at the silage pit. He gestured toward it with his gun. "How long has this been here?"

"It came with the place."

"That silage looks old. Why isn't it being used?"

"It smells *off*. The cattle won't touch it."

Primo spoke up. "I see. Well, farmer, here's the deal. You're gonna help us search your farm. Because I am a very generous man, I will not kill you if you help with that search. If you decide to be uncooperative, your house and barn and all living things here will burn, and I and my men will search at our leisure. Both methods have their advantages. Choose."

That afternoon Arnold and Red searched the barn, including the huge still room. They pried up planks, and looked behind stacks of boards, and under old and broken equipment. Then Red left to go talk to the Dacias, and Arnold searched the house, top to bottom, all the while with Primo *supervising* with his drawn .45 automatic.

Chapter Sixteen
A Wolf in Sheep's Clothing

Late that afternoon as the Dacia men were pitching manure from the barn into the manure spreader, a dilapidated Model-T Ford truck pulled in the driveway and continued slowly down to the barn.

A bony-looking man dressed in striped overalls and a blue work shirt climbed out of the truck. He wore a sweat-stained straw hat and farmer shoes, and his long face had the red skin of a permanent sunburn. He spoke across the nearly-filled manure spreader as Josif, Uncle Jon, and Michael-Joseph peered silently and suspiciously out the barn door.

"Don't stop on accounta' me," the man said. "Course I suppose you wouldn't mind lettin' up a little. Shovelin' manure on a hot day in June ain't never been my favorite pastime."

He raised a hand and grinned across the manure. "Your neighbors say you're the Dacias. Red McGuire's my monicker, and I stopped in to see if you folks knew about anybody 'round here needs a farm hand. You prob'ly don't need any help with that manure job now that you're about done."

He jerked a thumb at Peter and Paul. "That sure is the best looking team I seen in a long while. What are they, about six-year-olds?"

"They eight-year-olds," Josif said.

"I never woulda' thought it. I bet they can work the rear end off any team in South Dakota."

"They good horses." Josif felt his suspicion fading. "This my uncle, Jon Dacia. Boy, my son, Michael-Joseph."

"Well I sure am glad to meet you folks." McGuire took off his hat and fanned his face, revealing a mop of faded red hair. "I won't keep you folks from your work. I'll just mosey along and try a few more farms, maybe find a barn to sleep in."

He looked at the orchard that lay between the house and the creek. "Somebody who knows about fruit trees sure did a nice job of prunin' in that orchard. I don't think I ever seen a better lookin' one."

Josif felt that the man could be a good friend. "Is my uncle's orchard."

"Is that so!" McGuire made an army salute to Uncle Jon. "I gotta congratulate you, Sir! Only a military man could make those rows of trees stand at attention like that!"

Uncle Jon spoke to Josif in Romanian. "What is he saying? I can only understand about half of it."

"He is looking for work. He admires Peter and Paul. He also admires your orchard. Somehow he knows that you were in the army."

Uncle Jon straightened his back and shoulders and ran a finger over both sides of his mustache. "These things can be seen. Tell him I thank him."

Josif explained to McGuire. "We came from Romania. My uncle does not speak well in English. He thanks you for what you said about his orchard. He was Master Sergeant in the Army of Romania."

"I could tell that." McGuire saluted Uncle Jon once more. "Private McGuire! I was in the war, too. Helped kick the Krauts outta France." He saluted Josif. "You was in the war, too. I can tell."

"Yes."

"Well, that sure is great. How'd you folks ever happen to come to America?"

"Our country become bad after the war. We come here to find land of our own."

"Well, you sure found it." McGuire gazed at the buildings and fields. "I don't know when I seen a farm as tidy as this one. A lotta farmers just let their junk lay where it falls, but this place has everything neat as a pin, and not a weed showing! How long you been livin' here?"

"Three years."

"Only three years? Most farms go to wrack and ruin when the owners get old and move into town. You folks have every building painted up nice, and the fences clean and tight. I gotta hand it to you. You're good farmers." McGuire gestured toward the fields. "Without no rain though, it must be kinda hard-goin' right about now."

Josif nodded. "Storms come, but no rain."

"Ain't it the truth." McGuire jerked his thumb toward the south. "I been workin' my way up from Oklahoma. It's ten times worse there. Just about all the top soil has blowed away. Them farmers are packin' up everything they got and headin' for California. But there ain't no work for 'em out there, so they set around them camps like a bunch a' hobos, starvin' to death." He pointed to the cottonwoods and willows along the creek. "You folks were smart to find a farm with some water on it."

"Creek almost dry now."

"It'll come back. You wait'n see. You get any snow next winter and that creek is gonna be full." McGuire rubbed his chin. "You folks ever think of dammin' it up and makin' a little lake? You could irrigate about half your fields."

"What is *irrigate* ?"

"Why, it's bringin' water to your fields. They couldn't

raise a thing out in California if they didn't irrigate. They dam up the water in them big rivers and pump it onto their fields. They have irrigation ditches a' water runnin' over that land thick as wrinkles on a prune."

Josif led Uncle Jon and Michael-Joseph around through the central aisle of the barn and out the door so they could talk better with McGuire. He held his hand out and shook Red's hand. "You think we could irrigate fields here?"

"Sure thing. You just move the dirt out to make a big hole, then you put a dam across the creek."

"Our kids want us to make little pond for ducks and geese that way. Would have to move much dirt to make a pond big enough to water fields?"

"Coupla acres about ten-fifteen feet deep. I could do it with a good team a horses and a Fresno scraper in a coupla months." McGuire jerked his thumb toward the farm where the Lambs had lived. "Your neighbor kitty-corner to the south there has got one. I saw it when I stopped to talk to him about work. His name was Ariosto or somethin'. I guess he just moved in a coupla years ago. He might lend it to you."

Michael-Joseph piped up, "We wouldn't borrow anything from the damn Lamb place."

Josif cuffed Michael-Joseph. "Watch your language," he said giving Michael-Joseph a stern look.

"Yes, Papa," Michael-Joseph said automatically.

McGuire seemed to see Michael-Joseph for the first time. "Where'd you learn that kinda language, toughie?"

"He learn from Wagner brothers." Josif pointed north.

"Them two oversize guys with the big red barn and the old coot with the crutch who looks like he could chew nails and spit out rust? I ain't surprised your boy here has picked up a few choice words."

He paused and looked thoughtful. "What's this about a sheep place?"

"Farm belong to man name Lamb," Josif explained. "More came from Chicago."

"From Chicago?"

"Brought big machine to make alcohol. Were bad men."

McGuire's pale blue eyes narrowed. "You mean a still? A whiskey still?"

Michael-Joseph became serious. "Julius kicked my brother until he died."

McGuire looked at Michael-Joseph, then at Josif. "Julius is one of that Lamb bunch?"

"Was son of Verne Lamb."

"Was? You mean they went away?"

"They all dead."

"Dead? How many?"

"Five."

"What killed 'em? The flu?"

"Men all kill each other. Woman was sick."

"Well I'll be." McGuire scuffed at the ground. "It ain't none a my business, but that sure is some story. Four guys kill each other!"

Michael-Joseph chimed in again. "Clarence shot Verne and Verne split Clarence's head open like a pun'kin with an axe. There was brains and blood all over the place. Vince and Julius blew themselves up when they brought gasoline to burn down our house. The explosion was like a great big fireworks rocket. Vince and Julius looked like two black fried chickens."

McGuire shook his head. "That is the damndest story I ever heard." He looked at Josif. "How'd them Lambs get a big still out here?"

"They brought from Chicago in two big trucks."

"Was they some sorta gangsters?"

"United States Marshal say that,"

"Why in hell's half-acre did they come way out to

South Dakota? Chicago's about six hundred miles from here."

"Marshal think they come here so other gangsters not know where they are."

McGuire rubbed his chin. "I s'pose that could be it. Did the boy here say one of 'em was called 'Clarence'? That sure is a funny name for a gangster."

"Was little old man. Not look like he would kill sheriff."

"He killed the sheriff?"

"In court house. Wore old lady's clothes."

"Clarence's Model-A had armor plates and bullet-proof glass so nobody could shoot him," Michael-Joseph added.

McGuire stamped on the ground. "If that ain't the dangdest story I ever heard!" He looked thoughtfully at Josif. "There's somethin' kinda funny here. You say they brought the still in two big trucks, and now it turns out that this Clarence Lamb had a special-built car. This Verne and his kid Julius lived on the farm. Now how in blazes did Clarence Lamb and Vince Lamb bring two trucks and a car out from Chicago?"

"I ask Marshal that."

"And what'd he say?"

"He thought must have been more men come from Chicago."

"But nobody saw them?"

"No."

McGuire stared across the fields toward the Lamb farm, then said, "Well, it ain't none a my business, but that sure is funny. They tell me these Chicago gangsters are usually kinda heavy-weight Italians with oily faces and black hair. You'd think somebody in this neck a the woods woulda noticed them, what with most everybody around here bein' Swedes and such."

He shook hands with Josif, then Uncle Jon and Michael-Joseph. "Well, I gotta be moseyin' along if I'm gonna find a place to sleep tonight." He walked toward his truck, then turned around. "There's just one more thing. It ain't none a my business, Mr. Dacia, but what with you folks livin' so close to these Lambs, did you ever notice anything like gunshots from that direction, maybe like the machine guns you heard in the army?"

Josif shook his head. "We hear no machine guns."

"Thank you. I sure enjoyed meeting you folks. Maybe I'll be back some time, and we'll have another gabfest." McGuire climbed into his truck and cranked it into life, then he circled around the barnyard and headed out into the road.

Michael-Joseph watched the truck go over the bridge and disappear behind cottonwoods and willows. He turned to his father. "Papa," he said. "There sure is somethin' damned funny."

"What? And Michael-Joseph, you quit that swearing, or I'll take my belt to you!"

"I'm sorry, Papa."

"What did you want to tell me?"

"Remember that night we went with Fritz and August up by Sioux Falls where all that dynamite exploded and we found that woman who was shot, and the man's finger?"

"Yes."

"Well, it prob'ly ain't none a my business, but it sure is funny."

"What is funny?"

"Well, that man that was just here...."

"What about him?"

"I saw him that night. Up there by the ditch where we found that woman."

Chapter Seventeen
Zeke Volakis

Gina and Frankie arrived in Sioux City late that afternoon. Gina's suitcase contained make-up, scented bath salts, toiletry items, jewelry, and two sets of clothing: one for evening wear and one for farm wear. Her purse contained lipstick, powder, twenty-five dollars, and a .32 automatic.

Frankie looked up the address of the Athens Supper Club in a phone book, located it fairly easily, then drove about three blocks out around its perimeter until he located the Cattleman's Hotel and rented two adjacent rooms.

After a relaxing scented bath, Gina donned her undergarments and black silk stockings. Then she carefully applied her make-up, did her hair, and stepped into a calf-length tight black dress with a slit up the side and a low neckline which flattered her full figure. She applied her perfume and jewelry, then stepped into black silk pumps. With her black hair cut *Cleopatra-style* and ample diamonds around her neck, wrist, and fingers, Gina looked like a movie star.

The doorman hailed a cab which Gina took to the Athens Supper Club, the headquarters of Zeke Volakis, ruler of the Sioux City underworld.

She tipped the cabbie fifty cents, then entered the restaurant and tipped the maitre'd a dollar, introducing herself and asking to see Mr. Volakis. The maitre'd, Nick Constantine, spoke into a telephone and Achilles Papadopoulos came into the room. He introduced himself as Zeke's nephew, and escorted Gina to an exposed table in the middle of the room.

Achilles was of medium height, but as solid and agile-looking as a boxer. His features and mustache were dark, and he was handsome, but he moved like a bully, and his eyes betrayed no hint of friendliness or mercy.

He smirked and looked at Gina appraisingly. "Relax, doll, someone will be out to see you in a minute." Then he sauntered to a door at the back of the restaurant and entered Volakis' office where his brother Kostas and his uncle Zeke were discussing the various projects which sustained them in Sioux City.

"We have company," he said. "From Chicago. Primo Moretti's woman."

Zeke showed big tobacco-stained teeth beneath his thick mustache. "Which one?"

"The singer, Gina Campanella. I'll be happy to take care of her, Uncle Zeke."

Volakis scowled. "Not yet. Let's see what message Moretti sends."

Kostas added, "We have to find out why she's here. I agree with you, uncle, talk first."

Achilles fingered his switch-blade. "He insults us. He comes into our territory. He brings only two guns and the woman. He sends the woman alone. He implies we are sissies! I say we send him a message."

Volakis looked hard into Achilles' eyes. "*You* say? *You*, who shot Helen Stephenos five times and got nothing from her? *You*, who blew up the powder house in Sioux Falls and killed Primo Moretti's guy, Tony Turello, bringing us unwanted attention from Chicago and maybe from the cops? *You*, who have bungled things so badly that we will never find the money and jewels that Clarence Lamb hid. *You* will tell me how to do this?"

Achilles looked down at the table briefly. "No, but Uncle Zeke, Helen was supposed to be my woman and just go undercover to trick Tony into telling what he knew. She double-crossed us and betrayed me! She was covering for Tony, pretending they hadn't found out anything about the money. They were at the powder house to steal dynamite to blow something up. What else could it be but where the money is hidden? They both lied to me. How else was I supposed to get them to talk in a hurry? It was that rat-bastard Tony that moved in front of the storehouse just as I was beginning to question him."

"Achilles, if you weren't my sister's boy, you might accidentally blow up. For now remember this: you do only what I tell you to do. If something like an idea begins to grow in your head, shoot it! Keep your hands off the woman! Primo Moretti could bring twenty more men out from Chicago anytime he wants. When I want to send a message, I will tell you. Do you understand?"

"Yes, uncle."

"Good. Now, Kostas, go and talk with Primo's woman. Have some *ouzo* with her and tell her she is to be my guest for dinner. Achilles will cover you while I bring in more men. She may not have come alone."

Kostas straightened his necktie, and put on the dark blue silk jacket of his suit. Then he strolled into the restaurant where Greek *bouzouki* music played softly, and plaster statues of Greek gods looked down at the diners from their light blue niches in the walls.

He came smiling to Gina's table. Kostas was taller and broader than Achilles, not as handsome, and he had an air of cold practicality which made him seem steadier, but more calculating than Achilles. He extended his hand to Gina. "We are honored to have you here. I am Kostas

Papadopoulos, nephew of Zeke Volakis."

Gina shook his hand and flashed him her hundred dollar smile. "I'm Gina Campanella. Mr. Moretti asked me to stop by to pay my regards to Mr. Volakis."

"My uncle will be pleased to see you. He asks that you be his guest for dinner."

Gina smiled demurely. "It would be disrespectful to turn down such an honor. I accept with pleasure. Please join me and tell me of your uncle. He is well?"

Kostas slipped into a chair across from Gina. "He is well. And Mr. Moretti? I trust his health is good also."

"Yes," replied Gina, "his health is good. But there are many annoyances in running a large business which plague him. I'm sure your uncle would understand."

Kostas laughed harshly. "Yes, I'm sure he would." He snapped his fingers for a waiter and when he came, ordered *ouzo*. "Have you tried *ouzo* before?"

Gina shook her head. "What is it?"

"It's a very famous Greek liqueur. It tastes like licorice or anise."

"I like that flavor; I would like to try it, but are you not somewhat concerned to be serving liquor in public?"

"We are *benefactors* of the local police. There is no problem."

The waiter returned with a bottle of *ouzo*, a carafe of water, two highball glasses and a plate of sliced cucumber, tomatoes and olives on a silver platter. The waiter placed the items on the table and left. Kostas poured each glass about half full of the clear liquid, then added water from the carafe. With the addition of the water the *ouzo* turned milky, and Gina smiled in appreciation of the unique drink. He and Gina clinked glasses, and he smiled coldly and said, "Here's to an end of annoyances."

Gina sensed the controlled violence behind his smile and felt a sudden flash of vulnerability. She sipped the *ouzo* and marveled at its exotic flavor and sweetness. "This is good; I've never had anything like it," she said innocently while sensing that this liqueur was the kind that would sneak up on those drinking it, and lay them flat. She helped herself to the olives and tomato wedges.

Kostas smiled smugly and topped off her glass.

Twenty minutes later Achilles came to Gina's table and escorted her to the back room. Volakis greeted her warmly and seated her at a large round table with a starched, white linen tablecloth. There were place settings for two, a bottle of red wine, and two crystal goblets.

Volakis looked at Gina admiringly, and she avoided his gaze by looking around the room. There was a preponderance of marble: marble busts of Greek gods on marble pillars; a marble fountain with softly flowing water between two large palms; a marble façade of pillars and arches against one wall with a mural behind it of vineyards sloping down gentle sun-washed hills to sparkling azure water.

Against another wall was a huge studded leather sofa bracketed by potted palms. A substantial marble coffee table with an intricate mosaic of leaping dolphins sat in front of the sofa. Volakis' desk was at the back of the room. It, like everything else in the room, seemed oversized, solid, and heavy.

Gina brought her eyes back around to Volakis, who had seated himself across from her at the table, and was regarding her with a satisfied smile. His large right hand, with a heavy gold ring on every finger but his thumb, smoothed his coarse black mustache.

"You like what you see?" he asked her.

"Oh yes, it's all so beautiful and strong-looking."

Volakis smiled proudly. "Yes, there is beauty in strength. Not everyone understands that." He poured a dusky red wine into their goblets. "Now let's have some dinner. I have ordered *moussaka*, bread and salad for us with some excellent *baklava* for dessert."

Gina raised her glass to Volakis, "I don't know what all of that is, but I'm willing to take a chance on something new." She smiled sweetly at him and took a sip of wine.

A waiter appeared and served their dinner. Gina took delicate bites of the strange food and found that she liked it. After dinner the waiter appeared again, cleared their places, and left a round, brown crockery bottle and two brandy snifters.

Volakis pulled a large, heavy crystal ashtray over in front of him, and the waiter hurried back with a humidor and cigar cutter. Volakis selected a cigar and snipped off its end. Then he smelled it appreciatively while the waiter picked up a large brass pedestal lighter with both hands and lit it. He then rested the cigar gently in the ashtray, and uncorked the crockery bottle. "This is *Metaxa*," he said, "a very special Greek brandy and wine combination. I hope it is not too strong for you." He poured two glasses and handed one to Gina.

Gina smiled, took the snifter, swirled the rich reddish brown liquid, and took a sip. It burned her throat and warmed her down to her toes. "As I said, I appreciate strength."

She was thankful she hadn't coughed or sputtered, and hoped the drink would settle her nerves for the next topic of conversation with Volakis, the real reason for her visit.

"You have been very kind and generous to me, Mr. Volakis. I will tell Mr. Moretti of it."

Volakis smiled and nodded. "I am sure there is something more to your visit than the pleasure of new experiences. Please feel free to speak."

Gina folded her hands on the table. "Mr. Moretti's brother, Angelo, is missing, as well as a friend of the family."

"I'm sorry to hear this; what happened?"

"Mr. Moretti doesn't know, but he feels their disappearance may be related to the treachery of Clarence Lamb."

"I read in the newspaper of C.D. Lamb's still in South Dakota, at his family's farm. The article said all the Lambs are dead. Beyond this, I know nothing." Volakis smiled showing his yellowed teeth, and leaned back in his chair with his hands folded behind his head.

"Mr. Moretti will be pleased to hear that. He is a man of honor, and will not rest until his brother is found."

"He may be dead."

"That is what Mr. Moretti fears. And if it is so, he wants to find Angelo's remains so that they can be buried in the family plot, in consecrated ground."

"Of course, any Catholic understands this."

"Mr. Moretti wonders if Angelo's remains might be somewhere on the Lamb farm now."

"That would be a logical conclusion."

"That is what he figured. And that is why he wants to make sure nothing gets disturbed at the Lamb farm."

"I know of no one with any such plans."

"That's good. Mr. Moretti will be pleased to hear that. There is also a matter of some missing money."

"I have heard the rumors."

"Yes, Mr. Moretti was very upset to learn that while he was away, C.D. Lamb betrayed him. He stole money and jewels from him."

"Oh? How much?"

"For Mr. Moretti, even a nickel would be too much."

Volakis threw back his head and laughed. "In that respect Primo *the Bull* Moretti and I agree."

Gina continued on, knowing she must get the last part out. "Mr. Moretti is determined to get that money back, and he wants it clearly understood that anyone who might find it should return it to him, or he will treat them as if they had stolen from him personally. He would consider it a sign of great disrespect."

Gina realized that she had rushed to get through this veiled threat to Volakis. She looked at him apologetically. "I'm sorry to sound so unfriendly. Perhaps there is something more pleasant we could talk about."

Volakis picked up his cigar and pulled gently and deeply on it. He exhaled slowly then leaned forward and looked in Gina's eyes. "There is something you and I might talk about."

"What's that?"

"You are a brave woman to come here by yourself."

"I come in friendship. Mr. Moretti wants you to know that."

"Of course, you are the messenger. But I wonder about certain things. I do not like to wonder, I like to have answers."

"Of course, everyone likes answers."

"Yes. Well, perhaps you can give me some answers."

"I'll try. What do you want to know?"

Volakis leaned back some and puffed on his cigar so that the ash began to grow. "If Mr. Moretti has many men, why does he send a woman to speak for him? Why does he not come himself? This is what I wonder about."

"Mr. Moretti is a careful man."

"Ah yes. Very careful. But he is not careful of you." Volakis leaned forward menacingly.

Gina glanced at her wrist watch. "If I do not answer the telephone in my room in thirty-five minutes, you will die. If I give the wrong answer, you will die. This is certain. You will wonder no more." Gina held her breath and kept her eyes locked on Volakis. She was rehearsing in her mind how she could roll from her chair and get her gun out of her purse in case Volakis lunged at her.

He stared at her intently, then laughed, a big booming burst of sound. "You are one tough woman."

Gina relaxed somewhat. "Mr. Moretti angers very easily."

Volakis smiled. "I have heard that."

"I have found that doing what he says makes life easier."

Volakis snorted derisively.

Gina stood up. She could feel the effect of all the alcohol which had been served to her, and prayed that she could make her exit smoothly. "Thank you for your excellent dinner and drinks. I must go now to answer the telephone. Perhaps you and Mr. Moretti can talk about this another time."

Volakis laid his cigar in the ashtray and came to his feet, making a slight bow. "It has been my pleasure to have you here. Thank Mr. Moretti for sending such a beautiful messenger. Tell him that I will be almost as happy to speak to him as I am to you. Hah!" Volakis smiled. "There is one more thing."

"Yes?"

"If at any time you feel that Mr. Moretti is too careless of your safety, I would be pleased to have you be under my protection. I have a recent opening for someone with your skills. Also, I am much easier to love than Primo *the Bull* Moretti! Ha! Ha! Ha!"

Gina smiled coyly at him. "I'm sure you are."

Volakis handed her his card. "In the meantime, here is my telephone number, my personal, private line. Whatever that fat Italian is paying you, I'll double. And if you really want to become important to me and my future plans, I would be very appreciative and generous if you were to help me increase my wealth and eliminate any *foreign* influence in my territory. I think you know what I mean. Think it over."

Gina took Volakis' card and slipped it into her purse. She regarded her purse a moment, then looked up, locked eyes with Zeke and said, "I will, Mr. Volakis. I will think it over."

As soon as Gina had left the restaurant, Volakis met with his nephews. "Things are beginning to happen quickly. Moretti must be close to finding the money or he wouldn't be trying to scare me off. And I don't think he has many men with him yet, or he would have found another way to send me a message."

Achilles butted in. "Uncle Zeke, this is a perfect time to go up to Sioux Falls and wipe him out. I bet anyone up there could tell us where the rich, fat wop lives, and then we could ambush him and any guys he has with him."

Volakis looked coldly at Achilles. "Do you remember what I told you to do if you got an idea? We don't want to be noticed by the cops. We don't want witnesses. We want the loot. We want to be rid of Moretti and his men.

"Here's what we'll do. Kostas, you get on the phone with your people in South Dakota. Find out how to get to that Lamb farm. Achilles, collect our best guns and plenty of ammo. Then pack your clothes. We are going to take over that Lamb farm quietly, just the three of us. When Moretti shows up, we'll help him look for the money. Then we'll fertilize the corn with him. We leave in the morning."

* * *

Early the next morning, Gina dressed in her *farm wear* of a mid-calf length, perky navy blue and white polka dot dress with a white lace collar and navy blue, leather belt. She wore sturdy one-and-a-half-inch heeled navy blue leather shoes with an ankle strap. Her black hair was pulled back and tied with a white ribbon.

Gina had plenty of time to think over her conversation with Volakis. Frankie was singing Italian opera with the car radio while he was driving, and paying her little attention as he drove the Packard back to South Dakota from Iowa. True, she was Primo's favorite, but there were always others – younger and more ambitious. Without marriage, she would always be disposable, and Primo seemed very disinclined to tie the knot. Besides, as Volakis had pointed out, Primo was not easy to love, or pleasant. She did not enjoy his attentions, only his rewards – of the gold, diamond, and folding green variety. And Volakis had offered her more. And truly he was better looking.

If Primo Moretti and his boys, Red McGuire and Frankie Maldonado, could be eliminated, her trail could go cold to anyone who cared to look back in Chicago. Gina could stage her death too and settle in with Volakis and his crowd. But to really ensure her place with Volakis, it would be good to bring a present – like that missing money (after a bit had been stashed for herself, that is). Mob protection was essential for Gina to feel safe, but sometimes a girl had to protect herself from her protectors.

By the time she and Frankie had pulled into Arnold Ariosto's driveway, Gina had made her decision. She would play it straight with Primo until they found the money. Then she would contact Volakis and make plans. Of course, she would have to negotiate carefully with Volakis. One didn't let go of one rattlesnake to grab another without careful planning.

Chapter Eighteen
The Best Laid Plans

When Frankie and Gina arrived at Arnold Ariosto's farm later that morning, they found Arnold, Red, and Primo out behind the barn. Red and Arnold were working at opposite sides of the silage pit with pitchforks. Piles of sweetly sour silage with an *off* scent were beginning to build on each side of the pit. Primo was upwind of the two workers, leaning against the back of the barn in a thin strip of shade, picking his teeth with a silver toothpick.

"Any luck yet, Boss?" Frankie asked as he stepped gingerly over clumps of silage to stand in the sun next to Primo.

"Does it look like it?" Primo kept his eyes on the work in the pit. "How'd the trip go?"

"Fine on my end, Boss. In and out like a duck mating. We didn't get seen by nobody, and none of the farmers that we saw dropped their teeth when we went by, so I figure we blended in pretty good." He waved a fly away from his hair, the diamond in his pinky ring sparkling brightly.

"Frankie, I don't care if you were covered in pig shit, you don't blend when you're in a Packard in clodhopper country. Did you hide it in that shed we left open?"

"You bet, Boss. I closed and fastened the doors on the shed, and brought our guns and ammo inside. We're set real good for whatever goes down."

"I'll be the judge of that," Primo growled.

He next turned to Gina who had joined them and was watching Arnold and Red working. "Gina, did you deliver my message without incident?"

"Yeah, Primo, it went just like you said. I told Volakis only what he already knew; I told him to stay away from this farm, to stay out of your territory, and that any money or jewels that turn up belong to you. That you would take it as a sign of great disrespect if these directions were not followed."

"That's good. Did he make any moves on you?"

"No, but he did like you said and tried to tempt me over to his side. He will be easy to set up when you're ready."

"Were his low-life nephews there too?"

"Yeah, Achilles and Kostas were there." Gina shuddered inwardly at their memory.

"Were you able to find out any new information?"

"No, but rumors of C.D.'s theft have spread widely, and the amount stolen is not known, so I suspect the amount grows with each telling."

Primo spat on the ground. "No doubt, and that is why we will defend this territory until the money and Angelo are found. Then we will tidy things up, secure our interests in Sioux Falls, and move back to Chicago. I'm gettin' real tired of this country-bumpkin living."

Red squinted into the distance to the north. "Someone's coming," he said warily.

Arnold followed Red's gaze. "It looks like my neighbors, the Dacias."

Primo's eyes narrowed. "The Gypsies? What would they be doin' goin' out with their horses and wagon? Is there any reason they'd be comin' here?"

Arnold looked Primo in the eye. "Not that I know of."

They all silently watched the progress of the wagon to see which direction it would turn at the crossroads.

146

When the horses turned their heads west, toward Arnold's farm, Primo growled, "They're comin' here and if we try to get to the house before they arrive, we'll be seen. Me, Frankie, and Gina will go through the door on the far side of the barn, and go into the still room. Ariosto, get rid of those bohunks. Red, make sure he does."

Primo, Frankie, and Gina hurried along the back of the barn, turned left and entered the hay barn through a small side door. Primo led them to the still room. He reached inside the door and flicked the switch, but no light came on. "What the fuck?" he said and flicked the switch several more times with growing annoyance.

"Why is this fucking light out?" he called out furiously to Arnold who was just entering the barnyard with Red behind him.

"The bulb blew out and I haven't gotten around to changing it yet. You'd better close the door, Josif and Jon Dacia are just turning into the driveway."

Primo swore quietly under his breath in Italian and closed the door leaving a thin crack open to see and hear through. He whispered harshly to Frankie, "That light worked perfectly yesterday when he showed me and Red around."

"He's trying to cross us, Bull; we gotta watch him extra good."

Josif directed his team, Peter and Paul, over to the east side of the barnyard, stopped them by the chicken coop, and climbed out of the wagon. Uncle Jon came around from the far side of the wagon, and gently rubbed the horses' noses as he passed in front of them to join Josif. Arnold and Red walked out into the barnyard to greet them.

Josif and Uncle Jon's eyes lit up when they saw Red McGuire. "Well, is good to see you again so soon," Josif said.

"Likewise," said Red, extending his hand.

Josif looked at Arnold to explain. "Yesterday afternoon Mr. McGuire stop by our place to look for work. We glad to see he find some with you, it seems."

"Why yes, Red's helping me with some work out back of the barn."

"That good. Mr. McGuire say you have Fresno. We ask to see it and how it work. Maybe borrow, if okay with you."

"Well sure," said Arnold. "I don't see why not. I keep it back here where we're workin'."

He led the way along a path to the silage pit behind the barn. The Fresno was off to the side of the pit. As they gathered around the Fresno, Red positioned himself so that he could see around the corner of the barn and into the barnyard.

"You folks decide to dig that lake for your kids?" he asked.

"If not take too long or too hard on horses," Uncle Jon replied with a twinkle in his eye. "They not so young as used to be."

"Well, this is just the tool you need," Arnold said nodding toward a metal contraption which looked like a huge broad scoop shovel with a thin strong metal scraper at the bottom, a long handle out the back, and two large curved pieces of heavy duty metal which protruded from the top and bottom of each end in two large arcs. "You just hook it up to your team and lift up on the handle when you want to scrape up some dirt, then when the bucket part is full, you let the scraper come up and slide it along until you get to your dump pile, then you tip it up and over and dump out your dirt. It's pretty easy to work, but it sure helps to have two men to do the dumping."

"I can see how that would be. If okay with you, we borrow after harvest this fall."

"You bet, Arnold said."

FRESNO SCRAPER   J. Dunn

"What is it you do here?" Jon asked indicating the silage pit.

Arnold hesitated for a moment to come up with a story. Red's eyes burned into him and he had put his hand into his overalls' pocket where Arnold had seen him put his gun. "I want to add another room to the barn and the old silage pit is too unstable. I'm digging out all of this old stuff and gonna put it on some poor acreage in the east section. Then I'm gonna dig a small pond for ducks and geese, and use that soil to fill in here," Arnold replied.

"Is very good idea," Josif said looking at Uncle Jon.

Red visibly relaxed. "Yeah, two ponds in the neighborhood. That'll be nice. Well I guess we should get on with our work. Is that right, Mr. Ariosto? I didn't mean to speak for you."

Arnold opened his mouth to reply, when the distant sound of a car engine was heard to the south. Everyone paused to glance at the sound then continued to stare at the

149

unusual site of a shiny black Packard approaching. Red felt an adrenalin rush and casually moved around behind Arnold and the Dacias. The Packard paused at the end of the driveway, then turned in. Three men were visible inside.

Red peered around Arnold's shoulder, looked hard at the men, then recoiled and moved back around the corner of the barn. He pulled out two revolvers. Josif and Uncle Jon blinked in disbelief, then mentally prepared themselves for action.

"Listen to me," Red said quickly. "Ariosto, you go bring those three Greek bastards back here to see the pit. I'll be standin' behind these two, ready to plug 'em before they see it's me. I've already got the drop on these two bohunks, so don't try anything."

Arnold nodded grimly and headed around the side of the barn to the barnyard. The Greek's Packard was parked on the west side of the open area, and its occupants had gotten out. The three men were solid looking, and had a predatory air. One was older than the other two, and had a thick black mustache. The youngest appearing one had a coat draped over his arm, which appeared to be about three feet long, with a tommy gun barrel sticking out the end of it. The car had Iowa license plates. The oldest one spoke. "Is this the Lamb farm?"

Arnold felt like he was in a movie. He hoped this one would have a happy ending. Now he had to focus on not getting killed or getting the Dacias killed. And one other thing. "This used to be the Lamb farm, now it's the Ariosto farm."

"This is the right place. We're takin' over your farm for a while, Ariosto. We've lost something here."

Arnold opened his mouth to speak when he noticed Sheriff Butch Bennard's car approaching from the south. His visitors did too. "Kostas, Achilles, get into the barn. Ariosto, show us where that still room is. Get rid of the sheriff or we'll mow you down, farmer."

Sheriff Bennard's car was nearing the driveway. Arnold led the Greeks into the barn and back to the still room door. There he motioned for them to stop. He lightly rapped on the door which he could see was slightly open. "I know you know who's here. Well, the sheriff and his deputy are just now pulling in the driveway. I'd turn you all in if McGuire didn't have the drop on the Dacias. Send out the woman, or I'll burn my own place down."

There was a slight pause, then a command was uttered from inside the still room, and in a moment Gina appeared at the door, blinking as she entered the bright light. Volakis froze when he saw her, and instant understanding of his predicament dawned on him. Kostas and Achilles were muttering angrily under their breaths behind him. He quickly considered entering the room with guns blazing, but there were too many people around, and McGuire was outside somewhere. If Ariosto could get the cops and Dacias to leave, he might have a chance at neutralizing the Italians.

"Truce," he whispered loudly.

There was brief swearing in Italian, then, "Truce, for now."

Arnold pulled open the door and stood to the side. The Greeks slid into the dark room, with the Italians. He closed the door and stepped away quickly, as from a coiled rattler. It seemed as though he could feel the hatred radiating from the still room behind him. He expected it to explode any second. Arnold grabbed Gina's arm and quickly escorted her away from the still room toward the bright light of the barn door.

Sheriff Bennard, and his deputy were discussing the finer points of police detection as they pulled into the Ariosto driveway.

"Look for subtle things, Harold. Things that just don't fit in or look right."

"Like what?"

"Jesus H. Christ, Harold! That's the whole point of why we're here. We have to find those things."

"Oh. Like maybe that shiny black Packard parked over there with Iowa plates?"

Butch pulled in behind the Packard. He got out of the car, hiked up his pants, and adjusted his sheriff's hat, pushing it down more squarely on his head.

Arnold Ariosto was just coming out of the barn with a beautiful, black-haired woman on his arm. She showed none of the wear and tear of the average farm wife. Her clothes were more stylish than practical, not faded or thread worn, and her face and arms showed no history of exposure to sun and wind.

Harold nudged Butch with his elbow and whispered, "Looks like another possible clue. A real beaut!"

Butch ignored Harold and walked up to Arnold and Gina. "Howdy Mr. Ariosto, ma'am." He gestured with his hat toward the Packard. "Got company, do you?"

Gina was still blinking and trying to adjust to the bright sun after being in the dark still room. When she saw the sheriff, she tensed up, and seeing no good options for flight, was resigning herself for the inevitable arrest. Arnold patted her hand which was resting on his arm, looked down at her and smiled. "Why yes, sheriff. This is my cousin, Gina Ariosto from Iowa. Sioux City to be precise. She just got here."

Butch was preparing another pithy question in his mind, when Arnold said to Gina, "Remember you said you wanted to call Aunt Connie as soon as you got here? Why don't you go in the house and do that while I visit with the sheriff. The phone's in the hallway, just off the kitchen. We can continue our tour after that."

Gina felt weak in the knees. Arnold had saved her. Just that easily. And with such courage and determination. And now he was getting her even farther out of harm's way and giving her a way to get help. She looked up into his brown eyes, and smiled from her heart. "You're right, Arnold. I'll do that right away." Then she stood on her tiptoes, hugged him, and kissed him on the cheek. "It's so good to see you again, cousin."

The three men silently watched her walk across the barnyard, up the porch steps, and into the house. Then they turned to face each other. Butch looked around vaguely for a moment, then gestured with his head toward the Dacia's wagon with Peter and Paul hitched to it. "That your wagon and team?"

Arnold opened his mouth to answer when suddenly the Wagner's Pontiac came roaring down the road and almost tipped over as it made a high speed ninety degree turn into his driveway. Fritz, August, and Grandpa Wagner had their heads out the windows and huge excited grins on their faces. They looked like three happy hounds getting to go for a ride.

"What's goin' on?" Fritz yelled from the window as he slammed on the brakes just behind the sheriff's car. The Wagners got out of the car and gathered around the sheriff. "We saw that first Packard come in here this mornin', then the Dacias in their wagon, then another Packard, then you, Butch."

Grandpa Wagner hobbled up to the sheriff with his crutch. "Who got shot?" he yelled. "What's goin' on? Speak up!"

"No one got shot, Grandpa," August yelled into his ear. "Hang on, we're findin' out what's happening!"

"No you're not," Butch said. "This is official police business. I'm in charge. Just go on back to your farm."

Fritz snorted. "We're just over here visitin' neighbors; there ain't no law against that. Say, there's the Dacia's team and wagon. But where are they?"

"I saw them from the car, they're back there," August said and headed along the path next to the barn with Fritz and Grandpa in tow.

Red had kept his guns pointed at Josif and Uncle Jon. All three were behind the barn and couldn't see the happenings out front, although they did see the sheriff and the Wagners arriving. Red was becoming more and more agitated with each arrival.

Uncle Jon said to Josif in Romanian, "He is like a rabid dog. Something good which has gone very wrong."

"Shut up!" Red growled. "You two keep quiet and don't move a muscle. You're becomin' a problem for me, and my job is to get rid of problems. Get the picture?" He paced back and forth in front of them, stopping randomly to point his guns at their heads.

Suddenly the voices out front became louder and they could hear August and Fritz arguing and getting closer. Red snapped to attention. "Get your hands up and get movin'," he said to Josif and Uncle Jon, indicating with a

gun that they should head out around the barn to intercept the Wagners.

Josif and Jon raised their hands and stepped out onto
the path that ran next to the barn.

"Holy shit!" exclaimed August when he saw the three
approaching.

"All of you get your hands up and back away," Red
called out. "Any funny stuff, and first I wipe out the bohunks, then you."

Fritz and August raised their hands and slowly began
backing up. Grandpa lifted his crutch, then lowered it and
turned around. He carefully hobbled out into the barnyard
with Fritz and August behind him. Red directed his little
herd toward Butch, Harold, and Arnold.

"Get your hands up sheriff and everyone else. I've got
enough bullets to blow a lotta brains out. I'm takin' that
Packard and a hostage, so everyone stay calm, and no one
gets hurt."

Red continued to move the group across the barnyard
in front of the barn. He planned to grab one of the Dacias,
make them release Bull and Frankie, lock everyone else up
in the barn, and head for Chicago.

Abruptly, from deep inside the barn, came the sound
of yelling and Greek and Italian swearing. Then the loud
clap of a door being pushed open and slamming against
the wall, followed by the sounds of scuffling in the dirt.
Then the burst of a tommy gun and a cry of pain.

At the sound of the tommy gun, everyone in the barnyard reflexively ducked, and Uncle Jon used the opportunity to kick Red's feet out from under him, causing him to
fall and drop one gun. Before Red could regain control,
Josif had him pinned with his knife at his throat. "Get
rope," he said to Uncle Jon who looked around quickly for
something to use.

"Aw hell," said Fritz as he picked up a shovel leaning

against the barn, and smashed it into Red's head. "That's how you deal with a weasel." Red's form went limp, and the Dacias kicked the guns away from him.

More gunfire erupted from the barn, and Kostas and Achilles emerged looking back over their shoulders and firing into the darkness.

Fritz let out a whoop of joy and charged into Kostas, while August grabbed Achilles' collar with one hand and swung him around so that he could punch him in the jaw with the other.

Grandpa Wagner looked sublime as he tossed his crutch straight up into the air, grabbed the business end with both hands as it came down, and swung the arm support end against the front of Volakis' knees with a loud *thwack*. Volakis grimaced in pain and fell as Uncle Jon and Harold Torklesson lit on him.

Inside the barn, Primo quickly assessed the situation, and decided there was no benefit to staying. Frankie was bleeding from the right thigh, but was still on his feet and functional. "We've gotta make a break for it now while everyone's busy and before more cops show up. Head for the Packard."

Frankie and Primo ran from the barn, blinded by the bright sun, but with guns drawn and firing. Josif spotted the blood on Frankie's right thigh, and threw his knife into the back of Frankie's left leg. Frankie pitched forward and fell hard. Primo, unable to stop his momentum, fell over him. Grandpa bore down on them like an avenging angel, and proceeded to bludgeon them with his crutch. Butch kicked away their guns, tried to avoid Grandpa's crutch, and managed to cuff Primo, then Frankie.

Seeing that Butch had everything under control, Josif joined Uncle Jon and Harold in helping to subdue Volakis. Soon they also had him in cuffs.

Fritz and August were still fighting with Kostas and

Achilles, although it appeared that Kostas and Achilles might be willing to fall down and quit, but the Wagner brothers kept holding them up to punch them some more.

It all ended when Fritz and August picked up their opponents and heaved them in the pig pen. While the brothers were arguing over which of them had the idea first, an ambulance, paddy wagon, and three more squad cars showed up. Volakis had been grazed on the arm, so he, Frankie, and Red were sent off to the hospital in Sioux Falls, accompanied by two squad cars. A Federal Marshal took custody of the other prisoners.

Gina turned herself in to Butch, who turned her over to the Sioux Falls sheriff. When he learned that it had been Gina who had called for police backup, and that she was also *Mrs. Johnson*, the sheriff declined to cuff her, and had her sit in the front seat, next to him.

Arnold wished her well, and gave her his phone number. He got the Sioux Falls sheriff's business card, and told Gina that he would check up on her, if she didn't mind. She assured him that she didn't.

Butch Bennard and Harold Torklesson stayed behind. Butch secured the crime scene by sending Harold out to the end of the driveway in the squad car to prevent curious neighbors from coming over. Then he prepared to question the witnesses.

"Say Arnold, perhaps I could interview everyone involved in this dust-up at the kitchen table. Maybe with some cold water or pop if you got any. Subduing perpetrators is hard, dry work."

"Sure, Sheriff, I've got a big jug of iced tea. I'll go get the kitchen set up for you." Arnold headed for the house.

Butch retrieved a medium-sized pad and pen from the glove box in his squad car. Then he cleared his throat and addressed the Dacias and Wagners. "I'll be questioning all of you one at a time. I want to get all the details straight, so I don't want you swappin' versions with each other. I'll start with Gerhard Wagner first. The rest of you just keep quiet and relax in the shade or somethin'." He turned and ushered Grandpa Wagner toward the house.

By the time Butch and Grandpa had climbed the porch steps and gone into the house, Fritz had fetched a bottle from the trunk of the Pontiac, Uncle Jon had produced a flask of *tuica* from the wagon, and Arnold was coming out of the house with a loaf of crusty bread and a hunk of salami. The neck of a small bottle protruded from his hip pocket. He headed over to his neighbors who were laughing and talking in the shade of a large cottonwood by the pig pen, re-enacting the various fights they'd been in, and arguing over who had the idea first to throw the Papadopoulos brothers in with the pigs.

Chapter Nineteen
Hard Times

By the end of June, the Dacias were praying for rain. Black thunderstorms formed in the west and advanced across the plains, only to sweep over the dry land without spilling a drop from the boiling clouds.

The blazing sun beat down without mercy on the parched earth, and the corn and small grain which had looked so promising a few weeks before began to die. The soft, green leaves of the corn turned brittle and dry, while the oats and barley plants shriveled and turned yellow. The alfalfa field still remained green, but the plants were small, not boding well for feeding the horses and cows in the coming winter. In addition, the Dacias gathered from their infrequent trips to Centerford that everyone in their new country of America was suffering from something called a *Depression*.

While enjoying a game of pitch in the Dacia kitchen, the Wagner brothers explained to the Dacia men what was happening. Fritz spoke while building a cigarette. "First we ain't had enough rain to soak up a fart, and the idiot bankers is shuttin' up their blankety blank banks so you can't get a goddamned dollar out. Second, the stupid car companies is layin' everybody off, and third, the price on hogs and steers is so low that you can't even ship a dad gum steer to Chicago without the damn railroad chargin' you more than you get from the gol dang steer."

August added, "Then them guys that were in the war have gone to Washington to get their bonuses, and the damn government won't give it to 'em."

"Shut up, August," Fritz said. "Who asked you to come buttin' in? Them guys goin' to Washington don't have nothin' to do with it not rainin'."

"It does too. Some of them guys are farmers, and they don't have no more money than we have."

"Well, everybody knows that, for Christ's sake. But them bein' camped out in that Hooverville in Washington don't have nothin' to do with the price a oats." Fritz took a drag on his cigarette. "The trouble is, we ain't gettin' any crops."

"Jesus Christ," August replied, "That don't have nothin' to do with the government not payin' them guys."

Fritz ignored this. "Old Harry Peterson tried to take three steers down to Sioux City last week, and a buncha them crazy Iowa farmers wouldn't let him go through. If they try that with me I'm gonna wrap a monkey wrench around their necks."

"We ain't never took any steers to Sioux City," August said. "Sioux Falls is a lot closer."

"Well, I just might decide to take some to Sioux City. I'd like to see them Iowa dummies try to stop me."

"Why Iowa farmers don't want South Dakota farmers to take steers to Sioux City?" Josif asked.

Fritz tapped cigarette ashes into his overalls' cuff. "Because them dummies think if South Dakota farmers don't sell any cattle to the packing plants, the price will go up."

August leaned forward in his chair. "It ain't just the South Dakota farmers. It's all the farmers."

"Jesus H. Christ, August, who asked you? You got it all wrong as usual. There ain't no way you can stop all the

farmers from all over the country from shippin' their livestock. The minute I don't sell a steer, some smart aleck in
Nebraska is gonna sell his steers for a higher price. But is
he gonna thank me? Not on your patoozie. Them guys in
Iowa is prob'ly doin' the same thing, keepin' us from selling our steers while they're makin' big money off theirs.
I'm gonna knock the shit outta them if they try to stop
me." Fritz looked at his coffee cup. "I don't s'pose there's
any more coffee?"

Josif nodded at Michael-Joseph, and the boy brought
the coffee pot from the big cookstove. As he filled the
Wagner brothers' cups, he said, "Damnit Fritz, I wanna go
with you when you and August take them steers down to
Sioux City."

"There ain't gonna be no room. Grandpa says he's
gonna go with us and beat the crap outta them Iowa guys
with his crutch."

Josif spoke to Michael-Joseph in English so the Wagners could understand. "I told you to stop that language!
and you not old enough to go fighting with Iowa farmers."

"Well, when I get to be as big as Fritz, I'm gonna
knock the tar out of 'em."

Fritz glanced at Michael-Joseph. "You ain't never
gonna be as big as me unless you start eatin' sauerkraut."
He felt Michael-Joseph's arm. "Holy Christ, when I was as
old as you I could pick up a two hundred pound calf."

"You couldn't neither," August said, "He's only seven
years old. It wasn't 'til you was ten that you could pick up
that red calf."

"You don't know nothin' about it, August. I picked
up that calf when I was nine."

"Sure, but the calf only weighed one hundred then.
When he got to be two hundred you was ten."

Fritz slammed his cards down on the table. "You got
that all wrong, as usual. I remember I was nine 'cause I

weighed a hundred and twenty nine pounds then."

"I ain't got it wrong. It was all wrote down on the wall of the calf pen 'til that calf with the scours shot crap all over it." August looked at his cards. "Three."

"And I'm telling you I picked that calf up when I was only nine years old. If you say I didn't one more time, I'm gonna knock them cards right down your yap. And you can't bid three. I already did that."

"Yeah, but I'm the dealer. The dealer can take the bid over anybody."

Fritz slammed his chair back and loomed over August with a fist an inch from his nose. "Now I'm gonna knock you right through that window."

"Mr. Bowman said is going to be farm sale over by Viborg," Josif said. "You think I could maybe buy car there?"

The Wagner brothers slowly turned to look at him. "You wanna buy a car?" Fritz asked.

"Maybe."

"Well, I sure as hell wouldn't buy it from them Danes over at Viborg. Time they get through with a car it ain't nothin' but a pile a junk."

August added, "They never heard about changin' oil. They just keep puttin' in more until everything freezes up."

Fritz scowled at August. "Who asked you to come buttin' in? Joe knows about puttin' oil in a car."

"Well, it don't do no good even if he does. Them Danes don't know, and by the time Joe buys it from 'em, the thing's already shot."

"Whaddaya think I just been tellin' him? Now shut up and let me and Joe talk." Fritz started building a new cigarette and spoke to Josif as he shook tobacco into the paper. "You tell me what kind of a car you want and I'll see that you get a good one."

"We go to visit Izabella's uncle in east coast of America. He is very ill. Car must run good for long way." Josif looked slightly guilty as he lied to his neighbors, and shot a warning look at Michael-Joseph to keep quiet.

"Well, that ain't no problem." Fritz lit his cigarette. "When I take them steers down to Sioux City, I'll go to one of them used car lots and pick out a good one for ya."

"You don't hafta go to no Sioux City to get a car," August protested. "Al's Garage right in Centerford has got all sortsa cars. Them big city guys in used car lots will cheat you blind."

"Jesus Christ, August, they cheat them dumb-lookin' people that don't have no idea about what a good car is." Fritz tapped ashes into his cuff. "They ain't gonna pull nothin' on me." He spoke confidently to Josif. "Don't you worry about nothin'. I'll find you a good car."

Chapter Twenty
Izabella

The Wagner brothers' voices penetrated the living room door as though it were a thin curtain. Izabella felt a shiver of excitement down her back. Josif had made the first move in getting a car! But even as she thrilled at the promise of action, she quailed before the challenge of finding and rescuing Irina.

How could they find their way across America to the huge city of New York? Where would they find shelter for the nights? How would she be able to cook meals? Would they have money enough to buy a car; to pay for gasoline? How could they help Irina escape? Would they be pursued by members of the Iron Guard? By the police of America? Would they be thrown in jail? Shipped back to Romania? What would happen to her family, her children?

Uncle Jon, the old soldier, and Aunt Magda, the strong woman: the elders of the family. They would care for the children, the farm, the animals. But both were growing old. Izabella saw that in the stiffness of their motions in the morning, the fading of their skin and hair, and the slight decrease in their energy and endurance. Yet they still stood straight and erect and worked as hard as ever. And they loved the children, as the children loved them. But if she and Josif were killed, what would happen to the children after Uncle Jon and Aunt Magda were gone?

She heard the Wagners depart, the scraping of chair legs, the clumping of heavy feet, the loud voices fading as the two brothers went out through the porch and into the night.

Josif opened the door into the living room. "They have gone. We are letting the smoke blow out."

Aunt Magda pulled the bottom of her apron up over her mouth and nose. "Shut the door, Josif. We will all die."

The men and Michael-Joseph came into the living room, and Uncle Jon shut the door behind them. He smiled at the women and girls. "It is like after a storm. Thunder and clouds blow away."

Michael-Joseph came to Izabella. "Fritz is going to find a car for us!"

"We heard." Izabella hugged him.

"*We* will decide what car we want," Josif said. "You have seen how Fritz and August pick out horses."

Uncle Jon nodded. "The car would be sway-backed with knock knees and the heaves."

The girls giggled. Caroline staggered forward with her knees in and her feet out. "It would go like this."

Izabella gently scolded them. "They want to help us. You must not make fun of them."

"We won't, Mama." Marie gave Caroline's braided hair a little tug. "Brat."

Caroline stuck out her tongue at Marie. "Marie has a crush on August."

"I do not!" Marie made a face at Caroline.

Josif frowned at Marie. "What is a *crush?*"

Marie blushed. "Those little girls in the third grade think everybody is in love with somebody. They call it to have a *crush.*"

"You are in love with August?"

Marie blushed more deeply. "No, Papa. How could I be in love with August? He is a grown man and I hardly know him."

166

"It is just children talking," Izabella said. "Marie would never marry such an ill-bred man."

Aunt Magda agreed. "Shame on you, Josif. Marie will marry better than that!"

"She is almost through with school." Josif looked at Uncle Jon for support. "Girls should find a man with land. The Wagners have a good farm, but August is the second son. Fritz will inherit the farm. August would have to buy a farm of his own."

Marie stared at Josif, then at Izabella. She said nothing, but her eyes filled with tears. Izabella came to her and put her arm around her. She looked defiantly at Josif. "Marie will have the chance to go to high school before she marries any man."

"If she is getting *crushes* she will be married before she finishes high school. She will not be a wild girl who gets in trouble!"

"Of course not, Josif! Marie is a good girl; she won't get in trouble, but all our children can go to high school. Pioneer High School is only five miles away."

Izabella paused and spoke gently to Josif, "Do you remember when we came to this house, this farm, three years ago? You said we would have books in our house. We have some books, but we cannot teach our children all they need to know. The high school has many books, a library, professors. If our children do well in high school, they can go to college. They can become professors, scientists, doctors. All these things are possible in America."

"We have no money to send them anywhere. They will work on the farm. Michael-Joseph will own this land. The girls will marry men who own land." Josif gripped the back of a chair. "Land is the most important thing in the world!"

They all stared at him. Michael-Joseph spoke. "Darntootin'! When I get this place, I'm gonna build a barn and

silo as big as Fritz's and August's. I'll get a John Deere trac-
tor that can cultivate three rows of corn at a time. I'll buy
all the land these dumb Swedes don't know how to farm!"

It seemed to Izabella that August Wagner had spoken. She had a mental image of Michael-Joseph as big as
the Wagner brothers, clumping throughout the house in
huge work shoes, swearing with every sentence.

Josif slapped Michael-Joseph lightly on the back.
"Good boy. You have remembered my grandfather's rules,
'Owe no one. Fear no one. Get horses and land and a good
wife.'" He looked at the family. "We men will go to town
tomorrow to start looking for a car. In America we must
add one thing to my grandfather's rules. 'Get a car.' Everybody in America has a car."

Chapter Twenty-One
A Trip to Town

"I want to go to town with you today when you go to look for a car," Izabella informed Josif the next morning at breakfast.

"Oh?"

"Ellen Johnson asked me to come see her the next time we come to town. She is a good friend."

Josif knew that Izabella was right. Alan Johnson, the banker, and his wife, Ellen, were good friends. When Alexander lay dying and Josif and Uncle Jon were in jail, accused of killing the sheriff by the murderous Lambs, Ellen had taken Izabella to the hospital in Sioux Falls to be with Alexander. And Alan Johnson had helped fight off the lynch mob that had gathered outside the jail.

"If you go," Josif said, "everybody will want to go. I will not have girls giggling around us while we men look at cars."

Aunt Magda smiled sweetly at Josif. "I will take the girls to the grocery store with me. We need more coffee and sugar. Somehow we seem to use a lot of these particular things."

Josif scowled. "When friends come we must be good neighbors. We cannot refuse them a cup of coffee and a little sugar."

Michael-Joseph agreed. "August can make his coffee

so thick that it's like honey. He can drip it down into his mouth without hardly spilling a bit."

Aunt Magda said nothing, but patted Michael-Joseph's head.

Josif knew he was beaten. "So everybody will come. But we will buy no candy. And we leave as soon as we get the harnesses on Peter and Paul."

The girls screamed with joy, and within fifteen minutes Peter and Paul were harnessed and hitched to the big wagon that had brought them from Oklahoma, and the family had climbed in.

Josif clucked at the horses, and they drew the wagon out of the driveway and along the road that led south across the stone bridge that arched over the creek. They turned east at the first intersection and headed for the town of Centerford, eight miles to the southeast. The road led toward the distant tall white spire of the Orkadallen Lutheran Church where Alexander lay in the cemetery, and when they reached the church, Josif turned the team into the church yard.

They all climbed down from the wagon and trooped into the cemetery. They stood silently around the grave and the small stone marker on which was chiseled: *Jon Alexander Dacia; 1917-1929; With God.*

Izabella knelt and pulled a single weed that had sprouted among the wild roses she had planted on the mound of black earth. She placed her hands gently on the mound as though touching Alexander's forehead, holding them there for a moment before she arose. Despite the drought and blazing sun, the rose's delicate pink petals were perfect, and their light perfume filled the air.

Then each of the family knelt and touched the earth, and it seemed that Alexander stood among them.

Izabella gathered the girls and Michael-Joseph into her arms. "Alexander would have become a great man.

You must live your lives so that he would be proud of you."

"We will, Mama." Marie, Rose, Caroline, and Michael-Joseph spoke as one.

Izabella kissed each of them. "You are good children. We are proud of all of you." She opened her arms. "Now we will go to town."

Aunt Magda smiled at the children. "And you girls can look at all the things in the stores while Michael-Joseph goes with the men to find a car."

As the team pulled the wagon down the road again, the distant water tower of Centerford became visible across the flat land. The tower brought a feeling of excitement to the family, signifying belonging and acceptance, tribe and clan, civilization and progress. Below the tower were paved streets, fine houses, churches, stores, a lumberyard, a bank, running water piped to each building, electricity created in a giant power house lighting every street and building, a fire department, doctors, dentists, even the county Court House, sheriff, town marshal, and jail.

Josif and Uncle Jon knew that jail well. Knew it too well. When they first came to Centerford in March of 1929, Josif had been arrested and jailed by the fat marshal for bringing the horses and a cow down the main street. And when Clarence Lamb had killed the sheriff and convinced the marshal that the Dacias had done it, Uncle Jon and Josif had been thrown into the jail and almost lynched by an angry mob.

But now Clarence, Vince, Verne, and Julius Lamb were dead, the fat marshal was back to sweeping the streets, the townspeople had given Josif a new violin to replace the one stamped on by Vince Lamb during Josif's arrest, and the Dacias were accepted by the townspeople as good friends and neighbors.

It was still early morning. Meadowlarks sang from their fence post perches, and the air was cool. The enor-

171

mous blue sky vibrated above, the slant-lighted fecund earth stretched away into infinity, and the family felt the exhilaration and sense of space and eternity that the Great Plains could bring at certain times. Almost forgotten were the brown clouds of choking dust, the merciless afternoon sun, the withering crops.

Uncle Jon began to sing *Maidens Fair*, and the rest of the family joined in, their clear voices floating across the land, causing the horses to prick up their ears and walk more briskly, the meadowlarks to sing more strongly, and the horses and cattle in the dry pastures on either side of the road to raise their heads from their dusty and futile grazing.

They arrived in Centerford at 10:00. Josif carefully avoided Main Street and guided the horses to the empty lot behind the blacksmith shop designated for teams. They unhitched and unbridled Peter and Paul and tied their halter ropes to a wooden railing, leaving them with two buckets of water and a generous forkful of hay.

Josif looked at his family. "The big whistle on the electric power plant goes off at noon. All of us will come back to the wagon when we hear it."

The men and Michael-Joseph headed for the two garages on the edge of town, Aunt Magda and the girls went toward Main Street and the grocery stores, while Izabella walked into the wealthy residential area where the big white houses and their groomed lawns stood proudly beneath huge elm and oak trees.

She loved this part of town. The beautiful houses, order, stability, quiet good taste, gracious people, and the feeling of culture and wealth closed around her like a rich garment. But today she noticed a change since she last visited Ellen Johnson in May. The normally green lawns lay dry and yellow, the carefully-trimmed hedges drooped, and dead leaves from the elms and oaks covered the sidewalks and driveways.

The Johnson house was at the corner of Elm Street and Third Avenue. In spite of the dry lawns and fallen leaves, the house, with its great porches and columns, its wide windows, and its majestic chimneys, still seemed a magnificent mansion to Izabella.

She walked along the rose-bordered path and up the wide steps that led to the porch and the massive oak door with its gracious side windows of heavy beveled glass, and shining brass knocker and handle.

Ellen opened the door as Izabella came to the top of the steps. She ran to Izabella and hugged her, then expressing her delight, led her in through the doorway and the paneled entry room across soft oriental rugs into the spacious living room with its sofas and easy chairs, dark mahogany tables, and huge oil paintings of flowers and landscapes. A grand piano stood in one corner of the room, and shelves of books covered the walls on either side of the wide archway that led into the dining room with its massive table, china cabinet, and carved chairs.

Ellen seated Izabella in a beautiful antique chair inlaid with needlepoint of roses. Ellen sat in a similar chair, facing Izabella. The two women were in striking contrast to one another, each beautiful in her own way: Izabella dark-haired and dark-eyed, Ellen golden-haired and blue-eyed, one from Romania, the other from Swedish parents. Both had the lithe and shapely figures of dancers: one an accomplished performer of the wild and beautiful ethnic dances of eastern Europe, the other a trained ballet dancer. Both had lovely and expressive eyes and features, now showing their pleasure at being together.

Ellen leaned forward and squeezed Izabella's hand. "I am so happy you have come! Tell me of all the children!"

"Marie, Rose, and Caroline are happy and busy. They love school, but in summer vacation they have tea parties in the grove. A mother cat had a litter, and each girl has a kitten. They all play together on a blanket in the shade."

"How wonderful. I had a kitten when I was a little girl, and I loved her so." Ellen's eyes became sad. "I had to leave her behind. She died of old age while I was gone. I feel so badly about that." Then she smiled at Izabella. "But I must not make you sad with my memories."

Izabella's eyes showed her sympathy, then they brightened. "If the mother cat makes more kittens, do you want one?"

Ellen drew in a breath in joy. "Could I? Oh, that would be so nice!" Then she hesitated. "But I will have to talk with Alan about it first."

Izabella nodded. "Josif says cats are for killing mice and rats, that they belong in the barn, but sometimes he lets Micheal-Joseph and the girls bring one in the house for a little while."

"Michael-Joseph! What a fine little boy! I will never forget the first time I saw him. He wanted to take me to see the wild geese in your big pond." Ellen smiled at the memory. "Alan had brought me out from the bank with him on our way to Sioux Falls."

"You had your beautiful blue shoes with high heels."

"And I had to tell Michael-Joseph I would bring boots next time we came." Ellen's eyes became sad again. "But Julius Lamb shot the geese." She rose from her chair and put her arms around Izabella. "Forgive me. It seems that when we talk of good memories I come to the sad ones."

"We have the good memories and the sad ones together. I can talk of them now. That same day Julius Lamb hurt Alexander, you were with me while Alexander died. I will never forget your kindness."

The two women hugged each other and cried softly.

After a time they drew apart and sat in their chairs again. Ellen wiped her eyes. "Tell me of Michael-Joseph. He is such a bright little boy that he must have done well in school."

"Yes. The teacher said he learns everything so easy." Izabella smiled ruefully. "You know how he learned to say all the bad words from Fritz and August Wagner. Now he wants to be a farmer just like them."

"Perhaps he will forget the bad words?"

"I try to make him do that." Izabella looked down at her hands, then up at Ellen. "I have a wish for Michael-Joseph and for our girls. I hope they go to high school and college. I dream that Michael-Joseph will become the great man that Alexander would have been!" She looked down at her hands again. "Even though Michael-Joseph is destined to become a farmer like all the men he is descended from, I want him to have choices about possibilities for his future." She looked at Ellen apologetically. "I'm sorry. I'm a greedy woman; I ask too much for my children."

"You are not!" Ellen rose from her chair in her enthusiasm. "I think it's wonderful that you want them to become educated!" Ellen took Izabella's hand in hers. "I am so happy that you have told me of your hopes and dreams! I want to help you make them come true!"

Izabella stared at Ellen. "You would help us?"

"I would love to."

"We cannot ask this of you." Izabella lowered her eyes. "Josif would not let you. I should not have spoken of it."

"I know how proud he is never wanting to accept help. But there are ways for your children to become educated without offending him. Will you go for a walk with me after we have had tea?"

"A walk?"

"Yes. I want to show you something."

"What?"

Ellen's eyes sparkled with excitement. "I want to show you something in the town library."

* * *

When the family returned to the wagon all of the children tried to tell of their adventures at once. Izabella hushed them. "Let the men speak first. They will tell us of the cars."

Josif shrugged. "We went to both garages. The cars we can afford are junk. The good ones are too expensive."

"Art had a new Pontiac," Michael-Joseph said. "It smelled good inside and will go eighty miles an hour. It's blue. When I get big I'm gonna get one of them."

"Seven hundred dollars!" Josif slapped his pocket. "We have fifty."

Uncle Jon winked at the girls. "Michael-Joseph is going to save his money. All the girls will want to ride in his blue car."

Aunt Magda frowned at him. "Don't be giving him bad ideas. Just because you wanted all the girls."

Uncle Jon did a little dance step. "Hoo Ha! If I had a new blue car like that!"

Aunt Magda covered Caroline's ears with her hands. "Don't listen to him. He is getting worse as he gets older."

Marie held up a big paper bag. "We got sugar and coffee and a surprise!"

"Don't tell them!" Rose jumped up and down. "We can't eat them until we get in the wagon!"

Caroline jumped up and down with Rose. "They are going to taste so good!"

Izabella hugged them. "What good girls! To get a surprise for us!"

The men hitched Peter and Paul back to the wagon

and put their bridles on, while everyone told the horses how good they had been to wait so long. When the family was back in the wagon, the girls could wait no longer, and opened the bag to show everyone their surprise.

"Doughnuts!" Caroline said. "All covered with cinnamon and sugar!"

Aunt Magda smiled. "They wanted something for all of us."

Marie gave the bag to Caroline. "Give one to everybody."

While they ate the doughnuts and exclaimed how delicious they were, Josif clucked the team forward. Peter and Paul stepped out eagerly and pulled the wagon through the side streets and out of town, leaving the tall water tank and the streets and stores behind. While the family loved to visit the town, they felt happy that they were going home. Going home to their farm, their cozy house and barn, their big grove of cottonwoods, their creek, their orchard, their wide fields, their own land.

When they were back on the country roads, Aunt Magda asked Izabella about her visit with Ellen Johnson.

Izabella smiled happily. "We had such a good time talking together. We had tea, then we walked to the library. Next time we come to town we must all go there. There are hundreds of books, and other wonderful things to see and read. Things that can help our children become educated. Even go to college."

Josif frowned. "I told you we do not have enough money for our children to go to college. Only the rich can do that."

"We do not have to be rich. In the library were books telling of the colleges and universities in America. Some of them are expensive, but here in South Dakota they are not expensive." Izabella took a folded sheet of paper from her handbag. "I wrote down some of the things about them. In Brookings, south of here, is the South Dakota State College. They charge only about sixty dollars a year for what they call 'tuition', and students can sometimes be awarded *scholarships* which pay for their tuition."

"Michael-Joseph will be a farmer," Josif said. "He will be the man someday and run our farm. The girls will marry men with land."

"At South Dakota State College," Izabella said, "young men learn how to be better farmers. If Michael-Joseph goes to high school and then to State College, he could be the best farmer in the whole state."

Josif shook his head. "Farmers do not need to go to college to learn how to farm. The boy learns from his father, who learned from his father." He looked up at the blazing sun. "We will get no crops this year. We will have to use our money from the band to make our mortgage payments to the bank. There will be no money for a car. Barely enough to send the children to school, and no money for college. No money for anything except keeping our land!"

Chapter Twenty-Two
Decision

After the children were in bed, the four Dacia adults sat at the kitchen table trying to decide what to do. The time was drawing near when they must rescue Irina. They had not found a car they could afford, and their crops were dying in the drought and heat. As usual when the adults were alone, they spoke in Romanian.

Aunt Magda touched the cross at her neck. "I have dreamed of Irina. She is in great danger. I saw her running in the mountains with wind and lightning all around her."

Izabella shuddered. "I pray that she is safe. She has waited so long to come to America."

Uncle Jon pulled at his mustache. "She will survive. She grew up fighting in the mountains and forests. I remember her as a little girl, barefoot like a Gypsy, carrying a pistol."

Josif nodded. "Sofia fought like a man. Irina learned much from her. She will get to America with the dance company, and I know she is brave and strong enough to make her way here somehow. But it would be best if we go to meet her."

"We need more money to pay our mortgage and still get a car that can go to New York City and back and not fall into pieces. We will find more weddings to play at, but people are so poor that we will never get enough money in time."

"I could go to New York on a bus or train," Izabella said. "When Irina escapes from the theater, we would go to the station in the darkness."

Josif scowled. "You will not go alone to rescue her!"

Uncle Jon agreed. "The train station might be miles from the theater. We have to have a car."

"So you men are going to rescue her?" Aunt Magda raised her eyebrows. "Have you thought how you will find Irina, how she will find you? You could stand waiting for her at one door while she comes out another. Someone has to go into the theater and find her before she flees. A woman should do that. A woman in costume. I will go rescue her."

"We will go together." Izabella smiled at Aunt Magda. "They will think we are part of the dance ensemble."

Josif slapped his hand on the table. "You women are not going alone! My mind is made up on that. We will go in a car and I will drive it!"

"It must be planned like a military attack." Uncle Jon stroked his mustache. "We need maps. Maps of the roads to New York. Maps of city streets, a map showing where the theater lies. Everything must be planned and rehearsed. We must reconnoiter the area thoroughly. Set up observation posts. Choose an escape route."

"You will take an army." Aunt Magda patted her hair. "Two women can do all that without notice. All they need are a car and driver."

"I will be the driver," Josif said. "But we are back where we started. We have no car."

At this moment a car's lights shone in the driveway, and from the roaring of the engine the Dacias knew that the Wagner brothers had arrived. The car lights went out, doors banged shut, and the brothers clumped up onto the porch, arguing as usual in loud voices. Josif opened the screen door.

"I come to tell you I found you a car," Fritz announced. "It's just what you want."

"Dammit, Fritz," August protested, "I seen it first. You wouldn't have never even seen it if I hadn't gone over to it."

"I seen it before you did," Fritz said. "I just didn't go rushing over to it like some greenhorn. You ain't got brains enough to know how to handle them slick salesmen. You gotta act like you ain't interested, not go jumpin' up and down like some idiot." He spoke confidentially to Josif. "August don't know beans about buyin' a car."

August snorted. "I know a lot more'n you do. You was gonna give that guy a chance to back out on the whole deal."

"That shows how much you know! I was bringin' him in like I was catchin' a fish."

August spoke to Uncle Jon who was peering out over Josif's shoulder. "When we towed it home, Fritz claimed he was the only one that could do it right. He don't know beans about towing. If I hadn't steered your car it would've rolled over goin' around the corners. Fritz never even slowed down."

"I been tryin' to teach August about towing," Fritz responded, "but it don't do no good."

"Please come in house so we can talk about car," Josif said.

"We don't need to come in the house," Fritz said. He pointed to the Dacias' lanterns that hung on the porch wall. "Bring them lanterns out so you can see your new car."

Josif lit the lanterns and the Dacias followed the Wagner brothers out to the driveway. Behind the Wagners' Pontiac, they saw in the lantern light a black sedan in fairly good condition.

"Ain't she a humdinger?" Fritz kicked the front wheel

tire. "Solid as a rock."

"What kind of car is it?" Josif asked.

"Why it's a 1928 Hudson Super Six. One of the best cars there is."

"Car must be expensive?"

"It would be for most people. But we got a real bargain."

"What car cost?"

"You ain't gonna believe this... ten bucks."

"This car for only ten dollars?"

"That's right. Ask August. He was there."

August modestly scuffed his big work shoe in the dust. "It woulda been a lot more if we hadn't talked that guy down."

"Whaddaya mean, we talked him down? I was the one that got him to come down."

"You know that ain't so, Fritz. I was the one that told him that without no engine or spare tire, his car wouldn't be worth even five bucks."

Josif stared at August, then Fritz, then the car. "This car not have engine?"

"Well don't you worry about that. That's where we really pulled a good one on that salesman." Fritz patted the hood of the car. "This here car is gonna be good as new. My cousin Floyd kinda forgot about how he wrecked his Super Six one night, and left it at the bottom of the gravel pit."

"It looked like some old tin can somebody had hammered with a crow bar."

Fritz scowled at August. "Will you shut up when me and Joe here are tryin' to talk? Joe knows what a car would look like after it flipped over about ten times. The important thing is that the engine is almost brand new. All we gotta do is move it outta Floyd's car and into this one."

Josif looked at Uncle Jon, then at Izabella and Aunt Magda. Uncle Jon growled in Romanian, "They are going to charge us ten dollars for a car with no engine?"

"Yes, but they know of a car that is a wreck, but still has a good engine."

"It sounds like one of their ideas that will probably go bad. How much would we owe for this car of many pieces?"

Josif spoke to Fritz in English. "We only have fifty dollars. What will your cousin want us to pay for the engine?"

"Pay? Why he ain't gonna charge you nothin'. That Hudson of his is a total wreck."

"Ol' Floyd's too lazy to fart," August said. "He left that Hudson down at the bottom of the gravel pit for junk. Besides that, he collected insurance on it. Told that insurance guy the brakes went kerflooey."

"Joe ain't interested in all that, August. Everybody knows you can make them insurance guys believe anything." Fritz opened the hood of the Hudson. "Hold your lantern up here, Joe. All we gotta do is connect the drive shaft and a few of these wires and tubes and you'll have her purring like a cat drinking cream."

"How did car not have engine?" Josif asked.

Fritz snorted. "That stupid guy in the junkyard claimed it was built that way."

"Fritz was gonna beat the crap outta him," August said.

"I wasn't neither." Fritz glared at August. "I was just tryin' to help his memory a little bit. He prob'ly sold that engine to somebody, then claimed it got stole. He prob'ly sold the spare tire too. I woulda got all that straightened out but then he offered to cut the price in half if I let him down on his feet again. It's kinda like tradin' horses."

Three years before, Fritz and August had brought a team of the most ill-favored horses Josif had ever seen, offering to sell them to the Dacias. Now Josif felt a premonition of trouble to come with the engineless car. He spoke to the Wagners, "We thank you for getting car. But we are farmers, not mechanics. I work on trucks in army, but might not know how to put engine in car."

"Why, everybody knows how to do that. You just hoist the engine up with your horse power, lower it down into place and connect a few things. Even August could do it."

"Whaddaya mean, 'even August could do it'?" August said. "Who fixed the Pontiac when you couldn't get it started?"

"Fixed it? You call putting gas in it fixing it?" Fritz spoke to Uncle Jon. "This idiot took it out the night before and run it outta gas just as he got it in the driveway. He pushed it in and didn't bother to put more gas in it! Then he thinks it's real funny when I try to start it!"

August grinned. "He never woulda figured it out. He was startin' to pound on the engine with a wrench."

"I'll pound on you with this if you don't shut up." Fritz said shaking his huge fist in front of August's nose.

Uncle Jon spoke in Romanian to Josif. "They are going to start fighting in a minute. Send the women inside."

Josif looked at Izabella and spoke in Romnian. "Would you think I am foolish if I buy this car?"

Izabella smiled at Josif and responded in the privacy of their native tongue, "I know nothing about cars. But you have tried in vain to find a car we can afford. I believe Fritz and August are honestly trying to help us. If you think it is best to buy the car, then do it. I will never think that you are foolish. I know that what you do will be because you are trying to do the best thing for our family."

Chapter Twenty-Three
The Gravel Pit

The Wagner brothers' truck roared into the Dacia driveway the next morning as the family was finishing breakfast. Josif, Uncle Jon, and Michael-Joseph went out to meet them, staring at a tower-like structure of heavy planks that rose from the truck bed, extending out beyond the back of the truck.

Fritz spoke through the open window of the truck. "Grab a jug a water, your hats, and a big hay rope and pulleys. We're goin' over to the gravel pit and haul that engine out."

"We don't need horses?" Josif asked.

"Horses? Hell, no. We're gonna do this scientific-like."

August added, "I had to talk Fritz into it."

Fritz glared at August. "You didn't talk me into nothin'." He spoke to Uncle Jon. "August ain't got no idea how to use pulleys."

"I do too!" August came around from the far side of the truck. "I'm the one that figured out we should use pulleys."

Fritz climbed out of the truck and glared at August. "I was using pulleys and ropes before you could pull up your overalls. Now shut up about it bein' your idea or I'm gonna slug you one."

185

Josif tried to distract the brothers before they started fighting. He pointed to the tower of planks. "Can lift heavy car with this?"

"We can." Fritz slapped one of the planks. "I sure as hell built it strong enough. But the way I got it figured, we'll just lift the engine out. That car is just a hunk a junk."

"You built it?" August scoffed. "Who did all the work? You know damn well I did!"

"You couldn't build a hog pen if I didn't show you how." Fritz slapped the tower again. "It took some brainwork to build a derrick like this."

Josif said, "Is good. We thank you both for making it. We get rope and pulleys from barn now."

They loaded the Dacias' rope and pulleys into the back of the truck on top of the Wagners' ropes and a pile of heavy tools. Izabella, Aunt Magda, and the girls came out into the barnyard and Izabella handed a small sack to Josif. Then Josif, Uncle Jon, and Michael-Joseph climbed up into the front end of the truck box. As Fritz circled the truck around the barnyard and out the driveway, the Dacia men waved to the women and girls, feeling the cool morning air rushing across their faces as the truck bumped over the stone bridge and down the country road past the fields and farms of their neighbors.

Michael-Joseph climbed on top of the pile of ropes, holding onto the front boards of the truck box, shouting with excitement as the fences and ditches streaked past on either side.

They went south for five miles, then Fritz turned to the right and went west for three miles, then south again for half a mile. He nosed the truck up against a wire gate that led into a rocky field filled with cockleburs and sunflowers. A crude sign painted with garish red letters on an old board was spiked to the gate post. It said: "Keep out. This means you."

August climbed out of the truck, tore off the sign and threw it in the ditch, then opened and shut the gate after Fritz drove the truck through; Fritz not pausing to let August get back in the truck.

About fifty yards ahead of them the Dacias saw a large pit. Fritz stopped the truck at the edge of the pit, and the Dacias climbed down as August came panting up to them. He yelled at Fritz through the open truck window. "Next time you can open the goddamn gate, Fritz. You ain't pullin' that on me again!"

Fritz ignored him and walked to the edge of the pit. He pointed down to where a big yellow car lay crumpled with its tires splayed out, and its roof and sides caved in, about twenty-five feet below. "There she is. All we gotta do is unconnect the engine and haul 'er up."

"How did people get gravel out?" Josif asked. "Walls are steep all around."

"Old *Dynamite* John Hoyer blew up the roadway." Fritz started building a cigarette. "He got mad because of all them dumb high school kids."

August added. "They was doing all their neckin' down there."

Fritz scowled at August. "Joe can figure that out. We don't need your two cents worth."

"Well, for cripes sake, Joe wasn't here then!" August spoke to Uncle Jon. "Fritz thinks you folks should know everything that ever happened around here."

"Shut up, August," Fritz said, "and haul that stuff outta the truck. We ain't got all day."

The Dacias helped August unload the ropes, pulleys, and tools. Josif selected two of the big wrenches. "I go down and get engine loose."

Fritz said, "Me and you are both goin' down." He spoke to August. "Turn the truck around and back up so the tail gate hangs over the edge. And don't run over the ropes and stuff."

"You're the one that thinks he's such a wonderful driver," August replied. "You do it."

"Damnit, August. We need somebody with brains to tell you when to stop. I gotta do that. All you have to do is stop when I tell you to."

"Oh, sure. Like when you told Floyd when to stop. If he hadn't a jumped, he'd be down there with his car, pushin' up daisies."

"Jesus H. Christ!" Fritz said. "Floyd was too busy showin' off to that girlfriend a his to pay any attention to what I told him."

August explained to Uncle Jon. "They was having a contest to see who could back up closest to the edge."

He said to Fritz, "I ain't as dumb as Floyd. If you wanna hang the tailgate over the edge, do it yourself."

"Listen, August. I just told you to back that truck up to the edge. If you don't do it I'm gonna beat the holy crap outta you!"

While the brothers glared at each other, Michael-Joseph whispered something to Josif. Josif spoke to the brothers. "Michael-Joseph have idea. Many big rocks here. We measure from truck wheels to tailgate, then make line of rocks almost that far from edge, keep truck from going over edge when back up."

The Wagner brothers stared at Josif, then at Michael-Joseph. Fritz said, "August, you dummy. Why didn't you think of that? Then you wouldn't be so damned scared about backin' the truck up."

"I ain't scared!" August replied angrily. "And I didn't notice you comin' up with it. Maybe if you're so smart you would've told Floyd about it."

"For cryin' out loud, we was havin' a contest! You don't go puttin' a line of rocks up in a contest. That's why I didn't say anything to Floyd."

"Well, this ain't no contest now, and you still didn't

think of it. I sure don't remember you sayin' anything about it."

"Well, don't keep harpin' on it! I'll measure a few things and we'll get this show on the road."

They collected big rocks and made a barrier two feet from the crater's edge. August backed the truck out into the field, did a boot leg turn and backed at high speed toward the crater.

Fritz waved both arms and roared, "Slow down, you idiot! Stop the goddamned truck!"

August slammed on the brakes and grinned down at Fritz. "I was just seeing if you was payin' attention."

"I'm payin' attention all right! Climb down outta there and get the hell outta the way while I back it up right!"

"I'm driving, damn you, Fritz. You get outta the way." August backed toward the line of rocks as Fritz pulled the door open and leapt onto the running board, pounding at August as the truck neared the edge of the crater.

Josif ran out from behind the truck and held his hands apart, frantically trying to show the struggling brothers the lessening distance from the wheels to the line of rocks.

The rear wheels hit the rocks with a *thud* as Fritz and August rolled from the truck onto the ground, cursing and fighting like two grizzly bears while Uncle Jon drew Michael-Joseph back and Josif leapt into the truck and turned off the ignition switch, stopping the wild spinning and bucking of the wheels.

The fight suddenly ended with Fritz sitting astride August who lay on his back, still struggling. Fritz said, "You dummy, you ain't never learned that I can wrassle better'n you can."

"You was just lucky." August wiped blood from his nose. "You jumped me while I was drivin' the truck. Next time you'll see."

Fritz stood up and slapped sand and dirt out of his overalls. "I'll see all right. I can lick you with one hand tied behind me." He glanced at the truck. "If I hadn't jumped you,the damned truck would be down on top a that Hudson. Now if it ain't too hard for you, start stringin' those ropes and pulleys together while me and Joe go down and unconnect that engine."

He tossed a crowbar, a huge pipe wrench, and two log chains over the edge of the pit. "Throw what tools you want down there, Joe, and we'll go down and get started." He tied one end of a long rope to the truck box and threw the coil over the edge. "Just grab this when you go down."

Josif dropped the tools he had chosen over the edge and then followed Fritz down into the pit, holding onto the dangling rope as he made his way down the precipice. Luckily the Hudson had landed right side up.

Fritz pried the battered hood of the car open with his crowbar and they peered in at the engine.

"Look at that," Fritz said. "Like new. If she ain't cracked some place we got us a new engine. I'll work on this side, you handle the other one, and that way we ain't gonna be bashin' each other's knuckles. When we come to the crank shaft and transmission you better let me show you how it goes, unless you had a lotta experience."

Fritz crawled under the car. "Lemme just take a look under here before we waste a lotta time taking off all the damned wires and cables."

Michael-Joseph called down from the edge, "I wanna come down, Papa, and see how you do it."

Josif replied, "You help August and Uncle Jon fix ropes and pulleys. Then you come down."

"All right, Papa. But don't go too fast. I wanna see how you disconnect the transmission."

Fritz spoke from under the car. "Things look good under here. Hand me them log chains, Joe. Grab 'em when I push 'em up."

As Fritz passed the ends of the log chains up around the engine, Josif pulled them up and laid them over the car's fenders. Fritz crawled out from under the car and they bolted the ends of each chain together forming two big loops, one at each end of the engine.

August and Uncle Jon slowly lowered their block and tackle of ropes and pulleys until the lower end touched the car, then Fritz and Josif fastened the chain loops to the pulleys with heavy twisted-wire cables. Fritz shouted upward. "Pull the damned ropes up tight and tie 'em. We don't want this engine droppin' down when we pull the bolts outta the motor mounts."

August yelled back, "Jesus Christ, Fritz, we know that. You don't hafta tell us every damned thing." He turned to Uncle Jon. "He thinks he's the only one that knows anything."

As Fritz and Josif now began the work of separating the engine from all the wires, hoses, tubes, and mechanical connections which held it to the body of the car, Michael-Joseph came down into the pit. "We got things all fixed up there, and Uncle Jon and August can handle it," he said. "I came to help you get this dang engine outta here."

Fritz motioned to him. "Crawl up on top of the engine. Keep your eyes open and you'll see how a coupla real mechanics do it."

Josif cautioned the boy, "Don't get in way. If big wrenches slip could be dangerous."

Michael-Joseph stuck out his lower lip. "I ain't gonna get in the way, Papa. I'm gonna help you."

Fritz said, "Grab yourself a monkey-wrench and a pliers, Mike. Take care of the things you can handle. If you can't figure out whether to leave something with the engine or with the car, just ask me."

Michael-Joseph found the tools and crawled up onto the engine. "I know which ones to leave with the car."

"How in hell do you know that?" Fritz asked.

"Because I saw which ones are in the car you and August got in Sioux Falls. If they're in that car we don't have to take them from this car."

Fritz stared at Michael-Joseph. "You got all that memorized?"

"Sure."

Josif said, "His teacher tell us he got memory like a picture. He remember everything he sees. Even pages in book."

"Holy Christ!" Fritz pointed to an ignition wire. "We take that?"

"Hell, no. We already got it."

Fritz touched the radiator hose. "How about this?"

"Take it."

Fritz shook his head. "I gotcha that time. There's already one in your car. I seen it."

"Yeah, there's one there, but there's a slit in it. Some idiot cut it when they were taking the engine out."

Fritz's cigarette dropped from his lip. He retrieved it and said casually, "I knew that. I was just testing you. I got one of them picture memories, too. It just seems to come natural to me."

August shouted down from the edge of the pit, "He can't remember shit. If you're so smart, Fritz, how come you almost flunked in school?"

Fritz glared up at August. "Listen, you dummy! I remember important things, not some stupid pages in a book."

"Oh sure. Like when grandma made you get confirmed. That preacher was just about ready for the looney bin by the time he got you to say the right words!"

Fritz shook his fist at August. "I'm coming up and beat the crap outta you, August. I got confirmed better'n you did and you know it. Now shut up and let's get this engine ready to hoist up."

August spoke quietly to Uncle Jon, "That preacher quit and went into selling washing machines. He said he thanked Fritz for showing him the way to make more money than he did preaching."

Three hours later the engine was free, resting on the frame of the car with the block and tackle above it. Fritz used a sledge hammer and an axe to demolish the parts of the car that blocked a clean lift, then he, Josif, and Michael-Joseph climbed up out of the pit with the help of the dangling rope.

The block and tackle consisted of four big pulleys, two at the top, two at the bottom, with a stout hay-lifting rope running up and down between them and finally rising up to the truck where it was fed through another pulley so it could be pulled laterally. At the top the pulleys were chained to the derrick at the back of the truck; at the bottom the two lower pulleys were chained to the engine. Fritz examined the system with a jaundiced eye, then positioned Michael-Joseph to one side of the truck near the edge of the pit to watch the engine.

August seized the pulling rope. "You guys stand back. I'll haul that engine out myself."

"The hell you will," Fritz bellowed. "I ain't havin' you drop everything when it's half-way up. Gimme the rope."

"I ain't gonna drop anything."

Fritz forced himself in between August and the pulley. "Joe, you grab the rope in back of August. Jon, you better keep back so you don't get hurt."

"In army I have helped drag cannons up mountains," Uncle Jon said. "It is best to have an anchor." He wrapped the end of the rope around the front bumper of the truck and off to the side. "As you bring the engine up I will keep the rope tight."

Fritz shrugged his shoulders. "We ain't gonna need that, but it ain't too bad an idea. August here is prob'ly gonna have to make a cigarette or somethin' about half-way up." He braced one foot against a big rock. "Let's pull 'er up."

The rope creaked and the pulleys squealed as the four men hauled on the rope, and the engine began to move. Michael-Joseph shouted, "It's coming up out of the car!"

"This is gonna be easy," Fritz said. "I could do it by myself."

Slowly, the big rope ran through the top pulleys, and in a few minutes the lower pulleys, the chains, then the top of the engine appeared above the edge of the pit. Then the lower pulleys came up against the top ones and the engine stopped moving upward, its bottom about six inches below the pit edge.

Fritz gave a tremendous and useless yank on the rope and then emitted a blast of profanity that sent a flock of cliff swallows fluttering into the air from their nests in the pit wall. Uncle Jon, seeing the problem, quickly did a double half hitch around the truck bumper, securing the engine in its precarious position and allowing the men to release their hold on the rope.

Fritz turned to August. "You dummy, you didn't make the goddamned derrick high enough!"

"I didn't make it high enough? Jesus Christ! You're the one who claims you built it!"

"I told you how to do it, but you didn't have brains enough to figure out that the damn chains and cables would be too long! Now we got the goddamned engine hanging there like a stuck load a hay!"

Josif quickly intervened before a fight could erupt. "We all make mistake, didn't think cables and chains would stretch out so long. Maybe we find way to get engine over edge. We jack up rear wheels of truck, make road of rocks. Get engine over edge and on ground, then shorten chains and cables."

Fritz and August stared at him. "A road of rocks?" Fritz said looking thoughtful.

"Make higher than engine below edge."

August said, "I was just gonna mention that. We gotta take the rocks away as the truck goes ahead so the engine don't drag on 'em."

"Will you shut up, August," Fritz said. "Anybody could figure that out if they had half a brain. Get the god-damned jack out."

They jacked up each rear wheel in turn, then built a road of rocks under them and going forward, high enough for the engine to clear the edge of the pit, as Josif had suggested. When they finished, Uncle Jon drove the truck slowly forward a foot at a time, waiting until Josif and Michael-Joseph removed the rocks behind the wheels. In fifteen minutes the swaying engine hung safely out of the pit and away from the edge, and as Uncle Jon stopped the truck, Fritz and August lowered the engine to the ground.

Fritz squinted up at the sun. "It's noon. Grandma sent along a big jug a coffee and some sandwiches and cake. Get 'em outta the cab, August, and we'll have lunch before we shorten up them chains and cables."

Josif smiled, "Women send Romanian bread with-cheese."

Uncle Jon pulled a sack from the truck box "Good crop of plums last year made much *tuica*." He winked at Michael-Joseph. "You good mechanic like Fritz and August and your Papa. Now we got engine for car. We celebrate."

Michael-Joseph reverently touched the engine. "Boy howdy!"

Chapter Twenty-Four
Bucharest

As Deben and Irina neared Bucharest in Deben's car, he spoke glowingly of the dance tour.

"We leave the day after tomorrow. You are lucky that I found you. Now you will get to see Vienna, Paris, London, New York, Washington, D.C., and Baltimore."

He glanced at Irina. "You look ridiculous dressed as a shepherd boy. When we get to my apartment you will dress as a woman should."

"I have no other clothing. I had to leave everything behind when I fled from the men with the black cars."

"I brought your things to my apartment."

She stared at him. "My things? My clothing?"

"Of course."

"You were in my apartment?"

"We came to help you when we learned that Duca's men were going to arrest you."

"And you took my clothing to your apartment? Why?"

"Because you are going to stay in my apartment. You will be safe from Ion Duca there. We will keep you hidden until we leave on the tour."

"It is not proper for me to stay in your apartment with you! Besides, how can you keep me safe? Ion Duca rules Romania."

"The men you saw at the castle are more powerful than Ion Duca."

"He has the army behind him. How can you fight tanks and machine guns?"

"Ion Duca will die. Then the army will come to us. Corneliu Codreanu and the Iron Guard will rule Romania. We will purge our country of the Jews and Communists. We will form a greater Romania!"

Irina felt her body grow tense with anger and revulsion at Deben's words. Her Jewish friends had been killed by the Iron Guard. She replied sarcastically, "I didn't know you were so powerful."

"Because you are ignorant. What Ataturk is to Turkey, Corneliu Codreanu will be to Romania. I am close to our leader. I will have an important post in the new government."

"Of course."

Deben slowed the car and brought it to the curb in front of a shabby apartment building. "We are here." He got out of the car and came to Irina's side. He opened the door and gestured for her to come out. "Come quickly. No one must see you looking like a peasant." Then he swore and abruptly shut the door before Irina could step from the car. "Lie down on the seat!" he ordered.

An elderly couple and a young woman hurried down the sidewalk toward the car, waving. Deben stood with his back to the car, trying to hide Irina.

"You have found her!" the elderly woman cried. "Thank God! Christina was so worried about you." She peered around Deben, staring at Irina. "Where have you been, dear girl? And why are you dressed like that? I didn't recognize you until you let your hair down."

Deben whirled to glare at Irina, then he said smoothly to the woman, "She has been visiting a relative in the mountains. She was helping herd the sheep."

Christina, the young woman, clapped her hands. "We are so glad she is back; we were so worried! Let her get out of the car, Deben, so that I can hug her."

"She smells of sheep."

"That doesn't matter." Christina brushed Deben aside and opened the car door. "We heard that your apartment had been ransacked; I was afraid that you were in terrible danger."

Irina stepped from the car and the two hugged each other. When they separated, they wiped their eyes. Christina hugged Irina again. "You must stay with us until we go on tour. You will be safe with us."

"She will be safe here," Deben said. "She will have her own room with a lock. All of her clothes and things have already been brought to my apartment. Since we go on tour the day after tomorrow, it would be silly to move everything again, and I will make sure that she is not harmed."

The older woman smiled at him. "You are a good man, Deben. It is improper for a woman to stay at a man's apartment, but since her life may be in jeopardy it is the safest thing for her. And since her room has a lock she will not be in a vulnerable position. We know you will do the right thing and also watch out for Irina and Christina on the tour. They are so young and inexperienced...."

Deben kissed her hand. "I will protect them with my life."

The elderly man shook Deben's hand. "We appreciate your kindness and concern. But we expect no less from the lead dancer of the troupe. Since Irina's parents are dead, she has no one to look after her to make sure that no harm of any kind comes to her. I'm sure Irina will be safe with you. Thank you, my boy."

When the Romanescus had all hugged Irina and continued down the sidewalk, Deben snarled at Irina, "I told you to lie down on the seat! Instead, you let your hair down and let them see you!"

"Christina recognized me before you spoke," Irina replied. "I would have looked silly lying on the seat. You act as though you want to keep me hidden."

"Of course I want to keep you hidden! Ion Duca's men still search for you! I am the only one who can protect you." Deben held Irina tightly by the arm as he hurried her into the apartment building. "If you are taken by them, it will be your own fault."

Deben left Irina behind locked doors at his apartment and drove to the secret home of Corneliu Codreanu, a small farm on the outskirts of the city.

He found the lawyer grooming his white horse in the barn. "We had an excellent gathering at the castle," he said to Deben.

"Yes."

"We are strong. Soon we will rule Romania." Codreanu stroked the horse's soft nose. "You have the girl secured in your apartment?"

"She's locked in. She thinks it is for her own safety."

"She believes she will go on the tour?"

"Yes."

"She must not escape again. She must be made to hate Ion Duca. I will have the men come for her tonight."

"She doesn't think it was Ion Duca's men who came for her the first time."

Codreanu frowned. "What caused her to think that?"

"I don't know. For some reason she believes it was our people."

"When she is in the hands of the inquisitors, she will be convinced otherwise."

Deben spoke uneasily. "There is something else."

"What?" Cordreanu's eyes became icy.

"She was seen when we returned."

"By whom?"

"Nosey neighbors. An old couple and their daughter. The daughter is a member of the dance troupe."

"Where did they see you?"

"Outside my apartment, just as we arrived."

Codreanu spat with anger. "You idiot! You should have kept her hidden!"

"I couldn't help it. They came to the car. Then they recognized her."

"I should kill you!" Codreanu stroked the handle of the pistol at his waist. "Now your whole dance troupe will know that she has been found and is at your apartment. If she is taken now, you would be blamed."

"What should I do with her?"

"We cannot touch her here. She will be of little use to us now in killing Duca; but she knows too much. She must be silenced, but without suspicion."

"How?"

"We must change our plans. Take her on the tour."

"Take her?"

"There can be many accidents at sea."

"You mean…?"

"I do. People often fall overboard."

"Yes."

"Can you do it?"

Deben smiled, relieved that he had been spared. "I can do it."

Chapter Twenty-Five
The New Car

Using the horse-powered wagon hoist at the base of the Dacia grain elevator, the engine salvaged from the gravel pit was lowered into the engineless car from Sioux Falls. After two days, with the help of Michael-Joseph and the cursing and arguing Wagner brothers, Josif and Uncle Jon finished connecting the engine to the car. They filled the radiator with tank water, put in oil and gasoline brought from Centerford, and connected the used battery supplied by the Wagners. All was ready.

Josif sat behind the steering wheel and pushed on the starter. The engine growled weakly and became silent.

Fritz glared at August. "I told you to get that dang battery charged up!"

"I did, but I told you it wasn't no damned good." August spoke to Uncle Jon. "Fritz thinks he can use the same battery for about twenty years."

Fritz seized the crank from the pile of tools that lay on the ground. "All you gotta do is get the goddamned engine goin'." He inserted the crank and turned it with such force that the front end of the Hudson bobbed up and down. The engine roared to life as a cloud of blue smoke belched from the exhaust pipe.

Fritz removed the crank and tossed it onto the floorboards of the Hudson. "There ain't nothin' to startin' a car. A coupla turns with a crank beats them stupid starters, and you don't hafta be worryin' about some battery all the time." He patted the hood. "Why don't you take your whole family into town, Joe? Show 'em what this baby can do."

"Go into the court house while you're there," August added. Get yourself a license plate. Butch Bennard is touchy as hell about that."

Fritz scowled at August. "Will you shut up, August? Joe here knows about license plates."

"We have to have paper license to drive car?" Josif asked.

"A driver's license? Hell, no. Not in South Dakota. Some of them dummies in states like Iowa hafta be taught how to drive a car. Everybody knows how to drive here."

"Can drive car in other states without driver license?" Josif asked.

"Why sure. All you hafta have is your South Dakota license plate. Anybody sees that, they know you don't need any stupid paper license."

As the men talked, a dark wall of clouds boiled up in the southwest sky, and a hot wind began to moan across the dry fields. "That's the damndest lookin' cloud I ever seen." August said. "There ain't no lightning or thunder."

Fritz turned to look at the strange cloud. "You dummy, August. It's about fifty miles from here. You ain't gonna hear no thunder that far away."

"Well, I can see lightning that far away, and I don't see none. And I ain't never seen a cloud like that." August gazed at the cloud. "It looks like a wall covered with cow shit."

An eery darkening of the sky was taking place, and Josif felt a strange unease, a feeling of depression and hopelessness as though something huge and evil was approaching. He spoke to Uncle Jon, "We better put horses and cows in barn quick."

Fritz nodded. "We're gonna head for home. Them heifers ain't very bright and we sure as hell don't want 'em climbin' the fences when that storm hits." He jerked his thumb at the idling Hudson. "If I was you Joe, I'd ram this into a shed. If it starts to hail this car might end up lookin' like that wreck in the gravel pit."

The Wagners climbed into their truck and roared out of the driveway while Josif drove the shiny Hudson into a shed. Then he, Uncle Jon, and Michael-Joseph ran to the barn, opened the doors to the small pasture, and called to Peter and Paul, who were nervously circling inside the fenced area. The horses galloped toward the barn and thundered through the open door and into their stalls as though something was chasing them.

The cows and calves huddled by the big straw stack, their eyes wild, and they readily followed the big red and white cow named Grace into the cattle side of the old barn. The men haltered the horses and poured oats into their feed boxes to quiet them, then left the barn, closing all the doors behind them.

The women and girls had come from the house and were driving the chickens into the coop, while Uncle Jon and Michael-Joseph closed the hog house doors and then braced shut with two old planks the doors of the shed that held the Hudson.

The rolling brown wall rushed toward them from only a few miles away now, and the Dacias stared at it in disbelief while the wind whipped their clothing and flocks of birds circled wildly.

Aunt Magda crossed herself and grimly said in Romanian, "*Strigoi* are the cause of this! They suck the life out of everything!"

The three girls stood close to Izabella. "Is it a tornado?

Caroline, the youngest, asked. Will it take the chickens up into heaven, like it did when we came from Oklahoma?"

Izabella patted Caroline's head. "Our chickens are safe in their house. When we came from Oklahoma the chickens were in a crate at the back of the wagon."

"I remember that. Papa said the chickens had lots of grasshoppers up in heaven."

Michael-Joseph spoke. "This ain't no tornado. August said it looked like a wall covered with cow shi..." Michael-Joseph bit off the word as Josif scowled at him.

"I think it is dirt," Josif said. "In Oklahoma the ground was red. Red dust blew over the land. Here the ground is black and brown. I think it is a big cloud of dirt."

The sky was darkening rapidly now, and as the sun faded, the family hurried into the house and closed all the doors and windows, then gathered in the kitchen and gazed out in amazement at the great wall of dirt that approached their home. Then the storm swept over them, and the house shuddered in the wind as the roaring monster enveloped them.

The family drew silently together, crossing themselves, the adults holding the children close. They could not see the barn or the windmill, and the pump that stood ten feet from the house was a grey ghost in the blowing dust. A feeling of sadness fell upon the family, for it seemed that all the goodness and beauty of their world, their farm, had been destroyed. Their grove of green rustling trees, their gurgling creek, their bountiful orchard, their carefully-watered flowers, their vegetable garden – all the things that they cherished – were lost under the dust.

Izabella lit the kerosene lamp that stood in the middle of the kitchen table. Currents of dust could be seen in the air, and small piles of dirt were building on the floor wherever there was a small gap between the wallboards. "We will make coffee and eat now."

Uncle Jon nodded. "This is nothing. We have survived tornadoes and blizzards. This dust will blow on by, and all will be as it was. I will get a bottle of *tuica* to clear the dust from our throats."

A dense stream of dust poured from the keyhole of the door and formed a thick, brown drift on the floor. Josif scooped up some of the dust into his hand. "This is good topsoil. If it falls on our fields we will have even better crops when the rain comes again."

Aunt Magda hurried over with a dishtowel and twisted a corner of it between her fingers to make a small point which she jammed and pushed into the keyhole until the flow of dirt stopped. "I will be thankful for the good dirt when it is time to plant again, but right now I would like to see less of it."

While the women and girls set the table and prepared their noon meal of coffee, milk, bread, fried pork and fat and *mamaliga* with white cheese, Uncle Jon brought a bottle of *tuica* to the table. He poured it into four glasses after wiping out a thin coat of dust from each of them first.

"The animals are safe in the barn and sheds. We are in this fine house. Let the wind and dust do their worst. We laugh at them."

"Will our new car be all right?" Michael-Joseph asked.

"It will not be hurt," Josif answered. "If we were driving it now it might suck dust into the engine. That would be bad."

Thirteen-year-old Marie spoke up. "In school, Mrs. Horsefall said people who breathe lots of dust get sick. The dust gets into their lungs. When any of us go outside, we must tie a wet cloth over our mouth and nose."

"I ain't wearing no sissy wet cloth," Michael-Joseph protested.

Izabella looked at him sternly. "In the war, brave soldiers tied wet cloths over their faces to keep out poison gas. We will do the same for the dust."

All that day the dust storm raged over the land. The moaning of the wind, the swirling dust, and the darkness gave a feeling of deep depression to the family. A thickening layer of dust was building on every level surface in the house. Everyone's hair was becoming dull grey-looking, and their skin felt gritty.

It seemed to Izabella that they crouched in a dark cave while beasts roared outside and blocked the light of day with their writhing bodies. She forced herself to speak cheerfully, and she played games with the children, but she felt nervous and anxious. It seemed as though for every step forward they made, there was a new challenge which threatened to move them backwards.

She prayed silently to God, asking for the strength to endure so that she could protect her family.

Chapter Twenty-Six
Disaster

In the morning the storm had passed, but the family looked out at a changed world. High drifts of dirt blanketed the barnyard and driveway like snow after a blizzard, and the leaves of the trees were torn and dirty. The sky was a depressing brown color, and the morning sun shone weakly on the dirt-covered fields.

When Josif opened the kitchen door, he found a two-foot-high drift blocking the porch. The men and Michael-Joseph put on their overshoes and waded through the drifts to the granary. They brought scoop shovels with which they cleared the porch and made paths to the privy, barn, and chicken house.

The water in the stock tank had turned to thin mud. The men started the windmill and brought buckets of clean water to the horses, who responded with soft nickering and grateful tossing of their heads as they drank. The cattle were released into the small pasture by the barn, and they drank from a wooden trough filled from the pumping windmill.

The men went into the fields. The oats, barley, and rye fields were choked with drifts of dirt, and the cornfields were the same. Uncle Jon tenderly brushed the dirt from a hill of corn and lifted the wilted stalks and leaves. "They could live if we had a heavy rain."

Josif looked at the gloomy sky. "It would rain mud."

"This damn weather ain't never gonna change," Michael-Joseph said. "I'm heading for California!"

Josif cuffed him. "Stop that swearing. What makes you think you are going to California?"

"I'm goin' with August. You can sit on the beach there and drink orange juice under a palm tree."

"August has been saying he is going to California for the last three years. What do you think you could do out there to make money?"

"August is gonna get a job playing his guitar for the movies. I'll play my clarinet."

"August is grown up. When you are grown up you can go to California. But now you must stay with our family. Have you thought how your mother would feel if you went off to California?"

"She could come visit me."

"It would cost much money for you to go to California. It would cost more for your mother to go there. We will get no crops this year; our only money will be from any cattle that we can sell. We will have to save every penny."

"August says all we have to do is hop on a freight train. We'll get out there for free. Lotsa guys are doin' it."

"Would you want to ride in a box car with strange men?"

"You bet I would. That'd be fun. August said we'll knock the crap outta anybody that looks cross-eyed at us."

"But there is something else, Michael-Joseph. You and Uncle Jon have to be the men of the family for awhile."

"Why?"

"Your mother and I have to go away in the car for a little while. You and the girls will stay here with Uncle Jon and Aunt Magda."

Michael-Joseph stared at his father. "Are you and Mama gonna go get Irina?"

"Yes, but we must keep it as a family secret."

"Because of the Iron Guard?"

"Yes."

Michael-Joseph thought for a moment. "Is that why you lied to Fritz and August about why we need a car?"

"Yes."

"I guess I better stay here with the family for awhile," he said.

"I think that is a good idea," Josif said smiling. "You will help keep our family together."

They saw the women and girls coming from the garden, wearing their overshoes and stepping around the highest drifts. They joined the men and knelt to examine the dirt-covered corn plants.

Izabella looked at Josif, her face sad. "The poor corn. We brushed the dirt off the potatoes and tomatoes and onions. They are still alive because we gave them a little water when the rain stopped, but these plants are dying."

"It would take a hundred people clearing the dirt away, and at least an inch of rain to save the corn," Josif said. "There is no way to save the small grain. The only thing that might survive is the alfalfa. Its roots go down so deep they find moisture in the soil."

Marie looked sad. "The corn was so beautiful this spring."

"There is one good thing," Josif said. "Hundreds of tons of rich dirt have blown onto our fields. When the rain comes again, we will get better crops than we ever had before."

"Where did the dirt come from, Papa?" Rose asked.

"It blew in from the southwest." Josif scooped up a handful of dirt and examined it. "There is some red in this. Our farm in Oklahoma had red dirt. I think the poor people in the states to the south and west of here have lost much of their good soil."

Carolyn recited: "Nebraska, Kansas, Oklahoma, Colorado. From all those states?"

Michael-Joseph said, "You forgot Texas and New Mexico."

Carolyn stuck out her tongue at him. "I didn't forget them, smarty. Maybe they're too far away."

"I know something you don't know!"

"You do not!"

"You children stop that before I take my belt to you." Josif said. "I am going to tell all of you something now. It is a secret, and I don't want you to start arguing about who knows what."

He spoke sharply to Michael-Joseph. "When you have a secret, you do not talk about it. Do you understand?"

Michael-Joseph stood straight. "Yes, Papa."

Josif looked at each of the girls in turn. "Do you all understand that?"

"Yes, Papa."

"Good. Now listen. A week from today your mother and I are going on a trip in our car. We may be gone for over two weeks. We are going to get Irina. You will stay here on the farm with Uncle Jon and Aunt Magda. You will obey them. You will talk to no one about our trip. Do you all understand?"

"Yes, Papa."

"If anyone asks you directly where we have gone, and you feel you must answer, tell them that we have gone to get your mother's Uncle Bela on the east coast, who is very sick and wants to be with his family when he dies. We are asking you to lie, but only to keep our family safe from the Iron Guard. Do you understand that?"

"Yes, Papa."

"Uncle Jon is the man. If anything should happen to Uncle Jon, listen to Aunt Magda. Do you understand that?"

"Yes, Papa."

"Good. Your mother and I will not be able to contact you while we are away, but we will be very careful and we will come back to you. Do you understand?"

"Yes, Papa."

"Good." Josif pointed toward the house and buildings. "We will work to save the garden. The water in the tank is full of dirt, and the animals shouldn't drink it. We men will bring that water to the garden; then the windmill will pump clean water into the tank. Usually we must use as little water as possible from the well so it won't go dry, but we have no choice, we have to use it now."

Izabella added, "And we women and girls will uncover every plant in the garden as the men bring the water. We will have tomatoes, potatoes, squash, peas, beans, onions, and garlic for the winter." She smiled at Uncle Jon. "And I think you should water the fruit trees. We will have apples and pears, cherries and plums."

Uncle Jon's eyes gleamed. "If we have plums and cherries we will have *tuica* and *visinata!* We will live like kings!"

Chapter Twenty-Seven
A Slight Change of Plans

That night the adults stayed up late making plans for the trip to New York. As was usual for them, they spoke in Romanian. Uncle Jon had laid out the map they had brought with them from Oklahoma. He was seated at the table with a sheet of paper, a pencil and a ruler, and was carefully measuring roads and calculating mileage. He had a long column of numbers. The calendar was on the table, and open to August.

Izabela looked at the distance from Centerford to New York City. She compared it to the distance from Centerford to Oklahoma. It was longer, and that trip had taken months. Of course this time they would be in a car, not a horse drawn wagon, and they would not get caught in a snowstorm in August.

She was beginning to feel slightly more hopeful when Uncle Jon sat up straight, scratched his head, and jabbed at the sum with his pencil. "It is only about fourteen hundred miles. If you drive two hundred miles each day, you will make it fine in seven days!"

Josif stared into space with a distasteful look on his face. His brow wrinkled and he closed his eyes. He held on to the edge of the table and gently lowered himself into a chair.

"Do you think two hundred miles a day is too much?" Izabella asked Josif softly.

Josif held up his hand indicating he was okay, took a deep breath, and looked up with a look of sorrow and horror on his face. "I have had a very difficult realization," he said.

Izabella and Aunt Magda crossed themselves and looked with concern at Josif. "What was it?" Izabella asked gently.

Josif held up his hands in resignation. "We need to take someone with us."

Izabella's eyes widened. "Why?"

"Because even though it is only two hundred miles a day, things can happen. We may have to read road signs quickly, and maps. Because we will have to find our way around New York and read newspapers. Because we may have to fight." He looked dejected.

"Who, Josif?"

Josif looked up sadly and said nothing.

"No!" Izabella gasped and crossed herself.

"Yes."

"Is there no other choice?"

"None that I can think of."

"Which one?"

"August."

Izabella grabbed the table and sat down. "At least the children will be safe at home."

Uncle Jon looked concerned. "I hadn't realized it, but of course you are right, Josif. Only when is the best time to ask him? If we ask too soon, he will announce it to all of South Dakota. If we ask too late, he may not be able to go for some reason, and we will have to find someone else."

Josif slid the calendar over. "The performance in New York is Saturday, August twentieth. I think we need to give ourselves a little extra time, so I think we need to leave Saturday, August thirteenth. That will give us eight days, including the twentieth. Today is Sunday, August seventh. We should ask August no later than Friday night, the twelfth."

Izabella frowned at Josif. "Josif, that would be difficult for August. I'm sure he will need time to bathe, and wash his clothes and pack."

Josif raised an eyebrow and Uncle Jon guffawed. "No doubt. Maybe we should go ask him now." Josif tapped the calendar and shook his head. "Izabella is right. After this dust storm, he will have more work at their farm. He needs to know as soon as possible."

Aunt Magda nodded her head in agreement, but continued to look concerned. "The Iron Guard is involved. Irina's life is involved. Can we trust this young bull with so much? Will he be able to keep a secret?" She paused and looked shocked. "I have just had a realization, too." The others looked at her uneasily. She looked at them solemnly, "Fritz will have to know too."

Uncle Jon and Josif opened their mouths to protest, paused and closed them, opened them again, looked at each other and closed them. "Of course she is right," Uncle Jon said. "Only I was just getting used to August knowing."

"Yes, Fritz will need to cancel engagements for the band. He also might wonder where his harness-mate has gone," Josif added.

"And his opponent. He will have to argue with the cows," Aunt Magda said with a laugh.

"And they both will have to agree on a story to tell their grandparents about why August is gone, and where he went," Uncle Jon said. "Of course when August gets back from New York, he will not be able to contain himself. He will probably write a cowboy song about his adventures."

Josif became serious. "This is a big thing to ask a neighbor for such help. My chest feels tight when I think of it. If he says *no* I will feel foolish for asking. If he says *yes*, we become indebted to him. He becomes like family. This is a big thing, but I can think of nothing else to do. No one else to ask. If he agrees, Fritz will be okay to manage their farm by himself. I pick August instead of Fritz because Fritz is oldest. He should stay with the farm. August is the only choice. Uncle Jon and I will go talk to them tomorrow. If they agree to the plan, we will make them understand the importance of secrecy."

Suddenly Izabella clutched the edge of the table. Her eyes were wide. The others looked on warily. "Who is going to feed August on the trip?" she asked quietly.

"Holy Mary, she's right!" Uncle Jon exclaimed.

The others looked dejected.

Izabella looked at Aunt Magda. "We will pack as much food as we can spare and hope that August brings some with him."

Uncle Jon spoke up with authority. "You should take a tent and blankets in case there is no place to stay. And a lantern and fuel, canteens of water, plenty of matches, a compass, cooking pots and pans, plates, silverware, flashlight and extra batteries, oil for car, extra fan belt, spare can of gas, shovel, jack for car, spare tube and pump, kit to fix holes in rubber, and...."

Josif interrupted Uncle Jon. "Maybe we should tow our wagon behind the car? We will take what we must have and no more. Remember, we must grab Irina and run. We must travel light. We must blend in and not look like Okies with everything we own tied to the car."

Chapter Twenty-Eight
Guarded Expectations

After lunch on Monday, Josif and Uncle Jon got in the Hudson and drove over to the Wagner farm. Izabella and Aunt Magda tried not to let the children see their anxiety. They sent the girls out to the garden to continue cleaning pulverized dirt off of fragile leaves and stems. Michael-Joseph was assigned to shoveling piles of drifted dirt into a wheel barrow and then dumping it in a large pile to the side of the barn where it would be out of the prevailing winds, and ready for re-distribution onto the fields in the spring, just before planting.

The women continued sweeping, shaking, washing, dusting, and watching for the return of the Hudson. Every car that went by carried a twisting cloud of reddish-brown dust around it, which made it difficult to see them. Izabella and Aunt Magda followed each dust cloud from the north with their eyes to see if it slowed by their driveway.

Finally, around 4:30, the Hudson materialized from a cloud of dirt in the barnyard. Josif and Uncle Jon emerged from the car and greeted the children. They all talked for a moment, then Josif patted each on the back or head, and they returned to their tasks.

Josif and Uncle Jon stamped up onto the porch, hitting at their overalls with their caps, and raising small clouds of dust. They removed their work shoes and entered the house. The women watched them closely and searched their eyes for information.

Josif spoke first. He looked exhausted. "It's all set." He smiled wanly.

Aunt Magda looked demandingly at Uncle Jon.

"It's true. August is very excited and happy to go."

"And Fritz? Is he okay, too?" Izabella asked hesitantly.

"He's fine. August had to promise to bring him souvenirs," Josif said.

"Like what?"

"Like postcards, shot glasses, pennants, hats, shirts, and little statues."

"Fritz is not angry at us?"

"No, he understands the importance of the trip and why we need August."

"He also said, 'Damn right, I'm the one that should stay on the farm'," Uncle Jon added, grinning.

"What story will they tell everyone?"

"That August has an audition in New York to sing for a record, and since we have to drive to New York to get a relative, *our Uncle Bela on Izabella's side*, we will all go together." He looked up at Izabella. "He will bring his guitar. He will practice while I drive."

"Maybe we should let August do most of the driving."

"That is what I think. He will bring food."

Izabella looked relieved, then serious again. "Do you think they can keep our secret?"

"It is to be hoped. August said he once kept a secret for two weeks. We will leave before then, so there is hope."

"Yes, that is very hopeful, and Fritz?"

"He said he could keep a secret twice as long as August. But he also wants to keep being the bouncer for the dances. If he drinks, he may not be able to keep quiet."

Uncle Jon looked at Aunt Magda. "Josif and I agreed to let the family play at dances while they are gone. We will earn more money for winter. And maybe we can keep an eye on Fritz."

Josif spoke again. "They both seem to understand Irina's situation. I think they will do their best for her safety."

Izabella nodded, then asked, "Did August seem excited?"

"Like Christmas Eve. It took almost one hour to calm him down enough to discuss plans. And of course, both brothers argued about everything."

Uncle Jon nodded in agreement. "Biggest argument was about the story to tell their grandparents and neighbors about why August is gone. August wants to say he was contacted by a big record company and is going to make a record. Fritz had other ideas. He wanted to say August was run out of town because of yodeling, or that August has run off to join the Navy, or that Myrna wants to marry him and he ran away because he doesn't know what to do with a girl." Uncle Jon slapped his thigh with his cap. "That argument was the most fun, but we didn't laugh until in the car on the way home."

Josif looked bemused but weary. "The worst part was when Grandpa Wagner came out. It took a very long time to explain to him. That was when August told the story that *big shots* in New York heard about his playing and singing and sent for him. So that is the story. Now I only have to fear for my immortal soul. I have caused boys to lie to their grandparents and neighbors."

Aunt Magda put her hand on Josif's shoulder. "Don't worry too much, Josif. I doubt this is the first time."

Uncle Jon stroked his mustache and looked at the others. "I just had the biggest realization of all. Now you have to tell Michael-Joseph that August is going to New York with you, and he still is not."

Chapter Twenty-Nine
A Miracle

The week was speeding by and suddenly time was short. Everyone continued to clean up the farm after the dust storm, and the women cooked and baked everything that would travel well.

Josif and Izabella counted their money and calculated the amount they should take versus the amount they would need for the winter and the mortgage a hundred times. Their total cash on hand from their savings, the band's earnings, Uncle Jon's *tuica* and the embroidery was three hundred and six dollars and twenty five cents. If they only paid the interest on the mortgage and could survive on about two hundred dollars until next year's uncertain harvest, they would need three hundred and twenty eight dollars.

They calculated that they would need seventy-five dollars for the trip. Always one side came up short and required that they spend their survival money to go after Irina. Izabella was developing a permanent look of worry and seemed distracted.

Aunt Magda took her aside one morning when the rest of the family was outside. They sat at the kitchen table and spoke in their native tongue. "You have become an unhappy woman. Everyone is tense. Worries about money have become bigger in your mind than finding time to care for your children."

Izabella looked up, sadly acknowledging the truth of Aunt Magda's words. "I wish it were not so," she said. "I can think of nothing else. I worry about us freezing and starving this winter. I worry about losing our farm. I worry about not being able to get to New York to find Irina. I worry about not having enough money to get home even if we do find her. I worry these worries and more, over and over." She looked defeated and studied her hands.

Aunt Magda spoke gently to Izabella. "God will protect you and the children. You must have faith. Let me tell you another approach besides worrying."

Izabella looked up hopefully.

"Instead of making pictures in your mind of failure and sorrow, make pictures of the best possible outcomes. See Irina bright and happy. See you and Josif rescuing her and feeling full of joy. Feel yourself free of worry and looking at your well-fed, happy family this winter. You have done everything you can to save and raise money. Now assume that there will be enough. Have faith in God and look ahead with joy and confidence and with thankfulness in your heart."

Izabella smiled and Aunt Magda beamed. "Just hearing you say that makes me feel better. I am going to do what you said right now. I am going to go sit on the porch and look at my beautiful family working on our land and think only happy thoughts and good outcomes with joy and thankfulness in my heart." She got up briskly and went through the kitchen door to the porch.

Aunt Magda smiled to herself, closed her eyes, and imagined money raining from the sky, everyone's pockets full, and happy faces everywhere. She felt her heart expand to encompass her whole family, and Irina wherever she was, and all of America and Romania, and the whole world. She loved that feeling, and kept it going as long as she could, her heart also full of joy and gratitude.

Suddenly she was routed from her state of relaxed contentment by the sound of Michael-Joseph yelling: "The dad gum sheriff's here."

She chuckled to herself, then hurried outside to see what was going on. Josif, Uncle Jon, and Michael-Joseph were greeting Sheriff Butch Bennard. Aunt Magda joined Izabella, and they watched from the porch. The girls had stood up from their work in the vegetable patch and were listening from there.

There were the usual preliminary discussions of the weather, the dust storm, and the crops. Then Butch tipped his hat back, stuck out his chest, and said: "I brought you folks some real good news."

"Oh?" said Josif. "We like good news. What is it?"

"Well, it seems that there were some rewards posted for some a them jewels that we found in Arnold Ariosto's silage pit after that dust-up we all had with them gangsters."

The men smiled fondly at the memory.

"Was a satisfying fight," Uncle Jon said. "What are *rewards posted?*"

"That's when people *reward* you for finding something that was lost or stolen from them," Butch replied, speaking loudly.

"Oh?"

"That's right. There was also a reward on Red Mc-Guire and Achilles Papadopoulos. We finally got him red-handed."

"That good."

"That turns out to be real good for you folks, Arnold Ariosto and the Wagners. Say, I heard that August Wagner is goin' to New York with you folks to make a cowboy record. Apparently there'll be a parade for him and everything. Anyway, he said he sure could use the money for the trip. Seems he has to buy Fritz a new suit and some cowboy boots."

Josif and Uncle Jon exchanged cautious glances.

"So, you folks are goin' to pick up some uncle from Romania?"

"Izabella's uncle, Bela. He is old and want to die with family around," Josif lied as casually as he could. Uncle Jon nodded with a sad look on his face.

"Well, that sure should be some trip!" Butch raised his eyebrows and looked proud. "So, the total rewards come to $2500. Split three ways that comes to eight hundred and thirty three dollars and thirty three cents per family."

He reached into his shirt pocket and pulled out an envelope with "Josif Dacia" written on the front. He handed it to Josif and smiled. "Congratulations, I know this will come in handy."

Josif opened the envelope and took out a check for eight hundred and thirty three dollars and thirty three cents. "This for me?" he asked incredulously.

"That's what I been tellin' ya'!" Butch said. "You're loaded!"

On the porch Aunt Magda and Izabella hugged. "It's a miracle! All will be well now," Izabella said laughing. She could hardly wait for the sheriff to leave so that she could run outside and rejoice with her family.

Chapter Thirty
Departure

Finally Saturday morning arrived. The Dacias were up at dawn, packing the car, checking lists, and trying to put a brave face on the family's upcoming separation. Uncle Jon and Aunt Magda helped lug things out to the car and gave the children lots of reassuring smiles. Michael-Joseph was having a hard time accepting his *duty as one of the men of the house to stay home and look after the family.*

When he heard that August was going, he almost cried. Josif was painfully aware of Michael-Joseph's internal struggle, and knew he was asking a lot of a seven-year-old. However, Irina's rescue could be dangerous, and he did not want his only son anywhere near the reach of the Iron Guard. This concern had protected him from giving in. Michael-Joseph had been avoiding him this morning, and Josif approached him as he was standing behind the car watching supplies being packed.

"Michael-Joseph, you have been avoiding me. I know you are disappointed, but this is not how to behave."

"I'm sorry, Papa. I just want to go so bad."

"I know that, and I will not forget how good you are being. This is what it really means to be a man. You put your family ahead of yourself. I am very proud of you."

Michael-Joseph wiped his nose with the side of his hand. "I'm not in such a hurry to be a man anymore."

227

Josif laughed and picked him up and hugged him. "I am glad that you are content to be our boy a while longer."

Michael-Joseph smiled and hugged him back, then struggled to get down when he saw Rose and Caroline watching.

A large pile of items to pack had accumulated along the side of the Hudson. All the doors were open. Josif and Izabella had squeezed their clothing into one old medium-sized pressed cardboard suitcase, although Izabella's dance outfit and red boots had been neatly folded and placed in a strong cardboard box which was tied with cord.

When Josif and Uncle Jon drove into town to deposit the reward check and get traveling money, they had also gotten a tire pump, spare and tube, and a tube repair kit. The Hudson's original jack and tire iron had been in the car's trunk, so they felt confident about any tire repair that might be needed.

The pump, repair kit, jack, tire iron, and other maintenance supplies were neatly packed in the box trunk on the rear of the car. A shovel, a jug of water, four blankets, another cardboard box of dishes and cooking utensils, and at the last minute, for *self-protection*, Josif's violin all awaited loading next to the Hudson.

The sound of a car pulling into the driveway caused everybody to stop what they were doing and look up. The Wagner's car was approaching. Fritz was driving and looked serious. August had his head out the window and was waving. He was wearing a Tom Mix style ten-gallon cowboy hat. Fritz maneuvered the Pontiac up next to the Hudson. The brothers got out and Fritz opened the rear door of the Pontiac. Inside, August had a large square, brown leather suitcase, a sleeping bag, his guitar, two large paper sacks of food, and a five-gallon white crock. The scent of sauerkraut gently wafted out of the car.

Izabella's eyes widened and she tried hard to disguise her feelings of dismay and horror with a cheerful smile. She wanted to say something gracious, but she was speechless.

Josif struggled silently for a moment, then stepped forward. "If we put August's suitcase on seat and pile other things on top, I think we have room."

Izabella kept the forced smile on her face, and nodded weakly. "Yes, although a tipped crock of sauerkraut would not be good. Maybe we put on floor and brace with sleeping bag. Maybe we have old blanket we could wrap around lid to keep... flavor in?"

"Is good idea."

Josif arranged the suitcases, boxes and bags on the backseat, and wrapped a blanket around the top of the crock, and the sleeping bag around its base. August put his guitar on the floor of the front seat, and grabbed the two paper bags which he put next to and in front of it. The Dacia's food had been packed in a cardboard box and two paper bags, and these were also jammed into the backseat. Izabella kept a portion of the backseat behind the front passenger's seat clear for herself, and opened the window.

Fritz and August were unusually quiet, and what barbs they did throw at each other lacked their usual gusto. "I hope you're ready to get thrown out of New York City. When those city snobs hear August sing, they'll prob'ly puke and kick him outta town."

"How would you know? You're not musical. You wouldn't know good music if it bit you on the rear end!"

"The hell I wouldn't!" Fritz was going to continue, but looked around at the wide eyes of the women and girls and shut his mouth. "Just so you're prepared for the worst," he said.

Suddenly everyone looked around and realized that the car was packed and ready to go. Silence hung over the group and Izabella felt sudden butterflies in her stomach. She ran to her girls and hugged and kissed them. "I will miss you all so much. I know I don't have to tell you to be good. Listen to Aunt Magda and Uncle Jon, look out for your brother, and we will be back before you know it with your cousin, Irina!"

Then she turned to Michael-Joseph and knelt down to hug and kiss him. "You are such a fine, big boy. I know you will be good and listen to Uncle Jon and Aunt Magda. Your cousin Irina will be very impressed by you. I will miss you and we'll be back soon." Then she hugged Aunt Magda and kissed both her and Uncle Jon on both cheeks and got in her spot in the back seat, dabbing at her eyes with a hanky and shoving back the bags of food with her elbow.

Josif kissed the girls on their foreheads, patted Michael-Joseph on the head, and gave him a special smile. Then he shook hands with Uncle Jon, kissed Aunt Magda on the cheek, and got in the driver's seat.

August looked at the ground and stuck out his hand to Fritz who did the same. They shook hands brusquely. "Try not to fall in the pig pen," August said to Fritz.

"Don't disgrace the family name," Fritz replied.

They cuffed each other on the arm and August turned and got in the front seat. He rolled down the window and waved to the Dacias and Fritz. He looked solemn. Michael-Joseph ran over to August. "I guess maybe I'll go next time," he said.

"You bet, Mike. When we get back, I'll teach you how to play the guitar and yodel. And I'll even bring you something special from New York."

"Really? Thanks August!"

August and Michael-Joseph shook hands through the car window and Michael-Joseph backed away from the car looking less glum.

"Well, I guess we go now," Josif said. He started the car, circled the barnyard with everyone waving, calling good bye and the women blowing kisses, then slowly headed out the driveway. Suddenly the car stopped and backed up.

"Forgot map," Josif said sheepishly when they reached the watching group. Uncle Jon saluted and ran into the house, returning in a minute with the folded map. In the meantime, the children and Aunt Magda had gathered around Izabella's window, and they were hugging and kissing through the window again.

"Now we go," Josif said, and put the Hudson in gear. The car rolled out the driveway and turned south. It was soon enveloped in a cloud of brown dust which became smaller and smaller and, like the remnants of a dream at dawn, was soon gone.

The group in the barnyard was silent. A feeling of loss and abandonment was beginning to settle on them.

Fritz took off his hat and scratched his head. He looked over at the house, then at Uncle Jon and Michael-Joseph. "There's something I been thinkin' about," he said.

The others looked up, eager for a diversion.

"Maybe it's none a my business, but I've been in your house, and it's a mite small. Especially if you're bringin' home a cousin."

"There no argument there," Uncle Jon said.

The others nodded in agreement and watched Fritz closely.

"Well, I was just thinkin', with August gone, I can get my work done in about half the time, him bein such an interferin' fool and all."

"Sure," Uncle Jon said.

"Well, we got a pile a extra boards lyin' around takin' up room. Most farms do."

"Sure."

"We also got a lotta nails. We've been collectin' 'em for years."

"Sure, we got some collecting too."

"Mike's growin' up. I bet he can handle a hammer."

"You're g.d. right!" Michael-Joseph chimed in.

Uncle Jon coughed and choked a moment, and Aunt Magda slapped him once on the back, looking stern. Then she put her hand on Michael-Joseph's shoulder and gave it a gentle squeeze.

"He pretty good," Uncle Jon said.

"Well, I was just wonderin' if you'd be interested in addin' some bedrooms to your house in the next two weeks." Fritz looked around at the group for a response. "Say, you'd better all close your mouths," he said. "This is fly season."

232

Chapter Thirty-One
Saturday, 8/13/1932 - Road Trip

Josif drove the Hudson away from the farm, and out to Highway 77, which would lead south to Sioux City, Iowa. From there he planned to go further south through Nebraska to Omaha and Council Bluffs, and then head east straight to New York on Route 6. He was comforted by the thought that they only had to travel two hundred miles a day. They had two hundred dollars with them; August to help with reading, heavy work, and fighting; and lots of food and supplies. He felt vulnerable being away from the farm and the rest of the family, but Izabella was with him, and he had certainly succeeded in making difficult trips before.

Josif leaned back in the driver's seat, rested his elbow on the open windowsill, tipped his cap back, and looked at August fondly. "You good friend to help us. I not forget."

"Aw hell, this ain't no hardship. Spendin' every blasted day buttin' heads with Fritz, now that's a hardship! Haw! Haw!" August picked up his guitar and played a few chords and strummed it, humming notes to himself as he tuned it. "I'm gonna write some ballads," he said. "They're stories written as songs. I already started one about our fight with the gangsters."

"Oh?"

"Yeah, it's called, *The Dakota Six*."

"Sound exciting."

"It's not done yet, I'll sing what I got for ya." August turned around in his seat to address Izabella. "Don't worry Miz Dacia, it ain't got no cussin' in it. Grandma said I was to watch my language real good around you." August cleared his throat and began to sing and play:

"I'm August the Yodeling Cowboy,
And I'm here to tell ya the tale,
Of the weak and the strong and who's in the wrong.
Of the Dakota Six who jumped into the mix,
And sent six gangsters to jail.
Yeah, we sent six gangsters to jail.

Our neighbor, Arnold, got left a half section;
He was farming it like a man.
The fields were dry and the crops were small,
But his buildings were tight and his livestock were full.
He was doing his best to pull them all through.
Yeah, he was doing his best to pull them all through.

His farm had belonged to his sister, her husband had ties to the mob, who had brought a huge still from Chicago, and had killed, burned, tortured and robbed.

Then they ended up killing each other, and we thought the whole thing was done.
We went back to our farms and the things that we knew: not enough rain and bills that were due.
Yeah, not enough rain and bills that were due.
Yode a lay dee, yode a lay dee, yode a lay dee hoooooo.
Yode a lay dee, yode a lay dee, yode a lay deeeeee.

Then Primo Moretti came looking for treasure.
Came looking for loot and his dead gangster brother.
'Til the Greeks arrived and he had to take cover.
Deep in the barn, away from his foe.

234

Then neighbors and cops showed up at the farm, and in with
Moretti, Zeke had to go.
Yeah, in with Moretti, Zeke had to go.

The two mobs hated each other; but hated the law even worse.
They tried to break out together, but then they met their curse.
Six men were there to stop them, six heroes strong and true.
They were rock hard and tough, they wouldn't take no guff,
And they sent six gangsters to jail.
Yes, they sent six gangsters to jail.
Yode a lay dee, yode a lay dee, yode a lay dee hoooooo.
Yode a lay dee, yode a lay dee, yode a lay deeeeee."

August stopped singing and playing. "That's all I got
so far. How do ya like it?"

"Is good. Any time I am *hero strong and true* in song,
is good song."

Izabella leaned forward from the back seat."I like
song too. Now I find out what really happen during fight."

Soon they saw a sign which read, "Sioux City, 5
miles." Josif turned to August. "Okay with you to drive
through cities? I not read English enough to follow signs
safe."

"Oh sure, that's fine. I've been readin' since I was ten,
and drivin' even before that. Piece a cake," August said
jovially.

Josif pulled over and they switched seats. Izabella
crossed herself and prayed for protection. Josif leaned back
in his seat, and tried to look relaxed.

August looked behind him before pulling into traffic,
and Josif and Izabella noted this with relief. August drove
smoothly and carefully into Sioux City, following signs
which would continue their progress south-southeast. The
road went through a rambling shanty town, then followed
the edge of the city. Suddenly August let out a whoop and

made a hard left turn. "I just saw a sign for the Athens Supper Club. That's where the Greek mob had its head-quarters. It's somewhere on this street; let's go see it!"

Realizing that the decision had already been made, Josif smiled grimly, "Okay, but we should not take long. So far we only travel about fifty miles."

"Sure, Joe."

Progress was good until the detour sign which led the travelers into the business district. Undismayed, August followed the signs until he made a sudden U-turn, then a hard right. "Hell, they're just leading us around in circles like a dumb steer. If I cut through here, I can get us back where we wanna be. Don't worry, Joe and Miz Dacia, I got a real good sense a direction. We'll be there in no time."

About a half hour later, August slowed the car to a stop across the street from the Athens Supper Club. Shades were drawn inside, and there was a *closed* sign in the window.

"Well, how about that!" he said. "I guess we caused 'em to close up shop."

"Look like it," Josif replied.

"I'm glad they're in jail; this would make 'em pretty mad," August said thoughtfully.

They gazed at the restaurant a while longer. Then August put the Hudson in gear and looked at Josif and Izabella. "Well, if you folks are done sightseein', I suppose we should get goin'."

Within another half hour August had the Hudson back on the road, headed south toward Council Bluffs.

About forty miles later, they entered a shady section of road near the Missouri River. August pulled the Hudson off the road under the shade of a large cottonwood tree. "Well, who's starvin' besides me?"

Is 2:00 PM.. Time go by fast. We eat, use woods, and continue. We still need to travel one hundred miles today."

Izabella got out of the car and headed for the woods. "I use woods first, then eat. We ride in car long time."

Grandma Wagner had fried up two chickens, and they decided these should be eaten first. Izabella contributed a loaf of bread, white cheese, and some hard-boiled eggs. They sat on a blanket in the shade savoring the meal, cool shade, and the steady sound of the Missouri flowing by. Bees hummed in nearby honeysuckle bushes.

August leaned back against the tree, tipped his cowboy hat forward over his eyes, and was soon snoring. Josif and Izabella looked at August and shrugged. Their eyes were heavy, and the stress of the last week was catching up with them. "Just for twenty minutes," Josif said.

"Twenty minutes," Izabella echoed, curling up on her side next to Josif with her head on her arm.

Sixty minutes later the group was back on the road looking chagrined. August was the first to recover. "I suppose we'll be stayin' at one of those tourist cabin places for the night."

"Too early to think of that," Josif said sternly. "Is only 3:30; we still have to travel one hundred miles today."

Josif was driving again, and had pushed their speed up to fifty miles per hour whenever possible. The roads were mostly good, but had sudden potholes and uneven surfaces. Izabella smiled bravely whenever he looked back at her, but her teeth were clenched and her fingernails dug into the arm rest on one side and the seat on the other. August's question was a welcome distraction.

"What is tourist cabin?" she asked.

"What it amounts to is a wood tent. Sometimes they have two rooms with a wash room in between. They're small but cheap. We've got one up by Sioux Falls and one over by Spirit Mound."

"Oh, that sound good, if Josif think so."

"Too early to think of stopping yet, but that sound

237

okay, after we drive rest of two hundred miles for today."

"Sure."

"Of course, Josif."

They continued south awhile with Josif's eyes fixed on the road ahead, and August's out the side window at his right hand which was oscillating in the wind.

Josif looked at him. "Where map? I think we should be turning soon."

August sat upright, pulled his arm back in, and opened the glove box. He pulled out the map and opened it up. "Where are we now, Joe? You seen any signs lately?"

"No, I have not seen signs. If I do see sign, what do I want it to say?"

August folded the map to show Iowa. "It should say, 'This way to Route 6 or Des Moines'." He looked out the window. "There! There's a sign for 6!"

"Where?"

"Right on the other side of that tree, where that truck just turned. Turn now!"

Josif made a hard left turn, and felt the car lean heavily to the right. He glanced in the back to see if Izabella was okay, and just in time to see her bracing the teetering stack of boxes and bags, and looking in horror at the sauerkraut crock. There was a dull *thud* followed by quiet, feminine muttering in Romanian, and a growing scent of sauerkraut.

"Boy howdy, don't that smell good," August said, looking fondly back at the crock. "I'm sure glad that didn't tip all the way over. Now I'm gettin' hungry again."

"I think we stop in about fifty miles," Josif said. "Maybe another hour, hour and half at most." He kept his eyes fixed on the road.

Around 6:00 Josif gave the okay to look for the next tourist cabin, and by seven o'clock they had located and checked into Corny's Roadside Tourist Cabins. Theirs was a small wooden cabin with two double beds about two feet apart. At the back of the cabin was a door which led to the left along a short, narrow hallway to the *necessary* room, which was shared with another cabin on the other side.

It was getting dark, and the travelers were hungry and road weary, but in fairly good moods as they brought in food for supper and supplies they would need for the night.

Josif and Izabella sat on their bed facing August on his. They balanced plates on their knees, and each had a cup of water from the jug they had brought. They finished off the first of Grandma Wagner's chickens and most of the second as well as the loaf of bread.

Then August excused himself, and went out to the car. He pulled a large bowl and fork out of one of the food bags on the back seat of the car, and filled it with sauerkraut from the crock on the floor. The blanket which had been wrapped around the crock was damp from being tipped, but only a little juice had found its way down to August's sleeping bag, which was jammed around its base. He returned to the cabin and offered some of the pungent cabbage to Josif and Izabella, who each took small helpings.

"Is good," Izabella said. Josif nodded in agreement. 'We use sauerkraut in many Romanian dishes."

"It's what we mostly live on in the winter. It's real good with big hunks a sausage floatin' around in it," August said.

"That sound good, we serve with stuffed cabbage rolls and sour cream," Izabella added.

"That sounds good, too. That little crock in the car is 'bout all we got left from last winter," August said. "We'll sure be ready for our first fall crop a cabbage!"

Mention of the farm took everyone's mind back to their homes. Josif looked at Izabella's face and brought their attention back to their mission. "I think we drive more than two hundred miles today. Maybe as much as two hundred and thirty!"

"I bet you're right, Joe. The last sign I saw said Des Moines, twenty miles."

"That is hopeful news. Even with late start, and unexpected happenings, we keep our schedule, and even do better." He picked up the map from the pile of their belongings on the bed, and pulled a folded piece of paper and a pencil stub from his pocket. "Uncle Jon write schedule of where we should drive each day. I will cross off today." He opened the map all the way, then folded the bottom half up behind the top and laid it across his knees. "We go straight across from Des Moines to New York. Route 6 take us all the way there, except at very end when we head south right to New York City. Tomorrow we need to go to Davenport, Iowa. If we get early start, we may go past there."

"Piece a cake, Joe."

"I am sure you are right, my husband. We will do even better tomorrow. But now I think is time for sleep if we make early start." She looked uncomfortable.

August also looked uncomfortable. "Uh, if you want, I could go sleep in the car. I ain't never slept in the same room with a woman before." He looked longingly at the door.

Josif looked at August, then Izabella. "This long trip. Not good for August to sleep in car. Maybe we hang blanket between beds?"

"Oh, that good idea," Izabella said happily.

"Yeah, that'll work," August said, sounding relieved. "I'll go get some stuff from the car."

"I clean up food."

"I take it back out to car."

August and Josif returned with two blankets, a hammer, and three nails. "Fritz called me a dummy for bringing a hammer and nails, but they can come in just as handy as baling wire," August said as he nailed the corner of one blanket over the middle of the front door, and a corner of the other blanket over the middle of the rear door which led to the hall. Then he overlapped the two opposite ends in the middle of the room and nailed them to the ceiling. The blankets didn't reach the floor, but provided adequate privacy, and suddenly August had disappeared.

"That good job," Izabella said to the curtain.

"Thank you, Miz Dacia," it replied.

Josif and Izabella looked at each other wanting to discuss the day and how it was going with August, but knew that they really couldn't say anything. No one changed into sleeping clothes after their trips to the necessary room. They only took off their shoes and socks, and loosened their belts. It was hot and humid, and no breeze was coming through the screens over the front windows. They all lay still, trying not to make noise and to cool down. Finally August began to snore, then Josif's deep breathing could be heard, and finally Izabella heard neither and fell asleep dreaming of home and family.

Chapter Thirty-Two
8/14/1932 - Storm in Iowa

The travelers awoke just before sunrise. Roosters and crows were welcoming the sun, and mourning doves were cooing in nearby cottonwood trees. Songbirds made a full chorus. The morning was still, and it remained hot and humid. Each made their trip down the hall and cleaned up as much as possible. August took down the blankets, and they breakfasted on *mamaliga*, cheese, and pickled eggs. August had a small bowl of sauerkraut as well, and finished off the chicken. Josif looked at his cup of water. "Cup of coffee sure be good now."

"A pot of coffee sure would be good now," August added, taking out the fixings for a cigarette.

"We have pot and coffee with us, but no stove. We think we use if we have to camp and build fire."

"Well hell, I can have a fire built in nothin' flat. There's some woods at the end of the parking lot." August stood and headed out the door. Josif and Izabella looked on helplessly. "Well hell, I fill coffee pot with water," Josif said to Izabella. She playfully pushed him. "You become as bad as Uncle Jon. I go get coffee and sugar without swearing."

In about forty-five minutes the fire was made, had burned down some, and a leaning coffeepot was percolating away, emitting inviting smells of fresh coffee. When the liquid in the glass knob was sufficiently brown, Izabella grabbed it off the fire with a folded towel. August and Josif scattered and stomped out the small fire, then poured water on the ashes. Izabella filled everyone's cup with coffee, and passed around a jar of sugar and a spoon.

They each managed to get in two cups of coffee while they repacked the car and reviewed the map and plan for the day. By 7AM, they were heading east on Route 6. Since they were near Des Moines, August was driving and Josif and Izabella were intently watching the road for route signs.

As they neared the city, they passed through the inevitable Hooverville with its flimsy huts and raggedly dressed inhabitants. Small groups of children and loose dogs ran into the road without looking, and the road became rougher with more and deeper potholes.

Traffic picked up, and by 8:00AM they were approaching downtown Des Moines. August had both hands on the wheel and was peering intently ahead. "I think I see a detour sign. Maybe I should turn to avoid it. That last one didn't work out so good."

"No!" Josif and Izabella cried out in unison.

Josif spoke. "We think it best to follow detour signs. Maybe they take us back to road."

"Well, it's your car." August followed the orange signs, the smell of hot tar permeating the car. "Well, at least it smells like they're trying to fix these blame roads."

Izabella felt slightly nauseated and rolled up her window. The others followed suit, causing the car to become stiflingly hot. The car bumped along over an unfinished road which eventually was reunited with a nicely paved Route 6. They all breathed a sigh of relief, and rolled down their windows, almost welcoming the hot blast of humid air.

Soon they were leaving the city and feeling confident, although the road had deteriorated again. August was managing forty miles per hour on sections of the road with potholes if they were far enough apart for him to dodge and weave. But in sections of washboards, he had to slow down to twenty-five.

He was having fun speeding up and slowing down, and dodging and weaving until he missed and hit a pothole dead on. The sauerkraut crock bounced, and Izabella eyed it warily as the scent of sauerkraut grew. She pulled away a corner of the blanket wrapped around it, and saw that more juice had spilled out and saturated part of the blanket and sleeping bag. She adjusted the crock's lid and recovered it.

The Hudson bounced and bumped along for the next few hours with occasional stretches of relatively smooth road. They averaged about thirty-five miles per hour.

When they saw an ESSO station, August pulled in to fill up. They all used the restrooms, then Izabella got back in the car, and Josif and August went into the office to pay. They came out a few minutes later; Josif appeared to be holding a map, and August was drinking a Nehi soda.

"I have map of just Iowa. It has big map of Davenport, the next big city we drive through." Josif looked ecstatic. "Now we cannot get lost. Man in station say we can get free map for every state we go through as soon as we cross borders!"

"Hell, I coulda' told you that," August said, finishing his pop and tossing the bottle in the fifty-five gallon drum waste can.

Josif shook his head. "Next time tell me what you *coulda* told me before I do not need to know anymore."

August looked slightly puzzled. "Sure, Joe." he said.

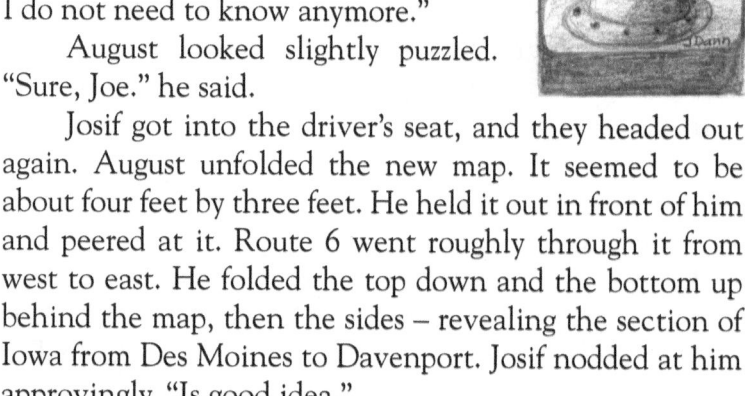

Josif got into the driver's seat, and they headed out again. August unfolded the new map. It seemed to be about four feet by three feet. He held it out in front of him and peered at it. Route 6 went roughly through it from west to east. He folded the top down and the bottom up behind the map, then the sides – revealing the section of Iowa from Des Moines to Davenport. Josif nodded at him approvingly. "Is good idea."

In another hour they decided to stop for lunch, and pulled off the road near a small grove of trees with some logs lying on the ground to sit on. Josif stopped the car in the shade, and they spread a blanket on the ground. August brought out six baloney sandwiches wrapped in wax paper and set them on the blanket. Izabella sliced *mamaliga* and set out the container of white cheese and a jar of eggs. The travelers were hungrier than they had realized, and ate most of the food. They washed it down with cups of water, packed up, and were back on the road within an hour.

They traveled along without incident until around 4:30PM. They had been enjoying evaluating the Iowan farms they were passing. August was being particularly critical. "Any fool can see their soil ain't nearly as black as ours. And look at them weedy fields. And that puny corn. Any farmer farm like that in South Dakota would get run outta town."

"Look at that farm's beautiful roses," Izabella said turning back to look at the garden as they passed by. "I almost smell them." She looked back at the sky and felt her stomach sink. "Josif. Storm coming!" She said ungently.

August and Josif looked backwards out of their windows. A black bank of clouds covered the southwest sky.

"Maybe we can stay ahead of it," Josif said.

"Nothin' much else we can do," August said. "Try to outrun it, and if that don't work, look for cover. You better hit it, Joe."

Josif hunched over the wheel and pushed the speed up to fifty miles per hour. He had to concentrate on the road to prevent hard impacts with potholes. They stayed well ahead of the storm for about thirty minutes, then realized that they were losing the race.

"Better look for a barn we can hole-up in pretty quick," August said. "Looks like that storm's haulin' hail." Large, dark, greenish-grey *mammatus* clouds were dropping out of the cloud bank, and the wind was beginning to howl.

They sped and bounced along for another mile when they spotted an open barn at a farmstead to their right. The farmer was hurrying horses into the stalls in the barn, and his wife was shooing the chickens into the hen house. The sky was darkening quickly, and the wind had picked up even more. Hard rain was pelting down.

Josif pulled into the driveway and stopped by the farmer who was heading for the house with his wife and

247

dog. August opened the window. "Mind if we get outta the weather in your barn?"

"Go ahead," the farmer yelled back. "You made it just in time. Close the big door behind you." He and his wife and dog dashed into the house, and Josif steered the Hudson toward the barn just as the first hail stones fell. They seemed about marble-sized and pinged off the car leaving random dimples in the metal. The wind screamed, and a flash of lightning lit the sky, followed almost immediately by a boom of thunder. Josif pulled the car into the barn.

"You don't have to count to know that was close," August yelled over the sound of the storm.

Izabella looked uneasy, and wrapped her shawl more securely around her shoulders.

Josif and August jumped out of the car and went outside to pull the doors shut. They swung them shut and slid the latch closed. The barn became even darker, the only light coming from two small windows by the side door. But the wind was blocked, they were dry, and the car was safe from more hail which was hammering the roof high overhead.

Josif looked around by the small side door of the barn and found a light switch. He flicked it on, and everyone relaxed at the familiar sight of horses. The horses were nickering nervously and moving about in their stalls. The visitors walked up to the stalls and held out their hands, speaking gently to the animals. There were four plow horses, and they made sure all of them got equal attention. Pretty soon, the people and horses were feeling calmer.

Josif and August consulted the map. "Where you think we are?"

"Somewhere west of Iowa City. Maybe here, around Homestead." August pointed to a town about fifteen miles west of Iowa City. "Looks like fifty or sixty miles to Davenport. Almost another two hours' driving."

"I wish rain stop soon."

"Well, you know what Grandma always says."

Josif looked at August with a puzzled expression. "No, what she say?"

"'If wishes were wings, we'd all be flyin'.' Ain't you never heard that?"

"No."

"Heck, we grew up on that. Grandma says that a lot."

"I remember that to tell Uncle Jon."

"He'll like it."

"We can drive in rain, but roads will be slippery and if get a flat tire, will be difficult."

"Right now we could drown in a pothole. Or get stuck pretty good. This Iowa soil's so poor, it's prob'ly mostly clay."

"If we ask farmer, he might let us stay in barn for night."

"Most likely. It wouldn't be no skin offa his nose. You heard that one before?"

"No. I tell Uncle Jon that one too."

"Good."

"If we leave and drive the sixty miles left for today, we have to spend night in Davenport, in hotel. I do not want to drive at night unless we must. We wait a while longer. If stop raining in time, we drive to Davenport. If not, we ask farmer to stay and leave before dawn."

As Josif turned to go tell Izabella his decision, the farmer entered the barn through the side door. He was wearing a heavy oil cloth slicker and carrying a covered cast iron pot in one hand, a coffee pot in the other, and three plates under his arm. His pockets were bulging. He set the items down on a nearby hay bale, and stomped off the rain.

"Howdy, folks, I'm Herman Hoffstetter. I hope you're hungry. Mrs. Hoffstetter sent you over some supper!" Herman Hoffstetter was in his early thirties, of medium height, but large-boned and well-fed, with an open and friendly face.

Josif walked up and shook his hand. "Hello, I am Josif Dacia. That my wife, Izabella." Izabella nodded to Herman from behind the car.

August stepped up and stuck out his hand. "Howdy, I'm August Wagner. We're from over south a Sioux Falls."

"Ya? Well you've sure come quite a ways! You get hit by any hail?"

"Some, but Joe here pulled us in just before it got real bad."

"Well, that was sure good. The fella on the radio said this is a big one. Movin' slowly east. Lots of hail, but no tornadoes yet." He moved along the stalls, checking on each horse, and making sure each had hay and water. He spoke gently to them, using their names.

"We had hope to leave today, but maybe no," Josif said.

"I sure wouldn't. It's getting late in the day. Gully washers like this take out a lot of bridges and sections of road. I'd wait until they get the detour signs out in the morning."

Josif looked despondent. "We not go fast enough."

"Where you folks headed?"

"New York City," and anticipating the next question he added, "We go to meet relative. Must be there by Saturday."

"Well, that sure is a drive. I can see why you're anxious to keep going." He thought a moment. "Well, I guess I'd say, *better safe than sorry.*"

August looked approvingly at Herman. "Yeah, that's a good one. I'd say that too." He looked sideways at Josif.

"Say, maybe you'll run into better roads further east. You're sure welcome to stay in the house tonight. We have a spare room and a Chesterfield. I'm sure we could make do."

"You very kind, but we sleep here, if okay with you. We want to make very early start in morning."

"Suit yourselves." He pulled three forks and a mug out of one pocket, and two mugs out of another. "I hope you enjoy your supper," he said. "Just leave the dishes, I'll get them in the morning. Feel free to use that straw to sleep on, it's real clean. I sure enjoyed talking with you folks. Have a safe trip." He waved and left out the side door.

August went over to the cast iron pot and took off the lid. "Holy Hannah," he said reverently. He turned to Josif and Izabella with a look of wonder on his face. "It's sauerkraut with sausages floatin' in it."

All three savored sauerkraut and sausages that evening. Izabella knew that Mrs. Hoffstetter would be pleased to see that they had cleaned it all up. She searched her mind for something they could do to repay the Hoffstetters.

As if reading her mind, Josif said, "Stalls look pretty clean, but maybe we can brush horses good and clean hooves. Hoffstetters very kind, we should give back."

"Is very good idea, Josif."

"Yeah, that'd be okay. That Herman Hoffstetter was somethin' else. He coulda' even been from South Dakota!"

After currying and brushing the horses until their coats shone, Josif and August cleaned their hooves, and returned the equipment to the small tack room. Izabella had fashioned two beds on either side of the Hudson out of the clean straw, and spread a blanket on each one. She made pillows for herself and Josif out of folded shirts and sweaters, and spread another blanket on top.

Suddenly she felt very sleepy. But first she and Josif took a quick trip out behind the barn. It was night and rain was still pelting down, but the thunder was only a distant growl. They hurried back through the side door in the barn, and shed their wet coats. August was already snoring on his straw bed with a look of total contentment on his face.

Josif turned off the light and whispered to Izabella, "Sometimes he can be such a good boy."

Izabella chuckled, and they crept over to their bed and crawled in. Izabella snuggled up against Josif and he put his arm around her. The straw was soft and smelled fresh and sweet, the thunder was far away, there were the smell and the gentle sounds of the horses nearby, and rain on the high barn roof. She and Josif stayed awake as long as they could enjoying it all, but were asleep within five minutes.

Chapter Thirty-Three
Sunday, 8/14/32 - *The Atlantia* Sails

On Sunday, August 7th, the Romanian State Dance Ensemble left Bucharest for Vienna by train. In seven days they traveled to, and performed in, three great European capitals: Vienna, Austria; Paris, France; and London, England. The concert halls were glorious with rows of tiered seats and gilded side boxes, sparkling chandeliers, and plush velvet seats and curtains. The performances went well, and the dancers received a warm welcome from all audiences.

The only drawback for Irina was Deben, who was becoming more and more bold and possessive, always finding a way to touch her breasts or thighs during a performance, and then smiling smugly. He seemed determined to show his dominance in public, and Irina felt that he would like to rape her on stage. It took all of her will-power to smile happily during her dances and to willingly twirl into his arms and allow him to lift her.

In London, Irina noticed that Deben was beginning to pay attention to her understudy, Mariana Miron, and knew that soon he would be making an attempt to kill her. She guessed that he would either try to throw her overboard on the Atlantic crossing, or arrange for her death in New York, after their performance. She vowed to herself that she would never be alone on the voyage, and that she would not spend time at the rail gazing out to sea. She was in a fight for her life as surely as if she were facing a man with a knife.

Deben's two followers, Dragos Amanar and Petru Buscan, were just as depraved as Deben, but would probably not kill her. They would save that for Deben. Irina prepared herself mentally for the challenges ahead, and boarded *The Atlantia*, a three- funnel steamship liner out of Southampton, with watchful gaiety and a constant preparedness for fight or flight.

The Atlantia sailed with the tide on Sunday, August fourteenth. The troupe consisted of twenty-five dancers, ten musicians, five wardrobe women, one dance director, and one tour manager and his two assistants.

The tour manager, Mihai Celac, was a tall thin man in his late forties with thick grey hair, a salt and pepper mustache, and kind eyes. He was experienced with tours, and had reserved rooms for the men on the starboard side of the ship, and on the port side for the women. He had found that an ounce of prevention was worth not bringing

a dancer home pregnant, and he did all he could to prevent opportunity from knocking.

He and his assistants shared a room at the head of
the women's string of rooms, and he set a curfew of 11:00
PM, and required that each woman stop by his open door
and sign in on her way to a room shared with two other
women.

While some of the girls chafed at these rules, Irina
breathed a sigh of relief, and felt that she was relatively
safe during the night. She requested a room at the farthest
end of the hall with her friends, Christina Romanescu and
Mariana Miron.

As a *courtesy to the ship*, which had given the Ensemble a sizable discount and allowed the group to travel
first class, the troupe was expected to add color and en-
tertainment to the voyage. This began with dinner at the
captain's table with Captain Arthur Stanford. He was a
trim, wiry man in his fifties with a neat grey mustache,
sideburns, and a competent air.

Irina and Deben were dressed in their dance outfits,
and sat either side of the captain. The tour manager sat
next to Irina, and the ship's activity director, Eamon Jones,
and two of the ship's senior officers filled out the table.

Neither Irina nor Deben spoke English, and the others didn't speak Romanian, so Mr. Celac, who spoke both,
spent most of the meal translating.

Mr. Jones seized upon the opportunity. He was a tall,
blond young man who looked like a university student,
but who was probably around thirty. He was full of fun and
energy, and seemed perfectly suited for his job. He pro-
posed that in exchange for daily English lessons, perhaps
some of the dancers would teach a few dances to interested passengers.

Irina visibly brightened at the idea, and suggested
that children be included. Deben smiled blankly and

longed for the meal to end. It was agreed that Mr. Celac would find dancers to participate, and Mr. Jones would announce the classes to the other passengers. The English classes would be taught by Mr. Jones, and would be open to any non-English-speaking passengers. They would begin at 9:00AM and last for an hour. Romanian folk dance lessons would follow that, and also last for an hour, ending in time for 11:00 tea.

Irina felt periods of safety beginning to fill in her daily schedule. Periods when she could let her guard down somewhat and enjoy herself. She sipped her wine and permitted herself a leisurely look around the dining room.

The Captain's table was on an elevated platform at one end of the room. Elegantly- dressed passengers draped in furs and jewels, or tuxedos and gold, filled the tables. Potted palms stood by pillars, and an elaborate three-level fountain trickled merrily near the orchestra, which was softly playing Strauss waltzes. Chandeliers shed gentle light, and each table had fresh flowers in a porcelain vase painted with a bamboo design, sitting on an Egyptian linen tablecloth.

After her flight through the mountains, being locked in Deben's apartment, and their hectic tour through Europe, the ship seemed like a slow-moving dream. She wanted to float away on the music and give herself up to the abandon of the dance.

The sound of Deben's voice responding to Mr. Celac brought Irina's attention back to the table and sent a flash of adrenalin through her system. She needed to be away from him. In a quiet voice she asked Mr. Celac to accompany her to her room as she was tired, and wished to retire. She asked him to thank Captain Stanford for his kindness, and to assure Mr. Jones that she would be at the Solarium at 9:00AM as promised.

It was after 9:00PM, and diners were beginning to

leave their tables and head for the ballrooms and lounges. Deben did not even say *good night* to Irina and Mr. Celac, but bolted off in search of his friends. The tour manager took Irina's arm in his and walked her back to her quarters. He did not like or trust Deben either, and was glad to remove Irina from his presence.

Irina's friends were already in their room and glad to see her. They locked the door and marveled at the elegance of the ship, and how lucky they were to be going to see America on an ocean liner which seemed as magnificent as a palace.

They turned out the lights, and soon their voices quieted and all that could be heard were the constant dull throbbing and vibrations of the ship's engines. Irina closed her eyes and felt herself being propelled powerfully and inexorably toward America and her remaining family. She fell asleep with a gentle smile on her face.

Chapter Thirty-Four
Monday, 8/15/32 - Illinois

Josif had decided to follow Herman Hoffstetter's advice and not leave before dawn. He did not want to drive off a washed-out bridge. At the first lightening of the eastern sky, he got up and wakened Izabella. The rain had stopped. August was stirring. Josif opened the side door of the barn to a hazy sky. The ground was saturated, and there were large, brown puddles scattered around. The air was thick and moist, and smelled of wet grass and earth, pigs, cows, and chickens. He was joined by August.

"Looks like we got a couple a gol dang flats. It prob'ly happened when we were slammin' over those potholes tryin' to outrun that storm. Or maybe in the barnyard; there's usually a few loose nails lyin' around there. I warned Fritz that this might happen. That Hudson prob'ly sat in that lot a long time since it didn't have no engine. That salesman prob'ly sold the new tires and substituted old ones. There's prob'ly some weak spots in the tubes and we musta hit em."

Josif re-entered the barn and looked at the Hudson. Both front tires were flat. "Well, there go early start, but we do not fix tires in mud."

"I got no complaints about that."

Izabella shook and folded the blankets while the men got started on fixing the tires. She was busy reorganizing the food bags and boxes when Herman Hoffstetter knocked on the door jamb and stuck his head into the barn. "Everybody up?" he called, then seeing the activity, strode in. "Well, flat tires, that sure is a common site. Ain't it nice to get to fix 'em in here. You folks sure are lucky!"

He walked over to the stalls to check on the horses. "Say, don't these horses look pretty. Their coats shine like gold, and their feet are clean as a whistle. That sure was nice of you." He gazed at the horses fondly.

August raised his eyebrows and looked pointedly at Josif, who nodded slightly, then addressed Herman.

"We glad to clean horses. We want to thank you for your kindness."

"I'll tell you what, that sure was some good sauerkraut and sausage," August said grinning.

"Yes," Izabella added. "Please tell Mrs. Hoffstetter her food is very good."

"Well, Mrs. Hoffstetter and I are real proud to help out. You folks have quite a trip ahead of you."

August nodded toward the door. "How'd your crops hold up in the storm?"

"Well, what there is of the corn is pretty far along, and held up okay against the hail. The rain helped."

He looked at the Hudson. Josif and August had the driver's side up on a jack, and had just been in the process of wrestling the wheel off. "Say, I have a jack. We could block those back tires, and get that other tire up. Save some time if we were working on both tires at the same time."

"Kill two birds with one stone," August said glancing at Josif.

"Well, I'll go get my jack and patch kit." He picked up the cast iron pot and coffee pot and headed out the door.

Josif and August continued working on the tire,

while Izabella used a pitch fork to move the straw from their beds back to the area by the open bale.

Herman returned with his jack, tire iron, hand pump, and patch kit. They blocked the back tires with two four by four remnants from a pile of boards by the side of the barn, and jacked up the other side of the car. Josif and August continued their work on the driver's side tire, and Herman began work on the other. Soon Josif and August were done, and helped Herman finish.

They were just lowering the jacks when a clanging was heard from the house. Herman wiped his hands on a rag. "Sounds like Mrs. Hoffstetter has breakfast ready." He hurried out the door.

Josif, Izabella, and August repacked the car, and picked up Herman's tools. "I sure hope Mrs. Hoffstetter is includin' us in that breakfast," August said, adjusting a box in the trunk. Josif and Izabella exchanged slightly guilty looks of agreement.

Josif and August were studying the map which they had spread on the hood of the car, when Herman returned. He had the coffee pot again, and a large, covered frying pan. There were three crockery plates under his arm, and three forks sticking out of his pocket. He set everything on the bale of hay from the night before, removed the lid of the frying pan, and said, "Help yourselves." There were three large sausages, and nine fried eggs. A spatula rested across the food.

August visibly struggled with himself, then stepped back. "You go first, Miz Dacia. Ladies first."

Izabella stepped up and helped herself to two eggs and one sausage. She nodded to Herman. "Your wife is very kind. Please thank her for us." She poured coffee into a mug.

Herman smiled broadly. "I sure will! She'd be out here herself, but she's pretty shy with strangers."

"I understand," Izabella said, and sat down on a bale of straw with her breakfast.

Josif and August finished up the eggs and sausage, and they all finished up the coffee. Then they said good bye to the horses.

"Well it sure has been a pleasure visiting with you," Herman said as they climbed in the car. "I sure wish you continued good luck and Godspeed."

"Thank you and Mrs. Hoffstetter again; we will not forget you."

"I'm gonna write you in a song," August said. "I'm a singin' cowboy, and I'm gonna write a ballad about this trip."

"I'll listen for it on the radio," Herman said, laughing.

Josif backed the car out of the barn, and headed it out the driveway. Everyone waved, and called good bye to Herman.

By now, it was 7:30. The sun was moving up off the horizon, the haze was dissipating, and fluffy, white clouds were forming. Potholes were full of water and easy to spot, and although they were no longer traveling in a dust cloud, the Hudson kicked up muddy gravel on itself as it swerved and bumped along.

Josif had decided to drive through Coralville and Iowa City, and they were soon in the country heading east. They changed drivers just outside Davenport. Josif and August had studied this section of the map carefully, and felt confident in being able to navigate through Davenport, south across the Mississippi River into Moline, Illinois, then across the Rock River, and east again.

"Remember, we follow signs for Route 6 and all detours. No shortcuts. We do pretty good today."

"Sure, Joe, I'm ready."

They entered Davenport easily and followed two detour routes around road repair. The third detour route,

however, led them away from their route south and roughly northwest, where the signs seemed to peter out.

"Well, don't that beat all," August exclaimed in frustration after about twenty minutes of trying to get back
on Route 6. "Just when I was gettin' to feelin' more kindly
toward them Iowans, they go and do somethin' ignorant
like this! They give us a map that don't have all the streets
on it!"

"Drive to high spot," Josif said. "Maybe we can see
Mississippi, drive to it, and follow to bridge."

"Sounds like as good a plan as any," August said,
heading up a street which led up a long hill. When they
reached the summit, they got out of the car and searched
for gaps in the trees which would provide a long view.

"There big river," Izabella said standing on tip toes
and pointing over the tops of trees below to a line of
brownish water to the southeast.

"Okay, we go that way," Josif said. "Head for river."

They got back in the car and headed in the direction
of the river. Although they could no longer see it, August
wound their way down the hill, up another, and southeast,
until the Mississippi appeared straight ahead. They looked
up and down the river and headed for a bridge about a mile
downstream. To their delight, Route 6 was the road which
crossed the river. It took them across the Mississippi River
and into Moline, Illinois. Only one easy detour met them
there, and they crossed the Rock River and headed east
into the gentle, wooded hills of northern Illinois.

Josif pulled Uncle Jon's schedule and the pencil stub
from his pocket. He crossed off Sunday's goal of Davenport, Iowa. "Now we are on schedule for today." Josif
looked at his pocket watch. "Is 10:00, and now from here,
we must go two hundred miles. About sixty miles east of
Gary, Indiana. We get there maybe four."

"Yeah, we already had our flat tires, and got lost. It

should be clear sailing from here on out."

In the back seat, Izabella crossed herself and said a quick prayer.

* * *

Illinois was hillier than Iowa, and the roads were wet, as the storm had also traveled east across northern Illinois.

They changed drivers and Josif managed to keep their speed at around forty miles per hour, dodging water-filled potholes and slowing over washboards.

August was practicing his guitar and yodeling, and Izabella was enjoying the scenery and imagining what her children were doing at home.

It was around 11:30, and Josif was beginning to think about the noon meal when he brought the Hudson over the crest of a hill and startled a doe and her two half-grown fawns browsing along the right shoulder.

They saw the car and bolted across the road in front of it. Josif braked and quickly steered the car to the right to miss the deer, plowed through the gravel at the edge of the road, the narrow muddy shoulder, and onto long, wet, grass. While the car still had some momentum, he turned the wheels to the left, gave the car a little gas, and managed to get the Hudson parallel to the road before the wheels began spinning in the grass and mud, and forward progress ceased.

"Everyone okay?" Josif asked, looking back at Izabella and over at August.

"I am fine, Josif," Izabella said picking things up off the floor and putting them back on the seat.

August inspected his guitar which had fallen off the front seat. "Looks like everything's okay." He opened the car door and looked at the wet ground below. "Well, let's get out and see what kind of a mess we're in."

Everyone got out of the car and looked at all four wheels. The two left tires were on the shoulder, although the rear one looked stuck. The right rear tire had dug up earth and was imbedded four to six inches. August offered his assessment. "Heck, this ain't too bad. Fritz an' I've hauled cars outta worse than this lotsa times."

"Before we start to push, I get shovel and move away dirt in front of tires. Izabella, you go back to top of hill and signal to cars coming to slow down and move to other side of road."

Josif got the shovel out of the trunk and moved wet clods of dirt from in front of the three stuck tires. Then he carefully scooped up gravel from the side of the road and spread a shovelful in front of each tire.

He got into the car and started the engine. August positioned himself behind the car with his hands on the trunk ready to push. Josif put the car in gear and gave it a little gas. The Hudson moved forward about three inches before the tires slung gravel up and dug into the mud even farther.

Josif got out and studied the situation again. "Maybe we do same thing, but this time I put car in neutral and we both push."

"It's worth a try."

They cleared in front of the tires, gathered and spread gravel, and positioned themselves with August pushing from the back and Josif pushing on the left window frame and trying to steer, by reaching through the open window to his right. On the count of three they pushed, gritted their teeth, dug in their feet, and pushed again. The car moved almost an inch, then rolled back into place.

"Well, we're sure goin' nowhere in a great big hurry," August said looking at the rear tires. "I think we're gonna need someone to pull us out."

"If I had Peter and Paul here, they pull us out easy."

"Yeah, a coupla horses or a truck would come in real handy about now."

Josif called up the hill to Izabella, "Anyone coming?"
"Three cars."

Josif and August discussed the situation further and decided that there was nothing more that they could do until a truck came along to help. They gathered up the still edible food which they had brought from South Dakota, a large bowl of sauerkraut, a jug of water and a blanket, and headed up to the crest of the hill to have lunch with Izabella and watch for help.

Several more cars drove by, but most were lighter than the Hudson. The drivers studied the picnickers, saw the car at the side of the road, summed up the situation right away, and shook their heads in understanding as they slowly drove by the stuck vehicle.

They had finished eating and August was in the process of building a cigarette when they spotted a large vehicle coming in the distance. After awhile they could see that it was a partially-loaded flatbed truck. Josif and Izabella carried things back to the car, and August stayed at the crest of the hill to flag down the truck.

Stanley Cleveland was the name of the truck driver. He was a middle-aged, lanky, taciturn man in work shoes, heavy brown pants, striped work shirt, suspenders, and an engineer's cap. He parked in front of the Hudson, got out of his truck, and walked around the car assessing the situation. "You're stuck all right. Got any rope?"

August opened the trunk and rummaged around in the cardboard box he had brought. "No rope, but how about ten foota log chain?"

Soon they were ready. Izabella was waiting to redirect traffic at the crest of the hill. The chain had been hooked to the frames of the truck and car. The car was in neutral. Stanley slowly moved the truck forward, took up the slack in the chain, and then gave the truck some gas. Josif and August put their heads down and pushed. The car crept up out of the holes the tires had spun in the mud, but seemed caught on something. Stanley gave his truck more gas, the men pushed harder, and suddenly with a grinding crunch, the car leapt forward. Josif and August didn't have time to even try to keep their feet; they both fell, face-down into the muddy gravel.

Stanley expertly kept the truck ahead of the car and managed to stop both without the car ramming into the back of the truck. Both vehicles were now out on the road.

Josif and August pulled themselves out of the mud and wiped off their muddy faces with muddy hands. Josif made his way to the Hudson, opened the trunk, rummaged around, and handed August a rag. He had another one for himself.

They joined Stanley at the front of the car and helped detach the chain from both vehicles. "Well, it looks like you're all set now," Stanley said, shaking hands with Josif and August.

"We thank you. You help very much," Josif said.

Stanley nodded briskly, climbed back in his truck, and drove off with a brief wave out the window.

Izabella joined them at the car and helped Josif wipe the mud and gravel off his clothes. August was using a large handful of grass to clean his clothes. "Maybe we can find a pond or stream to clean up in a little."

"Good idea," Josif said.

Izabella said nothing to keep from laughing at the two, and got in the back seat. Josif and August took their places. Josif started the car. A horrible loud noise and cloud of blue-grey exhaust blasted up from under the rear of the car.

August looked at Josif. "The dad gum muffler's busted."

They all got out of the car again. Izabella headed up the hill, and Josif and August rummaged in their boxes.

Forty-five minutes later, Josif and August emerged from under the car. The muffler had been *repaired* with a flattened section of a tin can and baling wire. A kink in the exhaust pipe had been almost worked out with skillful use of the tire iron, and the pair were now muddy both front and back. When she saw that they were done, Izabella hurried down the hill, and when she saw what they looked like, she quickly spread a blanket across the front seat.

They all got in the car again. Izabella crossed herself. Josif started the engine, and they found that the noise and exhaust had been decreased by almost twenty percent. Izabella rolled up both back windows, Josif put the Hudson in gear, and they resumed their journey.

Not too much farther down the road, they found a small pond. Josif and August got clean clothes out of their suitcases, and their soap and towels. They hurried down to the pond, and while Izabella kept watch on the road, stripped and jumped in. They returned to the car in about fifteen minutes, minus the mud and gravel, but with bits of duck weed in their hair.

They had rinsed their muddy clothes, and August stuffed the wet pile down next to his sleeping bag and the sauerkraut crock.

It was around 2:00, and they were almost half way across Illinois. Josif had decided that he should drive through Joliet and the outskirts of Chicago, and that August should follow the map and give directions as needed. August took over driving until just outside Joliet, where they stopped to get gas and an Illinois map. Josif hoped that they could reach their goal for the day, and get the muffler repaired after that.

As Josif started the car, August picked up the map and looked confidently at him. "Don't worry none, Joe, we're gonna slide through these cities slicker'n snot."

In the backseat, Izabella hung her head and prayed silently.

Route 6 was paved at this point, and had fewer pot-holes, and no washboards. Traffic began to pick up, and the noise of the vehicles soon rivaled that of their muf-fler. As they entered Joliet, the road made several ninety degree turns and began to be called by street names rather than route number. August realized the problem almost immediately and unfurled the map. "These Illinois idiots are worse than than those Iowa idiots back in Davenport."

He held the open map out in front of him and turned it around until he found the enlargement of the Chicago area. He looked out the window for street signs, then back at the map, then back out the window, and back at the map. "Where we are ain't on the map. Again. If I ever meet one of those idiot map makers, I'm gonna take his gol dang map and make him eat it! Just try to head east, Joe. We should run into 6." August continued to study the map and street signs.

Josif felt totally out of control of the situation. There were cars everywhere, purposefully turning here and there. There were buildings everywhere, and billboards, and storefronts. East was difficult to determine, and the map was proving useless. The city seemed to go on forever, and there was the intermittent stink of the stockyards, and the annoying noise and smell from the muffler.

August had been tracing roads on the map with his finger and he suddenly spoke. "Holy shit! We're way over here! Turn left on Cicero up there, then right on 159th, which is also Six. Finally the g.d. map is some g.d. help! 'Scuse me, Miz Dacia."

As soon as Josif turned the Hudson onto 6 again, he relaxed his grip on the wheel considerably and leaned back against the seat. "Good thing map help, or I do some-thing else with it to map maker."

August gave Josif a sideways glance. "Careful, Joe," he whispered. "Miz Dacia can hear ya."

They continued on 6, with only one brief detour, for almost an hour, until they saw signs indicating they were in Gary, Indiana. Josif drove east out of the city and pulled over at a wide spot in the road to change drivers. When they were on the road again, he consulted Uncle Jon's list and the map. "Okay, we go about sixty miles to town of Nappanee, Indiana. If we get there in time, maybe we get new muffler. We cannot drive in heat and not open all windows."

"Not unless you want to kill wife," Izabella said from the back. "The noise, and smell, and heat make me feel sick."

Josif looked back at his wife. She looked pale and a little green. He turned to August. "Stop over there." Josif got out and changed places with Izabella. "We will stop at next auto repair. We must get new muffler before we continue."

They soon found an auto repair garage. The mechanic diagnosed their problem as they pulled in. Luckily, they had a muffler that would work for the Hudson. However, it was close to closing time, and too late in the day to begin the job. The mechanic referred them to a hotel several blocks away, and told them to return at 8:00AM when they opened.

August drove them to the Hoosier Hotel where they took two adjacent rooms for two dollars and fifty cents. Josif put his arm around Izabella and walked her up the stairs to their room. She gratefully lay down on the bed while Josif opened the windows, then returned to their car for the luggage.

They decided to wait a couple of hours before going downstairs for dinner to give Josif and August time to wash the rest of the mud from their bodies, and duckweed from their hair, and for Izabella to recover.

By 7:30, Izabella felt better, Josif and August were clean, and all were feeling hungry. They went downstairs to the hotel restaurant where they ordered the Monday Blue Plate Special of liver and onions, bacon, mashed potatoes and gravy, and canned peas, with apple pie and coffee for dessert for ninety cents each. They were behind schedule again, but with their early morning appointment, Josif remained hopeful that they would catch up again the next day.

After supper, Izabella insisted that they retrieve Josif's and August's dirty clothes from the car so that she could wash them in the bathtub. After doing her laundry, Izabella took a shower, then hung the clothes over the shower curtain rod to dry. She and Josif could hear August playing his guitar and singing and yodeling in the next room. They got in bed and turned out the light, delighted to be in each others arms again, and to be able to discuss the trip so far in hushed tones so that August wouldn't hear their words or laughter. Soon they were making love, and they forgot the cares of the day.

Chapter Thirty-Five
Monday, 8/15/32 - Plans on The *Atlantia*

Irina went to the 8:00AM breakfast with her friends. Since most of the dancers came from families with little extra money, and since the troupe was supposed to *add color* to the voyage, it had been decided that the dancers would wear ethnic dance outfits whenever they traveled about the ship. For them to try to compete with the wealth of the other passengers would have been impossible. But in their embroidered blouses, bright skirts, and red or black boots, they were exotic, and as beautiful as any jewel-clad debutante. Heads turned to watch them wherever they went, and they received constant admiring smiles from the male passengers.

Christina and Mariana were as excited about the English and dance lessons as Irina. As they were eating their English breakfast of two fried eggs, fried tomatoes, toast, sausage and tea, they discussed which dances to teach, and decided on two fairly easy circle dances with the beautiful grapevine step, and some twirling across the floor.

At 9:00AM they reported to the Solarium and were pleased to see that most of the troupe and several other passengers were showing up. As Irina had hoped and expected, Deben, Dragos, and Petru were not there.

Mr. Jones gathered the group together, and began by teaching everyone to say, "Hello, my name is .... I am from…." Everyone repeated the phrases several times, then he went around the room and had everyone introduce themselves. He followed this with, "How are you today? I am well." Then he acted out other responses such as, "I am happy, sad, sick, tired, hungry, and lost."

Mr. Jones was funnier than he realized, and he soon had everyone laughing and imitating his expressions, as well as his words. The hour flew by.

At 10:00 the class ended, and passengers interested in learning Romanian dances were arriving. Mr. Celac was there to help translate instructions, and the troupe musicians readied their instruments of violins, *tambals*, pan flutes, clarinets, and a mandolin. Irina was amused to see how many men were interested in learning Romanian folk dances.

They began the class by demonstrating the steps and then putting them together in the dance. After the demonstration, the dancers interspersed with the passengers, and each passenger had their own private instructor. The male dancers worked with female passengers, and the female dancers worked with the male passengers. A small group of children had also attended, and Irina and her friends worked with them.

The haunting, compelling music filled the air, and soon everyone was grapevining, twirling, and laughing in the pure pleasure of dancing and enjoying each other's company.

The hour ended too soon, and all agreed to meet again the next day. Passengers and dancers slowly drifted away from the Solarium to go to the Promenade Deck for 11:00 tea, or to the swimming pool or some other activity.

Christina and Mariana wanted to go swimming in the indoor pool, but Irina did not know how to swim, and realized that she could drown as easily in a swimming pool as in the ocean if *sharks* were present to pull her down. She declined their invitation, and decided that she would sit on the Promenade Deck and have tea in full sight of passengers and crew. She waved good bye to her friends and turned to carry out her plan.

Suddenly Deben stepped out from behind a corner with Petru and Dragos. They encircled Irina and pressed in close. Deben was looking at her with cold disdain, and Petru and Dragos were smelling her hair and neck and giggling. Deben backed her into Dragos, and was about to run his hands over her body, when a woman's loud and cheerful voice stopped him.

"Oh, there you are. You are all so beautiful and graceful. It makes my heart feel light to dance with you. Let me give you all a big hug and kiss!"

Deben turned to see who had spoken. It was a grey-haired woman in her early fifties. She was of medium height and build, with a broad and friendly face, wearing impressive diamonds and jewels, and with a bearing of total confidence and openness. She was also wearing a Star of David.

Deben and his friends recoiled in horror and backed away from the approaching woman. She ignored this and flung her arms open to hug them, and puckered her lips as if to kiss them. In two seconds they were gone. The woman turned to Irina with her arms still open, and Irina gratefully hugged her and rested her head on her shoulder. Then she stood upright and looked at the woman.

"Hello, my name is Irina Tataranu. I am from Romania."

"Hello, my name is Mrs. Ida Epstein. I am from New York."

The two regarded each other solemnly and knew that they would be friends.

"I was in your dance class. I also saw your troupe perform in London."

Irina did not understand what she said, but recognized her from dance class, and recognized the word *London*.

Mrs. Epstein took Irina's arm in hers, patted it gently, and they walked together to the Promenade Deck for tea.

"I think you need more English lessons, Irina. I think that we should spend very much time together studying English so that we can have proper conversations. I feel we have much in common and much to share. I hope that is okay with you."

Irina sensed what Mrs. Epstein was saying, and she felt flooded with relief. She did not want to put Mrs. Epstein in any danger, but she needed a strong ally and knew that this woman would be one. She smiled at her gratefully and enthusiastically said, "okay."

They spent the rest of the morning practicing English and laughing together. At lunchtime, Irina invited Mrs. Epstein to join Christina, Mariana, and herself, and when she saw Mr. Celac, she eagerly included him to serve as translator.

Mr. Celac graciously spent most of his mealtime translating again, and was pleased with Irina's new friend, although he knew Deben would be furious.

During the meal, Mrs. Epstein shared that she had been in London visiting her brother, Jakob, who was a jeweler there. She lived in New York City with her son David, his wife Rebecca, and their children, Deborah and Daniel, ages eight and seven. She had seen the Romanian State Dance Ensemble perform in London with her brother and had been impressed with their skill and grace. She also said that as soon as she saw Irina and Deben dance together, she had wanted to meet Irina, as she felt they had *things in common.*

Irina shared that her family in Romania was dead, and that her only relatives had moved to a farm in South

Dakota. She knew of her aunt and uncle, Izabella and Josif, and her great aunt and uncle, Magda and Jon, and four cousins: Marie, Rose, Caroline, and Michael-Joseph. She had written to them, but did not know if they would be able to come to New York to see her.

In her heart, Mrs. Epstein had already adopted Irina. She knew that Irina was being persecuted, and that her safety, and maybe even her life, were in danger. She suspected that Irina might try to defect in New York, and she planned to do everything she could to help and protect her. She also sensed that Mr. Celac understood Irina's danger, and subtly enlisted his help.

"Mr. Celac. Please excuse an old woman for meddling, but I have noticed that the lead male dancer does not always treat his partner with respect on the dance floor. His hands go where they should not, and it is not the clumsiness of an inexperienced dancer. It is predatory." She spoke these words in a smiling and gentle way so that Irina and her friends would not guess what she was saying.

Mr. Celac responded in a similar manner. "I feel the same way. The political situation in our country is changing, and evil is gaining in strength. People spy on one another and do cruel things. Those who resist disappear, or their families do."

"I have seen this before, and I want to help protect your female lead dancer, without endangering others, of course."

"I also. I am grateful for your help. Perhaps between us, we can keep watch over her without endangering others."

"I have some ideas, Mr. Celac, that may allow us to keep watch over our little doe without suspicion to you."

"I would be pleased to hear them if you feel you can trust me."

"I do." She smiled at Mr. Celac, and gestured toward

the window as if they were speaking about the weather. "What can I do to help this girl stay safe from harm, I ask myself. Three things. Number one: she should never be alone. Number two: she should never be alone with three male dancers; you know who I mean. And number three: her face should be as common to the passengers of this ship, and people of New York, as the Statue of Liberty." She pointed to the menu. Mr. Celac nod‑

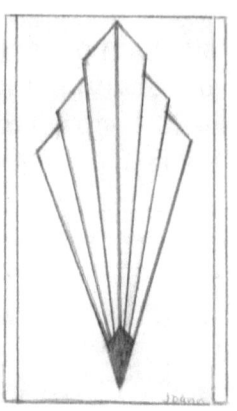

ded, and gave Mrs. Epstein a knowing look. She contin‑ued. "I will take care of number three. I have more ideas. Numbers one and two, we do together. I am going to do‑nate $1,000 to your ensemble. You cannot refuse this, and you will be obligated to pay me much attention. You could not be blamed for associating with me." She nodded to‑ward a wall sconce, and Mr. Celac looked thoughtful.

"I will ask that you‑know‑who becomes my compan‑ion for the rest of the voyage. I will teach her more Eng‑lish, and she will accompany me to concerts, play cards, shuffleboard, badminton, and activities such as that. You will also be around to help translate, be attentive to me, and keep an eye on you‑know‑who in case I have to leave her side for some reason." She smiled at Mr. Celac. "What do you think?"

Mr. Celac picked up a corner of the tablecloth and showed it to Mrs. Epstein and smiled. "I think you are a very smart and kind woman."

Mrs. Epstein and Mr. Celac continued smiling and turned to the others. Mr. Celac addressed Irina in Roma‑nian. "Your new friend, Mrs. Epstein, has a proposal. She says that she is alone on this voyage, and would like a companion. Someone she can walk, play cards, and attend concerts with. She feels a connection to you and wonders if you would spend your spare time with her in exchange for intensive English lessons."

Irina agreed enthusiastically, and Mr. Celac translated what he had said to Irina to Mrs. Epstein who nodded in agreement. Irina expressed regret to her friends that she would not be able to spend as much time with them as she had thought, but that she very much wanted to accept this opportunity to study English. They also expressed regret, but said that they would have fun together in their morning classes, and catch up on the day's events at night in their room.

Irina looked at Mr. Celac and Mrs. Epstein, and wondered what they had really been talking about.

After a dessert of petit fours and coffee, Mrs. Epstein rose and excused herself, stating that she had some business to attend to. She looked at Mr. Celac and asked if she could meet Irina and him in about forty-five minutes in the lounge near the Purser's office. He readily agreed, and poured more coffee for himself and Irina. Mariana and Christina said good bye and headed back to the pool.

* * *

Mrs. Epstein had two pieces of business to attend to right away. First she contacted the activity director, Mr. Jones, and told him that she wanted to present a gift to the Romanian Dance Ensemble. She wanted the event publicized, and was hopeful that it could occur on the bridge with the captain in the presentation photograph. She assured him that the picture would be in *The New York Times*. Mr. Jones was confident that he could arrange it.

Next, she wired her son David, a contributing editor of *The New York Times*: "David, purchase four front row, left seats at Carnegie Hall for Aug. 20th for the Romanian State Dance Ensemble performance. Bring Nicolae to translate, and a photographer from the paper. I will be bringing photographs for an article in the paper. Love, your mother."

Then she requested a Parcheesi game, and headed into the lounge to await Irina, Mr. Celac and Mr. Jones.

Irina and Mr. Celac soon joined her, and they began a game of Parcheesi. The three were well into the game when Mr. Jones arrived looking pleased. "Captain Stanford would be delighted to oblige your request He will be free before the first dinner seating, around 5:00PM, if that's not too early."

Mr. Celac smiled at Mrs. Epstein. "I have Irina here already; all I have to do is page Deben to the wheelhouse, and I'm sure he'll show up; 5:00 should be fine."

Mrs. Epstein looked pleased. "And, Mr. Jones, will you bring a photographer?"

"It would be my pleasure, ma'am."

At 5:00PM Irina, Mrs. Epstein, Mr. Celac, and Deben showed up at the wheelhouse. Captain Stanford gave them a tour, and Irina was awed by how tall the ship was, and what a path it cut through the water. She might not be able to spend hours gazing out to sea from the rail, but she had seen the sea from this viewpoint. It was vast and steely blue, looked calm, and no threat to this mass of steel and power which sliced through the waves with such ease and persistence.

When it was time for the presentation, Mrs. Epstein took a check for $1,000 made out to the Romanian State Dance Ensemble from her purse. Deben made sure to get a good look at it and his eyes widened when he saw the amount. Greed showed in his face as if he expected to receive the money himself.

The photographer had Mrs. Epstein stand between Irina and Deben. Mr. Celac was on Deben's left, and Captain Stanford was on Irina's right. Mrs. Epstein smiled kindly, and leaned forward slightly so that her Star of David was clearly visible. She reached across Deben, and handed the check to Mr. Celac.

In the photograph, Captain Stanford looked official, Irina looked beautiful, Mrs. Epstein looked gracious, Deben looked hateful, and Mr. Celac looked thrilled.

Mrs. Epstein thanked the captain, as did Mr. Celac and Irina. Then they headed off the bridge and down the stairs to the dining room. Deben walked quickly away from them and went to find his friends. He knew that he had been used and insulted by that Jewish woman. Why was she hanging around Irina? What did she want? He was confused and uneasy. He was supposed to make people feel uneasy. He would talk to Petru and Dragos. They listened to him. They would all make a plan. First to drive away the Jew, then to arrange an *accident* for Irina. But only after they had been repaid for all the trouble she was causing. Repaid repeatedly.

During dinner, two junior officers approached Irina and inquired if they could escort her to the evening's concert: selections from Gilbert and Sullivan. They also included Mrs. Epstein and Mr. Celac in their invitation, and the five spent the evening together, enjoying brandy and delicate puff pastries after the concert. Mr. Celac escorted Irina to her room at 11 PM concluding another day spent in safety.

Chapter Thirty-Six
Tuesday, 8/16/32 Ohio

After an early morning breakfast of fried eggs, bacon, toast, and several cups of coffee in the hotel café, Josif, Izabella, and August headed back to the auto repair shop.

The mechanic seemed skilled and experienced and took the car in right away. August grabbed his guitar, and they headed into the customer waiting room. There were three folding wooden chairs, a rickety card table with several old and torn magazines, a dog-eared calendar with pictures of cars that was covered with greasy fingerprints, and a wall clock. The smell of grease and oil was pervasive and the Hudson had added an overlay of exhaust fumes.

August strummed his guitar and sang and yodeled quietly to himself while Josif and Izabella thumbed through the magazines and glanced frequently at the clock. The sounds of banging, clanging, metal scraping on concrete, and ratcheting encouraged them, and in spite of several frustrating interruptions by other customers and phone calls, the mechanic and his assistant finished the job in two-and-a-half hours.

Josif paid the bill of thirteen dollars and sixty cents and silently thanked God again for the reward money. The mechanic backed the car out of the garage, and all got in and settled themselves for the day's drive. Josif was in the driver's seat. He took out Uncle Jon's schedule.

"We have sixty miles to finish from yesterday, then we must go far as Cleveland, Ohio. There are more cities and towns along this part of the way. Maybe there will be more paved roads, and we can drive faster. Izabella smiled encouragingly from the back seat.

"Sure Joe," August said. "We can prob'ly even go past today's goal for a change. I've heard of stranger things happening."

Josif started the engine. August opened their new map of Indiana and folded it to show their route. He laid it across his lap, then picked up his guitar and began strumming.

Izabella unrolled the window next to her, leaned back, and marveled at all the cars, buildings, billboards, and stores. She had lived in a city in Romania, but American cities were different. They seemed bigger and more sprawling. The roads were wider, parking lots bigger, and many of the buildings looked new and constructed of wood. In Europe, most buildings were made of stone and often looked cold and unwelcoming. In America, there were many painted buildings and big billboards. Nothing seemed very regimented, and there was always something new and different to catch the eye.

Josif's grim announcement of "detour ahead" interrupted her musings and she sat up to try to help keep track of the detour route. August had stopped playing and became as alert as a bird dog.

"They ain't gonna get us this time. We're gonna win this detour!" he said emphatically.

Josif meticulously followed the route, with August and Izabella pointing out each turn up ahead. It wound around and changed direction several times, but eventually brought them back to Route 6. August let out a whoop and slapped the outside of the car door with his hand. "We did it! I told you we'd do it this time. Maybe these Hoosiers ain't so bad."

Finally they left all signs of the city behind and entered the countryside of Indiana. Like northern Illinois, there were rolling hills and hardwood forests, streams cutting through valleys, and occasional wetlands and ponds. A few horse ranches were interspersed with the farms. The roads were gravel again, with the usual washboards and potholes.

Around sixty miles from Gary, they drove through Amish country. Even August was impressed by their tidy farms and communities, but puzzled by their avoidance of modern conveniences. "I appreciate a team and wagon as good as the next fella, but why not use a car or truck if you can? Heck, we never could be makin' this trip so fast if it weren't for this here Hudson. I wonder why they don't understand that."

Josif was relieved he hadn't waited until this part of the state to try to get a new muffler.

They stopped for the noon meal at a café and had fried bullhead catfish, hot German potato salad, green beans, and a dinner roll, with blackberry pie and coffee for dessert.

Josif reluctantly paid the bill of two dollars and five cents and left a twenty cent tip. "Even though we have plenty of money with us, I still hate to pay for one meal what it would cost to feed our family for several days," he complained to Izabella in Romanian as they left the café.

August took over driving when they stopped for gas, and it was around 2:30PM when they entered Ohio. Josif rifled through the stack of maps which August had folded in eighths and placed on the seat between them. "Would be good to fold maps as they were. Then name of state easy to see, and right map easy to find. Not like this."

August snorted, "No thanks, Joe. Fritz tricked me into tryin' that once, and I lost half a day before the dad gum map fell apart. I ain't no good at trick foldin'. I just do it regular."

Josif ignored him and pulled out the U.S. map. He unfolded it and pointed to Route 6 through Ohio. "Road go through big cities; we need Ohio map before then."

"Sure Joe, we can stop at the next gas station."

"We will stop for night in west side of Cleveland. Tomorrow we drive many miles in city. We are behind again, we must not stop unless is important!"

August sat up straighter and put both hands on the wheel. He stared intently at the road and pushed the Hudson up to forty-two miles per hour without hitting many more potholes. "Don't you worry none, Joe, we'll make it on time, even if we have to drive all night. I got some sauerkraut left, so we don't have to worry about food."

Josif smiled wanly at August, and Izabella crossed herself and looked sideways at the sauerkraut crock. They bounced and bumped along for another few hours, and finally stopped for gas and a map outside of Fremont.

Josif resumed driving, and August unfolded the new map. Suddenly there was a sound similar to hail hitting the windshield. Visibility dropped dramatically. A mass of yellow splotches began to cover the windshield. Josif turned on the wipers and the yellow mess smeared across the window. "Need to pull over and clean window, but cannot see shoulder."

"Hang on, Joe, I'll stick my head out the window and see where's a good spot." August stuck his head out the window, and Josif and Izabella heard dull *thwacks* muffled swearing, silence, then abrupt hacking and coughing. August pulled his head back in the car and gestured that it was okay to pull over. His face and hair were covered with leggy, yellow goo, and red, raised welts, and he was coughing vigorously. Veins were bulging, and his face was turning red when he finally brought up a yellow mass of wings and insect legs.

Josif successfully pulled the car over and braked. August had spat the yellow mass out the window and was energetically wiping the insect guts out of his mouth and off his face with the map. When he finished wiping his face, he used the map on his hair like a towel. When he finally emerged from the map, his eyes were watering, his hair was stuck together, and he had a disgusted look on his face. He hawked and spat out the window a few more times.

Izabella handed the jug of water up to him, and he took a large mouthful, swished and spat, another mouthful and gargled and spat, another rinse and spat, then several long swallows. Finally he poured the last of the water in his hand and wiped it over his face, drying himself with the back of the map.

"Holy heck! That was the most god-awful crap I ever tasted! That was worse than the time Fritz fooled me into drinking warm curdled milk, saying it was melted ice cream. You're lucky I don't puke up all over the car. I still might. That was pure horrible." August went on a while longer, then looked at the windshield. "We can't drive like that, Joe."

They all got out of the car and went looking for ways to clean the windshield. Josif went to the trunk and found a rag, but no more water. Izabella looked through the food box, but the closest thing to liquid she could find was plum jam. August went over to some clumps of grass and began pulling them up. He scrubbed the windshield with a handful of grass which only smeared the sticky yellow fluid and left grass stuck to the window.

"We need liquid," Josif said.

"I know where is some," Izabella said quietly, glancing at the sauerkraut crock.

August looked aghast, then crestfallen. "I s'pose you're right, Miz Dacia. Come to think of it, that juice just might do the trick." He found two large bowls and a large spoon in the food box. August scooped as much of the sauerkraut as he could into one bowl and juice into the other. He took the juice bowl and the wadded up map of Ohio and dunked the map in the juice. Then he wiped the dripping mess over the windshield. "Maybe we should let it soak for awhile," he said, setting the bowl on the hood. He turned and walked to the back seat. "No reason to let this go to waste," August said picking up the bowl of sauerkraut, and rummaging in the food box for a fork.

Josif and Izabella watched in wonder, then went to the front of the car to look at the windshield again. Josif noted that the radiator was also covered with insects which could cause it to overheat. He and Izabella began to pick insects out of the radiator with small twigs from the side of the road.

After about five minutes, August commented on the situation. "Well, I sure hate to use our last clean rag on that mess."

"Yes, we should save for last cleaning of window. I think we must use another map first."

"I'll get Indiana." August reached through the window and grabbed the top map under his guitar. He wadded it up and put it in the juice to soak, then wiped vigorously at the windshield, causing the yellow goo to smear. "Well, it's loosening up some." he said.

After several more applications of sauerkraut juice, and wiping with Indiana, Illinois, and the clean rag, two roughly circular, clear areas were achieved on each side of the windshield. Insect parts, blades of grass, bits of maps, and sauerkraut pieces were stuck in the remaining yellow goo, which seemed to have hardened to an impenetrable glaze.

August took what was left of the sauerkraut juice, and carefully poured it back into the empty crock. "This here's too good to waste. We don't know what other bug messes we're gonna get into down the road." He looked at Izabella. "Just don't forget and have a little snack of this while we're driving, Miz Dacia; it's got a lotta bug parts in it."

They resumed their places in the Hudson and continued toward Sandusky, resolving to stop and get another map of Ohio as soon as possible. As they entered the outskirts of Sandusky, Josif spotted a gas station up ahead. But before the entrance, they were directed down a side road by a detour sign.

The travelers instantly became alert, and began calling out turns as they spotted them. Traffic was building in the city, and the narrow detour route was becoming choked with cars. They passed three gas stations, but Josif was reluctant to lose his place in traffic and kept on. The detour route rejoined Route 6 briefly several times before leading away from it again. Josif resolutely drove on, straining to see through the small opening of clear glass. Finally the detour route ended and they rejoined 6 just as it bordered Lake Erie. A road sign said, "Cleveland 35 miles," and they all let out a whoop of joy.

It was getting dark, and thoughts of supper and a room for the night were entering their minds. There were few lights along the lake, but the moon was full, there were few clouds and Josif was able to bring them safely into Cleveland city limits.

Gas stations were closed by then, but they found a hotel, paid for two rooms, gave August time to wash off the bugs, and headed downstairs for supper in the hotel restaurant. The Tuesday special was pot roast with potatoes, carrots, and onions. They had chocolate cake and coffee for dessert. Josif parted with one dollar and eighty-five cents, with a fifteen cent tip.

Eyelids were heavy when they got back to their rooms, and they were all asleep within thirty minutes after having agreed to get another early start in the morning.

Chapter Thirty-Seven
Tuesday, 8/16/32 - Deben's Three Bad Plans

What Deben had thought would be easy: disposing of Irina, was proving to be difficult. He had presumed that the affairs of the members of the troupe would be private; that he would be able to make and carry out plans without interference.

But that was not the case. Wearing their Romanian dance outfits, they stood out like red tulips in a field of yellow daffodils, and eyes seemed to follow their every movement. Irina and Mrs. Epstein were always together, and even Mr. Celac was becoming involved with them and being very friendly toward the Jewish woman. Of course, in light of her $1,000 contribution to the troupe he could see why, but now that they had the money, he felt that Mr. Celac should pull back and not encourage personal contact and friendliness.

It was Tuesday. The ship was due to dock in New York on Thursday afternoon. If he did not kill Irina while on the ship, he would have to wait until after the performance on Saturday or Sunday.

Mariana was good, but to fill in for Irina she would need several days of intense practice or she might embarrass him during their most difficult duos, and detract from his skill and manly beauty.

Deben valued his connection to the Iron Guard. He

planned to become very prominent in that group. But he also loved to be the subject of admiration and envy. A mirror was his best friend, and dancing in front of an audience was his passion. Often during his daily activities, he imagined that he was on stage, naked, and that a rapt audience of thousands was watching, mesmerized by his beauty and grace.

Now though, he focused on his assignment from Corneliu Codreanu. Irina had foiled his plans in Bucharest, when she had let her hair down and revealed herself to Christina and her parents. This failure had lessened his prestige with Codreanu. It was essential to rebuild it, and to show Codreanu that he was competent and capable of any assignment, no matter what was involved.

Irina must die, and the Jewish woman must be taught a lesson. His feelings of inadequacy must be turned into feelings of power and control. He was becoming angry and impatient, and he wanted to strike out and destroy any who stood in his way. He had two tools to help with this. Two tools who also liked to wield fear and power, and who liked to be told to indulge themselves.

Petru Buscan was Deben's age. He was slightly taller and thinner, with chiseled features and thick black hair. He lacked Deben's grace and agility, but he made up for it with his muscularity and stage presence. His only detracting features were his arrogant expression, which always seemed on the verge of turning into a disdainful sneer, and his eyes which reflected a shallow and mean spirit.

He realized that Deben was moving up in the Iron Guard, and he wanted to ride his coattails as one of his enforcers. He didn't like to worry about what he could get away with. He just liked to be given orders to cause pain and fear, and to have his actions legitimized by someone else. Petru Buscan was a very willing follower.

Dragos Amanar was perhaps the worst of the three.

He liked to follow orders too, but he liked to suggest em-
bellishments, and he often seemed to be daring Deben to
push the limits even beyond their usual cruelty. He had
been a bully all his life, and he liked the idea of an organization of bullies. He followed Deben's orders now, but he
knew he could surpass and replace him in the Iron Guard.
Now he would use Deben to get noticed. Later he would
pick the opportune moment to shame him and demon-
strate his superiority in front of Codreanu.

Dragos was the shortest male in the dance troupe,
and his face was scarred from acne. He had dark brown
hair and a wiry build. He also lacked Deben's grace, but
he attacked each dance with a precision and force which
enthralled and also intimidated. He was hungry for action,
and eager for Irina's capture and slow torture, followed by
a painful death.

It was these two to whom Deben had turned on Monday night. Together they had come up with three plans to
torment Irina and Mrs. Epstein. They hoped to scare Mrs.
Epstein off so that they could isolate and pick off Irina.

Deben's turn came first. His favorite form of intimi-
dation was sexual, and he wanted to humiliate Irina in
front of her dance students after the morning English lesson. She would not be so proud when her class members
turned their heads in shame while she was in Deben's
hands; they would avoid her after that, and she would be
easier to corner.

The next morning Deben waited out of sight just outside the doors to the Solarium and listened. When appropriate music was played, he leapt gracefully into the room,
grabbed Irina, twirled her, and lifted her roughly, letting
his hands approach her breasts.

Suddenly he felt a strong hand on his shoulder and
turned to see an irate male passenger, backed up by three
other male passengers, staring down at him. "See here old

man," the first passenger said. "We're in the middle of our class now. Don't be a bore." The man was not smiling, nor were his companions.

Deben roughly pushed Irina away and lightly ran out of the Solarium. He turned at the door, and with a smile on his face, swore at the passengers in Romanian, and shot a cold look at Irina before disappearing down the passageway.

The Romanian dancers looked horrified at Deben's actions toward Irina and the passengers in the class. Irina felt frustrated and angry. Deben was bringing shame to the dance troupe, and thus to her friends and country. The momentum of the class had stopped, and people were standing around looking uncomfortable. Irina realized that Deben had accomplished his goal.

She tried to overcome her distress and anger, and to focus on a way to bring joy back into the room. Her eyes fell on the group of children with whom she had been working. She spoke to the musicians and asked them to play the music to an easy dance which involved partners, and skipping together between two rows of dancers who were facing each other, with hands joined above the heads of the skipping couple, like a bower.

There were twelve children in the class today, and she paired up each child with an adult. Then she and one of the troupe members demonstrated the dance and took their places in the facing lines. One by one, the pairs of adult and child skipped together under the bower and took their places in line. As Irina had hoped, the children laughed, the adults joined in, and many an adult had to try to skip under a bower which was only about five feet high at spots where the children were located. Soon Deben's ugliness was replaced by laughter, silliness, and friendship. The class ended happily, and many of the passengers approached Irina afterwards and shook her hand, or placed a gentle hand on her shoulder.

Ida joined Irina and looked at her proudly. "Well done," she said. "Laughter is one of the best tools to fight fear."

Irina understood the gist of Ida's statement and responded in her best English. "To laugh is good, to fear is not good."

"Very good English! Now let us go have tea on the Promenade Deck."

Irina smiled. "Okay," she said and took Mrs. Epstein's arm. "Let us go have tea."

They walked together out of the Solarium and down the passageway to the Promenade Deck. As they approached the spot where they had become accustomed to having their morning and afternoon teas, they were met by a small crowd gathered in concern around an elderly passenger, obviously in pain, who was lying on the deck next to an overturned and broken deck chair. Deck hands rushed up with a stretcher and lifted the passenger onto it, covered him with a blanket, and hurried off to the infirmary. Another deck hand was inspecting the chair.

"It looks like a supporting pin came out of the chair, but I can't find it anywhere around here." Other deck hands quickly checked other chairs and found that many had been tampered with. They gathered up the broken ones while others scurried off to obtain replacements.

Irina and Mrs. Epstein looked at each other knowingly. This had all the earmarks of Deben and his two followers. They seemed to be extra active today. Care must be taken to avoid being alone, and they must be vigilant every moment. They found seats together farther along the deck and enjoyed the usual hot tea, petite sandwiches, and pastries of *elevenses*, 11:00 tea.

Just as they took their last sips of tea and set their bone china cups back in their saucers, two junior officers strolled up to them and invited Irina and Mrs. Epstein to accompany them on a tour of the upper decks. They gladly accepted and silently calculated that they had at least another hour of guaranteed safety.

The officers, Richard and Albert, were ernest and humorous, and took turns naming items in English with Irina repeating their words, and naming the items in Romanian. Mrs. Epstein was amused to hear Irina learning words with an English accent.

They identified all the lower decks for Irina and Mrs. Epstein, and learned the Romanian words for *very pretty*, *handsome*, and *handsomer*. By the time they had returned to the Promenade Deck, the four were comfortable with each other and laughing frequently.

Mrs. Epstein invited the young officers to join them for lunch, and they readily agreed. Over a meal of poached Scottish salmon, boiled red potatoes with Hollandaise sauce, and a watercress salad, the conversation turned to the weather.

A bank of dark clouds was gathering to the northwest, and the wind was beginning to pick up. Richard explained that the captain had received reports of storms to the west, and thirty-five foot swells. The ship was due to intercept the weather around mid-afternoon, and he encouraged the women to visit the infirmary before then to receive anti-nausea injections.

When Irina looked alarmed and Mrs. Epstein began to ask questions about the seaworthiness of *The Atlantia*, Albert was quick to jump in with reassurances. He explained to Mrs. Epstein, with encouraging smiles to Irina, that *The Atlantia* was a very sound ship with more than sufficient life boats and preservers. He further explained that Captain Stanford was a stickler for safety and that in spite of steamship lines' constant competition for the quickest trans-Atlantic crossing, he always maintained moderate speed and put ship and passenger concerns first.

Richard added that some captains did not observe

moderate speed during inclement weather, and simply posted more lookouts and closed all watertight doors. "*Moderate speed*," he explained, "meant that a ship could come to a dead stop in half the distance of its visibility."

He illustrated this using the butter dish as a ship, and the salt and pepper shakers and other tableware as other ships or icebergs obscured by fog or heavy rain, which Albert provided by holding an unfolded napkin between the butter dish and the other objects. There were several minor collisions, but nothing was overturned.

Albert finished the reassurances with an explanation of four, three, and two funnel fogs. He told how, during fog and heavy weather, some captains would stand on the bridge and see how many of their funnels were visible. Some wouldn't even slow to moderate speed during two funnel fogs, but would live on the bridge, sounding their horns, and straining to hear the slightest sound from a nearby ship.

Captain Arthur Stanford would never take such a risk. He took his duties seriously, and his first duty was to his ship and passengers. The ship might arrive a little late, but at least it would arrive. The ladies need not fear, they were in steady hands. Besides, Richard and he were on duty, and they would keep an eye on things.

The four broke up from lunch around 2:30, and Mrs. Epstein and Irina decided to go get their anti-nausea injections as the cloud bank seemed much closer, and the ship was beginning to pitch and roll.

They followed the ship's signage down a deck and aft toward the infirmary. There were fewer passengers in this section of the ship, and the passageways were dimly lit and seemed almost deserted. Suddenly, they heard kissing sounds and derisive laughter behind them. Without turning, they knew that they were being followed by Petru and Dragos.

Ida and Irina tightened their grips on each other and scanned the signs and passageways ahead and to the sides for refuge. They quickened their pace toward the infirmary and heard the following footsteps also quicken. Now their stalkers were speaking in Romanian in low ugly voices full of threat and insult. Irina's face burned in shame at their depravity. She wanted to break and run, or turn and fight like an enraged wolf, but she knew neither action would ensure their safety. She centered herself as if preparing for a complex dance solo, and maintained a steady, brisk pace.

They were nearing a corner and Irina prayed that the infirmary would be just around it. Petru and Dragos were almost on them as they turned the corner and saw an open door to the left with warm light streaming out of it, and "Infirmary" on a sign above it. Three quick steps brought all four within view of those just inside the door.

Mrs. Epstein stopped at the entrance and turned, positioning herself so that Petru and Dragos could be clearly seen. In a loud laughing voice she addressed them. "Little boys, why would you want to make love to me? I'm almost old enough to be your grandmother. Run along and play or I'll tell your mothers."

Irina did not know exactly what Ida had said, nor did Petru and Dragos, but they all knew that she had insulted them in front of people who did. Irina regarded them with obvious loathing, and spoke in Romanian, "You bring shame to the dance troupe, to your country, but most of all to yourselves. You are a disgrace!" She turned her back on them and joined Mrs. Epstein in the line to get their injections. The other passengers enfolded them and turned to look coldly at Petru and Dragos who slunk back around the corner and out of sight.

By the time Mrs. Epstein and Irina were finished in the infirmary, the storm was upon them and the ship was rocking and rolling, and pitching and yawing in earnest.

The passageways were filling with queasy looking passengers, and they felt safe venturing out again.

The doctor had promised that the injections would take effect quickly, and should be repeated every twelve to sixteen hours. He advised against too much walking around, as it could be unsettling as well as dangerous with all the erratic ship movements. He also mentioned that during rough weather, movies were shown non-stop in the ship's theater as "getting one's mind off of one's stomach was almost as effective as the injection." Sensing that the doctor's advice was sound, Ida and Irina headed for the ship's theater.

Cimarron with Irene Dunne was scheduled to start in twenty minutes at 3:30, and the theater was already about one-third full. They found seats in front of a group of four male passengers, and felt secure that even if Deben and his followers felt well enough to look for them, they wouldn't chance harassing them with such witnesses.

By the time the movie started the injections were taking effect, and Irina and Mrs. Epstein were able to snuggle into their plush velvet seats and enjoy a saga of the Oklahoma Land Rush which was preceded by a newsreel and a Laurel and Hardy short feature. The ship's movements became less disturbing and when the movie was over, it was time for the second dinner seating. They decided to eat a small dinner and return at 7:30 for *The Champ* with Wallace Beery and Jackie Cooper.

Walking in the passageways and climbing stairs in the ship was indeed a challenge and dangerous at times when the ship would lurch suddenly, then seem to wallow for a moment only to lean forward and to the side at the same time. Mrs. Epstein and Irina clung to the handrails and cautiously made their way to the dining room.

In spite of the 6:00 seating being the most popular, the dining room was almost empty. Waiters skillfully carried trays with covered plates, and served beverages in glasses and cups that were only half full. Diners were taking tentative bites with one hand and hanging onto the table or their chair with the other.

Irina and Mrs. Epstein were feeling good but didn't want to tempt fate with a heavy meal, so they ordered beef consomme with saltines, and shirred eggs on toast, with coffee and tapioca pudding for dessert.

On their way back to the theater, they ran into Stefan, one of the other troupe members, who mentioned that Deben, Petru, and Dragos had refused to get anti-nausea injections and were very sick and staying in their room. Most of the others had gotten their injections and were feeling pretty good.

Mr. Celac was keeping an eye on those who didn't feel well, and was encouraging everyone to get an injection in the morning if the rough weather continued.

Irina and Mrs. Epstein stifled their amusement at the news of Deben's and his friends' discomfort until Stefan had left, then they laughed with guilty pleasure at their unkind thoughts.

After watching *The Champ* and several shorts and newsreels, Mrs. Epstein escorted Irina to her room, stopping by to check in with Mr. Celac. They decided to meet at his room at 8:00A.M. If it was still stormy, they would all go to the infirmary together.

Irina and Mrs. Epstein told Mr. Celac of Petru and Dragos's actions earlier. He was shocked and outraged, and promised to speak to them that evening. He escorted Irina to her room, then Mrs. Epstein to hers. He told her that he would send one of his assistants to escort her back to his room in the morning. Then he went to Deben's, Petru's, and Dragos's room to have a talk with them about behavior which would get them thrown off the tour and out of the troupe.

Chapter Thirty-Eight
Wednesday, 8/17/32 - Pennsylvania

Josif reviewed their destination for the day over breakfast. He proudly crossed off Tuesday's goal of Cleveland, Ohio. "Now we are back on schedule. Today will be better. We drive to Kane, Pennsylvania. Pennsylvania is next to New York. We are almost there!"

"Yes, Josif."

"Sure, Joe."

"First we find gas station, get Ohio map, and ask gas station man to clean window."

"That sounds like a good plan to me, Joe."

"To me also. We will shame Irina if car look like this."

They re-entered Cleveland traffic around 8:00AM. The road continued to follow Lake Erie and crossed countless railroad tracks. Barges could be seen on the lake, loaded with coal, steel, and lumber. There were no easily accessible gas stations in the downtown area, and Josif forged ahead, constantly scanning the road for Route 6 signs. They had a thirty minute delay crossing the draw bridge across the Cuyahoga River while a ship loaded with steel girders slowly passed underneath. Traffic became stop and go through the heart of the city, and they crawled along going east.

Gradually traffic thinned, and around 11:00 they re-entered the hills and valleys of the countryside. As Josif relaxed his grip on the steering wheel, August consulted the U.S. map. "You'll never guess what, Joe."

"What?"

"We might could make it through the rest of Ohio without a map. There's no more big cities and what I can see of Route 6 looks pretty straight forward. If we wait until we get to Pennsylvania, we'd save us a little time."

Josif thought about it and reluctantly agreed. "I wait until Pennsylvania like you say. I want to get window clean, but bugs on window help block sun in eyes."

They crossed into Pennsylvania and stopped at Conneaut Lake for lunch, gas, and a map. They found the gas station first. The service station attendant tried valiantly to clean the windshield and succeeded in removing some of the larger chunks, smearing the yellow goo around more evenly, and slightly enlarging the two view holes. He also worked at the headlights, which ended up coated in a yellow gel with a few wings and legs.

"Looks like you drove through a swarm of dirty devils. They're pretty thick this time of year. Keep having attendants work at it, leave it out in the rain, and try not to hit any more bugs," was his advice to Josif and August as Josif paid for the gas and picked up a map of Pennsylvania.

"That ignorant so and so! That advice was about as much good as tits on a bull," August exclaimed when they got back in the car. "That's about the kind of advice I'd expect from Fritz, about worthless!" August seemed about ready to go on protesting a while longer, but the mention of Fritz's name seemed to make him lose his train of thought, and he became quiet and thoughtful.

Izabella noticed his reaction and leaned forward from the back seat. She gently put her hand on his shoulder. "We miss our family back on the farm, maybe you miss your family too, especially Fritz?"

"Well, corn coulda' growed a foot since I had a good

fight. Fritz is the only one who can even come close to whoopin' me. I kinda miss that. Since that dust storm ruined most of our crops, he's prob'ly sittin' around pickin' his teeth. He can be real lazy sometimes."

August remained thoughtful until Josif pulled into a café, at which point his spirits rose dramatically. They had the local special of fried trout, sautéed red potatoes, sliced tomatoes, creamed onions, yeast rolls, with coffee and ice cream for dessert. August looked sublime. "Getting hit in the face with all those god-awful exploding bugs was almost worth it, if this is the reward. That food sure was good!"

Josif and Izabella heartily agreed. "That meal almost worth have to drive through Cleveland," Josif said.

"And almost worth have to ride in hot back seat with smells of car exhaust and sauerkraut," Izabella added.

Feeling refreshed, they returned to the Hudson and climbed back into their spots in the car. Josif started the engine and steered the car back onto Route 6, East.

At Meadville, the route turned abruptly north for about twenty miles before heading east again through increasingly hilly terrain. The roads were in terrible condition, and the frequently-encountered log and coal trucks explained why. Potholes were randomly spaced, large and deep, and washboards filled in the spaces between them. Josif was forced to slow to twenty-five to thirty-five miles per hour. The trucks didn't seem to share the same constraints, however, and often passed the Hudson, slinging up mud and gravel.

The countryside was lush and green, the hillsides picturesque with meandering streams through wooded valleys, but Josif saw very little of it. His eyes were fixed on the road and traffic as he peered intently through the clear space in the windshield.

August had been practicing his music while Josif was

driving, and after about two hours he put his guitar down, cracked his knuckles, and stretched. He turned to Josif. "Say, Joe, how about lettin' me have a little a the fun?"

Josif pulled over at the next wide spot in the road, and they changed places. August hunkered down over the wheel and peered through the clear area in the windshield. "Looks like we hit a few more bugs, only these have green guts."

He pulled the Hudson back out onto the road, and they continued their slow and painstaking drive. Josif tried to relax and enjoy the scenery, but his neck and shoulders were tight, and he was beginning to feel that he was a long way from the farm.

Soon they would try to rescue Irina. It must not go wrong. The Iron Guard must not kill his sister Sofia's daughter. He had helped Uncle Jon and Aunt Magda come over, and had been thankful ever since. Irina was just as vital a member of his family. He must think the rescue out carefully, and plan every detail. Irina would not flee for her life across the ocean to fail, nor would he and Izabella go through all of this to fail. While August drove, Josif leaned back, tipped his hat forward, closed his eyes, and planned.

In the back seat, Izabella was also planning. She had lost Alexander to violence. She would not lose her niece. Tonight she must discuss plans with Josif.

Josif and Izabella were roused from their thoughts by August announcing, "Kane, two miles. Looks like we're almost there."

Josif sat up and looked out the side window. It was getting dark, not so much because of the hour, but because the sun was behind the crests of forested hills. "Good. We find hotel and have supper. Tonight we must plan Irina's rescue."

They found a modest hotel, The Allegheny, booked

two rooms, hauled their suitcases upstairs, cleaned up a bit, and headed downstairs for supper.

Over heaping plates of meatloaf, mashed potatoes and gravy, canned corn, and sliced white bread and butter, the group discussed the plan. Josif set the tone. "This is life or death for Irina. It will not be death." August's eyes widened, and he slowly continued eating his corn without taking his gaze from Josif. Izabella set her fork down and looked intently at her husband.

"We arrive in America in New York City. It is big. It is crowded. It is fast. People speak fast. We must not appear unusual or like we don't know where we are going, or any of the Iron Guard who might be around will know that we are strangers. We need good map of city. We need newspaper which can announce dance performances. When we know where Irina will dance, we will go there early and look at all entrances and streets around theater. We find entrance where performers enter. We watch, and when we see performers go in, August and I make disturbance. Then Izabella sneak in with dancers when people look at us. If she is questioned, she says she is from local dance troupe, and was sent over to see if she can help in any way."

"We could be playin' cowboy songs. Guitar and violin, singin' and yodelin'. That'd get those city folk's attention," August added eagerly.

"That may be good idea," Josif said, looking somewhat doubtful. "After Izabella get in, she make contact with Irina. They decide good time for Irina to get out. When time come, they run outside, and August and I protect and get everyone in car, and drive to nearest police station. Irina ask for protection from Iron Guard, and they are made to leave. We take Irina and go home."

"Wow, Joe, that was great. Maybe we'll have to knock a few of 'em off, too!"

307

"I hope not. They should die, but I do not want to go to trial and be away from farm. I want them away from my family, away from farm, away from America. They are a bad sickness. I do not want it to spread."

Izabella smiled at Josif. "That is very good plan. When we get city map, we find theater and police station, shortest ways there, and immigration office."

"That is true. We want everything legal. Irina must become an American."

Up in their room, Izabella rubbed Josif's neck and shoulders. "Your neck is very tight. Do not worry. You have made a good plan. We will get Irina."

Izabella's conviction soothed Josif, and he was finally able to drift into a fitful sleep. Izabella snuggled up next to him and struggled with her own worries for the rest of the night.

Chapter Thirty-Nine
Wednesday, 8/17/32 - Weather

The storm was still raging in the morning although it had abated somewhat, and now the swells averaged fifteen to twenty-five feet. Irina, Mrs. Epstein, and Mr. Celac met at his room as they had planned, and they headed to the infirmary for their shots.

Mrs. Epstein inquired of Mr. Celac how his talk with Deben, Petru, and Dragos had gone. He looked at her with great sadness. "In spite of them being sick as dogs, they are still full of venom. When I related what they had done, and what the consequences would be for one more infraction, they threatened me and my family. Dragos was able to recite all their names, and where they lived. Even Deben looked surprised by his independent research. They have been infected by the Iron Guard which appeals to their basest feelings. They are lost to us. I have placed them on suspension, and informed the dance director not to tolerate any misbehavior, especially towards Irina."

"I guess that's the most we can do now," Mrs. Epstein said. "Do you think the dance director can control them?"

Mr. Celac looked doubtful. "Perhaps somewhat with threats to throw them off the tour, and out of the troupe. But they know they would be hard to replace on the tour, and the dance director has only one child, and is not very brave."

Mr. Celac translated their conversation to Irina who nodded in understanding. She wanted to protect Mr. Celac from danger, but knew it was too late. She decided to tell Mr. Celac about Deben's efforts to get her to kill Ion Duca and his threats of rape and torture.

The look of shock and horror on Mr. Celac's face confirmed Mrs. Epstein's suspicions of the seriousness of the situation, and Mr. Celac's translation filled in the details.

They stopped their conversation as they joined the queue to the infirmary. Other dancers were trickling downstairs to the infirmary, and concealing their relief, they learned that Deben, Petru, and Dragos were still sick and staying in their room.

With lightened hearts, the three clung to the handrails and each other, and followed the ship's passageways up to the dining room. They had a light breakfast of soft boiled eggs, toast, marmalade and coffee, and headed up to the Solarium to see if Mr. Jones was having the morning English class.

Since so many of the ship's activities, such as shuffleboard, tennis, and swimming were impractical under the current weather conditions, and with the pitching and rolling of the ship, Mr. Jones had substituted a sing-along for the English and dancing classes to accommodate more passengers. He had several of the ship's musicians with him, including accordion, violin, and clarinet players. Mr. Jones was playing the piano.

The piano was bolted to the floor, but the piano bench was not, and he struggled to keep it in place as well as his place on it. The other musicians were seated on stationary chairs, but also had to work to keep their seats. The passengers were in a similar predicament and the singing often included muffled, *uh oh's, hang on's,* and *pardon me's.*

Mr. Jones had a lovely tenor voice as well as a sense of the absurd, and as he clung to the piano he matched the rhythm of the songs to the movement of the ship. The passengers caught on, and *It's a Long Way to Tipperary* was soon full of improvisation, and hoots of laughter. Irina tried to join in with *la la las*, but dissolved into tears of laughter, and felt much of her tension evaporate. Mrs. Epstein and Mr. Celac were in similar straits. The session ended with voices of surprise that the two hours had passed so quickly.

Mr. Jones announced the schedule of movies for the day, and Irina and Ida decided to see *Tarzan the Ape Man* at 1:00PM. Mr. Celac excused himself to go check on the other members of the troupe, but said he would try to join them at one.

Irina and Mrs. Epstein stayed in the Solarium and conducted their own English class in which Irina would point to something, Mrs. Epstein would say the English word, and then they would discuss or describe it more.

Today's words revolved around the weather. They began with *wind*, then to *very strong wind*, *thunder*, *lightning*, *rain*, *gale*, and *low visibility*. From there they discussed the sea and such words as *waves*, *white caps*, *swells*, and *twenty-foot swells*. A queasy passenger on an outside lower deck yielded new words *seasick*, *nausea*, *green*, *unfortunate accident*, *deck hand*, *mop and bucket*, and *inadequate wages*.

Ida was teaching Irina verbs and their conjugations, and her student was beginning to construct short sentences. Irina also found that watching movies helped her pick up the rhythm and common phrases of English.

After another light meal for lunch, she and Mrs. Epstein worked their way cautiously back down the stairs to the theater, and met Mr. Celac in the small lobby. They found three seats together and ended up watching *Tarzan the Ape Man*, preceded by an episode of *The Little Rascals*, then *The Music Box* with Laurel and Hardy, followed by *The Royal Family Of Broadway* with Fredric March.

By the end of the last film, the rough movements of the ship had ceased, and the passengers got out of their seats to find a steady deck.

As wonderful as the cessation of the storm was, the three realized that Deben, Petru, and Dragos would soon be on the prowl again. The ship was due in port on Thursday afternoon, in less than twenty-four hours. They vowed to stay together for the rest of the evening, and to maintain their vigilance the next day when there would be increased activity and confusion in preparation for docking.

The ship's fog horn had been sounding frequently during the last movie, and when they made their way back to the upper deck and dining room, they could see why. Through every window and porthole, only grey could be seen. The movement and motion of the ship seemed minimal, and Irina and Mrs. Epstein knew that Captain Stanford was maintaining *moderate speed*. Irina explained the term to Mr. Celac and the risky behavior of some of the other captains to whom only speed and a schedule mattered. He shuddered at the thought of speeding through fog this dense without knowing if the ship could stop in time before hitting either another ship or an iceberg.

Mrs. Epstein taught Irina the phrase, *pea soup fog* which she found very humorous and memorable.

When they reached the dining room, they spotted Christina and Mariana and joined them for dinner. After so many light meals during the storm the passengers were ravenous, and anticipating this, the ship's cooks had prepared hearty meals. The group ordered roast beef, Yorkshire Pudding, mashed potatoes with gravy, and fresh petite peas with pearl onions. Fresh horseradish and pickled peaches were on the side, and gooseberry tarts with ice cream and a cup of coffee completed the meal.

Too stuffed to move, the five lingered over their coffee discussing the ship's slow speed and wondering when it would actually dock in New York.

As if reading their minds, a ship's officer at the head of the dining room struck a small gong and requested everyone's attention. Because of the storm and the fog, they were delayed by at least twelve hours and would not be docking until Friday. The exact time could not be determined as yet, but they would make another announcement in the morning.

Christina and Mariana were ecstatic to be able to spend another day on this floating palace, and begged Irina to go swimming with them Thursday afternoon. After some hesitation, Irina agreed. She had not spent much time with her friends, and after she defected, she might not see them again. Mrs. Epstein, who had been having the ship's photographer take pictures of Irina and the dancing classes, thought it would be another great photographic opportunity.

There were hand rails around the pool, and behind

them were small round tables and padded chairs. Light food service made lounging around the pool very pleasant, and art deco tropical murals on the walls added an exotic ambiance.

Mrs. Epstein declined to go swimming herself, but said she would love to sit at a table with a glass of iced tea and observe the swimmers. Irina felt more comfortable knowing she would be there, and began to feel excited about the next day's activities.

Mr. Celac reminded the dancers that the troupe had agreed to put on a performance for the passengers, and although they had to postpone it because of the weather, they would have time Thursday evening with a rehearsal right before it. He would set everything up with Mr. Jones, and let the troupe members know the particulars tomorrow.

At 8:00, the five decided to go to the last two movies, *Speak Easily* and *Scarface, The Shame Of A Nation*. *Speak Easily* starred Buster Keaton, Jimmy Durante, and Hedda Hopper. It was about a show troupe on their way to Broadway. The theme was close to home, and they laughed heartily and wondered if the New York City that they would dock at on Friday would be anything like that in the movie.

The Romanians had heard about gangsters, and were anxious to see what they were like. *Scarface, The Shame Of A Nation* had a reputation for being shocking and graphic, and was shown last, at a time when most children would be in bed. It starred Paul Muni, Ann Dvorak, George Raft, and Boris Karloff. The movie was violent and unsettling, and Irina saw many commonalities with members of the Iron Guard.

Irina felt a rush of butterflies in her stomach at the thought of her upcoming defection, and wondered if her aunt and uncle would be there to help her. She had come so far, and soon her future would be determined. Most of the time she felt cautiously optimistic, but other times she felt the Iron Guard was too big and powerful, and that she would be crushed by them like an egg by a hammer.

Mr. Celac accompanied the dancers to their room, then Mrs. Epstein to hers. Thursday would be a busy day, and Friday and Saturday even more so. Irina was safe so far, but he had a feeling her troubles were not over yet. He renewed his vow to himself to keep her safe, although he knew his responsibilities to the troupe and tour would demand much of his attention.

Chapter Forty
Thursday, 8/18/32 - The Worst Detour

As was becoming their habit, the three South Dakota travelers reviewed their progress and destination for the day over breakfast. Josif crossed off Wednesday. "We have kept schedule, and day after tomorrow we will be in New York City. We have had problems, but we are okay. We must continue slow and steady, and all will be well."

"Of course, Josif."

"Sure, Joe."

"We have only one city, Scranton, and that is where we stop for night. On Friday we have only about one hundred and fifty miles. We stop about fifty miles from New York City, so on Saturday we can arrive early and make final plans."

"You have planned well, Josif. I feel confident." Izabella said, smiling.

"Yeah, we're doin' great considerin' what we've been through," August added. "But say, Joe, after Scranton, we only have a total of two hundred miles. Whaddaya think of gettin' in to New York on Friday night?"

"I think of that also. If is early in day, maybe. But I do not want to enter New York at night. Is too big. We do not want to get lost in city bigger than Joliet or Cleveland."

August nodded in agreement. "You got that right. I've enjoyed about as much of drivin' through big cities as I can stand. Well, let's finish up our coffee and hit the road, I'm gettin' excited."

They resumed their places in the Hudson, with Josif driving. August spread the Pennsylvania map out on his lap, and folded it with Route 6 highlighted. "Looks like more of the same, only more squirrelly." He grabbed his guitar. "I'll play some; that'll make time fly by."

Josif took a firm grip on the steering wheel, peered through the round view hole in the windshield, and resumed their trip.

The road had not improved overnight, and they bounced and vibrated, swerved and braked, and avoided log and coal trucks as much as possible. They maintained a fairly steady thirty-five miles per hour.

Route 6 followed the Allegheny River for awhile, and they all admired its beauty as well as views from hill crests over the lush green valleys. Railroad trestles crossed rivers and valleys, and many hillsides showed signs of logging.

They reached Mansfield around noon and stopped for dinner. August was thrilled to see sauerkraut and sausages on the menu, and ordered that. Josif and Izabella tried the Thursday special of corned beef hash with two fried eggs on top. The portions were large, and when Izabella couldn't finish hers, August offered to help out. He polished off her portion, and exerted great control in not picking up the plate and licking it. "That sure was good. I ain't never had that before. If I see that on a menu again, I'm sure gonna order it."

August built and lit a cigarette, and they finished their coffee amiably, recalling some of the sights they'd seen that day.

When they left the café, they were somewhat dismayed to see that the sky had clouded over. Josif drove them to a gas station, where they filled up and let the attendant have a go at the windshield.

"Well, sir, this crap seems to have fused to your window. My cleaning solution ain't even touchin' it. I think you may have to soak some towels in ammonia and lay them across those windows overnight, or maybe for a couple days." He looked intently at Josif.

"Oh."

"Say, I recognized the bug parts and grass on your window, and some pieces of what appear to be a map, but it also looks and smells like you got some sauerkraut on there. How'd that happen?"

"Seem like good idea then. We had no other liquids to clean window."

"Sure, well I can see that, I guess. Just don't go pouring no syrup or honey on there!" The attendant guffawed and slapped his thigh at his joke. Josif and August didn't appreciate the humor, but couldn't think of an appropriate rejoinder, and leveled solemn, unblinking stares at him until he stopped laughing.

With as much dignity as he could muster, Josif paid the bill of two dollars and twenty-five cents, and they got back in the car and headed east on Route 6 again.

The clouds had thickened, and they could see the slanting grey signs of rain ahead. They met the rain in about twenty miles, and were through it in another twenty.

The roads were now muddy, the potholes full, and the grass on the shoulders slick. The wipers had little effect on the windshield situation, but at least they had not caused more smearing, and Josif still had fairly good visibility. He felt his neck and shoulder muscles tightening up again as he struggled with the driving conditions, and felt full responsibility for their mission.

They passed through Towanda, and August announced, "Scranton, sixty miles. Another couple hours. Want me to take the wheel for awhile, Joe?"

"That okay. I drive more, my hands clamped to wheel."

319

The road twisted and turned even more than usual, and flowed up and over an unending succession of hills.

As Josif rounded one hill, he saw a line of red tail lights ahead, and something large lying across the road. Josif slowed the car, August put down his guitar, and Izabella leaned forward and peered around August at the scene ahead.

As they got closer, they could see that a logging truck had tipped over. The truck's rear wheels were hanging off the road and out over the ravine which the road had been following. Logs were strewn everywhere. They had covered the road, and some had tipped off the shoulder and were jutting into the air, like huge accusing fingers. The driver appeared to be okay, and was walking around the truck inspecting the damage. The road was completely blocked.

Josif brought the creeping Hudson to a full stop, and the three regarded the accident. There was absolutely no way around it. There were no tow vehicles there yet, and even if there were, this accident would take some time to clean up. Josif felt weak. "This is not good," he said quietly.

August picked up the map and studied it closely. "What's the last town sign we passed?"

"I cannot say it, but I would know it if I saw it on map," Izabella said.

August showed Izabella the appropriate section of map, and after a few minutes she put her finger on Jenkinsville and handed the map back to August. He held the map up and traced a road with his finger; showing it to Josif. "All we have to do is turn around and go back to that Jenkinsville sign. There's a road from there that connects to another road that connects with Route 6 about five miles down the road from here, at Randall Hill."

Josif studied the map. "Is not what I would do if I had choice. This road is bad, and those roads are more small than this one. I do not like it, but we have no choice. I will turn car around."

Josif turned the car around very carefully on the narrow road. He had August get out to spot the rear wheels to be sure he didn't back up onto the slick grass. When they were facing west, August got back in the car, and they retraced their tracks.

Izabella felt strange heading in the wrong direction, and could see that Josif was even more tense. Even August seemed more quiet than usual and was not playing his guitar. After what seemed like twenty miles but was really only five, they spotted the Jenkinsville sign, and Josif reluctantly turned left onto the narrow, rocky road.

This road was less used than Route 6, so had fewer potholes and washboards. However, it also had more large rocks and an almost non-existent shoulder.

Izabella prayed fervently to herself in the back seat with her eyes closed. Josif forged ahead at about fifteen miles per hour, and August kept his eyes wide open, scanning the road ahead for signs or problems. Finally they reached Jenkinsville, which amounted to a combination general store and post office. A sign in the window said, "Closed."

August pointed to the map. "Okay, now we take this road to that road, to Randall Hill. All we have to do now is find where this first road is."

They drove around the area for a bit and identified three possible roads as the right one. There were apparently no people in Jenkinsville and no one to ask, so they debated and finally picked the road which most seemed to be going in the right direction.

Josif felt like he was traveling into a nightmare from which he couldn't awaken. He had few choices, he was in a strange place, they were probably going to get lost, the road was treacherous, they had no food, it was getting late, and he was responsible. He could think of no choice but to keep going forward.

After about three miles of bouncing over large, sharp rocks, they heard the inevitable *wop, wop, wop* of a flat tire.

Josif stopped the car, collected his tools, and jacked up the car. August built a cigarette and lit it, then he wrestled off the wheel, and they set about finding and repairing the hole. When they had finished pumping up the tire, they put everything away and got back in the car.

It was getting dark and cool, and they could feel the moisture in the air. With much more confidence than he felt, Josif smiled at his passengers. "Well, let's go. When we get back on Route 6 we will stop at first hotel we see, and have nice hot supper and warm bed.

"Of course, Josif."

"You bet, Joe."

They pushed on, searching the side of the road for signs or an adjoining road. The headlights were dim because of their yellow coating, and deepening twilight made visibility very poor.

Suddenly Josif saw movement as an animal darted in front of the car. He slammed on the brakes.

There were two almost simultaneous dull thumps, one from the front of the car, and one from the back seat.

There was silence for a moment while they each tried to figure out what had happened. Then suddenly, they all knew.

"Peeuoowee!" August exclaimed. "That wasn't no jack rabbit we hit." He sniffed the air from the back seat. "Smells like the dang crock cracked, too."

Josif looked at Izabella. She was huddled in the far corner with her shawl over her nose and mouth. Her eyes were not smiling.

They all got out of the car. Josif and August went back to the trunk. Josif fished a flashlight out of his tool box; August grabbed a shovel and looked under the car while Josif illuminated the area with the flashlight. He scooped up the dead skunk and tossed it down the steep slope at the edge of the road. "Best not to run over them things twice," he said.

Then they opened the back door by the crock. The strong odor of sauerkraut greeted them. August grabbed the crock and hauled it out of the car. "I'll never hear the end of this. Fritz said this would happen."

August's sleeping bag which had been wrapped around the crock's base had soaked up most of the juice. He took it out of the car and wrung it out as best he could, then draped it over large rocks at the side of the road. He mopped up the small puddle on the floor with the map of Iowa.

Izabella walked down the road about fifteen feet. It was totally dark now, and the moon was obscured by clouds. The air was cold and damp. The Hudson stunk of skunk and sauerkraut, and when August lit the lantern, she could see that the driver's side tire was low. They were cold and hungry and would probably sleep in the car, which was on a slight incline. They might be lost. They were in the middle of a road. Irina needed them.

She felt like flinging herself on the ground and weeping in frustration. She wanted to blame Josif or August, but it was no one's fault. She took a few deep breaths, wrapped her shawl more tightly around her, re-tied her headscarf more snugly, and headed back to the car.

Josif and August were discussing the pros and cons of continuing on that night. The pros of trying to make up time, and possibly making it to a hotel, were trumped by the con of possibly driving off the road due to the dim headlights and no moonlight.

They decided to build two fires, one in front and one in back of the car, to alert any other vehicles which might approach. If they could clear enough rocks off the ground by a fire, they could sleep there using all their blankets and warm clothes. Izabella pointed out the low tire, and they decided to fix it in the morning. Josif and August set about breaking small,

dead branches from the undersides of trees, and gathering any large dry limbs they could find. They each collected a good-sized pile of wood, and gathered up dry pine needles under a large white pine for starting their fires. Soon they each had a good fire going on the road.

Izabella opened the car doors to let it air out, then searched through the food boxes for anything they could eat for supper. She thanked God that she had thought to refill their water jug at the last hotel, and grabbed the coffee pot and coffee.

Josif and August met at the trunk-end fire, and Izabella spread a blanket on a nearby flat rock and began to gather their supper. Josif prepared the coffee pot and rested it on two large branches which were nestled in the fire. When he returned to the blanket, Izabella had laid out soda crackers, plum jam, a half pound of somewhat dried out baloney, about a third of a fruit cake, a bag of venison jerky, a partial small jar of pickled eggs, and some hard candy. Plates, silverware, their coffee mugs, and a jar of sugar were laid out on the side.

She stood back and gestured at the blanket with a

graceful curtsy. "I present you supper at the Sharp Rock Road Hotel. All who fix tires and drive go first."

They filled their plates as best they could, and stood around the fire eating. When the coffee was done, their spirits lifted considerably, and they were able to warm their hands on their hot mugs.

As Izabella was tidying up after supper, Josif and August discussed the flat tire. "How many patches we have left?" Josif asked August.

"I'm not sure, maybe only one or two."

"Maybe is time for new tube. Uncle Jon pack one in box of tools."

Josif ambled over to the box and rummaged around. He returned with a Mason jar of clear liquid, with a piece of paper tied around it. He opened the jar and smelled it, smiled, and slid out the note. "Is from Uncle Jon. Jar was wrapped in tube. He say if we need new tube, we may need jar of *tuica*. He is man who knows about fixing tires!"

He opened the jar, took a deep swig, and handed it to Izabella. "Have some; it will warm your toes." Izabella complied, and took a hearty swallow. She handed the jar back to Josif, who handed it to August. "Have *tuica*, August. After this trip I make you official Romanian!"

"Thanks, Joe." He took the jar, and took a large swallow, then wiped his mouth with the back of his hand. "So far bein' an official Romanian is okay with me! My toes needed a good warmin'!"

They passed the jar around again, and August went to the front of the car and came back with his guitar. "You folks have heard some of this, but you ain't heard all the verses put together. As you know, I bin working on my gangster fight song. I'm gonna call it, *The Dakota Six*." He blew on his fingers, rubbed his hands together, cleared his throat, and began.

"I'm August the Yodelin' Cowboy,
and I'm here to tell ya the tale,
of the weak and the strong and who's in the wrong.
Of the Dakota Six who jumped into the mix,
      and sent some gangsters to jail.
Yeah, we sent some gangsters to jail.
It was out in southeastern Dakota that justice made its stand.
I-talians from Chicago, Greeks from Sioux City.
What they had planned sure wasn't pretty.
No, what they had planned sure wasn't pretty.

Our friend, Arnold got left a half section;
      and was farmin' it like a man.
His fields were dry and the crops were small,
      but his buildings were tight and his livestock were full.
He was doin' his best to pull them all through.
Yeah, he was doing his best to pull them all through.

His farm had belonged to his sister,
      her husband had ties to the mob,
      who had brought a huge still from Chicago,
      and had killed, burned, tortured, and robbed.
But the mob ended up killing each other,
      and we thought the whole thing was done.
We went back to our farms and the things that we knew:
      not enough rain and bills that were due.
Yeah, not enough rain and bills that were due.
Yode a lay dee, yode a lay dee, yode a lay dee hoooooo.
Yode a lay dee, yode a lay dee, yode a lay dee heeeeee.

Then Primo Moretti came looking for treasure.
Came looking for loot and his dead gangster brother.
'Til the Greeks arrived and he had to take cover,
      deep in the barn away from his foe.

Then neighbors and cops showed up at the farm,
     and in with Moretti Zeke, had to go.
Yeah, in with Moretti, Zeke had to go.

The two mobs hated each other,
     but hated the law even worse.
They tried to break out together,
     but then they met their curse.
Six men were there to stop them.
Six heroes strong and true.
They were rock hard and tough,
     they wouldn't take no guff,
     and they sent the gangsters to jail.
Yeah, they sent the gangsters to jail.

There was August, Fritz ,and Gerhard, Arnold, Josif and Jon.
Neighbors all, we heard the call, and came to the aid of our
     friend.
We whupped the mob good, it didn't take long.
They didn't stand a chance; they were all in the wrong.
They thought they were big 'til we threw 'em to the pigs.
Yeah, they thought they were big 'till we threw 'em to the pigs.
Yode a lay dee, yode a lay dee, yode a lay dee hoooooo.
Yode a lay dee, yode a lay dee, yode a lay dee heeeeee.

Sheriff Bennard and his deputy, Harold, had some help,
     they weren't over a barrel.
Tommy guns blazed and pistols were firing.
The six stood strong, they didn't flinch.
They didn't give ground, not even an inch.
No, they didn't give ground, not even an inch.

The gangsters are out of the hospital now;
     they're all of 'em back in the hold.

Two bodies were found in the silage pit,
      and lots of jewelry and gold.
The six are back to farmin' again,
      and bein' just ordinary men.
They'll tend to their crops and they'll watch over their land.
And they'll always be ready to lend a hand.
Yeah, they'll always be ready to lend a hand.

There's some are said to be brave.
There's some are said to be true.
Some are called heroes and compared to Tom Mix.
But I'll tell you this 'bout the Dakota Six,
      there may be some that're just as good,
      but there ain't none any better.
Yeah, there may be some that're just as good,
      but there sure ain't none any better.
Yode a lay dee, yode a lay dee, yode a lay dee hoooooo.
Yode a lay dee, yode a lay dee, yode a lay dee heeeeee."

Josif looked at August in amazement. "That was most beautiful song I ever hear! I am proud you are my neighbor, my friend." He patted August on the shoulder and handed him the jar.

August wiped his eyes and took a drink. "I just love that last line. I think I made it up, but I may have heard it somewhere. Mrs. Horsefall was always makin' us read stuff like that." He looked soulfully at Josif and handed the jar back. "You're a good neighbor too. You and Jon run a tight ship, and you fight like a coupla badgers."

Josif tipped the jar up. He handed it back to August. "I save last sip for you, my good friend, August." He drained it and handed the empty back to Josif who stuck it in the food box. He faced August and regarded him seriously. "We may have to fight Iron Guard in New York City. I know you will do well."

"By heck I hope you're right, Joe. I'm sure ready for a good fight."

Izabella joined them. "Is time for sleep. What do you think is best?"

They added more wood to the fires, and looked at the ground. It was hard and wet with numerous small and large jutting flat rocks, many with sharp edges and points. Clearing sleeping areas would be a lot of work even though it would be nice to sleep by a fire. The car would be softer and drier, but it had strong smells of skunk and sauerkraut, and they would have to sleep sitting up.

The decision was made when it began to rain. Izabella got in the back seat and Josif sat in the driver's seat, with August in the passenger's seat. They each had a blanket pulled up over their noses, and eventually with the sound of the rain on the car roof and their meal and *tuica* in them, they relaxed enough to fitfully sleep.

Chapter Forty-One
Thursday, 8/18/32 - Drowning Attempt

The sound of the ship's engines and propellers, and the ship's forward movement, told the awakening passengers that they had resumed their normal speed. At breakfast an officer announced that the estimated time of arrival of the ship in New York would be mid-morning Friday. Although the skies were overcast now, weather reports were hopeful for sunny skies in New York over the weekend.

Irina, Christina, Mariana, as well as Mrs. Epstein and Mr. Celac, all breakfasted together. Today would be the last English and dancing classes, and tonight the troupe would put on an abbreviated performance for the passengers at 9:00. The troupe would have a dress rehearsal immediately preceding, at 8:00PM.

With her plans to go swimming after lunch, Irina would have a full day. She was grateful for any distraction which would keep her from worrying. She hardly dared to think of it, but if all went well, she would be with her Uncle Josif and Aunt Izabella the day after tomorrow, and free of the Iron Guard.

Or if they had not received her letter, or had not been able to come for her, she would be fleeing the Iron Guard in a strange city, not knowing where to go or to whom to turn. She knew Mrs. Epstein would help her, but her Jewish friends in Romania had died a horrible death at the hands of the Iron Guard, and she did not want to bring even the slightest risk to Mrs. Epstein. She maintained a cheery smile as the group finished their coffee, and then headed to the Solarium.

Mr. Jones focused the English class on names of kitchen items, sports, and animals. He ended the class with the group singing, *Old Mac Dougal Had A Farm*. As usual, the class ended with everyone feeling carefree and relaxed.

There were no untoward incidents in the dance class, and the passengers were able to learn a satisfyingly difficult dance, and to perform it with grace and joy. They hugged or shook hands with all the dancers after the class, and slowly filed out into the passageways.

Irina and Mrs. Epstein were joined by Mr. Celac, Christina, and Mariana for elevenses, after which they all strolled around the decks together enjoying the view from the upper decks, and spotting a group of dolphins keeping pace with the ship.

At 1:00 they had lunch, and at 2:30 they headed for the swimming pool. Mr. Celac excused himself to attend to arrangements for the troupe's disembarkation on Friday. Mrs. Epstein asked him to send the ship's photographer down to the pool, as had been previously arranged, and found a seat at one of the café tables near the railing at the pool.

Christina and Mariana showed Irina where to get a suit and bathing cap, and they took the items into the changing rooms where they donned the suits and caps and hung their clothes in a locker.

Mr. Celac made his way to the ship's radio room to send messages to the hotel and theater in New York about their delay. On his way, he ran into Deben and informed him of the scheduled rehearsal and performance and asked him to spread the word. With thick sarcasm, Deben said that nothing would make him happier and strolled off around the corner. There he stopped and turned around. He approached the corner as closely as he could without being seen, and listened intently for Mr. Celac's footsteps to move away. When he heard him proceed down the passageway, he peeked out and saw where he turned. He silently left the corner and followed Mr. Celac hoping he would somehow reveal where Irina was.

Deben was rewarded when Mr. Celac encountered a steward and asked him to inform the ship's photographer that Mrs. Epstein was waiting for him at the pool. Deben reversed course and hurried to the men's entrance to the changing rooms at the pool. He quickly formulated a plan and hoped the pool would be crowded enough to conceal his actions. He chuckled to himself in glee. He still had a chance, a good chance, of getting rid of Irina.

Deben changed into a swimming outfit quickly, and signed out a mask and snorkel. He put on his mask and cautiously peered around the doorway into the pool area. As he had hoped, the seventy-five-foot long pool was fairly full. He spotted Mrs. Epstein at a table and followed her gaze to Irina and her friends who were in the water and hanging on to the side of the pool at the three-foot depth. Mariana was demonstrating the dog paddle to Irina.

Deben walked quickly to the pool and slipped in. He ducked under the water and swam close to the women, keeping an eye on Irina's feet from under the water. Now she was hanging onto the edge of the pool with both hands, and practicing the flutter kick behind her. Mariana and Christina were on either side of her doing the same.

He swam past them to a cluster of bathers, and surfaced on their periphery. Now the three had pushed away from the edge of the pool and were dog paddling across the width of the pool together, still at the three-foot depth, too shallow to carry out his plan. Deben was determined not to be recognized, so he kept his mask and snorkel in place and swam around with his face under the water for what seemed like forever while Irina and her friends frolicked in the shallow end of the pool.

Finally he saw that they had moved into slightly deeper water and were now swimming at an angle that would take them to the eight foot depth. They had moved apart somewhat. He snorkeled to within ten feet of them, then dove underwater and swam beneath them.

Deben spotted Irina's feet and grabbed her ankles, pulling her down. She tried to kick and struggle, but he tucked her legs under his arms and pulled downward. He could hear her calling for help under the water.

Suddenly the water above him exploded with splashing and dozens of legs and arms. He felt numerous strong hands grab Irina and kick and push off from him as they wrenched Irina away and lifted her out of the water. Fearful of being identified as the one trying to harm Irina, he struggled to hold his breath and swam to the other side of the pool where he surfaced.

With disgust, he saw that Irina was sitting on the edge of the pool, coughing into a towel, with almost every male in the pool from age fourteen to eighty either in the water at her feet or behind her looking concerned. She dried her face and looked up smiling at her rescuers who beamed back at her.

There was a sudden flash of light, and Deben knew that the ship's photographer had arrived. He swam back to the shallow end and got out of the pool and into the changing room as quickly as possible while most people's attention was still on Irina. His left cheek and temple hurt, and his right shoulder was sore. There was a scratch across his nose. He was livid with rage and self doubt.

Mr. Celac joined the four women for dinner at 6:00PM. He had heard rumors of a near drowning of one of the Romanian dancers, and was relieved to see that Irina was alright. She related the incident to him and said that someone had grabbed her legs and pulled her down. She had not seen who it was, and did not mention any names in front of Christina or Mariana. Mr. Celac looked at Irina and Mrs. Epstein, and casually mentioned that Deben had also had a close call and had tripped over an unattended child and fallen down several stairs. He had bruises on his left cheek and temple, a sore shoulder, and a scratch across his nose. No one looked overly concerned except to en-quire if he would be fit to dance.

"Yes," Mr. Celac replied smiling. "Although the dance director does not want him to do any lifts tonight if his shoulder is going to be in top condition for Saturday." He translated for Mrs. Epstein and they all exchanged looks of pleased relief.

Deben showed up for the dress rehearsal with a heavy application of stage make-up over bruises on his forehead, cheek, nose, and around his left eye which appeared swol-len. His movements were stiff and he handled Irina rough-ly refusing to make eye contact, let alone smile.

The dance director commiserated with his injuries, but insisted he dance with his usual grace, and that he smile during the actual performance. Deben ignored him, and Petru and Dragos laughed out loud. The other dancers looked very uncomfortable and began to realize the extent of Deben's decay.

The performance was well received by the passengers although Deben's performance was lackluster, and he con-tinued not to make eye contact with Irina. Applause for him was tepid during the final bows, but Irina received a standing ovation. The photographer got several fine shots.

The women dancers returned to their rooms en masse and Irina and her friends quickly entered theirs. Irina promptly locked the door.

Christina looked at her. "It is clear Deben is after you.

Everyone knows he and his friends Petru and Dragos are in love with the Iron Guard." She paused and looked at Mariana and back to Irina. "Are you planning to defect?" she whispered.

Irina looked at her friends. "If I were planning such a thing, I would not tell my best friends. Such knowledge could get them in trouble." She took their hands and smiled at them. "I would tell my friends that whatever happens in life, and wherever I go, they will always be with me in my heart."

Christina and Mariana had their answer and hugged Irina and wept, knowing that soon they would see her no more.

Chapter Forty-Two
Friday, 8/19/32 - Approaching the City

The South Dakota group awoke to an overcast sky. Their necks and backs were sore, and they felt stiff. Josif and August had slight headaches. They opened the car door and eased out into the day. August stretched, hawked, and spat, and built and lit a cigarette. Josif stirred the coals and added more wood. Izabella prepared the coffeepot and brought it over. When the coffee was ready, they stood around the fire drinking coffee and chewing on venison jerky.

Finally Josif and August felt warm and limber enough for the tire job. They had decided to use one of their last patches instead of changing the tube, as they still had many sharp rocks to contend with before getting back on a main road, and there was no point in risking the new tube. Josif gathered the tools and a patch, and August prepared another cigarette. They followed their usual routine and were finished quickly.

They were lowering the car with the jack when they were startled by the voice of a man who was approaching from the front of the car. The man wore brown pants, heavy laced-up work boots, a work shirt, suspenders, and cap. His face, neck, hands, and clothes had the permanent black stains of a coal miner. He was slightly short of breath as he worked his way around the rocks to them.

"I saw your fires last night. With it bein' so dark and

rainin', and with not much you could do about your situation anyway, I figured you'd keep 'till morning. How're you all doing?"

Josif felt a wave of relief wash over him. "We all okay. Only lost. We just fix flat tire."

"I figured you might have had a couple. I guess you were trying to get around that log truck wreck up on Route 6?"

"Yes, was not clear in Jenkinsville which road to take."

"Yeah, well, this'll work, but most folks avoid it 'cause of the shale. It's a real tire killer." He looked up from the tires, and stuck out his hand. "Hello, I'm Elmer Collier. Lived and worked here all my life."

Josif introduced Izabella and August. "We come from South Dakota. We have farms there. We on way to New York City, and yesterday we have some problems. Can you tell us how far to 6?"

"There's a better road about a hundred yards up this road. Take a right on it, and it'll lead you right to 6 in no time. Hopefully you won't have any more flats between here and there."

Elmer declined the offer of a ride back to the road. He nodded at the sleeping bag. "Boy, don't that smell of sauerkraut! I can smell it from here, even over the skunk smell." He looked at the cracked crock. "Say, if you folks don't have any need of that broken crock, I could clean it up, and use it to store chicken feed. That'd keep the critters out all right. Like I said, I'll walk, but if you drop that off at my car around that bend up there, I'll gladly take it off your hands." August thought it over, and reluctantly agreed. Izabella smiled inwardly, and looked at August sympathetically.

The only item not in the car and ready to go was August's sleeping bag. He and Josif each took an end of it and twisted it in opposite directions. A stream of dark grey water poured from it onto the road, but in spite of their twisting efforts the bag remained very damp. August was not sure where to stow it for the rest of the trip. It stunk, and he sensed that Izabella was not eager to have it near her.

Indeed, Izabella was reluctant to have the bag in the car near her dancing outfit, even though the outfit was well-wrapped in a box. She considered offering to bury August's sleeping bag, or of throwing it over the edge of the road, or of tying it to the outside of the trunk, or to the hood, or the roof.... Finally she looked at August with resignation, and mustering all the grace she could manage said, "Put bag where crock was. That spot already wet and smell."

They put out the fires and scattered the ashes. Then they got back in the car, rolled down the windows, and cautiously made their way down the road at about ten miles per hour, waving at Elmer as they passed him. They rounded a bend and saw Elmer's car parked on the side of a fairly decent road which their road abutted. A sign pointed to their right and said "Route 6, 5 miles." They pulled over by Elmer's car, and August hoisted out the broken crock. He patted it fondly and set it by Elmer's car. "I bin eatin' sauerkraut outta this crock all my life. I sure hate to see it go."

Josif put his hand on August's shoulder. "We know is hard to leave things behind. We leave many things in Romania."

"I suppose you did. Some things just can't be helped." He turned to Josif and brightened some. "Oh well, we'll lose a crock, but gain you a niece. This'll give her more room to sit."

"You are very kind, August," Izabella said, smiling at him.

They got back in the Hudson, followed the sign to Route 6, and were soon back on course. At the first café sign, they pulled in, eagerly anticipating a large breakfast.

Within seconds of entering the café, patrons turned to look, and many put their forks down and covered their noses. The waitress spoke to them from about five feet away. "Smells like the skunk won. You smell of wood smoke, too. You folks been campin'?"

"We not mean to," Josif replied.

"Well, I tell you what. It's warmin' up pretty good outside. How 'bout I set you folks up at a table on the back porch? No offense intended, but it just might be easier on the other customers."

The three tried to hold their heads up as they were escorted through the café and seated at a picnic table on the back porch. Corned beef hash and eggs were on the menu, and they all ordered that with sides of toast and coffee. The waitress left them a bell. "Just ring that if you need anything, and I'll be right out."

When she left, the three looked at each other sheepishly. "I guess these folks never met anyone from South Dakota before," August said with a twinkle in his eye.

Josif and Izabella regarded him seriously for a moment, and then they all broke out in uncontrolled laughter.

Josif joined in. "Yes, people from South Dakota look and smell strong!"

Izabella spoke through tears of laughter "Even the women it seems; we like to put on our skunk perfume in the morning. What a fine place to live!"

Their eyes watered, their faces turned red, August snorted, and whenever they calmed down enough to try to speak, they all lost control and began laughing again. They weren't able to stop until the waitress returned with their breakfasts. Then they clamped their teeth together, froze their faces, and looked intently at their food, trying to stifle more laughter. It was the smell and taste of breakfast that finally brought them under control, and they tucked in and ate with relieved determination.

When they had finished, August built and lit a cigarette, and Josif pulled the schedule and pencil stub out of his pocket "I think we are about twenty-five miles from Scranton now. Today we drive to Montgomery, New York. Tomorrow we enter New York City, and tomorrow night we rescue Irina. Tonight we will go over our plan and try to think of anything we did not consider. The time is almost here. We must be more clever than the Iron Guard."

Josif paid the bill of one dollar and seventy-five cents with a casualness which he did not feel, wondering if his dollar bill smelled like skunk, while August and Izabella waited outside. With a renewed sense of urgency and purpose, the three briskly left the café and returned to the Hudson. August volunteered to drive and Josif let him, welcoming the opportunity to reflect on their rescue plans.

Route 6 continued to follow ridges and the hilly contours of the land, until it wound its way south, down into northeast Scranton.

Scranton's roads were in need of constant repair due to their heavy traffic, and they encountered four detours on their way through the city. The three travelers felt experienced and confident as they tracked the detour signs and even found the abrupt northeast shift that 6 made, with only one U-turn.

Finally they left the Scranton area and followed Route 6 up to Carbondale. Signs of coal mining were everywhere, and they were frequently stuck crawling behind a slow-moving, heavily-laden coal truck going up hill, or hurriedly bouncing and bumping down a steep incline pressed by a fast-moving heavily-laden coal truck behind them.

The road frequently rose and fell with long, flowing sweeps around hills. The countryside was beautiful with hardwood forests, small glacial lakes, deep valleys with streams and rivers at the bottom, occasional waterfalls, and train trestles crossing wooded gorges.

They made fairly good time and around 2:30, they crossed the Delaware River into New York, near Port Jervis.

August spotted a gas station and they pulled in. They filled up with gas and returned from paying with two maps, New York and New Jersey.

While they were in the gas station office, the attendant had been working at the windshield. After about a half bottle of window cleaner and four rags, the attendant was red-faced and perspiring heavily. He had managed to slightly enlarge the view holes. Tracks of the cleaner were running off of the hood through dried mud. He looked up unhappily at Josif and August as they returned to the car.

"Normally I take pride in my work. I like to send cars out of here with bright, clear windows. But this window has got me beat. They don't even make glue this good. And how about this grass and paper and what looks like sauerkraut? What happened? Did you run into a swarm of flying skunks carrying grass, reading papers, and eating sauerkraut?" He guffawed at his joke and Josif and August, still unable to come up with a suitable retort, again clamped their mouths shut and glared at him until he stopped laughing.

"We thank you for trying," Josif said curtly.

"Well, that's my job, no matter how smelly or impossible." He gathered up his bottle of cleaner and rags and backed away from the car, then turned and went into the station.

"Boy, I'm sure gettin' tired of these smart-alecky gas station attendants," August said quietly to Josif. "If somethin' like what happened to us happened to them, they'd pro'bly pour oil and battery acid on the windsheild, or somethin' like that."

"That would be big mess!" Josif replied. "Much bigger mess than what we have. They would destroy their car."

"You got that right! Boy, are they dumb!" August said with satisfaction.

"They are idiots." Josif agreed.

They got back in the Hudson and pulled in at the next café they spotted for lunch. The Tri-State Café boasted home cooking and featured a Friday special of a fish basket and fries, with a milkshake, either chocolate or vanilla, for fifty-five cents. They chose a table by an open window and all ordered the special with chocolate shakes. Josif and Izabella were uncertain what *fries and shakes* were, but accepted August's assurances that they were "real American food, and almost as good as sauerkraut, but in a different way."

When their food arrived, it only took Josif and Izabella a few bites of the fish and fries and one big swallow of their milkshakes to agree. They were intrigued by the catsup and tartar sauce, and soon felt like real Americans as they dipped their fries in catsup and sucked on the straws in their shakes.

When they returned to the Hudson in the parking lot, they were pleased and somewhat surprised to see that they didn't have any flats.

August rolled a cigarette, lit it, and took a deep pull. "It's a good thing we don't have a flat. I'm so full right now, if I had to bend over and wrestle a tire, I might just puke up all over the car, and it shore don't need that. It looks plenty bad enough already."

The three regarded the car with fresh eyes. Traveling across farm country, the dust and mud layers had looked natural. And in the logging and coal country, the mud and rain-streaked look also blended.

But now, as they approached New York and the cities of the east coast, there were more shiny, clean cars in the parking lot. And none of them smelled like skunk, wood smoke, and sauerkraut. And none of them had lumpy, yellow windshields with bug parts, grass, paper bits, and sauerkraut stuck on them around two *portholes* for viewing. Not to mention the lumpy yellow headlights and random collection of insects from the northeast quadrant of America in the radiator, and the polka dot effect from the hail.

Josif looked at the Hudson and shook his head. "As Michael-Joseph would say, 'Car look like shit!'"

343

Izabella and August looked at Josif with astonishment, then burst out laughing. Izabella felt strengthened by hearing Josif evoke Michael-Joseph, and she fought back tears of pride, joy, and longing for her son.

"What we need's a good pump and bucket, and soap and rags." August said. "But where's a fella gonna find that around here?"

"I now decide what we do tonight." Josif said. "We do not go into city early. We find small hotel in Montgomery, just as we plan. We park in back and borrow bucket. Then August and I wash car while Izabella prepare clothes for tomorrow. We study map and make plans for how to find theater Irina will dance in, and where we can wait and change clothes. We clean car and ourselves. We plan, eat good meal, and sleep in good bed. Tomorrow we be ready."

* * *

Josif continued driving as they left Port Jervis, and they were amazed and delighted to discover that the roads in New York were macadam, and the car felt like it was floating compared to the bumps and jolts of driving on the average gravel road. The terrain in this part of New York was similar to that of Pennsylvania, and Josif actually began to enjoy the sweeping curves, hills, and dips, which he could travel at forty-five miles per hour.

August was holding his right arm out the window watching his hand oscillate again. He was making large movements with his hand in the increased wind speed, and trying to make the wind inflate his shirt sleeve. After a while he persuaded Josif to let him drive, and they arrived in Montgomery in about an hour.

They spotted a modest-looking hotel with a back area that looked suitable for car washing, and after inquiring at the desk about the loan of a bucket, and permission to wash the car out back, they got two adjacent rooms and set about their tasks.

Izabella opened the box with her dance outfit and hung it by an open window. She also got out her best dress and shoes, and Josif's best shirt, pants, vest, and shoes. She hung the clothes on hangers and hooked them on a curtain rod in front of another open window. In the bathroom she found paper hand towels, and she moistened one and wiped off Josif's and her shoes. Then she took a long hot shower and tried to wash off the grime and smells of the last few days.

Out back Josif and August were washing the car with water they had hauled from a spigot at the side of the hotel. They each had two rags, and they were sharing a bar of extra-strength lye soap which Grandma Wagner had sent along.

They lathered the soap as best they could and scrubbed away at the car. The ground around the Hudson turned a rich dark brown with its newly deposited soil. They picked as many bugs as possible out of the radiator and scrubbed the fenders and wheels. Then they hauled bucket after bucket of clean water and rinsed the car from top to bottom. They rinsed the rags, hung them on a bumper to dry, returned the bucket, and headed to their rooms for their own wash just as it was getting dark.

After a dinner of fried chicken, fried potatoes, summer squash, bread pudding, and coffee, the three met in August's room to study the maps and finalize plans. They made the excuse that Izabella had feminine things hanging all over the room, but in reality, they didn't want August's inevitable cigarette smoke to foul their marginally fresh clothing.

Each room had a table and two chairs, and Josif brought one over from Izabella's and his room, as well as the maps of New Jersey and New York. They all sat around the table and looked at the New York map. They would leave Route 6 tomorrow and travel down 9 West into New Jersey. There the road would follow the Hudson River to the

George Washington Memorial Bridge which they would cross into Manhattan.

The map had several enlargements of the city, and an especially large and well-labeled one of Manhattan. It indicated the theater district and showed Central Park and many other features of the city. A street named Broadway ran diagonally across the city from the George Washington Memorial Bridge to the southern end of Manhattan. Except at the southern end, the roads ran straight, either north and south, or east and west. It looked very logical, and easy to follow, especially since the east and west streets were all numbered consecutively.

Josif pointed to Central Park. "Here is where we wait. When we enter Manhattan, we buy newspaper. We park on side street, and walk to park for picnic." He pointed to a street on the map. "It look like 72nd Street go into park. We will park there. We buy food in park, sit on blanket, and study newspaper. When we find where Irina will be and what time performance is, we drive there early and look. Then we plan how to rescue her in detail. Now we think August and I sing and play to get guards to look at us while Izabella sneak in with dancers. Then she find Irina and they plan when to escape. When they run out, we all get in car, and hurry to police station where Irina will be safe, and Iron Guard stopped and sent home."

"That should work, Joe. And if they give us any trouble, we'll beat the living sh..." August paused and looked at Izabella. "Ah, cr.., ah manure! out of 'em. No offense, Miz Dacia."

"Of course not, August."

They visited a while longer, then Josif and Izabella returned to their room. They agreed to meet at 7:30 for breakfast.

Chapter Forty-Three
Friday, 8/19/32 - Disembarkation

Friday dawned with a clear sky. Sun glinted off gentle waves; there was a soft breeze smelling of salt water, and gulls swooped and dove and cried out that land was near.

The ship was a-buzz with activity as the passengers enjoyed a last hearty breakfast and scrambled to pack up all their belongings and to prepare for disembarking.

Irina and her friends had breakfasted with Mrs. Epstein and Mr. Celac; then the group had split up to go pack. They planned to meet on a forward deck when the announcement was made that New York was in view.

Irina was full of conflicting emotions. Her goal was near, and soon her fate would be decided. She longed to see her aunt and uncle, but didn't know if they would be able to find her.

She had given them a huge task, and she didn't know for sure if they had even gotten the letter or if they would recognize each other. Would they learn that the troupe would be performing for two days and come on Sunday instead of Saturday?

They had already fled Romania and found safety in America; was it selfish of her to ask them to put themselves at risk again? If they were not there, she would have to find a way to get to South Dakota by herself, providing she was able to escape the clutches of Deben and his friends of the Iron Guard.

347

Soon she would say good bye to Mrs. Epstein, something she dreaded, as they had become fast friends and endured much together. And tomorrow, with either success or failure, she would be saying good bye to her friends in the dance troupe for the last time. There was no going back, or changing of her mind. She would defect. She would stay strong and focused, and run for her life.

Her musings were interrupted by the voice of a steward going down the passageway calling out, "New York in view. New York in view!" The three stopped what they were doing and together hurried up to the forward end of the Promenade Deck.

There they found Mrs. Epstein, and Irina squeezed in next to her and took her arm. Christina and Mariana also found room at the rail near them. In the distance land could be seen, and gradually the shapes of many buildings and several skyscrapers came into view. Out of habit Mrs. Epstein taught Irina the words: skyscraper, Empire State Building, Chrysler Building, The Statue of Liberty, cars, buses, taxis, and subways.

Irina repeated the words several times, then looked at Mrs. Epstein with tears in her eyes. "To say good bye is hard. You are my good friend. I miss you."

Mrs. Epstein hugged her, then put her hands on her shoulders. "We will see each other again. I am coming to your performance tomorrow." She reached into her purse, and pulled out a small envelope. Inside was a gold locket on a gold chain. Mrs. Epstein opened the locket to reveal a small picture of herself. She closed it and fastened the chain around Irina's neck.

"I have many pictures of you with me from the ship's photographer. I will see that you get copies." She reached in her purse again and pulled out another envelope. She handed it to Irina. "Here is my address and telephone number. Please write to me wherever you are. If you write in Romanian I will find a translator. There is also some emergency money. Do not try to refuse it; I will feel better if I know you can have more choices."

Irina nodded and held the envelope close to her heart. Mrs. Epstein looked intently at Irina. "If by some circumstance you should not be on the ship when it returns to Romania, you will always be welcome at my home. Do you understand?"

Irina wiped away tears. Mrs. Epstein knew. Again this good woman was willing to risk her own safety for her. It was good to know she had a refuge, but the last thing she wanted was to bring harm to Mrs. Epstein or her family. She smiled at her friend. "Yes, I understand."

The ship's horn sounded, and they turned to watch *The Atlantia* steer to the north into Lower New York Bay. Gradually land came closer on both sides of the ship, then opened again in Upper New York Bay. Makeshift shacks were present wherever there was space between warehouses and other buildings, and the port bustled with activity.

But as the Statue of Liberty came into view, it captured everyone's attention. Irina felt a lump in her throat and squeezed Mrs. Epstein's arm. Lady Liberty looked so strong and certain. Others had found freedom and justice here and, God willing, so would she. She drank in every detail of the statue, clouds, and water, and knew that for the rest of her life she would cherish this memory.

Soon they cruised past Ellis Island and north up the Hudson. Numerous docks were crowded with other liners and freighters, and three tug boats approached to tie up to *The Atlantia* and pull her up to her berth on the west side of Manhattan.

Passengers were leaving the rail and turning to attend to their luggage. Mrs. Epstein looked at Irina. "Stay close to Mr. Celac and your friends. Call me if you have any problems. I will see you again soon. Do not be afraid, you have many friends."

349

Irina hugged her. "Thank you for being good friend. You help me very much. I will write to you." They left the rail and walked with Christina and Mariana back to the sleeping quarters where the dancers and Mrs. Epstein parted.

The next three hours were spent transitioning from the ship to the hotel. The troupe had to be collected and funneled through customs, then herded onto buses which took them to the Algonquin, an expensive hotel with an owner who supported performers, about ten blocks from Carnegie Hall.

Four dancers were assigned to each two-person room, and cots had been set up in the rooms to accommodate the extras. Irina, Christina, and Mariana were joined by Elena in their room, and soon the four women had unpacked, and their dance outfits were hanging from doors and hooks to air out and lose some of their packing wrinkles.

Mr. Celac sent his assistants around to each room to make sure that all were settled well, and to announce that they were to meet in the hotel's restaurant for a meal. Then they would be taken by bus to the theater for a non-dress rehearsal.

Irina felt safe. This close to a performance the troupe stayed together and was very busy. She didn't expect any trouble with Deben and his friends until Sunday after the final performance. That would be the most obvious time for her to defect. She hoped making her move on Saturday would give her an element of surprise.

Irina had no clear idea of how she would defect. She had not felt that she could confide in anyone, both for their safety and hers. During most performances in large cities, extra policeman were assigned to protect the wealthy patrons going to and from the theater. She imagined that she would run out of the theater, yelling the word *help* which Mrs. Epstein had taught her on their first day together.

She would find a policeman and run to him calling for help. If there were no policemen around, she would jump in a taxi and say "police station, hurry!" – another phrase Mrs. Epstein had taught her.

If her aunt and uncle were there, she would run to them, but only if she were not being chased by dangerous people. She would die herself before bringing harm to them. She hated to abandon the dance troupe, but Mariana was a fine dancer and knew Irina's dances. She would be a good substitute and even gain some fame after replacing *the defector*.

She made a mental note to tuck Mrs. Epstein's envelope into her dance outfit. When she ran, all she would be able to take with her would be what she was wearing.

Chapter Forty-Four
Saturday, 8/20/32 - Locating Irina

After a tense breakfast which they hardly remembered, Josif, Izabella, and August returned to the car for the last leg of their journey to rescue Irina from the Iron Guard. The car looked much less muddy, but the extra strength lye soap had left dull smudges where Josif and August had scrubbed it, and there was no shine whatsoever. The portholes of clear glass through the yellow bug varnish on the windshield looked like large eyes, and with the two yellow headlights, made the Hudson resemble a huge four-eyed bug. The effect was somewhat unsettling.

Josif drove as they left Montgomery and headed south along the Hudson River on 9 West. The roads were macadam again, and the driving was pleasant. Soon they passed from New York into New Jersey and continued through rolling hardwood forests of sumac, maple, elm, and ash to signs for the George Washington Memorial Bridge, and New York City.

With their first glimpse of the bridge, the three felt as if they were entering a different world. Its roadway appeared to be a tremendous height above the river, and looked like a tightrope. It was huge, graceful, bright, and shiny. Long sweeping reversed arches spanned the river, and silver cables connected the bridge to the arches, giving it a look of elegant strength. The bridge towers were open metalwork, bright, shiny, and modern, signaling one's entry into the wonders of New York City.

Most bridges were built of massive blocks of carved stone, or of combinations of wood, stone, and steel. They looked solid, dark, and strong, or as with the Brooklyn Bridge, reminiscent of a cathedral.

This bridge looked different. It definitely gave the message that times were changing, and good things were just around the corner.

As Josif steered the car onto the bridge, they passed a sign with its name, and "completed in 1931". After an initial, "Holy Hannah, would you look at that!", August had stared up at the cables and down at the water, clutching the arm rest. "Hang on everybody," he said. "We must be about two hundred feet above the water."

Josif and Izabella looked slightly uneasy as they regarded the river far below. Then they looked up at the bridge. "I never see such beautiful bridge," Josif mused.

"I wish we could show to children, and Aunt Magda and Uncle Jon," Izabella added.

"If I tried to tell Fritz, he'd call me a liar for sure," August said. He paused and thought a moment. "Grandma might believe me. Maybe we can find a postcard of it! That'd prove it!"

At the east end of the bridge, Josif followed signs to Broadway, then turned south toward Central Park as they had planned. The streets were wide and well-marked, and Josif felt fairly confident driving through the city in spite of a steady flow of traffic and multiple lanes.

Unlike the ultra-modern George Washington Memorial Bridge, the rest of New York was a combination of new and old. Most of the buildings were made of stone blocks, reminiscent of European architecture. Skyscrapers could be seen ahead, protruding high above the rest of the skyline, and these, like the bridge, signaled a new era and confidence in man's inevitable ability to prosper.

At ground level however, the poverty that the three had seen on their trip was still present. Down side streets laundry hung from fire escapes, kids and dogs played in the streets, and the usual make-shift shanties popped up in any empty lot or between buildings. Sanitation was not good, and litter piled up along fences and buildings.

Small groups of unemployed men lounged on steps or in doorways, their caps pulled low over their eyes as they studied the passersby. Numerous people had wheelbarrows or baskets with apples or other items for sale. Faces were gaunt, and eyes were watchful for any opportunity to make a dime.

At a stop light, a boy with a leather shoulder bag filled with newspapers approached the car window and yelled, "All the news that's fit to print! Get your paper. Only five cents a copy! Get your paper!"

August dug in his pocket and gave the boy a nickel for a newspaper. It was thick, and had more printing than pictures. It was called *The New York Times*. August held it up in triumph. "How do you like that? I bought a newspaper right from the car! Fritz'll never believe it."

"That is good," Josif said. "Now we go to Central Park and look in paper for Romanian Dance Ensemble." When the light changed, he pulled ahead and soon turned left on 72nd Street, parking about a block from the park, near 9th Avenue.

The three got out of the car and took the newspaper, the New York City map, two blankets, Josif's violin, and August's guitar. There was no food left to bring; they hoped there would be vendors in the park, or a store along the way.

They crossed into the park at the light and veered off to the left, looking for some shade and food. They soon found both, and while Izabella spread out blankets, Josif and August headed off to a nearby grouping of vendors' carts which were topped with red and orange umbrellas.

Izabella smoothed the blankets with her hands and arranged the instruments at one end. Then she picked up the newspaper and unfolded it. She glanced at Josif and August who were looking over the vendors' wares, wondering if she should wait until they returned to begin searching through the many pages. Seeing no particular reason to wait, she began leafing through the newspaper.

On the second page she abruptly stopped and stared at three pictures. Two of them showed people in Romanian folk dance outfits, and one was of a beautiful young woman in a bathing suit and cap, sitting on the edge of a swimming pool, surrounded by male swimmers. She looked familiar. Izabella stared closely at the photographs and then at the printing under the pictures. She saw the name Irina Tataranu mentioned several times and gasped in amazement, putting one hand to her mouth, and one to her heart. "I found her!" she called out to Josif, who was approaching with August.

Both men were carrying hot dogs and pop. When Josif heard her, he ran as fast as his open drinks would allow, set the food on the blanket and picked up the page with the pictures. He studied the picture and captions, then handed the page to August who had also arrived, set down his burdens, and was peering over Josif's shoulder. "What does printing say under pictures?"

August took the page and sat down. He cleared his throat and read the caption underneath the picture of the pretty girl in the bathing suit. '*Possible drowning attempt. Irina Tataranu, female star of the Romanian State Dance Ensemble, sits amongst her would-be saviors on board The Atlantia on Friday afternoon. The dancer reports someone grabbed her ankles and pulled her under while she was swimming with friends. Other swimmers came to her rescue, and she is fine for the performance tonight.*'

August looked up proudly. He had read most of the words well, and with minimal stumbling, but hadn't quite grasped the content; Josif and Izabella looked concerned.

"Read this one," Josif said, pointing at a picture of the troupe as a whole.

August cleared his throat again. '*Political unrest will not stop art. The Romanian State Dance Ensemble performing on board The Atlantia. The troupe is to perform in New York, Washington, D.C., and Baltimore. Their first U.S. appearance is to be held at Carnegie Hall, Saturday, August 20th, at 8:00PM.*'

"So at least we know we are in right place at right time," Josif said with relief.

"Yes!" exclaimed Izabella. "We are so near. She must be in the city now. We almost have her!" She looked at August. "What says under last picture?"

This was the picture of Mrs. Epstein giving Mr. Celac a $1,000 check for the Dance Ensemble aboard the bridge of *The Atlantia* with Capt. Stanford, Irina, and Deben.

August cleared his throat once more and read, with some difficulty. '*Renowned New York City philanthropist contributes to Romanian Dance Ensemble. Mrs. Epstein, a long-time supporter of the arts, presents Mr. Celac, manager of the Romanian State Dance Ensemble, with a donation of $1000 to help defray the costs of their international tour. 'In times of fear and insecurity, it is vital to dance and enjoy life all the more,' she told reporters. From left to right are: Capt. Arthur Stanford of The Atlantia, Irina Tataranu, Mrs. Epstein, Deben Ceascu, and Mr. Mihai Celac. Miss Tataranu and Mr. Ceascu are the lead dancers of the ensemble.*'

Josif sat back, visibly relieved, and Izabella had a look of concerned anticipation. August looked pleased, and took a hot dog and pop. Between mouthfuls he said, "Now that we know when and where she'll be, we just have to go and grab her. I sure hope there's a fight!"

Josif took a hot dog and drink, and handed them to Izabella, then took food for himself. "You may be right," he said. "But we must spend rest of day thinking and planning, and getting in position so there will not be one. We do not want women to be hurt."

"I suppose you're right," August replied, looking somewhat crestfallen.

For the next several hours the three looked at the map of the city, studied the pictures of Irina, determined where they would park the car to make a quick getaway, where the nearest police stations were, and how they would keep watch and get Izabella into the theater. With the excellent map, they didn't feel the need to drive to the theater beforehand.

They decided that they would eat dinner in a nearby café at 6:00, and that Izabella would change into her dance outfit in the ladies room after dinner. They would park near the stage entrance, and Izabella would sneak in with the others if possible. If not, she would walk in boldly, claiming that she danced with a New York Romanian dance group, and that it had been arranged for several of their members to be on hand for emergency fill-ins and translating as necessary. She would size up the situation and approach Irina when able to formulate a plan of escape.

Josif and August would stand across the street from the stage entrance playing their instruments, with August singing his original composition as well as standard cowboy and hillbilly songs. Josif would also sing Romanian songs with August accompanying him. They figured they would probably have to sing and play for about three hours.

"Two things I know for sure," Josif said. "We need to bring something to drink, and we better practice like hell."

August looked at Josif with wide eyes and grinned. "Atta boy, Joe," he said.

Chapter Forty-Five
The Plan Goes Forward

Josif and August moved about ten feet away from Izabella and the blankets, tuned their instruments, and after
a brief discussion began with *Red River Valley*. Both played
and August sang. Josif looked lean and dangerously handsome with his fine features, black hair, and mustache, his
cap pulled low over his dark eyes, and his sensual playing
of the violin in even such an old familiar ballad as this.

August was wearing his ten-gallon Tom Mix cowboy
hat, a red bandana, which he had just pulled out of his
pocket and tied around his neck, and his usual cowboy
boots. He looked very out of place in Central Park, but
also bigger, better looking, and more serious. His voice was
very pleasant, and he had a winning smile.

The pair sounded good together and were easy to look
at, and soon a small crowd had gathered. After each song,
some people would move on and toss some change in the
violin case, or at least give them an approving and thankful grin. More passersby would take their places and tap
their feet and clap their hands to the music, or close their
eyes and listen with blissful expressions on their faces.

Around 5:15 they stopped playing and packed up
their belongings. Their audience clapped and whistled,
and Josif and August felt a sense of pride and astonishment at the reception of their music. They grinned pri-

vately to each other as they scooped up the change and put it in their pockets.

"We do pretty good," Josif said quietly to August.

"Boy howdy!" he whispered back.

* * *

On the way out of the park, the three looked up at a tall, impressive, spired building with buttresses and balustrades reminiscent of Europe. Around its base was a wrought iron fence with dragons and other creatures. They all saw the name of the building at the same time. "The Dakota!" they said in unison.

"This very good sign," Josif said.

"Oh yes!" Izabella exclaimed. "It is sign from God. We will bring our Irina home, from Europe to South Dakota. It is clear, this is our fate!" She crossed herself and thanked God. A new expression of joyful determination replaced one of concern and anxiety.

August looked at the name placard and up at the magnificent structure. "Well that sure is spooky. If I didn't see it with my own eyes, I probably wouldn't believe it, especially if Fritz told me. But there it is, The Dakota!"

The three walked in almost reverent silence back to the car. Once there, they were faced with the next step in the plan: eating and getting Izabella into her outfit and into the theater. The Hudson still smelled distinctly of skunk, and a damp, sauerkraut-soaked and much-used sleeping bag. Izabella wondered if August would notice if she hauled it out of the back and flung it on the pavement. She was afraid he would.

They had noticed a small restaurant on the way to and from the park. They dropped off the blankets, map, newspaper, and instruments in the car and dug out the box from the pile on the seat which contained Izabella's dress and boots.

The three felt fairly calm during their dinner, in spite of the small knots in their stomachs, and ate their meal of grilled cheese sandwiches and chicken noodle soup with fairly relaxed conversation. It wasn't until Izabella emerged from the women's room in her dance outfit that the three really felt the immediacy of their mission. They paid the bill and walked briskly back to the car.

Izabella's clothes were wrinkled, but she really couldn't tell any more if they smelled or not. She suspected they might, and hoped walking in the open air would help with both problems.

Once in the car they plotted the course to Carnegie Hall and reviewed their plan to circle the hall first to locate the stage entrance, then drop Izabella off about a block away, before parking the car near the entrance. That way Izabella wouldn't be seen with them, and they could watch her as she approached her goal.

Their plan went well, and Josif was able to drop Izabella off and to park just around the corner from the stage entrance. He grabbed his violin case and bottle of pop, which he had purchased at the restaurant, and hurried out to the corner to watch Izabella approach through the steady stream of pedestrians.

She looked beautiful and vulnerable, and strong and determined, and Josif felt his heart swell with pride and love. She kept her face forward, but acknowledged Josif with her eyes as she passed by him and disappeared into the door marked "Stage Entrance".

Josif turned back impatiently to see what was keeping August and was astounded to see him shoving his suitcase back onto the seat while dressed not only in his cowboy hat, red neckerchief, and boots, but also in a large pair of sheepskin chaps and shiny spurs. He grabbed his guitar and sauntered toward Josif, spurs jingling.

"How do ya like this outfit, Joe? I got it in Sioux Falls.

Ain't it a dandy? We should really make some money now!"

"It look like you have sheeps tied to legs. I hope no sheep dogs loose around here."

"Shit, Joe, I bet these New Yorkers ain't never even seen a sheep; I'm really gonna show 'em somethin'.'"

Remember, we are here to save Irina, and now Izabella. That is most important. Can run in those?"

"Hell yes, Joe. Us cowboys can do everything in these. We're practically born in 'em."

"I never see anyone else wear them."

"Times are tough, Joe. Not everyone can afford 'em now. But everyone sure would be wearin' 'em if they could."

"Maybe, but now we need to set up across from stage entrance and keep watch on door, ready to save women."

"Right, Joe. I'm ready."

The two crossed West 56th Street, got out their instruments, consulted briefly, and began with *Red Wing*.

Chapter Forty-Six
Preparations for the Performance

Saturday morning Irina awoke with butterflies in her stomach. She felt slightly ill, and knew that her nerves were getting the best of her. She felt overwhelmed and very small. She was going to defect from her country and abandon the dance troupe. She felt somewhat cowardly and ignoble.

But it was too late to stop now, and she knew only torture and death awaited her if she returned to Romania; Deben's and his friends' actions had convinced her of that. Besides, her only family might be here, and they may have put themselves in harm's way to come for her. She had mentioned Saturday, August 20th, in her letter, and this was the day. She hoped that they wouldn't learn of the two-day performance schedule and come on Sunday! So many worries, not to mention remembering the dance steps.

Irina moved through the rest of the day with a serious and focused look on her face. She kept close to her friends during meals and going to and from the buses, but kept her own counsel and conversed little.

During the dress rehearsal, Deben behaved appropriately, but Irina suspected he was saving his usual *accidental touching* for the performance when it would be the most thrilling for him. She dreaded ever having him touch her again, but saw no way to avoid it. She would dance in New York as promised, once. It had to be. Mariana would fill in tomorrow. She was a good dancer, and now she would become the star. There was some satisfaction in that.

After the rehearsal, the troupe was bussed back to the hotel for a rest and the evening meal. As Irina was exiting the bus, she saw Deben walk away from the group to talk to two men who seemed to be waiting near the door. The men's eyes were studying the dancers as they entered the hotel, and she noted that a brief look of predatory satisfaction crossed their faces when they saw her.

Iron Guard! her mind screamed. *They are here!*

She felt like running up the stairs to her room and locking the door, but controlled herself and stayed with her friends, locking the door when they were all inside. There she tried to take a nap, but it was futile. Her mind was racing, and she had to content herself by acknowledging that she was at least resting her body.

The performance was at 8:00PM, and the dancers ate a light meal at 5:30, arriving at the theater an hour later. As she departed the bus and approached the stage door entrance, she heard guitar and violin music from across the street. The violin playing sounded Romanian, but the song was strange to her, and the singer was certainly not Romanian. The bus blocked her view of them, and she put it out of her mind as she entered the theater. Now she must focus. Now everything was at stake.

Deben was also experiencing butterflies in his stomach. He knew that since he had not managed to dispose of Irina himself, he had to at least deliver her into the hands of the Iron Guard, or he would lose all face with Codreanu, and probably die himself.

The two men he had spoken to outside the hotel were local agents of the Iron Guard. All he had to do was to make sure that they captured Irina.

Deben was quite sure she would try to defect, but whether on Saturday or Sunday he did not know. He didn't think she had any help in America, except maybe that interfering Jewess, Mrs. Epstein, and he felt that between Petru, Dragos, himself, and the Iron Guard, they would be able to complete their mission.

The two men he had spoken to would be present both nights. They would be waiting in a car outside the stage entrance and looking for Deben and his friends to deliver Irina to them. They planned to have fun questioning Irina and then to help her be struck by a car in her wild attempt to flee. Deben could claim to Mr. Celac that Irina had run, he had tried to stop her, but that she had been captured by two unknown men in a car. Such things were common in big cities, he would claim. Such unfortunate things often happened. He would be properly upset, and blame it on local crime in New York City.

Deben filled Petru and Dragos in on the plan. He instructed them to keep an eye on Irina, especially when he was involved in one of his solos. They agreed, and all seemed ready.

Chapter Forty-Seven
Flight and Fight

Izabella had arrived just before the dance troupe, and explained to the theater staff that she had been sent by a local Romanian dance group to help the performers prepare and to translate if needed. This story was accepted, and she found an inconspicuous spot to wait where she could observe the performers as they entered the backstage.

She didn't have to wait long, and as the performers entered, she could hear Josif and August playing across the street through the open door. She felt a flood of relief knowing that she wasn't as alone as she felt.

The dancers, musicians, and wardrobe people entered the theater in a good mood. Most seemed excited and talkative. Izabella studied their faces until she spotted a beautiful young woman with Sofia's eyes who seemed preoccupied and tense. She was the girl from the paper. She was Irina!

Izabella stopped herself from getting up and running to her, and from laughing and clapping her hands with glee. Her heart felt full of love and joy, but she kept an impassive look on her face and tried not to stare at Irina. She felt she must not approach her until well into the performance; she did not want Irina's behavior to change, and she didn't want to take her focus from the dance. She hated to see her so tense, but knew it was for her own good.

Izabella noted where the wardrobe women were getting set up and joined them. The offer of added help was gladly accepted, and the usual backstage smells of dusty curtains, waxed floors, old perspiration, and make-up seemed to conceal any scents from the road which Izabella carried with her. She settled into mending and ironing tasks, and kept as much out of sight as possible.

By 8:00PM everyone was dressed and made up, with the women's hair freshly braided and arranged, all shoes and boots polished, and all the long fringes on the dance aprons untangled and swinging freely.

The musicians were in their places, and the dancers lined up on each side of the stage ready to make a simultaneous entrance. Irina was on one side, and Deben on the other. In the first dance, they would meet in the middle and perform a strenuous duet, happily without any lifting of Irina by Deben.

The first strains of music began, and the curtain lifted. The audience applauded heartily at the dancers' appearance, and the performance was begun. Izabella had obtained a program and studied it for the best opportunity for Irina to disappear unnoticed. The last dance seemed most promising. In it, both Irina and Deben would have solos: Irina first, Deben second.

Irina would be at the edge of the stage while Deben performed. If Irina quietly disappeared from one side of the stage while Deben was at the other side, they would have a few moments to have a head start. It would be their best chance. Izabella could see the conceit in Deben and hoped his vanity would prevent him from noticing Irina. It was the best plan she could come up with. Now she needed to find a way to inform Irina.

Between dances and during intermission Izabella sought opportunities, but could find none. The dancers made costume changes, freshened their hair and make-up, and were never alone. Izabella wanted privacy to approach Irina. They couldn't risk being seen hugging or speaking together excitedly. Izabella was becoming more anxious, and she could see that Irina did not have true joy behind her smile as she danced.

My poor, dear niece, she thought. *You are so strong and brave, so near and yet so much could go wrong. You must be suffering greatly, not knowing if we are here, not knowing where to go, and being pursued by the Iron Guard. Just a little longer, my brave Irina. Be strong just a little longer, and we will rescue you if we have to fight the entire Iron Guard to do it!*

Deben had not actually touched her breasts during the dancing yet, but had come close, and when he did, there had been disapproving murmurings from the audience. He was dancing strongly and was beautiful to watch. His handsomeness and skillful technique were mesmerizing, but his disrespectful handling of Irina and arrogant attitude had cost him much good will, and the audience didn't reward him with the exuberant applause which they gladly offered Irina. His response was to look more arrogant and to behave more cavalierly. He would often alight from a dramatic leap too close to other dancers, causing them to graciously move out of his way, smiling all the while as if this were the norm.

Finally it was time for the last number. This piece had been specially choreographed to show off the talents of Irina and Deben. It began with the whole troupe performing an intricate circle dance which then transformed into a large arc with center stage open, Irina on one end, and Deben on the other. Luckily, Irina was at the end near Izabella.

The two lead dancers left their ends of the arc and danced together in the center. Then they moved apart and performed identical steps until Irina leapt into Deben's arms, and he lifted her and twirled around. This was the part of the dance Deben had been waiting for. As he lowered Irina to the floor, both hands slipped up over her breasts and he looked at her with a bullying leer. Louder angry murmurings came from the audience, and a few *boos*.

Irina kept a fixed smile on her face and inwardly held back the tears of shame and humiliation. After Deben put her down, she performed her last solo while he returned to his end of the arc to await his turn.

She danced without error and returned to her spot at the other end of the arc. *Now!* she thought frantically to herself. *Now I must run.* But her feet seemed rooted to the floor. She had been unnerved by Deben and was reluctant to abandon the troupe in front of the audience.

Suddenly she heard an urgent whisper, in Romanian, behind her. "Daughter of Sofia, step backwards slowly and come to your Aunt Izabella." It came from behind a side stage curtain.

Her heart lept with joy, and she found her will again. She quickly glanced at Deben, and when he was involved in a complex maneuver, she took three slow steps backward and disappeared behind the curtain. She hoped she hadn't been noticed, but a quiet gasp from the crowd and more murmurings told her this was not the case.

The audience's response alerted Deben, who stopped his dance in mid-stride and called out in Romanian, "Petru, Dragos, stop the bitch!" Romanian members of the audience called out in anger and booed loudly. Even those who did not speak Romanian understood the tone and were equally upset.

Izabella and Irina heard the commotion, and with hands clasped, ran for the stage door. Petru and Dragos left the stage and along with Deben chased the pair toward the door. Members of the audience had left their seats, and a small group of a woman with three men hurried up the stairs at the side of the stage and joined the pursuit.

Outside and across the street, Josif and August had played well, and August had sung every song he knew at least once, as well as accompanied Josif when he sang a few Romanian songs. Again a small crowd had gathered.

It was approaching 10:00PM, and a line of taxis could be seen arriving and lining up to receive the concert-goers when they exited the hall. The line extended from the front of the theater around the corner, and back almost to the stage door. Josif deduced that the performance was almost over and directed August to take their instruments back to the car and to bring it around while he kept watch.

The buses had returned and blocked his view. He crossed the street to better watch the door. There were still passersby on the street, and now a bunch of people waiting to catch a glimpse of the dancers when they left the hall. Josif hadn't expected so much interference with his plan.

He heard the distinctive sound of the Hudson approaching and turned to signal August to pull up near him. Then he heard the faint sounds of music from inside the theater abruptly stop, and the sounds of running and yelling coming closer. *This was it!*

The stage door entrance burst open, and Izabella and Irina emerged, hand in hand, looking frightened but determined. Izabella spotted Josif and pulled Irina's hand in that direction, but before either could take a step, two men popped out of the crowd and grabbed the women. It looked like one of the men had a gun pressed against Izabella's back as they roughly pushed them over to the curb and into a waiting car, a Ford.

Josif felt paralyzed for a split second as he considered trying to also enter the car. *Not enough time and too dangerous for the women,* he thought with extreme frustration. He turned and got in the Hudson with August who immediately set off in hot pursuit with an eager grin on his face.

Deben, Petru, and Dragos were close behind Izabella and Irina, and saw their abduction withJosif and August joining in the chase. Deben pointed at the nearest cab, and the three got in, indicating to the driver that he should follow the two cars.

Next out the door were Mrs. Epstein and three men. One carried a large camera with a flash attachment. They also quickly got in a taxi and followed the other cars. Streams of audience members and other dancers next crowded out the door, many of them also jumping into taxis.

The car with the women raced ahead and darted in and out of traffic, tires screeching around corners, trying to get ahead of its followers. August matched the driver's every move and kept him clearly in sight. Josif fingered his knife which was in a sheath hanging from his belt. He longed to use it.

Seeing August so close, the driver of the Ford made an abrupt right on 5th Avenue and pressed the gas pedal to the floor. August did the same and sped after the car which was again weaving in and out of traffic.

"Get beside him and force car to sidewalk. We must stop car!" Josif yelled at August.

"That's just what I was thinking, Joe. We need to show these fellas what's what, and I can hardly wait."

August gradually gained on the Ford and maneuvered alongside. Then with a sharp pull to the left, the Hudson banged into the Ford and, with steady pressure, forced it up across a broad sidewalk and into a short flight of stairs in front of a cathedral, St. Patrick's. The Ford managed to climb a few stairs, then rolled back, the front tires hitting the cement hard, causing the front of the car to bounce.

Josif was out of the Hudson in an instant. The right side of the Ford was pressed against the Hudson, so Josif had to run around behind his car to reach the other side of the Ford. Before he got there, however, the left back rear car door opened and Izabella and Irina struggled out, Irina kicking away a grasping hand from the back seat. August emerged from the right side of the Hudson at the same time, and seeing that the women were all right, flung open the door of the Ford, pulled the driver out with one hand, let go, and punched him in the jaw with the other. The man fell back in the car, unconscious.

"Well shit a brick," August muttered. "That was hardly any fun at all."

Within a few seconds, the taxi with Deben and his henchmen arrived, as well as a police car, the taxi with Mrs. Epstein and the three men, and numerous other taxis and private cars which had joined in the chase.

The policeman had spotted a gun in the hand of one of the men who emerged from the Ford and pulled his own. "I've called in for more units," he called to the man. "Your car is trapped; you have no escape. Drop your gun, and I mean now!"

The man complied, as did his accomplice in the back seat, and the officer began the process of cuffing them and sequestering them in the reinforced back seat of his car.

At the same time, Deben, Dragos, and Petru lept from their cab and rushed toward Irina. Izabella stepped in front of Irina, and Josif stepped in front of her, knife drawn.

August grabbed Dragos and Petru by the shoulders and spun them around. "Two at once, now this is more like it!"

The two henchmen stared at August with disbelief. He looked huge and wild and strangely joyful. Petru threw the first punch and Dragos tried to maneuver around behind August to kick him in the back of the knees. August punched Petru in the gut, then swung around and did the same to Dragos. Both men buckled, then painfully straightened up and attacked August again, with Dragos trying to get his arm around August's neck to choke him, and Petru trying to break his ribs and knock the wind out of him.

August grabbed Dragos's arm and pried it from his neck, then not letting go, he twisted it and swung him around and into Petru, who stumbled. The two regained their footing and tried a two-pronged attack on August again, this time Dragos trying to punch August in the face and side of his head, and Petru trying to pull his huge hat over his eyes.

"Now you're messin' with my new hat," August said. "I guess that's about enough."

He brought his right elbow up hard under Petru's chin, and saw him drop to the cement. Then he swung around and delivered a punch to Dragos's solar plexus, the strength of which he usually saved for one of the Sorgstroms. Dragos folded in half and also fell to the cement, unable to breathe, and beginning to gasp and heave.

* * *

Josif stared at Deben with contempt and spoke in Romanian. "You dishonor yourself and your country. You have become rabid. You need to die."

Deben's face twisted in fear and became a repulsive parody of handsomeness. Josif looked him in the eye closely and spat on the ground, seeing the hatred and frustration of one who would try to control others by violence. "You are not worth me having to clean my knife. I think if you go back to the Iron Guard a failure, that will be enough."

Behind him Izabella's voice said, "We do not think so." She and Irina had come up behind Deben with August's cold, wet, smelly sleeping bag. They had opened it up and each held a corner. They swung it behind them-selves, then forward at Deben with all of their strength, hitting him hard and knocking him over backward with the foul-smelling sleeping bag covering his upper torso and head. Muffled sounds of disgust came from the bag. "I have wanted to do something like that with that sleeping bag for a long time," Izabella said.

"Yes," said Irina. "That felt very good!"

By now the other police units had arrived and were dealing with Deben, Dragos, and Petru.

Mrs. Epstein approached with the three men. The one with the camera took a picture of Irina and her family. "This has been great!" he exclaimed. "I know I got some swell fight shots with that big cowboy."

"Excellent," said Mrs. Epstein. "Irina, I want to in-troduce everyone, but maybe we should go into the cathe-dral. There you can request sanctuary, and make a formal statement that you want to defect. Now no one can argue that your life was not in danger."

Chapter Forty-Eight
Safety

Inside, the cathedral was dimly lit, peaceful, and cool. A faint smell of incense clung to everything, and there was a bank of lit white votive candles to each side of the wide doors.

The Romanians crossed themselves, then gratefully fell to their knees in the last pew, and prayed heartfelt prayers of thanksgiving. When they were done, Father Fitzgerald greeted the group and led them to a small room at the side of the vestibule.

There the reverent air evaporated, replaced by eager introductions, quick catching up, laughing, tears of joy, and much hugging. Irina was overcome with relief, and the long-missed feeling of being encompassed by a loving family. Izabella felt as if a small part of the hole in her heart from Alexander's death had been filled. She felt full of life, as though she had found something she had lost. Mrs. Epstein looked on, dabbing her eyes with a lace-edged hankie. She put her arm around Irina and addressed the group.

"This one," she said squeezing Irina to her, "tried so hard not to put me in danger by not telling me her plans to defect. But I have been around. I have eyes to see. That Deben was a dangerous man, and Irina was in great peril.

For her to defect was the only good solution to her problem. I decided to help."

She explained what she and her son David had been doing behind the scenes to help Irina. She paused as Nicolae translated her words into Romanian. Josif and Izabella nodded, and smiled gratefully at Mrs. Epstein. August looked at Mrs. Epstein and nodded sagely, "That's what I'da done."

In spite of weak protestations, since they had nowhere else to go, and since Mrs. Epstein and David already felt like family, the Epsteins persuaded the Dacias, Irina and August to come to their home for the night. "David and his wife Rebecca live upstairs with their children, Deborah and Daniel. We have a brownstone, so there's plenty of room for everyone!"

August wondered what a *brown stone* had to do with plenty of room for everybody, and couldn't come up with an image in his mind that made any sense. He reassured himself that he could sleep in the car if he had to.

Father Fitzgerald blessed the entire group as they left the cathedral. Deben and his friends were gone, and the Ford had been towed away. Most of the crowd had been dispersed, but those who were left cheered and clapped when Irina and then August appeared at the cathedral door.

A policeman was standing at the bottom of the cathedral steps guarding the entry. His car was parked at the curb, behind the blotchy, yellow-eyed, skunk-smelling, pock-marked Dacia car. The Hudson sprawled kitty-corner across the sidewalk like a huge beat-up bare knuckle boxer resting between rounds.

"I'd usually write you up for this kind of parking," he said, indicating the Hudson.

"We sorry." Josif said, approaching the policeman. "We not from here."

"Tell me something I don't know. I saw what happened here tonight, so I'll let you go. Just move that mess off the sidewalk, and everything'll be jake."

Josif felt too tired to ask what that meant. The stress of the trip and the events of the rescue had finally caught up with him. He gladly agreed to let David drive the Hudson through Manhattan to the Epsteins' brownstone, with him as passenger, while the others followed in a taxi. Nicolae took the subway home, and the Times photographer caught a cab back to the paper to get started processing his photos for the morning edition.

August was relieved to see that brownstone referred to the color of the stones of three-story narrow buildings which were sandwiched together sharing exterior walls, with about seven stone steps leading up to heavy doors with thick beveled glass framed in black painted wood.

Inside the Epsteins' home, all the furnishings reminded the Dacias of the elegance of Europe. There were dark, wooden antique bookshelves, a sideboard and a china cabinet, a brocade-covered Chesterfield and matching chairs, a Victrola on a small chip-carved table, oil paintings on the walls, and thick oriental carpets. The focal point of the main room was a large rectangular table, covered with a white lace tablecloth and with eight ornate chairs around it. Mrs. Epstein and Rebecca quickly set seven places.

Hoping that Irina's South Dakota family would be able to find her in New York, Mrs. Epstein had made a large pot of matzo ball soup, and had a platter of fried chicken, *just in case*. She happily ladled out large bowls of soup, sliced up a loaf of pumpernickel bread, brought out a bowl of hard boiled eggs, a plate of sliced tomatoes, and a bowl of fruit. David made sure his guests didn't mind breaking prohibition *just this once*, got out wine glasses, and poured everyone a glass of thick sweet Manischewitz wine from his private stash. After dinner Rebecca made a pot of coffee and served an apple *kuchen* with white icing drizzled over it for dessert.

They all stayed up talking late into the night, catching up on family, world events, *the Great Depression*, the road trip, the trans-Atlantic crossing, the fight with the gangsters, August's family, the Lindbergh kidnapping, Amelia Earhart's trans-Atlantic flight, the new roles for women, the plight of the bonus marchers in D.C., and General MacArthur's attack on U.S. veterans, and finally politics and the upcoming election between Herbert Hoover and Franklin D. Roosevelt.

Eventually yawns became more frequent than comments, and everyone looked forward to a soft bed, pillow, and a good night's sleep. Mrs. Epstein and Rebecca assigned rooms and beds to the weary visitors, and soon all were asleep.

Chapter Forty-Nine
The Big Apple

Mrs. Epstein served bagels with lox and cream cheese, more hard boiled eggs, and fruit and coffee for breakfast. David and Rebecca's children joined the group. Both were dark haired and bright-eyed, and when August built a cigarette after breakfast and lit a match with his thumbnail, he had their rapt attention. Izabella and Josif hoped he wouldn't lapse into his usual tall tales as little ears so quickly picked up new ideas, and they didn't want to leave this fine family with such *souvenirs* from South Dakota.

Daniel looked up at August with wide eyes. "Can I do that, too?"

"Why sure," August started out, but was silenced by loud coughs from Josif and Izabella, who were staring very intently at him. "Uh, well, gee, little feller. I guess maybe you might be too young, even though I was only six when I started." Josif considered reminding August that he had said before that he had started smoking at age ten, but realized that would not really be all that helpful.

"Really? Well I'm almost eight!" Daniel said triumphantly.

"And I am eight!" said Deborah with a big smile.

Josif looked apologetically at Mrs. Epstein and Rebecca. "I think we start to walk down path which lead to cliff."

Mrs. Epstein slid a heavy, crystal ashtray over to August and shrugged. "He is what he is." She patted August's arm. "We love you just as you are." she said. Then she looked sternly at her grandchildren. "No smoking for you until you are as big as August."

The children were preparing to protest when their father came in with the Sunday morning edition of the *Times*. He lightly tossed the paper into the center of the table with the front page up. The headline read: *Romanian Dancer Defects; Saved by South Dakota Cowboy!*

There was a large picture of Irina looking at August, who had a big grin on his face as he was tossing Dragos into Petru. Deben had an ugly snarl on his face, and Josif's knife could not be seen.

"You're safe now," he said to Irina. "There's nothing like shining light onto darkness to make it go away. Once a story hits the press, everything is in the open. Then all the facts are known, and dark deeds are exposed. Now the law takes over and brings safety and order."

Mrs. Epstein looked proudly at her son. "It is not always so easy as that, but it is what my son, the editor and journalist, is working for. He is so much like his father. My Samuel was an idealist, too. Always trying to bring order and goodness into the world."

She turned to her friend Irina. "Now let's talk about your future. Forgive me for butting into your life so much, but you feel like a daughter to me, and well, you know mothers!"

Izabella translated and Mrs. Epstein continued. "What can a gifted dancer, so pretty and graceful, do in New York? You could teach dance; fall in love, get married, and have beautiful children; you could study the ballet; you could study English and then attend college. If you decide to live in New York, I would be so pleased to have you stay with me while you get started, or whatever you choose. So, there are many opportunities here in New York.

"I have also thought of another possibility. Here in America is a thing called Chautauqua. It is like a traveling university although somewhat different. Our former great president Theodore Roosevelt called it *the most American thing in America*. It is a big assembly, often in a tent, and it brings teachers, entertainers, musicians, and various speakers to people all over the country. They've had Sergeant York, Will Rogers, Calvin Coolidge, and Gilbert and Sullivan operas.

"Chautauquas don't travel around as much as they used to, but the place where it all started is right upstate from here. Just south of Buffalo and Niagara Falls, on Lake Chautauqua. They even have a Bohemian band started by a protege of John Phillip Sousa."

"Who is he?" Josif asked.

"He was a famous American composer and band leader. He wrote *Stars and Stripes Forever* and many other military marches. Sadly, he died in early March of this year."

"I would like to hear his music someday, and so would Uncle Jon."

"I will play some for you later. I have a phonograph record of his music. I also have an album of *Klezmer* music you might enjoy."

"Oh yes, we know *Klezmer* music. It is beautiful, and so long since we hear any," Josif replied.

Irina's head spun with ideas and possibilities. "So many good ideas. I need time to think. But first I want to know my family in South Dakota."

"Yes," said Izabella. "To see Deborah and Daniel make me miss my children."

"Our family and farm wait for us. We must return soon," Josif added.

"I can certainly understand your feelings," David agreed. "But I hope you'll stay a few more days so that we can show you the city. I know you arrived in the U.S. through Ellis Island, as you said last night, but you might be able to take it in better now, and that was thirteen years ago; things have changed some. Besides, I need to take Irina to the Immigration and Naturalization office to get some papers signed on Monday. I thought today we could go see the Statue of Liberty, the new skyscrapers, the Empire State Building, and the Chrysler Building, Central Park, and the Museum of Natural History, which is just up the street from here.

And there's one more thing to attend to," he said, looking at August. "You've become an overnight celebrity. Not only are you the *fighting cowboy hero*, you've also picked up the nickname of the *Singing Cowboy*."

"Yeah, well I guess both are right," August said, humbly examining his fingernails. "Joe and me made over ten dollars yesterday; I guess some folks like us. And as far as fightin' goes, heck I was born fightin'. You just ask my brother, Fritz."

"Well," David continued, "as you're such a celebrity right now, there's a recording company that wants you to audition for them. Maybe even record an album. They can see you tomorrow morning."

August let out a whoop that almost shook the windows. "Well that's what I told everybody back home I was gonna be doin'! Boy Howdy! I'm gonna be a singing cowboy star! Wait'll Fritz hears about this; he's gonna shit for sure!"

August paused and looked at the slightly stunned group of faces. "Oops," he said. "I kinda forgot my manners for a minute. Excuse my cussin', but that's exactly what Fritz is gonna do, I guarantee it."

The day was spent sightseeing and included most of the places David had mentioned. The group rode subways

and buses and ate at little cafés and from street vendors. There was a spirit of joyous abandon as the group traveled the city together. They bought a copious number of post-cards showing everything they had seen, and even pictures of construction workers on the Empire State Building sleeping and eating on steel beams high above the city.

"I kinda feel sick just looking at 'em," August noted. "Man, they've sure got a set!" He paused and looked questioningly at Josif, silently asking if that was cussing. Josif nodded slightly, and August mumbled another "excuse me".

Irina probably traveled twice as far as the others, as she kept running between Izabella and Josif, Mrs. Epstein, and Rebecca and David and their children. The weight of the world had been lifted from her shoulders, and everything seemed bright and wonderful.

David had learned from Mr. Celac that Deben, Petru, and Dragos, as well as the three men in the Ford, had been taken into custody, and charged with kidnapping and assault.

Mariana would fill in for Irina and become a star in her own right, as well as the three male dancers who would fill in for Deben, Dragos, and Petru. The ensemble would continue its tour, only gaining in popularity as word spread of the fight and defection. Even if the main players were gone, there was still an air of mystery and danger about the troupe.

Izabella and Josif deeply missed their family, but were also enjoying an unexpected vacation. The weight of the world had also been lifted from their shoulders, and Josif was as close to giddy as he had ever been. He felt great satisfaction and an expansive sense of generosity and love for the world. Irina looked so much like his departed sister, Sofia.

The Iron Guard had taken his country from him and many of his family. Now he, his wife, and a farmer had rescued this precious flower and saved her from being ground under the wheels of the brutal Iron Guard. He was full of love and gratitude for his new country, and the American attitude of optimism and fair play. He noticed that he was feeling especially fond of August. August, who only a few weeks ago had seemed like a quarrelsome, overgrown kid whose only goal in life was to best his elder brother. Now he was becoming his own person.

Josif shifted position in the group, and walked next to him. "August," he said. "I want to thank you. You have been big help. You have acted as a man, and I feel much gratitude. You will always be welcome at my home."

"Shucks, Joe, it weren't nothin'. Except for changing a few too many tires, those detours, that skunk, and those homicidal bugs, it's been a hoot. I especially loved that fight, it helped me relax."

"When we get back to farm, we have big party. Now people can know why we go to New York. I will tell of your help and bravery."

389

"Yeah, and we can sing and play together, maybe even collect some more dough-ray-me!" August guffawed at his joke, and slapped Josif on the back.

* * *

The next day August went to the recording studio. He played and sang old ballads and his favorite, *The Dakota Six*. Everyone but Rebecca and the kids accompanied him as there was concern that the children would fidget and cause a disturbance. Josif had brought his violin and played with August on a few numbers.

The man liked the music, cut an album, gave August one hundred dollars, and had him sign papers promising him fifty percent royalties on any albums which might sell. They also took his picture and told him to be listening to the radio for some of his songs, which would be airing either today or tomorrow. They gave Josif ten dollars for his playing on the album and ten percent of the royalties.

After the recording session, and on the way to the Immigration and Naturalization office, the group stopped for a late lunch at a deli with a seating section. Mrs. Epstein, aware of August's love of sauerkraut, recommended that he try a Reuben sandwich. A grilled sandwich with the combination of corned beef, sauerkraut, Swiss cheese, and sauce on toasted pumpernickel bread sounded intriguing, and Josif, Izabella, and Irina also ordered one. The Epsteins ordered corned beef on rye, and everyone helped themselves to cold lemonade from a large pitcher which had been placed in the middle of the table with six glasses.

"This sandwich is very good," Izabella said between bites. Josif and Irina nodded in agreement, and kept on eating.

August looked blissful. "Monday, August 22nd, 1932. So far, this is the best day of my life."

Chapter Fifty
Shopping

Mr. Celac had Irina's few belongings packed up and sent to her at the Epsteins'. These items were welcomed, but inadequate for a beautiful young woman beginning a new life. Irina had received some money from the ensemble for her performances in Europe, and the one in New York. Also Mrs. Epstein, Josif, and Izabella wanted to get her something. Josif, Izabella and August also wanted to buy gifts for their families at home, so one more day was allotted for shopping, with firm statements that they would leave the next day.

Josif and Izabella had a talk the night before. Propped up in bed, they had discussed their dreams for their children. As usual when by themselves, they spoke Romanian.

Josif had begun. "Owning land will always be the best security, and Michael-Joseph will have the farm. The girls may or may not marry farmers and live on their land. I always thought that's what they would do, but seeing all these smart women here, working and doing many different things, I am beginning to doubt that. I know Marie wants to have more schooling. How can I tell her *no*? Alexander would have been a scholar, why not Marie?" He looked at Izabella for her comments.

"You are a good and wise man, Josif," she said, beaming at him. "Any of our girls could be scholars. Marie is begging for more education, and although the others are too young to know what they want yet, we should be ready to help them. Also, although Michael-Joseph seems ready to farm next week, he is very smart, and we should encourage him to learn, too."

"How would it help him to farm?"

"He would know what other educated farmers know. He would not be left behind, and besides, he might learn something besides new cuss words."

They both laughed, and before Izabella's eyes could well up with tears in missing her son, Josif picked up the conversation. "Books," he said. "That is the way. We must get more books. Did you see how many Mrs. Epstein and her son's family have?"

"Yes," replied Izabella. "And since we have some money left from the trip, perhaps a radio so that they can hear the news. It has been very interesting listening to Mrs. Epstein's radio, and I think it has helped my English speaking."

"Yes, and then we can hear the *Singing Cowboy* too!"

* * *

The next morning, David returned to work at the *Times*, Rebecca stayed home with the children, and Mrs. Epstein, Irina, Josif, Izabella, and August hit the sidewalk by 9:00AM.

Mrs. Epstein hailed a taxi, they all piled in, and she said to the driver, "Wanamakers, please." Soon the cab pulled up in front of a huge, white building at Broadway and 10th Avenue. It appeared to be made of cast iron, and took up the entire block. Lines of storefront windows featured women's clothing, accessories, and other treasures.

Josif was filled with both wonder and dismay. "Thank God we left most of reward money home. I think we not come out of here with much."

"Okay," Izabella said with a look of pure joy and reckless abandon. She felt as if she were about to walk into a wonderland of pleasures for women. The contrast to her home in South Dakota made her feel dizzy.

August gallantly opened the door for the group and ushered them in with a wave of his cowboy hat and a small bow.

As the group entered the store, first Mrs. Epstein, a well-known face in the store and city; then Irina, the beautiful Romanian dancer whose pictures were in the *Times* and who had defected right from the stage, and finally August, the *fighting and singing cowboy* from South Dakota, were recognized by staff and customers alike.

A tall, shapely woman in a brown tailored suit, and with blond marcelled hair, approached the group. Miss Rutter, the store manager, welcomed them to Wanamakers and introduced herself. She chatted with them, understood that a lot of shopping would be occurring, and made the group an offer.

"You, Miss Tataranu, Irina, and Mr. Wagner, August, if I may use your first names, are overnight sensations. Everyone in the city knows and loves you, and we at Wanamakers are thrilled and honored that you have chosen to shop in our store. We would like to turn this happy event into a benefit for both you and the store. If you would allow us to take a few photos of you for advertising purposes, we would like to pay you in merchandise today, and more merchandise or cash in the future, per use of the photos. We would like to offer each person in your group here a new outfit, including shoes, hat, and coat. And a Brownie camera for each of you." She beamed at the group, who were speechless.

Mrs. Epstein put her arm around Irina and looked at her questioningly.

"What do you think, Mrs. Epstein?" Irina asked.

"I think publicity such as this is always good for a performer. I can see no disadvantages. August, what do you think?"

"Why heck, I say bring 'em on," he stated jovially. "Let's get this shoppin' started!"

Miss Rutter smiled happily and stepped over to a counter to write a quick note and send it off in a pneumatic tube. Soon two photographers and three fashion consultants showed up. She explained to the group that Miss Shaver would be assisting the men with accompanying photographer, Everett, and that Miss Starkenburg and Miss Jenkins would be assisting the women with their accompanying photographer, Roy. Miss Rutter would be checking back and forth between the two groups, and would begin by accompanying the women.

The two groups headed off to their respective departments, and Josif looked over his shoulder at the departing women with foreboding. Again things had gotten out of his control, and he knew he must remain clear-headed and strong. He was in women's territory now, and anything could happen. He squared his shoulders and quickened his step to keep up with August, who was happily chatting with Miss Shaver and Everett.

As the women rode the elevator to the floor where they would begin shopping, Mrs. Epstein mentioned to Irina and Izabella that she knew of a small Romanian store near-by, and that they could stop by there after Wanamakers if they liked.

"Oh yes, please," Izabella said. "We all have left so much of our old country behind. Maybe I could find something to take to Aunt Magda and the girls."

"Yes," said Irina, "mostly we bring memories with us."

Mrs. Epstein also told Miss Rutter that she had plenty of clothes, and that she would like Irina to have a second outfit instead of receiving one herself. Miss Rutter readily agreed, and Irina hugged Mrs. Epstein. "You are so kind to me. I will always think of you when I wear my new clothes!"

Soon the elevator operator opened the door, announcing "Ladies Dress Department," and the women emerged with joyful determination.

Miss Jenkins brought clothing for Izabella, Miss Starkenburg for Irina. Mrs. Epstein and Miss Rutter sat in comfortable stuffed chairs and offered comments on the various ensembles, while Roy took photos.

Three hours later, the two groups were escorted to the store cafeteria, where they were treated to lunches of cheeseburgers, fries, and vanilla milkshakes. Irina also marveled at the tastiness of this new food, and discovered that she loved catsup.

They all looked slightly flushed and excited as they compared notes. Mrs. Epstein looked at Josif proudly. "Josif, if you thought you had beautiful women in your family before, wait until you see them in their new outfits. They are stunning. Such beauty!"

"Thank you, Mrs. Epstein," Izabella said, blushing slightly. She looked at Josif with a slightly pleading look. "Josif, Irina and I now have such beautiful clothes, Aunt Magda and the girls will feel embarrassed next to us. Maybe we get new outfits for them, too? Our clothes cost us nothing; perhaps we could afford it."

Josif pretended to look gruff and to think about it. August rolled his eyes. Finally Josif's face broke into a grin. "When I see August and me in new clothes, I realize same thing." He looked slightly sheepish. "I already get Uncle Jon new trousers, shirt, shoes, jacket, and hat, same as me only different colors. Also clothes for Michael-Joseph." His voice trailed off slightly.

Izabella, Irina, and Mrs. Epstein looked relieved, then burst out laughing. Izabella confessed, "We do same thing for Aunt Magda and the girls already too."

August grinned. "Yeah, I look so good in my new duds, I knew I better get the same thing for Fritz, too, or he'd dress a scarecrow with mine. I even got him a Stetson hat with a broader brim than mine, so that he wouldn't accidentally punch his fist through mine. And I got Grandma and Grandpa new outfits too. Now I should be able to go home without anyone complainin' that they got left out!"

Mrs. Epstein told Josif about the Romanian store nearby. He looked interested. "First we shop for books and radio, then go to Romanian store. Maybe I can find knife for Michael-Joseph."

"And an icon of the Virgin Mary for Aunt Magda, and maybe something nice for the girls," added Izabella.

Josif kept trying to think of things they shouldn't buy or should return, but could think of nothing. They all needed new clothes and it made his heart feel full to think that Izabella and the rest of the women in his household would wear clothing befitting their beauty and importance in his life.

They were overdue. They had gone without and worn clothing with copious mending, no matter how skillfully done, for long enough. And the same for Uncle Jon, Michael-Joseph, and himself. There was no fault in spending some of the reward money on clothing. It would allow his family to hold their heads a little higher and to see that they were improving their lot in life.

Now they would get books and a radio. They were riding the wave of American progress. His children would become educated and able to do anything they could imagine. Times were hard now, but things would change. Things would improve, and when they did, his children would be ready.

Now Josif could hardly wait to go spend the money

he had earned playing with August in New York and may-be some of the extra they had brought for the trip in case of emergencies. He had a sudden image of this money as seed money and of his children as the most precious seeds he had.

At the book department Josif understood the prob-lem of too many choices. He was speaking English better, but reading it was another issue, so he looked to Mrs. Ep-stein for assistance.

"We want our children to learn the wisdom of others, and to make good lives for themselves whether or not they own land. We want them to become educated and smart. What are best books to bring home to them?"

Mrs. Epstein consulted with the clerk, Mrs. Vitalia-no, a middle-aged, studious-looking woman with a pencil protruding from the bun of black hair at the back of her head. Mrs. Vitaliano looked over the top of her glasses at Josif and Izabella and asked questions about the ages and tastes of the children, then set off with a wheeled cart to gather a selection.

She returned shortly with the cart piled high with books, and addressed Josif and Izabella. "Of utmost im-portance in the American home today are: *The Book Of Knowledge, Miriam Webster's Dictionary*, and a *World Atlas*. With these tools, a person can go far. There is not much that you can't find an answer to in these books."

Josif and Izabella eagerly nodded in agreement and the books were set aside.

Next she hauled out two large books called the *Set Of Great Literary Works*. "In these books are some of the greatest literary pieces ever written by mankind. They contain works by Shakespeare, Herman Melville, Tho-reau, Homer, Mark Twain, O. Henry, and others. Reading these books will give any child a head start in school."

Josif and Izabella looked at each other, back at Mrs.

Vitaliano, and nodded again. She set the books aside.

"Next is a very good book of poetry. In it you will find some of the best poetry of our time."

Josif and Izabella nodded, and a copy of *The Standard Book of British and American Verse* was added to the pile.

"Now we have some excellent works of fiction as well as some of the works in the set I just mentioned." She laid her hands gently on another stack of books. "Some people think that works of fiction contain no value in the modern world. But this is not true. In fiction the imagination takes wing, and the mind and soul delight. In my opinion that is where mankind's hopes lie.

"Anyone can learn facts, but the curiosity and imagination to go beyond that and say, 'what if?' is what makes us move forward and use our knowledge. They are our best skills. It is in that light that I suggest these books to you. Besides, there's nothing like a good story to get a child in the habit of reading."

Josif and Izabella nodded, and copies of *Little Women*, *Tales of 1001 Arabian Nights*, *Heidi*, *The Complete Works Of Jules Verne*, *The Adventures of Robin Hood*, and *Treasure Island* were set aside.

With Mrs. Vitaliano's help, August set aside *Tarzan the Ape Man* for Michael-Joseph, *The Standard Book of British and American Verse* for his grandmother, and *The Greatest Collection of Good Clean Jokes* for his grandfather.

Mrs. Vitaliano smiled at the group approvingly. "You have chosen a wonderful selection, I'm sure your families will be very pleased."

"Only if we can afford all this," Josif said quietly.

"Don't worry," she replied. There's a fifty per cent off sale in the book department today!"

"We must be most lucky family in New York," Josif said with resignation. As much as he wanted all these good things for his family, he didn't want charity from the store, or from Mrs. Epstein, in case she had a hand in this.

"Don't worry, Mr. Dacia," Miss Rutter said, sensing his mood. "The store will be making a bundle on this advertising. There is no charity involved. This is a business transaction. I'll be sending you all a contract to sign which will explain the terms and benefits."

Josif was speechless. She was right. He hadn't fully realized it, but Irina, Izabella, August, and he were advertising models. The thought put an ironic grin on his face which lasted the rest of the day.

In the radio and phonograph department, Josif selected an Emerson radio, and he and August looked at Victrolas. Josif had located a Klezmer album, and both had also picked out records of John Phillip Sousa. "I think Grandpa might be able to hear this," August had noted.

Suddenly the group became aware of a store employee rushing up to the counter and directing the salesperson to turn on a radio. "Quick! Tune to WJZ, they're playing August's music!" The station was quickly obtained, and August's voice singing The Dakota Six came through loud and clear.

August whooped, and Roy and Everett took pictures. Miss Rutter beamed and imagined the advertisement: *August Wagner, 'The Fighting and Singing Cowboy,' shopping in Wanamakers and hearing himself singing The Dakota Six on the radio for the very first time.* She gestured at the items on the counter. "Those Victrolas and that radio are on the house!"

Josif looked at August and the radio in amazement. Never had he dreamed this would happen. A crowd was gathering around August, girls were giggling, and autographs were being requested. Next the crowd spotted Irina and became even more excited. More publicity photos were taken, several of them being of August and Irina next to each other. They looked happy but slightly awkward together.

When they were able to break away from the crowd, Josif, Izabella, and Irina agreed that they were done shopping. August requested just one more stop at the musical instruments department. There he picked out a *Junior Guitar* for Michael-Joseph with an instruction and song book. He looked at Josif and Izabella. "I told him I'd bring him somethin' special. This way I can teach him how to play and sing cowboy songs."

"He will be very happy with your gift," Izabella said. "Thank you for your generosity to him."

Finally they were ready to leave the store. Miss Rutter informed them that the store would ship their purchases to their farms in South Dakota for free. "We ship our merchandise by train all over the country. It isn't much to include a couple of extra boxes," she explained.

"That is good news," Josif said. "I think we have to tie very big box on top of car otherwise."

Chapter Fifty-One
One Last Stop

The group left Wanamakers as they had entered, empty-handed, except for their Brownie cameras which they hoped to use to document their drive home and to take pictures of their new friends, the Epsteins.

"Did that really happen?" Irina asked. "We spend most of day there and get many things, and bring almost nothing out! It feel very strange."

"Yes," agreed Izabella. "I remember the beautiful clothes and all the interesting books, but now we have to wait another week to see them!"

"Yeah," August added. "When we get home it's gonna be like Christmas, only better'n most! I wonder if I'm on the radio back home yet? That'll sure blow their socks off when they hear me singin' on the radio while they're eatin' breakfast!" August's eyes went soft at the thought, and he looked as contented as if he had just polished off another Reuben sandwich.

Mrs. Epstein hailed a cab again and gave the address to the driver. In about twenty minutes they were deposited in front of a small but inviting store called The Shop of Romanian Treasures. Its name was printed in both English and Romanian, and with eager steps Josif, Izabella, and Irina led the way in.

As their eyes adjusted to the dim lighting in the store, the three Romanians paused and looked around in awe.

"There is so much from home here!" Irina exclaimed.

"Yes," Izabella added. "It is as though we stepped through that door and back into our old country. So much is familiar."

Finally they were able to move, and they walked around the store, tenderly touching items that reminded them of what they had left behind. Irina picked up a folded lace tablecloth, and opened it a bit to see the design. "Oh, Uncle Josif and Aunt Izabella, it is just like one my mother had." She hugged it to herself, and wiped tears from her eyes.

Izabella put her arm around Irina. "You must have it," she said gently. "We will get it for you." Then she brightened and picked up a beautiful cut lead crystal bowl. "I just had a good idea. If all the Dacia women and girls each get a piece of crystal tableware setting, we can set a beautiful table again, like we used to."

Josif smiled at the thought. Good food, drink, and company around a beautiful table set with crystal and lace. He had forgotten how much he enjoyed that. Since coming to America, they had *made do*, often with chipped crockery and unmatched dishes.

"That is a good idea," he said. "You pick out a piece for all the women, and I will go look at knives. He may not get it right away, but Michael-Joseph should have his own knife. One day he will be the head of his own family."

Izabella chose a decanter for Aunt Magda, a pitcher for Marie, a creamer and sugar set for Rose, salt and pepper shakers for Caroline, a platter for herself, and a medium-sized serving bowl for Irina. She also added an icon of the Virgin Mary for Aunt Magda.

Mrs. Epstein purchased a bible in Romanian for Irina.

"It is important to remember our origins. You will become an American in no time, and this will help you record your history and keep it with you."

Irina hugged Mrs. Epstein. "I will miss you so much," she said. "You are a good friend; you feel like family."

"Well, I feel the same way, and I want you all to know that you will always be welcome in my home."

"Us too," said Josif. "You and your family will always be welcome with us."

This time when they left the store, they carried their packages with them and knew that truly they would be bringing home treasures.

Chapter Fifty-Two
Heading Home

The morning of Wednesday, August 24th, was bright and sunny, and although the travelers were anxious to return home, they also truly regretted saying good bye to Mrs. Epstein and her family. The only things that allowed them to depart with some peace of mind were promises to reunite in the future. Josif, Izabella, and August had all urged David and Rebecca to bring Mrs. Epstein and the children out to South Dakota for a visit.

"There ain't much room at their house," August had stated, "but there's lotsa room at mine. Grandma would love to put you up; she gets kinda lonely sometimes."

David had the Dacia car stored at his garage, and they hardly recognized it when it was brought around that morning. It had been washed and waxed, most of the yellow bug residue was gone, and some of the hail stone dents had been banged out. There were new tires all around. "I had my mechanic check it over," David said. "He also did an oil change and tuned it up. When he found out it was your family's car that was involved in Irina's rescue, he said he wanted to do everything he could to help you, and charged nothing."

"You people are all very kind and generous," Josif said. "We cannot repay your kindness now, but if you come to

South Dakota, we will try. We are in your debt."

"Never mind paying us back," David said. "Moving to a new country is not easy, and defecting even harder." He looked at Irina fondly. "We are pleased and proud to have helped. You owe us nothing."

With that, they all hugged one last time, and Irina and Mrs. Epstein parted with much eye-wiping and nose-blowing.

August snapped a few pictures with his new Brownie. Josif got in the driver's seat, August got in next to him, and Irina and Izabella squeezed in the back seat next to the pile of belongings. Rebecca handed a large brown bag of food through the window to August as the back seat was totally full. He happily received it and placed it on the floor next to his guitar.

"Well, I guess this is it," Josif said, and started the engine which almost seemed to purr. They waved at the Epstein family one last time, and followed David's directions back to Broadway. There they turned right, headed northwest, and followed signs for the George Washington Memorial Bridge. This time August took pictures and had proof of his own to show Fritz about the bridge's height, length, and beauty.

Soon they were across the river and heading into wooded hills and valleys. Conversation between Izabella and Irina was non-stop and often in Romanian, although they made a determined effort to use English the majority of the time.

Josif and August also conversed and were easy and relaxed with each other. They relived their experiences singing for the public and marveled at how much money they had made.

Everyone praised August and his success, and imagined his developing popularity and *star* status. Irina described her experiences in Romania and the voyage on

The Atlantia. Josif, Izabella, and August contributed to the recounting of their cross country trip, and they all contributed to the telling of the rescue and fight.

Then Izabella and Josif described their children and told the story of Alexander's death. This led to a long discussion about gangsters, and Irina told them about the movie, *Scarface*, which she had seen on the ship. Then she described *Cimarron* and the story of the land rush that she had seen. Josif and Izabella told of their journey from Oklahoma to South Dakota, and four days and no flat tires later, they were heading north on Highway 77, near Sioux City, Iowa.

It was Saturday and nearing 5:30PM. Josif pretended to yawn. "Is getting late, maybe we stop for night, and get back to farms in morning." He glanced in the rear view mirror. Izabella and Irina had become silent, and Izabella's look had become stern.

August looked at Josif, grinning. "Haw! That's a good one, Joe!"

At 7:00PM the Hudson made its way slowly up the long Dacia driveway to avoid stirring up any dust. A large group of cars was parked in the barnyard.

"Hey, there's our car! I wonder how did Fritz know we'd be home tonight?" August commented.

Josif parked the car and they all got out. Suddenly there was a burst of happy voices, and a blur that looked something like Michael-Joseph slammed into Josif and held him in a tight hug. The girls crowded around Izabella and Irina, and Uncle Jon and Aunt Magda joined in the happy reunion. Fritz joined August and gave him a rough hug and slap on the back. "We heard you on the radio. Somehow it didn't break."

August grinned and punched Fritz lightly on the shoulder. "People are gonna shit," he said. "I've become a star!" He paused and looked around. "Say, what are all these people doin' here? There's Grandpa and Grandma!

What's goin' on?"

"Have you looked at the house yet? While some people were off singin' in the city, some of us back here were doin' real work."

August looked at the Dacia house. It had more than doubled in size. The Dacia children were herding Josif, Izabella, and Irina into it, as various neighbors stepped aside smiling. The porch and kitchen were the same, but that was all. There were now three new doors off the living room, and Josif and Izabella's cubby hole had been replaced by shelves. Uncle Jon's and Aunt Magda's cubby hole appeared to be a closet now, with a hanging bar filled with clothes on hangers, a shelf over the bar, and many sturdy coat hooks.

Michael-Joseph's bedroom had been converted into a closet for Josif and Izabella, who now would occupy the adjoining room which had belonged to the three girls. The three new doors off the living room led to: a bedroom for Uncle Jon and Aunt Magda, a bedroom for Michael-Joseph, and a large bedroom with two beds for Marie, Rose, Caroline, and Irina. The rooms were nicely finished with bureaus, curtains on each of the windows, and freshly drying wallpaper on the walls. Braided rugs were on the floor.

Irina beamed with delight. "This will be so wonderful to share a room. Now I have three sisters! This is a dream come true!"

"It was Fritz's idea," Uncle Jon said, speaking in Romanian. "As soon as you were out of sight, we started. Many neighbors helped. Since the dust storm there hasn't been that much to do, and working on the house has kept many people busy, and has helped some people not miss their parents too much. We used scrap lumber from many neighbors, who also brought over any extra furniture and rugs. Since so many farms have been foreclosed on, there's a lot of cheap furniture around.

"The children and Magda and I also used money that we earned playing at events for more nails, lumber, laths, plaster and wallpaper. Now we adults each have a nice room, the girls all share a room and don't have their brother coming through all the time, Michael-Joseph has a new room, we have closets, and we all have a bigger house!"

"I hope this dream never ends," Izabella said. "Everything keeps getting better. Irina, you have brought very good fortune with you!"

Aunt Magda brought out bread, pickled eggs, *mamaliga*, white cheese, and a pot of coffee. Women fetched baskets of food from the cars, and an informal picnic was set up on blankets near the house. Stories were told about building the addition, and about the trip and rescue. Mr. Bowman remarked on *Uncle Bela's* good looks and laughed heartily. Everyone greeted Irina and remarked about her courage and beauty. August and Josif played a few songs, and the children laughed and clapped.

Around 9:00PM the neighbors headed home with the understanding that the Dacias would host a big picnic and dance the next Saturday. August, Fritz, and their grandparents were the last to leave. August told Michael-Joseph that when the boxes from New York arrived, there would be somethin' real special for him.

"Thanks, August, that's damn nice of you," he replied, then looking at his father with some trepidation, he corrected himself. "I mean real nice."

"I see not everything has changed," Josif remarked.

"Yes," said Izabella. "Thank God."

Chapter Fifty-Three
Home is Where the Heart is

Wonderful things continued to happen all week. The boxes from New York arrived, and it was indeed the best Christmas they all had ever had, even if it was the last day in August. Everyone loved their gifts and the books. Irina and Marie were becoming close friends. August and Fritz were fighting less. Uncle Jon looked sublime while listening to his Sousa and *Klezmer* records, and all felt great satisfaction in regarding the tangible signs of progress and gain.

While Josif and Izabella had been away, Uncle Jon had gone into Centerford with Fritz and purchased a Delco Plant, a gas generator set with glass batteries, so they had electricity. They had a mailbox now and plans to get hooked up to the telephone line. Michael-Joseph was reading *Tarzan* and loving it, and Rose and Caroline were also reading their books and giggling with glee a lot.

Izabella, Aunt Magda, Irina, and Marie began cooking for the party on Thursday. Everyone planned to wear their new clothes, and August proudly reported that he had a newly composed song to sing. "It's real special," he said conspiratorially, but nothing more.

A large bundle of wrapped *New York Times* newspapers arrived at the new mailbox on Friday. It contained copies of the paper with pictures of Irina which the Dacias and August had first seen in Central Park. It also contained copies of issues with Wanamakers's ads. Photos of Irina and August were prominent. There was also a photo of Irina and Izabella together, and even one of August and Josif together.

The papers made the time in New York come vividly back to mind, and Irina realized that she was now collecting good memories, very good memories. She touched the locket at her neck which Mrs. Epstein had given her and smiled.

With the bundle of papers was a notice stating that the Dacia family had received a lifetime subscription to the Sunday edition of *The New York Times.* Josif shook his head in amazement. This was another very good way to educate his children. He pushed down feelings of his pride resenting charity, realized that if positions were reversed, he would have done something similar, and silently thanked the Epsteins for their wise generosity on behalf of his children. Still, he wondered how he ever would repay them.

Friends and neighbors began showing up at the farm around 6:00PM, when the sun was less intense. Arnold Ariosto, the Bowmans, Miss Horsefall, Ellen and Alan Johnson, the Wagners, the Lundstroms, Maud, Ansel and Ture Peterson, and the Sorgstroms were all there, as well as other neighbors who had helped with the addition.

The men made tables out of planks on sawhorses, which were soon covered with tablecloths and laden with casseroles, breads, preserves, cakes, rhubarb pies, pitchers of lemonade, and other pot luck items. Blankets were spread on the ground and chairs brought out for the women.

Everyone looked happy and proud in their new outfits. Young men were shyly talking to Irina, and August was strutting around in his new duds carrying his guitar and occasionally playing a few chords. Folks ate and socialized and marveled at the big addition to the house. Mr. Bowman and many of the other men took turns going into the barn *to look at the horses* and would return in very jovial moods. Uncle Jon couldn't stop chuckling to himself, and Aunt Magda looked years younger.

Around 8:00PM the tables were moved aside, a makeshift dance floor of plywood scraps with a 2 X 4 foundation was hauled out, and preparations for the dancing began. The Dacias got their instruments, and Ture fetched his sax.

August stepped forward with his guitar, and in a loud voice stated, "I have a special treat for everyone before the dancing. I wrote a song about rescuin' Irina. You're all the first ones to hear it. It's called, *We Brought Irina Home*." The crowd clapped, Fritz sighed in resignation, and August cleared his throat and began singing:

There was danger in Romania, Irina was doomed,
The Iron Guard was after her, they would catch her real soon.
She must run for her life, or all hope would be lost.
She must run for her life, no matter the cost.
She had done nothing wrong, this innocent dancer.
To find a new home was her only answer.
To find a new home where hope didn't end.
A home with safety, family, and friends.
A home with safety, family, and friends.

So she changed her name, and sent a letter,
        with no hope at all that things would get better.
The letter did make it; it arrived at the farm
of her family in Dakota who would keep her from harm.
She sailed from Europe on a big ocean liner.
The star of the dance troupe, she hoped they could find her.

Long Dance Home

But evil pursued her and made her life hard.
For she was still stalked by the cruel Iron Guard.
For she was still stalked by the cruel Iron Guard.

More than once they tried to hurt her,
     tried to shame her, tried to break her.
But she found a friend on whom she could lean,
     a strong and kind woman named Mrs. Epstein.
They stuck together, tight like glue.
No one could get between these two.
They bested the Guard time and again.
No one could break the will of these friends.
No one could break the will of these friends.

Back in Dakota, her family did worry.
They knew they must find her, they knew they must hurry.
But they had no money, no car, no plan; and tough as he was,
her uncle was only one man.
They thought, and they prayed; they must find a way;
     and soon things changed in just a few days.
The Wagners helped them build one car from two,
and the sheriff showed up with very good news.
Yeah, the sheriff showed up with very good news.

They had a reward, the amount would do fine.
 They got it from fighting the gangsters that time.
That fight at the farm with August and others.
That fight that sent gangsters running for cover.
Now they just needed someone who could fight.
Someone to help them make things turn out right.
Someone strong and smart and with a good voice.
That someone was August, there was no other choice.
That someone was August, there was no other choice.

So they packed up the car and headed out east.
They would bring back Irina, they would fight back the beast.
Uncle Josif, Aunt Izabella, and strong August Wagner,
> *they would do what it took to find her and save her.*
The trials and troubles they endured were rough, flat tires,
skunks, getting lost, and other stuff.
Homicidal insects, and log trucks turned over; and detour signs
that took you all over, then dropped you off cold in the middle
of nowhere.
Then dropped you off cold in the middle of nowhere.

There was one surprise that lifted our mood.
All 'cross country, we had real good food.
Especially in Iowa with Mr. Hoffstetter.
His wife's 'kraut and sausage just couldn't be better.
Finally we crossed the big Hudson River.
We bought us a paper and planned how to save her.
We learned when and where Irina would dance,
Then we got in position, we'd have just one chance.
Then we got in position, we'd have just one chance.

At Carnegie Hall, things got real tense.
There was only one plan that made any sense.
Izabella would sneak backstage to find her;
But then both women were in mortal danger.
Josif and August kept watch by the door.
Singing and playing; wanting to do more.
Then the door burst open and the shit hit the fan.
Both women ran out, but were grabbed by a man.
Yeah, both women ran out, but were grabbed by a man.

A man with a gun and a car with two waiting, stole the two
women, and took off racing.
But Josif and August in the trusty old Hudson, stayed on their
tail to teach them a lesson.

We chased 'em 'round town, with their tires all squealin'.
We kept 'em in sight; we knew with whom we were dealin'.
Then we forced their car over, up the steps of St.Patrick's.
And we lit into those bastards, our fists hard as bricks.
Yeah, we lit into those bastards, our fists hard as bricks.

And that's where the Iron Guard turned to rubber.
In just a few punches they started to blubber.
They thought hurtin' women was the right thing to do.
But the Dakota men taught 'em a thing or two.
The Guard's now in jail and their jaws might be sore.
But we're real glad to see them no more.
They meant no one well, they were all real mean.
So we went and spent time with good Mrs. Epstein.
Yeah, we went and spent time with good Mrs. Epstein.

We made real good friends in big New York City.
We shopped and we walked until we felt dizzy.
Irina was famous, the talk of the town;
          and August cut a record, showin' he was no clown.
Irina left Romania where all hope had died.
She came to America where love turned the tide.
They say where your heart is, that's where you call home.
Well, her heart is here now, Irina is home.
Yeah, her heart is here now, Irina's found home.

Be sure to check www.DannWorks.com
for links to music and articles related to
the *Good Neighbors Series*.

Biography

John R. Dann was raised on the family homestead in South Dakota during the *Dust Bowl* and the *Great Depression*. He served in World War II in the Navy. With a Ph.D., in organic chemistry and biochemistry, he did research for a world-renowned laboratory. He and his wife, Barbara, retired to an island off the coast of Washington, where he pursued his lifelong interests in science, creative writing, and international folk dancing.

* * *

Janet M. Dann is a daughter of John R. Dann, the author of *Fate Be Damned* John Dann began *Long Dance Home*, a sequel to *Fate Be Damned*, but asked Janet to complete it for him as his health began to fail. Janet was born in upstate New York, and spent many summer vacations with her family visiting their relatives on the farm in southeastern South Dakota. She also spent a year in VISTA in north central South Dakota., on the Standing Rock Sioux Indian Reservation. She has a B.A. in Anthropology from NYU, and a B.S. in Nursing from Alaska Methodist University. She is currently retired and with her husband, Tsolo, traveled the country for nine years in an RV. They are now living in the San Juan Islands in Washington. Her current interests are writing, painting, and Astrology.

www.ingramcontent.com/pod-product-compliance
Lightning Source LLC
Chambersburg PA
CBHW022240020726
47496CB00004B/995